THREE MINUTES

Also by Roslund and Hellström

Pen 33
Box 21
Cell 8
Three Seconds
Two Soldiers

Three Minutes

Roslund and Hellström

Translated from the Swedish by Elizabeth Clark Wessel

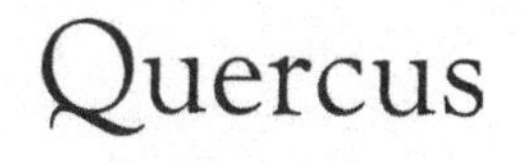

New York • London

Quercus

New York • London

First published in the United States by Quercus in 2017

ISBN 978-1-68144-413-0

Library of Congress Cataloging-in-Publication Data

Names: Roslund, Anders, 1961– author. | Hellström, Börge, 1957– author.
Title: Three minutes / Anders Roslund, Börge Hellström.
Other titles: Tre minuter. English
Description: New York : Quercus, 2017. | First published in Swedish as Tres Minuter ([Stockholm] : Pirat Förlaget, [2016]).
Identifiers: LCCN 2016039046 (print) | LCCN 2016055304 (ebook) | ISBN 9781681444130 (hardback) | ISBN 9781681444123 (paperback) | ISBN 9781681444116 (ebook) | ISBN 9781681444109 (library ebook)
Subjects: LCSH: Police—Sweden—Fiction. | Undercover operations—Sweden—Fiction. | Drug traffic—Sweden—Fiction. | Political kidnapping—Fiction. | Suspense fiction.
Classification: LCC PT9877.28.O77 T7313 2016 (print) | LCC PT9877.28.O77 (ebook) | DDC 839.73/8—dc23

Distributed in the United States and Canada by
Hachette Book Group
1290 Avenue of the Americas
New York, NY 10104

Manufactured in the United States

10 9 8 7 6 5 4 3 2 1

www.quercus.com

always alone.

IT'S A GOOD day. Sometimes you just know.

Hot, like yesterday, like tomorrow. But easy to breathe. It rained recently, and he takes a deep, slow breath and holds the air inside, lets it lie there in his throat before releasing it a little bit at a time.

He exits a city bus that was once painted red, that departed just an hour ago from a bus stop in San Javier, Comuna 13—a few high-rises and some low-rises, as well as buildings that aren't entirely walled in. Some call it an ugly neighborhood, but he doesn't agree, he lives there, has lived there for all of his nine years. And it smells different. Not like here, in the city center. Here the scent is unfamiliar—exciting. A large square that has probably always been here. Just like the fish stalls and meat stalls and vegetable stands and fruit stands and the tiny restaurants with only three or four seats. But all these people crowding around, jostling each other, surely they haven't always been here? People are born, after all, and die—they're replaced. That's how it works.

Camilo crosses the square through narrow aisles and continues into La Galería. Here there are even more people. And it's a little dirtier. But still lovely with all those apples and pears and bananas and peaches lying in heaps, changing colors. He collides with an older man who swears at him. Then he walks a little too close to the bunches of big blue grapes and some fall to the ground. He picks them up and eats as many as he can before a woman who resembles his mother starts screaming the same curses that the older man just screamed at him. But he doesn't hear them, he's already moved on to the next stall and the next and the next. And when he passes by the last stalls of fish and long-since-melted ice—and here the smell is not exciting, dead fish don't like the heat and the ones that haven't sold by lunch smell even worse—he knows he's almost there. A few more steps and there they are. Sitting on wooden benches and wooden chairs in front of the heavy tables that don't belong to the merchants or the kitchens, which someone put at the far end of the market, where everything is sold out. That's what they do, sit and wait together. Before this year he hadn't been here too many times, he's only nine. But he does as they do—sits down and waits and hopes that today, today he'll get a mission. He hasn't gotten one yet. The others are a little older—ten, eleven, twelve, thirteen, a few even as old as fourteen, their voices are starting to drop, cutting through the air and occasionally losing grip, falling out of their mouths and fluttering here and there just when they're about to speak. He wants to be like them, earn money like them. Like Jorge. His brother. Who is seven years his elder. Who *was* seven years his elder, he's dead now. The police came to their home, rang the doorbell, and told his mother that a body had been found in Río Medellín. They thought it might be him. They wanted his mother to come with them and identify him. She had. He hadn't been in the water long enough to become unrecognizable.

"Hi."

Camilo greets them timidly, so timidly that they don't even notice, or at least it seems so to him. He sits at the very edge of one of the benches where the other nine-year-olds are sitting. He comes here every day after school now. The voices that cut the air, who've been here longer, don't go to school at all, nobody forces them to, so they sit here all day. Waiting. Talking. Laughing sometimes. But meanwhile they keep glancing at the space between the last stalls—cauliflower and cabbages like soft footballs piled up on one side and large fish with staring eyes on the other—glancing, but pretending they don't care at all. Everybody knows they're fooling each other and still everybody pretends their eyes aren't glancing in that direction, when that's all they're actually doing. Because that's the direction *they* usually come from. You have to be ready. *Clientes*. That's what they call them.

Camilo takes a deep breath and can feel a cloud forming in his belly, white and fluffy and light. And a kind of pleasure fills his whole body, his heart beats faster, and the red on his cheeks deepens.

He wants it so much.

He's known since this morning. Today somebody is going to give him his very first mission. After today, he'll have *done it*. And once you've done it, you're forever somebody else.

It's hotter now. But still easy to breathe. A city that's fifteen hundred meters above the sea, and when people come just for the day, as customers often do, they complain about the lack of oxygen, their lungs seize up, and they swallow again and again trying to get more.

There. *There.* A cliente.

Camilo sees him at the exact same time as everybody else. And he perks up just like everybody else, stands up, and hurries toward him, flocking around him. A fat man with no hair wearing a black suit and black hat with small, sharp eyes like a bird. The man examines the kids flocking around him and after a fraction of a second, as intense as the beating of a drum, he points to someone in the middle. Someone who's eleven, almost twelve, who's done this before. And they go off together.

Shit. Camilo swallows what could be a sob. *Shit, shit, shit.* That might be the only one who comes today. And he'd been so sure it was his turn.

An hour passes. Then another. He yawns, decides not to blink an eye, counts how many times he can raise and lower his left arm in sixty seconds, sings the kind of silly children's song that gets stuck in your head.

Someone is coming. He's sure of it. Determined steps, headed straight for them. And everybody does exactly like last time, like always, jumping up, flocking around him, fighting to be seen.

A man this time too. Powerfully built, not fat like the other one, but big. An Indian. Or maybe not. Mestizo. Camilo recognizes him. He's seen him here before. He comes all the way from Cali, and he's older than Camilo's father. Or he thinks so anyway, he's never seen his father and his mother won't say much about him. The Indian, or

Mestizo, usually gives his missions to Enrique—Enrique who hasn't been around for a while, who's done this a total of seventeen times.

They are all filled with expectation. Usually no more than a few come here with a mission, and this is probably today's last chance before they all have to head home having accomplished nothing more than waiting. They surround the Mestizo, and he watches them try to look like adults.

"You've all done this before?"

They all answer simultaneously. "Sí!"

Everyone but Camilo. He can't raise his hand and say yes, can't lie. The others shout: *eight times* and *twelve times* and *twenty-one times*. Until the man looks at him.

"What about you?"

"Never. Or . . . not yet." Camilo is sure Mestizo is staring only at him.

"Well then, it's time for your first. Right now."

Camilo stretches as high as he can, while trying to take in what the man just said. He's going to do it. Today. And tomorrow, when he walks through those rows of stalls, everything will have changed, they will look at him with respect, because he'll have done it.

The car is illegally parked outside La Galería, near the square. A Mercedes G-Wagen. Black. Boxy. Large floodlights on the roof—Camilo counts four—broad and robust, which can be angled in different directions. Thick windows you can't see into, not even through the windshield. Bulletproof, he's sure of it. And inside the car smells like animals, as new cars do. This one has soft, white leather seats. It hardly makes a sound as it starts up and rolls away. Mestizo is at the wheel with Camilo in the passenger seat. He glances surreptitiously at the man, who is so tall his head almost grazes the ceiling. Square face, square body, a bit like the car they're sitting in. A squat, black braid of hair that resembles a burnt loaf of bread is tied back in a hairband woven with glistening gold threads. They don't say a word to each other. It takes twenty minutes to drive to their destination as the city transforms from shabby to dirty to renovated to expensive and then back to shabby. Over the Carrera 43A and onto a smaller road that's he's unfamiliar with.

Then they stop. Camilo looks at the street signs, they have stopped where Carrera 32 crosses Calle 10. The city is expensive again. A neighborhood called El Poblado that he's never been to before. A good neighborhood. His mother has said so. And, of course, people live here in their own houses with their own lawns and two cars in the driveway, not far from the city center.

From here, they can see the house without being seen. And Mestizo points.

"There. She's standing in the far window. Your mission."

Camilo sees her. And nods. Nods again when he's given a towel and puts it on his lap, unfolds it. A handgun. A Zamorana, made in Venezuela, fifteen shots, nine millimeter. Camilo knows that. Jorge taught him almost everything.

"And you know the rest, right? What to do?"

"Yes."

"How to shoot?"

"Yeah. I've done *that* a ton of times."

They had, Jorge and Camilo. Practiced. In the evenings they used to practice with the same kind of gun but an older version, which Jorge borrowed from a person Camilo was never allowed to meet. On a deserted lot quite far from here, in La Maiala.

"Good. We'll meet in two hours. Same place as before, at the market. You'll have to get back there by yourself."

His heart is hammering as much from joy as from expectation or excitement or fear. A sicario.

After the car has disappeared, Camilo walks over to some trees that line the roadside and sits beneath one of them. From here he can observe the house and the window, and the woman standing there, clueless.

Green dress. Not as old as he'd thought. She's framed by what appears to be the kitchen window, and he can't really make out what she's doing. He screws on the silencer just as Jorge taught him to do and loads the magazine with the five bullets that were also in the towel. That's what they give you.

Focus. That's what Jorge used to say, *Focus, little brother, keep breathing slowly, close your eyes, and think of something you like.* Camilo thinks of a boat. He likes boats, big boats with sails that float forward slowly when the wind is slow and fast when the wind is fast. He's never been on a boat, but he's thought about it so much he's sure he knows how it feels.

A few minutes. And he's ready. Stands up. Stuffs the gun into his waistband and makes sure his shirt covers it. Walks to the door of the house Mestizo pointed to. Bars. A security door. Extra thick. He's seen this kind of door before. And he rings the bell.

Steps. Someone is approaching. Someone is peeking through the peephole; he can tell from the shadow.

He pulls the gun out of his pants and pushes the small switch located at the far end of the grip, turns off the safety at the precise moment he hears her unfastening the door chain.

Then she opens the door, because she sees a nine-year-old child. And he meets her eyes just like Jorge told him to and raises his gun, aiming upward, she's so much taller than him.

He holds it with both hands just like Jorge showed him. And pulls the trigger. Twice.

The first shot hits her chest and she jerks, bounces a little, and looks surprised, in her mouth and in her eyes. Then he shoots again, at her head. And she sinks down, like a leaf gently falling from a tree, with her back against the doorframe and a bleeding hole in the middle of her forehead. But she doesn't fall backward or to the side, not like he'd imagined she would, like they do in movies.

He sits on the bus, afterward. And it feels like just a moment ago that his heart was pounding with joy and excitement, yet not at all like a moment ago—now there is no fear. Now he's done it. It will show on him, he knows, he can see it himself on others.

The car is waiting at the same place. Near the square. The stocky Mestizo is in the front seat, the thick braid hanging on his shoulder. Camilo knocks on the window, and the passenger door opens.

"Done?"

"Done."

Mestizo wears gloves as he takes back the handgun and pulls out the magazine. There are three bullets left.

"You only used two?"

"Yes. One in the chest, one in the forehead."

Me. A sicario.

The bus again. The back of the bus is full, and he sits down on the only free seat, which is right behind the bus driver. He returned the pistol in a towel and got two hundred dollars. Camilo's cheeks feel hot, red. Two hundred dollars! In his right pocket! And the bills are as warm as his cheeks, burning his thigh as if they want to come out, show themselves to the other passengers on the bus this evening, who don't have two hundred dollars in their pockets, not even combined.

Six zones along Rio Medellín turns into sixteen comunas and two hundred and forty-nine barrios. He is on his way to one of them a bit farther up on the slopes of Comuna 13, San Javier. On his way home. He's ridden this way so many times, with his mother and with Jorge and alone, but it's never felt like it feels now. The cloud in his stomach is no longer moving back and forth, it's made a place for itself next to his heart, and the fluffiness no longer presses out toward his chest, but inward. He leans back against his hard seat and imagines his home, which is crowded and messy and full of sounds, how he'll run there as fast as he can from the bus stop and rush inside and before he's even seen her he'll shout *Mom, I told you I'd fix the fridge and I did,* and he'll hand her half the money. And she'll beam with pride. And then he'll go to the room they sleep in and to his secret spot—a flat tin box that once held thin pieces of chocolate and that he can hide almost anywhere—and he'll put the other one-hundred-dollar bill in there, his first.

trust only yourself.

PART ONE

IF DAWN TURNS into morning. If July turns into August.

Piet Hoffmann rolled down the windows of the truck—a draft—it wasn't even eight in the morning yet, but the heat was already pressing against his temples, the shiny sweat covering his shaved head evaporating slowly as the wind whirred around him.

If an ending turns into a beginning and therefore never ceases.

It was on this day three years ago that he arrived in a country he had never visited. On the run. A void. Life was now just about survival.

He eased up on the throttle slightly, ninety kilometers per hour, just as they'd agreed. He checked the distance to the truck in front of him: two hundred meters, just as they'd agreed.

They had long since turned off highway 65. Mile after mile and to their left, on the other side of dense shrubbery, the Rio Caquetá flowed, roared, forming the border to the Putumayo Province—the river had followed them the last hour, keeping its distance but still stubbornly sticking to the road. He chewed on coca leaves to stay sharp, drank white tea to stay calm. And occasionally drank some of the mixture El Mestizo forced on him before every delivery, some version of colada: flour, water, sugar, and a lot of Cuban espresso. It tasted like shit, but it worked, driving away hunger and fatigue.

On several occasions, especially during the last year, he'd believed an ending really was an end, an opening, an opportunity to get back home. To Europe. Sweden, and the Stockholm he and Zofia and Rasmus and Hugo considered the whole of their mutual world. And every time the opening quickly closed, the void had widened, their exile continued.

He'd see them again tonight. The woman he loved, even though he'd once believed he wasn't capable of loving, and two small people that he somehow loved even more—real people who had real thoughts and looked at him like he knew things. He'd never intended to have any children of his own. But now when he tried to remember what it was like before they arrived, there was only blankness, as if the memories were gone.

He slowed down a little, he was getting too close. Maintain a constant distance, for maximum security. It was his responsibility to protect both of these trucks. They'd already paid for their passage through—this was the kind of place where if you joined the police or military, it wasn't because you wanted to catch criminals or fight crime, it was because you wanted to make a good living collecting bribes.

Protection. That's what he did yesterday, was doing today, and would do tomorrow. Transport. People. As long as he did it better than anyone else, nobody would question him. If El Mestizo, or anyone else in the PRC guerrillas, doubted for even a moment that he was who he said he was, if he was exposed, it would mean instant death. For himself, for Zofia, for his children. He had to play this role every day, every second.

Piet Hoffmann rolled up the two side windows, the heat neutralized for a moment—the breeze had scared away the foaming wave of sweat that slipped beneath his usual getup. The bulletproof vest with two pockets he'd sewn on himself—the GPS receiver that stored the exact coordinates of every route and destination, the satellite phone that worked even in the jungle. Plus, the gun hanging from a shoulder holster, a Radom, fourteen bullets in its magazine, the one he'd gotten used to wearing during his many years of undercover work with the Polish mafia, paid for by the Swedish police. In the other shoulder holster, he carried a hunting knife with a wooden handle, which he liked to hold, its two-sided blade newly sharpened. He'd carried it for a long time, since before the judges and prison sentences, since before he'd worked for Swedish special protection—*maximum damage with a single stab.* On the seat next to him sat a Mini-Uzi with a rate of fire of nine hundred and fifty rounds per minute and a customized collapsible stock that was as short as he needed it to be. Also, on the platform, just behind the truck's cab, secured with two hooks, he had a mounted sniper rifle. He even had registrations for all of them. Issued by El Cavo in Bogotá for the right price.

Over there. Beyond the unpainted shed that stood close to the road, just before the two tall trees that had long since died—naked and stripped branches that seemed to be waiting for someone who would never arrive. That was where they would slow down, turn right, and continue the last few miles down a muddy dirt road that was too narrow and whose deep potholes were filled with water. A fucking potato field. Thirty kilometers per hour, you couldn't go faster than that. So Hoffmann drove a little closer to the truck in front of him, half of the secure distance, never leaving a gap of more than one hundred meters.

He'd never transported anything to this particular cocina before. They all looked alike anyway, all had the same purpose—processing coca leaves with chemicals in order to spit out more than a hundred kilos of cocaine a week. About an hour along this godforsaken road, and they'd be in a PRC-controlled area—which had once been FARC-controlled—where labs are either owned by the PRC or by operators who rent their land from the PRC and pay to grow and produce. When he first got here, Hoffmann had assumed the mafia was in charge, that's what he grew up with, that's how myths were formed, took root. He knew now that wasn't the case. The members of the mafia might rule in Colombia, might sit on the money, but without the owner of the jungle they were nothing. The mafia. The state. The paramilitary. And a mess of other organizations running around making war on one another. But there was no power without the PRC guerrillas—the cocaine demanded the jungle, demanded the coca leaf, and they weren't cultivated on guerrilla land without guerrilla permission.

"Hello."

He'd planned on waiting to call. But he wanted it too much. Her hands on his cheeks, her eyes looking into his, wanting the best for him, loving, steadfast, beaming with confidence.

"Hello."

He'd been away for seven days. Like last time. That's how it worked. Distance, waiting, long nights. He endured it because she did. They had no other choice. This was his only way to support them. If he went back to Sweden he'd be locked up. If he didn't continue to play this role, he'd be dead.

"I miss you."

"I miss you, too."

"Tonight. Or maybe even this afternoon. See you then."

"Love you."

He was about to answer. *Love you too.* When the call cut off. That happened out here sometimes. He'd call again later.

The already tiny road was becoming more like a path, narrower and narrower and with even wider potholes. It was difficult to maintain the correct distance. Sometimes the second truck disappeared around tight curves and behind high ridges. Hoffmann had just rocked the right rear wheel out of a crater when two brake lights lit up ahead of him, glowing like red eyes under the bright sun. It felt wrong. The other truck should not be slowing down, or stopping, not here, not now. He'd designed every detail of this transport himself, it was his responsibility, and he'd made it clear that no vehicle should slow down to less than twenty-five kph without warning him.

"*Watch out.*" El Mestizo's voice in Hoffmann's ear, he adjusted the round and silvery receiver in order to hear better. "*Stop.*"

Hoffmann slowed too, then stopped just like El Mestizo. Eighty, maybe ninety meters away. And now he could see it, despite the sharp curve and bushes obscuring his view. In front of them on the road stood a dark-green off-road vehicle. And on either side of it stood more. He counted four military vehicles in a semicircle, like a smile stretching from one edge of the jungle to the other.

"*Wait and—*" It crackled sharply, that electronic scraping turned angry and tore into his ear, and Hoffmann had a hard time making out the whole sentence as El Mestizo moved the pinhead microphone to his shirt collar and locked it into transmit mode.

Hoffmann kept the engine running while he gazed at the green vehicles. Regular military? They'd already been paid. Maybe paramilitary? If that was the case, they had a problem. They weren't on El Mestizo's payroll.

Then every cab opened at the same time. Men in green uniforms jumped out holding automatic weapons, but not pointing them. And now he could see.

It *wasn't* paramilitary. Those weren't their uniforms. And he relaxed, somewhat. El Mestizo seemed to do the same, his voice became less of a growl, as it did when vigilance and suspicion took hold of him, the characteristics that defined him.

"*We know them. I'll be back.*" The door to El Mestizo's cab opened. He was heavy, tall, and wide, but when he landed on the muddy ground, he did so gently. Hoffmann had seldom seen so much body move with such coordination. "*Captain Vásquez? What's going on?*"

The transmitter on his collar no longer crackled, instead transmitting clear and clean sound. Reproducing the overly long silence.

Until Vásquez threw his arms wide. "*Going on?*"

"*These vehicles. It looks like a goddamn roadblock.*"

"*Mmm. That's exactly what it is.*"

Vásquez's voice. Hoffmann didn't like it. There was something missing. A resonance. It was the kind of voice a man unconsciously affected when he didn't mean you well. Hoffmann rose up gently from the driver's seat, exited through the cab's rear window, and crawled out onto the covered bed of the truck. The sniper rifle was held down by two simple brackets and he undid them, took out the bipod, lay down, and pulled the bolt upward and toward himself while pushing the muzzle through one of the prepared holes in the tarp.

The telescopic sight brought him close. It was as if he was standing there with them, among them, El Mestizo on one side and Captain Vásquez on the other.

"You've been paid what you asked for, Vásquez."

"And it's not enough."

Close enough to be part of El Mestizo's face. Or Johnny's face, he called him that more and more often. Shiny, like always when they left Cali or Bogotá for the jungle, mouth tense, eyes on the hunt, eyes that had once frightened Piet, but that he'd learned to like even though they so often turned from friendly to ruthless. And Vásquez's face—the bushy, pitch-black mustache that he was so proud of, eyebrows sprawled like wild antennas. He looked as usual. And not at all. Just like his voice, his movements were different, not heated, violent, more confident. Yes, that's what they were, slow, almost transparent, as if he wanted what he said to really sink in. He hadn't looked like that when they negotiated with him, paid him at a hole-in-the-wall restaurant behind a church in Florencia, compensation for allowing three deliveries to pass. On those occasions Vásquez wore civilian clothes, seemed nervous, talking and moving jerkily, only settling down after he ripped open the envelope and—mumbling—counted the money bill by bill.

"You never told me how big your transport was. I didn't know what it was worth. But I do now."

Hoffmann peered through the telescopic sight, focusing on El Mestizo's eyes. He knew them well. They were about to change shape. It always happened quickly—pupils dilating, gathering more light for more power, preparing to attack.

"I want double what you paid me."

Vásquez shrugged his uniformed shoulders, pointed to the diagonal trucks, and the four young men waiting outside them. And all of them simultaneously—without raising their weapons—put their right index finger on the trigger.

Hoffmann magnified the telescope on his rifle and moved the bull's-eye to the center of Captain Vásquez's forehead, aimed at the point between his eyebrows.

Eighty degrees outside. Hoffmann's left hand on the rifle's telescope. *Windless.* The small screw gently between his index finger and thumb. *Distance ninety meters.* He turned, one click.

TPR1. Transport right one. Object in sight.

"Be careful, Il Capitano . . . you know as well as I do that accidents happen easily out here in the jungle. So listen very closely, Vásquez—you're not getting any more money."

Through the telescopic sight, Hoffmann was almost a part of that thin skin, wrinkling up on the forehead, eyebrows drawing together. Captain Vásquez had just been threatened. And reacted. What had been confidence and self-control now became aggression and attack.

"In that case, I hereby confiscate your transport."

Hoffmann felt it. They were on their way there. Where he didn't want to go. Right index finger lightly on the trigger. Avoid all questions. Survive.

His official duty was to protect. That was what El Mestizo believed and must continue to believe.

Breathe in through your nose, out through your mouth, the calm, it had to be in there somewhere. He'd killed seven times before. Five times since he got here. Because the situation demanded it. To avoid being unmasked.

You or me. And I care more about me than about you, so I choose me.

But the others had been the kind who profited directly from the drug trade, which slowly took away people's lives. Captain Vásquez was just an ordinary officer in the Colombian army. A man who was doing what they all do, adapting to the system, accepting bribes as part of his salary.

"So that means your truck is mine now . . ."

Vásquez was armed, an automatic rifle hanging off his left shoulder and a holster on his right hip, and that was the gun he pulled—a revolver he pressed against El Mestizo's temple.

". . . and you're under arrest."

The captain's voice had become much quieter, as if this was just between them, and that's probably why the metallic click sounded so loud as the gun was cocked and the barrel rotated to release a new cartridge.

Breathe in, out. Hoffmann was there now, where everything could be broken down into its separate parts and built back up again. This was his world, and it made him feel secure. One shot, one hit. No unnecessary bloodshed. Take out the alpha, it worked every time, forcing everyone else to look around for where that shot came from, take cover.

"*Nobody puts a fucking gun to my head.*" El Mestizo spoke softly, almost a whisper, while turning around, even though the gun dug into the delicate skin of his temple—there'd be a round, red mark there later.

"*El Sueco.*" And now he looked straight at the second truck. At Hoffmann. "*Now.*"

One shot, one hit. Piet Hoffmann squeezed the trigger a little more. *And I care more about me than about you, so I choose me.*

And when the ball hit Captain Vásquez's forehead it looked just like it always did with this ammunition—a small entrance wound, just a centimeter wide, but a huge exit wound, an explosion as the whole back of his head disappeared.

HE HAD NEVER seen anyone die before. Not midstep. Breath, thoughts, love, longing, and then—nothing.

He had faced death, of course, had been hunted by cowardly, ugly, shitty death and learned to hate it, but in another way—he knew what it felt like to hold it in your arms while you said goodbye, to lose the one you love the most one glacial moment at a time.

Timothy D. Crouse stared at a screen covering an entire wall of the room that bore his name. The satellite, which had just filmed and recorded a bullet from a sniper rifle hitting the middle of a man's forehead, was floating right now according to the operator's computer at an altitude of one hundred miles, orbiting the Earth every eighty-eight minutes. An image angled from above.

The man in uniform—probably an officer, he'd moved that way in relation to the four other men in uniforms—had pressed his gun against the head of one of the truck drivers. Four military vehicles had formed a roadblock, and it was clear the commander and the driver had argued. Then his life had been extinguished in front of his men, who became confused, uncertain where the shot had come from. Soon they too were under fire. Shots to the side, in front, and behind them. It was as if the shooter, who so accurately hit the officer's head, was deliberately missing, content to intimidate, control. The four soldiers had thrown themselves to the ground. Not falling, just needing to get down to the ground as fast as possible. While the shots rained down, the burly, almost square driver with the thick, dark braid drew his own weapon and ran over to them, tying them up one by one, their arms pinned behind their backs and their faces in the mud.

Crouse was absorbed by the monitor. Everything had stopped. The burly man in the middle of the screen was waiting for something. Or someone. Then Crouse saw the shooter come running in from the right side of the image, slipping on the muddy, uneven road, a weapon in his hand.

"Eddy, you okay?"

A murder streamed live. Watched by two viewers. He himself on one seat and the satellite operator, one of the people responsible for monitoring Colombia, on the other.

"I'm okay, sir."

"Take a break, if you like. This shit . . . seeing this, it's rough."

"I'll be fine."

"In that case, Eddy, I'm gonna leave you here for a minute. I need some air." Crouse put a hand on the operator's shoulder and stood up. Threw a cursory glance at the two giant screens that covered other walls in the Crouse Room—one of which looked over the Golden Triangle—Laos, Burma, and Thailand—and the other concentrating on the Golden Crescent—Afghanistan, Iran, and Pakistan.

Cultivated coca on its way to cocaine kitchens in Colombia. Poppy fields headed for the opium factories of Asia. All of it ended up in drug transports, drug sales, drug abuse. Death. The sort that he'd just witnessed. Or the kind he'd given birth to, dressed up, and seen end.

Crouse opened the locked door with his plastic card and went into the endless corridor. Stifling, dusty air. The kitchenette was halfway down the other end of the hall, and empty, just as he'd hoped. He spooned some coffee grounds into the coffee maker, a little more than was necessary, had to make it really strong. He poured the water into the top of the machine and watched it start dripping, the condensation collecting on the glass pitcher as it slowly filled. With that first sip came the rush to his chest. He wanted to remain inside that wet steam and with that coffee, warming him from throat to stomach, felt so good sometimes to fall into the void, escape death and demands and responsibilities. The speaker of the House. Technically, the third most powerful person in the United States after the president and vice president. And here he stood, in a cramped kitchenette in the building he increasingly sought out, where for a moment he could be nobody at all.

He continued down the corridor, which seemed a little less sultry. Passed by the room where the sign still hung on the door even though the mission was completed, Operation Neptune's Spear—the information gathered there had formed the basis of the US military raid on a house in Abbottabad, Pakistan, where Osama bin Laden had been hiding. Passed by the room with a sign that read Operation Iraqi Freedom—the continuing hunt for the fifty-two most wanted men in the invasion of Iraq; passed by an entirely new room for something called Operation Aladdin and a room marked Operation Mermaid, which was not yet up and running.

Then the endless corridor came to an end.

He stepped into one of the world's largest rooms—an atrium with a glass roof big enough to house the Statue of Liberty. With mug in hand he sought a bench at the far end near the stairs, not particularly elegant but he liked sitting there, drinking his coffee and glancing up at the blue sky hanging above the glass roof, which hid the satellites much of his work depended on.

Liz.

He missed her every day. Many times a day. It never passed, never lessened. More death always stoked the grief. And even when he thought he couldn't bear it, he knew tomorrow would be worse. Crouse took slow, deep breaths as he looked around a compound that housed eight thousand employees, yet remained almost unknown, often confused with the NSA. National Geospatial-Intelligence Agency—the NGA—the US government agency tasked with analyzing images from aerospace, commercial satellites, other nations' satellites.

And our own satellites. One of which had just taken him to another part of the world. A reality he would soon return to.

"Sir? I don't like you sitting here."

"And I don't like you pointing that out. As usual." Crouse smiled at the tall, well-built man who had snuck up behind him. Dark suit, gun in a holster across his chest, a radio, he looked like all the others, but he wasn't. One of several bodyguards, Roberts was the one who had been at his side the longest, since he was elected minority leader and first started receiving threats—there was always someone who was angry or disappointed or needed someone to take it out on.

"You were supposed to let me know if you left the Crouse Room."

"And I didn't do that, Roberts. Because I wanted to be left alone."

"My job, sir, is not to respect the privacy of your coffee breaks. It's to keep you alive."

"And I'm alive. Aren't I?"

They walked back, and Roberts followed him all the way to the door that read THE CROUSE MODEL, and only then did he stop and stand outside. He'd still be standing there when Crouse came out again.

"It'll be just a minute, sir, until we get the live feed back." The operator at the Colombia desk nodded toward the giant screen on the wall. It was black. "A new window is about to open. Another satellite."

Crouse sank down onto a simple wooden chair he used so often that it almost felt like his own. A few years ago, when the Crouse Model was first initiated, black silence had dominated that wall, broken up only now and then in limited intervals by extremely low-res, hard-to-interpret images. Now it was the opposite. Only a few times a day did a short window of time arise when spy satellites, which circled the Earth closer and faster than other satellites, didn't overlap, thus making a specific location inaccessible.

"There. The window is gone. We can follow them again."

Crouse looked up at the screen. The satellite image had altered, now had a new center. The scene had changed. Half of the four military vehicles that had formed a roadblock were gone. But the four men in uniform remained on the ground, bound and guarded by the burly man.

"We're gonna get in real close now." The operator grabbed what looked like an electronic pen, held it over the disk on the desktop, and zoomed in on the burly man. "Close enough to almost be able to identify them."

Crouse watched a powerfully built man on a winding road in the Amazon jungle, unaware he was being watched, walk back and forth beside prone soldiers, giving them a sharp kick now and then if one of them moved too much. This image was also from above, the satellite's angle, but was vastly more detailed. That hadn't been possible in the beginning—the first time he sat here they'd been using spy satellites that conveyed sequences in which every pixel corresponded to ten-centimeter resolution—which meant that it was impossible to make out anything in these unprocessed images, no one was identifiable. A new generation, three-centimeter resolution, had also been inadequate. Now they were using satellites with one-centimeter resolution in anticipation of the next generation, *zero point one*, evolving—at that point they'd be able to read the fine print in a newspaper.

"Can we get any more detail?"

"Unfortunately not, sir."

The face dissolved into colorless squares. It didn't matter. Crouse had already guessed who it was—had watched him several times before, just like this, twenty-five hundred miles away and close enough to be able to touch him.

His physique, the way he moved. *It was him.* El Mestizo—Johnny Sánchez. Professional killer. The man the FBI had classified as the fourth most dangerous member of the PRC guerrillas.

But it was his companion that Crouse was more curious about. The other truck driver. The sniper. Who now came running for a second time from the edge of the image, this time from the left.

"I want you to change focus—go right up to *him* instead."

A new zooming in. More colorless squares. A hairless man with what appeared to be a large tattoo on his shaved skull. Slightly shorter than Sánchez, slender, a hunting vest worn over his shirt, jeans, boots, dark gloves.

Twelve seconds was as long as they were able to follow him before he jumped into one of two remaining off-road vehicles and drove away with it, back into the jungle. The man the FBI placed at number seven out of a total of thirteen on that same Most Wanted list of the cocaine-financed PRC-guerrilla hierarchy. The only one who had yet to be identified. El Sueco.

From his appearance, and according to their few sources, not South American. Not necessarily Swedish, as the name suggested, but probably northern European, or maybe Australian, even North American. That was as far they could get with facial recognition software.

"Every time we've seen him, *every time*, we've registered Sánchez at his side. Or rather—this guy is always at Sánchez's side. According to our patchy information, his closest companion. His right-hand man. He protects the cocaine fields, the cocaine kitchens, and cocaine deliveries. Protects weapons shipments. Protects Sánchez."

A murder streamed live. And they were still streaming, guarding the bound soldiers and moving the vehicles as if nothing had happened. Just another day in the drug trade, where a life was worth less than money. Crouse took a slow lap around the large room with that restlessness that never left him alone—he could feel it again, death brought death. He passed the next screen and the operator watching the anonymous factory buildings that handled opiates in Laos, then the screen showing the poppy fields in Afghanistan and the many farmers harvesting with simple tools. Farther into the room, those responsible for the development of the Crouse Force. He said hello and told them to prepare for a site visit tomorrow, and beyond them sat the leaders of the Crouse Group—the heart of the Crouse Model, the analysts who compiled the images taken in via the NGA's spy satellites, the audio intercepts and documents downloaded via their cousin the NSA's signal reconnaissance-program, and the insider information that came from the DEA's undercover work.

A slow second turn around the hall before returning to the Colombia investigative desk. By far the largest producer. Eighty-five percent of all cocaine that was snorted, smoked, or injected originated there and was transported by the Mexican cartels to six million Americans.

His own daughter was one of them. Had been one of them. Crouse closed his eyes, took a breath, held in the air, keeping it in his abdomen as he'd learned to. It didn't help. The restlessness turned to anger. The anger became more restlessness. What a fucking anniversary.

In 1915, cocaine became illegal. In 2015, more tons of cocaine are smuggled across the border than ever before. One hundred years of failure.

Crouse looked up at the screen and for a moment the resolution was perfect. The truck had been moved and was parked behind the one Sánchez drove. He was alone in the picture. The man they called El Sueco was no longer visible to the satellite cameras.

Sánchez seemed hesitant, as if he was waiting for something. Without being in any particular hurry. They'd murdered someone. And unlike those who were several thousand miles away watching that murder, they didn't seem haunted.

Then, suddenly, he moved, turning in the direction of the muddy road, clearly searching for something.

"Can you zoom out?"

The satellite operator took his electronic pen, pulled it over the plate on his desk. Zooming out five steps. Until Crouse saw what they were waiting for. A minibus and two motorcycles, men in uniforms, approaching rapidly.

PIET HOFFMANN ROLLED out his sleeping bag onto the rough, gritty truck bed. He'd spread out a newspaper, the center spread of yesterday's *El Espectador*, to cover the truck bed properly. And on top of the paper stood his disassembled weapon—twelve parts that needed to be sprayed, wiped clean of powder residue, and oiled.

He had killed a man. They would discuss it this evening, he and Zofia. Not that she would judge him, condemn him—she never did—but he'd learned that he *had* to talk about it. Or, she had taught him that.

Hoffmann looked at his wristwatch, counting. They'd been waiting for an hour and forty minutes. It wasn't far to Puerto Arango, but El Cavo would soon be here.

A revolver. Pressed against his temple. Johnny—he was Johnny at that moment—had stood ninety meters away. And slowly turned back toward him, whispering, *El Sueco, now*.

Johnny trusted him. Even when his life hung in the balance. The one person he shouldn't trust.

Four young soldiers from the regular military had been forced down onto their stomachs, tied up tightly with their faces in the mud and hands behind their backs. Hoffmann had moved his own truck closer to El Mestizo's and parked behind it. That was after he read the topographic map and found a slope half a kilometer into the partially cleared jungle—terrain that had not yet begun to form new walls of bark and leaves, fragile vegetation that was more reminiscent of the kind he and Zofia sometimes walked through far out in the Stockholm archipelago. The kind you could drive on. He drove the first military vehicle through the jungle to the precipice, backing up close to one of nature's own cavities, where a small, blue river wound by twenty-five meters below. He'd left the jeep in reverse, pressed down the clutch, and replaced his foot with a heavy stone attached to a string to hold the pedal down. After that it had been enough to pull up the hand throttle, jump out of the car, and with rope in hand gently pull away the stone. Until the car started to move. Then he snatched away the stone completely and the jeep coughed a couple of times before rolling backward over the edge of the precipice and down into the river. He had driven away the fatigue that came with oppressive heat and humidity, and time after time run back and picked up the next military vehicle. All four six-wheeled vehicles were now at the bottom of the ravine, scattered here and there like a wilted bouquet of flowers.

You pay if you threaten El Mestizo.

Hoffmann had finished spraying and wiping away any powder residue and carefully oiled the barrel, the very last part of his gun. Twelve pieces of metal on the open newspaper. Each of them harmless. But when they were bolted together again they'd be deadly.

That fucking image wouldn't go away. Right between the eyebrows. A small entry, an explosion as it exited the back of his head.

He crawled out through the gap near the back of the tarp covering the truck bed, sniper rifle slung over one shoulder. He chose a tree a hundred and fifty meters away, mounted the laser instrument, and checked the telescopic sight against a red point to make sure it was perfectly calibrated. He loaded a new magazine with nine bullets—ready to fire.

"They're here now." El Mestizo pointed in the direction they'd come from. You couldn't see them yet, but you could hear them. Two, maybe three vehicles coming along a muddy, narrow, waterlogged dirt road. Hoffmann went back up on the truck bed, fastened the sniper rifle to its two hooks, and jumped down again.

Two motorcycles and a minivan with six seats. Eight police officers. But only one of them counted. El Cavo.

El Mestizo waved them over to the edge, greeted a tall, skinny man who was a little pigeon-toed, rare among police officers.

"Sánchez. It's been a while."

El Mestizo seldom answered to his surname. But they had that kind of relationship nowadays.

"And every time the same . . ." El Cavo broke off suddenly. He'd just noticed the corpse. ". . . circumstances." Or rather, the uniform on the corpse. And recoiled. "A captain? From the regular army?"

"Shit happens."

"This is not even close to what's included in our agreement!"

El Mestizo had signed agreements with more people than Hoffmann could keep track of—and he'd been working by his side for almost two and a half years—still, someone new was always popping up. Some customs official who could manipulate declarations, prosecutors who don't bring charges, a judge who fabricated findings, soldiers who registered weapon licenses, police officers who turned a blind eye. There were a ton of those types, when it came to documents. But then there were the others. Hoffmann had met them in at least seven of Colombia's thirty-two provinces. High-up police officials who take care of something a little trickier than paper—dead bodies. For example, this El Cavo, whose jurisdiction was in the province Caquetá. Hoffmann had seen him once before, then it had been Johnny who'd done the shooting, someone who leased the land, grew the crops, and forgot a little too often to pay his fee.

"It was this boy here." El Mestizo pointed at Hoffmann. "He's from Sweden. And accidentally shooting someone here in Colombia could make it complicated with his papers. So I'd appreciate it if you took care of this."

Hoffmann didn't shake his head, but he wanted to. *Boy? I'm thirty-eight years old. Not much younger than you are.* But he understood what El Mestizo was up to. Marginalizing. Generating sympathy.

"So I'll give you nine million pesos right now. In addition to your monthly payment."

"Hey, man, there's eight of us. You want us to split nine mil?" The tall thin one, who squinted just as often at the blown-off back of the head as at the four soldiers tied up on the ground, spoke in a strange dialect that Hoffmann had never heard before. Even though his Spanish had become almost as good as his Swedish or Polish, he still had difficulty following these twisted words and sentences that seemed to form their very own language.

"What are you thinking here, Sánchez? There won't be anything left."

"I think you get a good salary from me already. Usually without having to do shit."

"If I, *we*, are gonna clean this up it'll cost nine million. Times eight."

"You better goddamn . . ."

"Look at me, Sánchez. If you shoot a military officer, that's just how much it costs. And I want it in dollars. Thirty-five hundred dollars each. That's twenty-eight thousand. How *do* you want it?"

El Mestizo rarely gave in in a discussion about money, or any discussion at all. But this time he did. He went to the cab of his truck, rustled around in the glove compartment, and returned with a brown envelope. El Cavo stretched out a slender arm and took it. They both knew what would happen next. A phantom image of someone who had never been there. A call over the radio, *a black man was noticed running from the scene.*

But that's not how things ended this time. El Mestizo handed over the envelope, nodded after the completion of the negotiation, and walked toward the dead officer. A machine gun hung around his lifeless neck. He unfastened it, nodded back toward El Cavo, and continued toward the four bound and prone soldiers—who you really could call boys—and set the weapon to burst mode.

Then he shot them one at a time, in the back, in the direction of their hearts.

"If you're getting paid that much, you might as well take care of this too." El Mestizo nodded a third time toward the chief of police, who was silently holding a brown envelope. "Twenty-eight thousand dollars. Divided by the five bodies. An average cost of . . . fifty-six hundred. That feels a hell of a lot better. Right, chief?"

* * *

Hoffmann reached out through the open window and adjusted the side mirror—El Cavo and his men were getting smaller and smaller, but not as quickly as he hoped. The two trucks were moving almost painfully slow, twenty kilometers on a road that started out undrivable and got even worse, which meant forty-five minutes of driving.

Side mirror again, still not quite right—needed to be turned a little more to the left. There. Maybe angled slightly downward. Perfect. He saw what he expected to see—El Cavo's little troop had already started digging. Not very deep, the forest dogs had to be able to catch the scent. He'd seen their tracks when he dumped the off-road vehicles, they were close by, hiding and waiting patiently. They usually came down quickly, working in teams like wolves, making it to the bottom of a two-foot deep grave in ten, fifteen minutes tops. And tore the bodies up quickly too—knowing their time was limited, ate quickly, the smell would spread and with it came competition. Condors and vultures would circle overhead, then start to attack the dogs who gave up and loped away. The big birds continued the meal, but more calmly—nothing would disturb them until nightfall when the Andean bear took over and cleaned up, first crushing the bones to get to the marrow. Until the jaguar challenged it. Until they both left with a femur. Only the skulls would remain, stripped to the bone, there at the bottom of the hole—by tomorrow morning five people would have disappeared.

The conversation with Zofia felt more heavy than usual, all the more fucked up. At first she would try to comprehend that her husband killed another man. Because he thought he had no choice. Then she'd attempt to comprehend that four boys had been buried and then dug up. Because El Mestizo had felt he had no choice and did what he always did when he felt threatened or wanted to position himself. She would try her best to understand why someone she never met, someone called El Cavo, and his men had cleaned up body after body for thirty-five hundred dollars each.

Hierarchy. Money. And it just kept going. As it does when the system outside of you becomes the system inside you. You are born into it, nurtured by it, embraced by it, until eventually you embrace it back. And your breath is no longer your own survival, it's the death of others.

"Zofia?"

Cell phone in hand. It took her a few rings to answer.

"Hello. Again. It cut off before?"

"I'm in the jungle, you know."

"I know."

"Tonight, Zofia."

"If you . . . I'll wait for you here."

"I love you."

The call broke off again. This time because of his index finger on the answer button. It was enough. She knew what it meant. She should put Rasmus and Hugo to bed early, and they would sit across from each other in the kitchen and talk through this until they were done, then sit next to each other on the sofa hand in hand without saying anything at all.

The jungle tightened around him. It was becoming more difficult to move forward as branches and leaves and lianas whipped against the windows. A road the guerrillas had built up, dug out, routes to meeting places and camps that no one else could find, a world of its own. And inside it, the sounds. The strange hum of hundreds of thousands of insects hovering in black clouds, herons and giant toucans and macaws amplifying each other's calls, and the monkeys, who sat in almost every tree, sounding their warning calls—a dark-green reality that formed a giant greenhouse with its own primordial soundscape.

Hoffmann read the map, again. And he was sure it couldn't be far away, a kilometer or so, not more. He wiped his shirtsleeve across his neck, face, scalp, but was no less sweaty, just added new moisture from the fabric. There. *There.* He glimpsed a zinc roof, and walls of bamboo and dried mud. Cocina. Work and home for ten people—the camp manager, two chemists, three chemist assistants, and four guards. He stopped the truck just as El Mestizo was stopping his, got out, said hello. First to the camp manager, El Comandante, who welcomed them in his slightly bigger caleta. He lived alone, a stained straw mattress on his floor, a simple desk under a bare bulb, and outside his door a large TV hanging from a tree, with an adjustable antenna, connected to the generator like the lamp. Then the older chemist, the only one not in camouflage, introduced himself as Carlos. Hoffmann smiled—all five head chemists he'd met so far had called themselves Carlos.

The two truck platforms looked identical, covered by tarps. Six rows with four large bags in each, stacked two by two, the bulky kind reminiscent of packs you see outside construction sites—all of them brimming with coca leaves. And then, at the back, four oil barrels filled with chemicals.

The crane rooted around like a hunting claw, an arm of metal sticking up between the cab and trailer, easy to maneuver. One by one sacks and barrels landed on pallets holding them up from the mud that drowned everything else, and with every step Hoffmann's hiking boots were stained by that soft, brown gruel.

Hoffmann, like El Mestizo, had handled this kind of load several times before—a half hour and the truck bed was empty.

"You hungry?" El Comandante tied mosquito nets to branches and nails and rolled out black plastic bags over the wooden planks that connected his own caleta to the guards' and chemists', creating an open living room in the middle of their jungle home. "Ajiaco? Today's main course. And for the first time we have the pleasure of serving cold beer to our guests."

There was a small shack behind the chemists' cocaine kitchen and the camp manager proudly led them inside and showed them a fairly new refrigerator connected to a generator. He smiled broadly as he opened it, revealing several rows of Aguila and Club Colombia bottles, light and easy to drink. El Comandante and the chemist Carlos settled down onto the plastic-covered wooden boards, invited El Mestizo and El Sueco to sit opposite, and they all ate potato soup with chicken and sweet corn and toasted with cold beers while the guards and assistants stood a bit farther away awaiting their turn.

Hidden by a wall of trees at least thirty meters high, which prevented sunlight from penetrating and satellites from discovering them. Inside this demarcated terrain, the cocina became an inaccessible fortress impossible to survey. The cocaine laboratories that Hoffmann had visited so far were all like this, or located in desolate regions close to Venezuela, which offered a different kind of protection—if the military attacked, and the PRC were at a disadvantage, the guerrillas could always flee across the border. The domestic troops never followed them there. A blown cocina was not worth the risk—armed soldiers in a foreign land could be interpreted as an attack and result in launching another war between two countries that were tired of fighting each other.

"Dessert?"

The camp manager was waiting for one of the chemist's assistants to clear the table and take the plates and cutlery to a primitive but functioning kitchen—water in a plastic can and a crumpled piece of metal as a sink.

"Not me . . . But maybe this young man?" El Mestizo nodded toward Hoffmann.

"Arroz con leche de coco. Any interest?" The camp manager smiled at his other guest, as proud as when he opened the refrigerator. "It's not every day I can offer you that out here."

"Thank you. But I'm good."

"You know the coconut, it . . . my friend, you can't even taste the rice."

Hoffmann patted his stomach lightly. "Still—I'm full."

El Comandante lifted a hand, held it up smiling, a gesture of defeat. "Well then. More for me. Right? But in that case I insist you take some tamales with you. We've got some ready to go. It'll do you good." Rice, chicken, vegetables. Inside a can of Coke. Hoffmann nodded and stood up, stretched, looked in the direction where he guessed the river flowed. He didn't see it. The green walls were in the way. But according to the map it lay close by.

He had to go there before they headed back. He had to be alone. *Only a criminal can play a criminal.*

He took a slow lap around the sacks and barrels, ran his hand through the tightly packed coca leaves, and knocked on the rounded metal—a muffled sound, filled to the top with chemicals. This was the heart of the cocina, the main building, which also had a roof of zinc, panels and walls of widely spaced bamboo. Earth-packed floor, which got looser near the middle and had a tendency to turn to mud. As soon as the others finished their meal, the coca leaves would be soaked in ethanol inside those sawed-open oil drums, methodically drained of their juice. Then moved to the next barrel where the gasoline would be separated out, and the coca mixed with ammonia, then filtered. A long time ago—before Zofia and the children, before the lies and the promises that he eventually started to keep—he'd smoked a lot of the sticky mass that was created midway through this process. Freebasing. That's what they'd called it back when he bought and sold it in downtown Stockholm; in this country they called it basuco and, according to Johnny, it was of an entirely different quality, gave a different buzz, total fucking paranoia, anyone who tried got stuck inside it for days.

Now and then he longed to do it again, but of course he never did.

That last step, from basuco to cocaine, the white powder, was the same—more chemicals. The ones he'd transported here today. Ether, butanone, hydrochloric acid. That was all he could make out from the waybill. And there was more, he couldn't decipher the contents of the last barrels.

"Something wrong in here?" El Mestizo put his hand on Piet's shoulder. That didn't happen often. He was in a good mood.

"Yes." Hoffmann had already scanned the laboratory as he always did when he entered a new space. Now he did it a second time. Workbenches made of empty shipping boxes. The other benches made of plywood balanced on sawed-off tree trunks. Plastic barrels, plastic buckets, metal containers, serving trays, fabric, microwave ovens, pallets, fragile racks of test tubes.

It all fit.

"Those seem a little . . . out of place."

There was a pile of bags in one corner. Bags stacked on top of each other. Purses on top of briefcases on top of suitcases of various sizes. All in the same color and material, some kind of leather.

"You're right. And wrong. They don't quite fit in. And yet they do. *Carlos?*" El Mestizo shouted through the gap-filled wall to the chemist standing outside with a cigarette in his mouth. "Come in here. I want you to show our European friend your little secret."

The head chemist dropped his cigarette into the mud, stomped on it with the heel of his boot, and went into the laboratory. Carlos. Hoffmann remembered his predecessor who'd borne the same name—just like *his* predecessor—had been the type to get a little too chatty sometimes and so last year El Mestizo had had to take care of him. Now this version of Carlos went over to the pile of bags, grabbed a mid-size suitcase, and put it on one of the workbenches.

"Show him."

Two unexpectedly calloused hands opened the suitcase, whose interior looked just like any other suitcase.

"This is our method for providing a customer with . . . selected samples." The head chemist pointed with one of his callused hands at the empty suitcase. "Small bag, not much cocaine. Big bag, lots of cocaine. This transports about three kilos."

Three kilos. Samples? Hoffmann didn't know much about street value these days, but back when he was dealing in Stockholm that amount of coke would have meant a huge party and a shitload of money.

"The exterior is made of leather. You see? And inside, some plastic, but mostly leather—here too, basically the whole interior—the compartments, the bottom, the sides." Carlos ran his hands over the leather, which was an unassuming brown. "The leather contains cocaine. Which I have killed. Or at least the smell, anyway. Completely odorless cocaine. You can get through any customs you want, pass by any dog you like."

El Mestizo gestured that he wanted the bag, and the head chemist handed it over.

"The first time I saw this, Peter, I was just about to kill him. Do you remember that, Carlos? I came in here and saw a huge saucepan with some black goo boiling inside it. I asked what it was and Carlos replied, *that's your cocaine.* It made me fucking furious. I've never seen it before. *What the hell are you doing, you idiot, you're destroying it!* I screamed until Carlos interrupted me. *I'm not destroying anything, let me show you.*" El Mestizo took hold of one of the bag's inside pockets, ripped it loose, and held up the bit of leather. "There are two steps. The first, you have to kill the stuff. I've never seen it done. And I haven't pressured anybody. I understand you, Carlos. I've explained that it's your technique, the livelihood of you and your colleagues, and you have to protect that."

The head chemist smiled guardedly, as if afraid El Mestizo could change his mind at any time, become less understanding.

"There aren't many who can do this. Just a few chemists. I know of one in Cali, one in Bolivia, one in Venezuela, and there's one more here in the Guaviare province, but much further into the forest. We kill the scent and then melt the cocaine into the leather. And when I do it, I don't let anyone in here. But step two, bringing the cocaine back to life, that I can show you. It's easier, and our customers receive instructions on how to do it themselves."

A blue plastic barrel stood in the corner near the stack of bags, smelling strongly of chemicals. Carlos picked it up, placed it on the workbench.

"Give me the leather." He nodded toward El Mestizo, who handed over the scrap he'd just ripped out of the suitcase. "Like this." And then he sank the oblong piece into the chemical mixture.

"Ether. I dip it, rub it, as if I'm washing it and, voilà . . . as you can see, it turns white. Or maybe not so much white as colorless. What do you think, maybe we should call it a whitish yellow?"

The leather's dark brown hue was gone. Carlos picked up another plastic container of chemicals—permanganate, sulfuric acid—and lowered the now colorless leather into it. Two layers slowly formed. A yellowish surface layer, and below that a second layer of pure water. Or, at least it looked like water.

"Now we restore it. Bring it back to life." He reached over to the shelf filled with test tubes and chose the one that stood closest. "A drop of this into the white. One more drop. One more. Do you see? It gets thicker, almost looks like semen. The more drops you give it the thicker the goo, as Sánchez calls it. Or maybe batter sounds better? And then, if we had more time, I would have heated the mixture to ninety-eight degrees, put it on a tray, and let it dry. In a few hours you'll have cocaine of the highest quality, ninety-four percent, sometimes even ninety-six. We call it fish scales. They don't have it where you come from, but there's nothing better and it glitters, like the scales on a beautiful fish."

Hoffmann had come across yet another form of the drug that once controlled his life. Now he possessed knowledge that few others did. But that was not what this was about. Confidence. That was the real message. El Mestizo, who didn't put his trust in anyone, had once again done just that, shown his confidence in him, and now seemed a little pleased with himself while waiting for the man he kept closest to realize that. It had taken two and a half years, but he was now more deeply embedded in the core of the PRC guerrillas than any other informant ever had been.

"The river? Is it that way?"

El Mestizo smiled.

"Are you going for a swim, Peter?"

"I need to wash off. Before we head back. This heat has crawled into my pores and won't let go."

"You know there are crocodiles, right?"

"Yes."

"And in this province, you know, they don't just bite off whatever's sticking out, they chew." His smile spread even wider.

Hoffmann also smiled and headed out alone down the carved tunnel, surrounded by the screams of monkeys and buzzing of insects. Ants formed thick black ropes as they crisscrossed the path in front of him.

A few minutes and he was there. It was beautiful. Wide, open water, he guessed seventy-five meters to the other side and a strong current in its middle. One of the many tributaries that carved the Amazon jungle into pieces, leading from nowhere to nowhere. A light wind, pleasant, cooling.

He stripped naked and took the first steps toward the shore and then saw a log lying not far into the water. He bent down, picked up a good-size rock, and took aim. A hit. The log moved in irritation, splashed as it disappeared below the surface, and swam away, small eddies following behind it.

He moved farther out, dipped his whole body, put his shaved head well below the surface of the water. Silence. Even more cool. It was like a cold balm against his blazing skin. He stayed in longer than he'd planned, needed a private moment without the punishing heat.

Johnny had shown trust in him when he urged him to shoot. And again when he showed him the bags. The one person he shouldn't trust.

Hoffmann waded toward the shore between jagged rocks, dried himself off as best he could with his damp shirt, dressed, and looked around cautiously. He was still alone.

The GPS receiver lay there in the fabric pocket of his vest. He took it out, pressed a button labeled *mark,*

57.308326, 15.1241899

and checked the decimal grade on the display. The precise latitude and longitude of this location—but in a coded program.

If the coordinates ended up in the wrong hands, if someone else got hold of the figures before he gave them to his handlers in Bogotá or Cartagena, they'd have no idea what the numbers meant. They would lead them to another continent—to one of the churches he liked so much, Korsberga in southern Sweden. And which they had agreed to always use as a diversion. The real coordinates of a PRC-controlled cocaine kitchen in the Amazon jungle would only appear after his DEA handler ran them through *her* encryption device.

He put the GPS receiver back in its place in his vest pocket and took a few steps back toward the water, squatted down, and rinsed his face again, staring down into a wavy mirror. Somewhere in the green behind him was the cocina. After about an eight-week wait, to keep from throwing any suspicion on his visit, the newly formed Crouse Force would crack down right here on the basis of the coordinates he'd just downloaded—and shut down this cocaine lab by force. And only a few people would be aware of what had happened, few would know how they'd been able to find their way here, the conditions necessary for an informant's survival. Not even the powerful US politicians who initiated his mission, who reaped the benefits of it, knew that he, a convicted prisoner on the run from a European prison, was actually working for them.

TIMOTHY D. CROUSE couldn't cry. Not anymore. It was as if he'd run out of tears four years ago, as if they'd all run down into the ground, making a softer bed for the one who rested there. Forever.

He didn't cry now either. Even though he was watching images for the seventh time of another grave being filled, other human beings who no longer existed. Rage. That's what he felt. That was why he moved away from the satellite operator, stepped over to the big screen on the wall, leaned in close to minimize reality. It didn't work. Sánchez, the burly man with the ponytail, who was also called El Mestizo by the PRC guerrillas, had taken the automatic weapon from the dead man's shoulder and fired it at the young men in uniform.

One death had become five. And another patrol, probably of police, had taken an envelope, probably money, and watched while Sánchez shot them. A patrol that then started digging.

Crouse didn't scream. He never did. That wouldn't solve anything. But he ended today's visit, nodded to Roberts guarding the door outside in the corridor where they'd parted, walked faster than usual, heels hard against the polished plastic floor.

"We're going there, Roberts. Tomorrow."

"Where, sir?"

"Where they dig graves for profit rather than grief."

The black car was waiting in his parking spot, just outside the entrance to the eight-story building. It wasn't much more than a six-mile drive from NGA and Fort Belvoir to the Pleasant Valley Memorial Park. He visited the project that bore his name at least three times a week, and on his way back to the Capitol, he always stopped to be with her. With Liz. The one who held all his tears.

"First to Liz, then to the House of Representatives, then home. That's today's schedule. Tomorrow we'll arrive in Bogotá just after lunch. I just let them know I'm coming."

"You're not giving me much time."

"Roberts?" It wasn't often he snapped at the man he entrusted his life to. But that's what happened now. Bodies shoveled into holes should call forth those who'd watched it. "Take care of it."

His driver parked by the chapel, next to the main road. Crouse always wanted to approach her headstone on foot, watch it grow from small and gray to something that comprised his whole world.

She only made it to twenty-four. Outgoing. Happy. Maybe too outgoing, too happy. Though he didn't think so at the time. On the contrary, he encouraged it without understanding how it slowly turned to a lack of boundaries. She never said no—she always followed along. She'd been fifteen years old when he confronted her about the pills the cleaning lady found in her room, and she told him they were given to her by somebody whose name she didn't even know. More confrontations followed, and it was clear that her drug use was becoming more frequent and her behavior to get ahold of the drugs more risky.

Beautiful green lawns surrounded a narrow, winding path toward the graves. Her headstone lay there, framed by two shrub-like trees, and was similar to the one that lay next to her plot. Mother and daughter together in life and death.

He'd contacted an addiction counselor to help him clarify issues that Liz didn't want to hear. Together they'd arranged an intervention. And he got his answers. The ones he didn't want. Starting at the age of twelve, she'd tried every drug he'd ever heard of and some he hadn't, and by then she was in the grasp of a mix of OxyContin, Valium, alcohol, and marijuana. He'd checked her into a private treatment center. After less than two weeks, her stay there resulted in new drug contacts and running away with a heroin addict nine years her senior.

"Sir?"

Roberts never usually interrupted him here. Not with her. When he did, it was important.

"Yes?"

"I apologize, but I've looked into it and I just can't get an acceptable security detail together in time for tomorrow."

"And *I'm* not gonna sit in front of a television screen anymore without participating. I need to do this. Because I can. This is why the Crouse Force exists. So tomorrow, Roberts, we're headed to Bogotá, no matter what, headed to the barracks."

He loved her headstone. Granite. A simple engraving—ELIZABETH CROUSE to the left, the day of her birth and death to the right.

"Not like last time, sir? When we were also supposedly staying in the barracks, and you left the outer perimeter of the security zone to inspect where the new recruits burned down some coca plantations on the border with Venezuela? Or the time before that, when you departed with a captain from the Crouse Force to oversee the dismantling of a warehouse full of chemicals outside Cumaribo without informing me?"

"One day and one night. Back the next day." Crouse squatted down, straightening the vase of flowers stuck into the grass just behind the stone, the roses inside starting to wilt, but they had a few more days in them.

"The outer security zone, five men. The inner zone, four men. Close-range zone, three men. Sir, that's not enough in my book."

"If that's what there is, then that's what you have." He snapped again. But this time he felt in the right. "Roberts, if you'll excuse me?"

The bodyguard retreated to a tree some distance away and watched while Crouse watered the heather growing in front of Liz's mother's stone. By the time their daughter was born they were already separated, but now some kind of connection had returned.

The sudden breeze blew a few dry, brown leaves down onto his daughter's grave. He ran his hand over them, as he used to do when she was little, spreading his fingers through her long hair, pushing her bangs a bit to the side, before she put them back the way she wanted them.

She was sixteen years old when she ran away from the rehab center. He tried to get her to come home, but they didn't speak much after that. A phone call here, an impromptu visit there, always shaky, nervous, broken. He got the call from the Sacramento police the day before her birthday. She was lying in a morgue with a steel frame beneath her head, and she looked the same age as her father. Weighed seventy-five pounds. He'd kissed her forehead and squeezed her stiff, bird-thin hand. An overdose-induced heart attack.

He'd decided long ago. And today he did so again. He would hunt down those drugs. Not to punish anyone—but to remove the source. He was no longer driven by a desire for revenge, but by grief.

HE STEPPED OUT of the car and into the protective darkness. There'd been a time when he feared what now engulfed him, drowning in it while it protected others—the ones who were there to attack. This darkness was like the light, leading him forward, holding on to his hand.

Piet Hoffmann lingered in the narrow backyard. Cool, dry air. Starry sky. And from where he was standing right now he could see into the kitchen, where she was sitting at a round oak table with a glass of wine in hand, a newspaper open in front of her, alone just as she promised she'd be.

So different from the hellish humidity and insects of the jungle. He'd taken the muddy path back to the road, and they'd exchanged their trucks for a car in Florencia, took turns at the wheel as usual. Eight hundred kilometers and neither of them had talked much, not because they'd decided not to, but they let each other be, neither one afraid of silence. He liked that about Johnny, there weren't many who could deal with silence, remain comfortable inside it. Not even when he dropped him off at the large hacienda outside Pradera did they say anything to each other, just nodded. They'd meet again in a few hours at the brothel anyway for a new day that would need new words.

The white plaster house with its semiworn tiled roof looked just like every other house in the district of Los Guayacanes in Comuna 5 of northeastern Cali. That's how it had to look. An ordinary car outside an ordinary house with ordinary people on a narrow, winding street with nonexistent street lighting. He'd bought it seven, almost eight years ago on a trip here from Stockholm with Erik Wilson as his guide. His Swedish handler had been the one who told him he had to find a way out and helped him to arrange it. They'd both known that if he was ever discovered by the group he'd infiltrated on behalf of the Swedish police, or burned and abandoned by his employer, he'd have to flee with his family—immediately. Flee from his own death sentence. A couple of successful crack deals in southern Stockholm—which the Swedish police turned a blind eye to as long as he continued to provide them with useful information on organized crime—had paid for the house as well as the caretaker who looked after it for the four years it stood empty.

Peter Haraldsson. That was the name he used on the deed. The very first time Piet Hoffmann entered into his new guise. A property transaction on another continent with a new identity. He hadn't even told Zofia about that.

He had lied so long that he forgot what truth felt like or how it looked. And when he'd finally been forced to tell her everything—or lose everything—he finally understood the way he'd pushed at the boundary between falsehood and truth, until he was never quite sure where a lie ended and a truth began, until he no longer knew who he was.

Now she poured a little more wine into her glass. Picked up a pencil, wrote something. Kitchen lamplight fell so beautifully over her face, so soft, present.

He remembered another house in Enskede, Stockholm, which after a sudden departure stood just as empty as this one had. Their home. He'd stood many times just like this outside it, just before going in, the moment equidistant between midnight and dawn. An empty house in another reality—overhanging fruit trees, wide flower beds, a lawn he should have cut more often. And a sparse hedge bordering the neighboring house that Rasmus and Hugo disappeared into as often as they could.

Zofia. His wife. She was the one sitting inside. Sometimes it felt so strange to think that. That a man who never intended to settle down had someone he could call his wife. The first few times he said it, *wife,* it sounded false, contrived, as if it were something other adults had come up with. *My wife.* The one who waited for him because she knew he needed her to.

"Hello." He leaned forward, kissed her, always twice. Always an even number. Held her and felt totally relaxed, only here, only in her arms. For seven days and several hundred kilometers he'd longed for this.

A Swedish newspaper sat in front of her, *Dagens Nyheter*, she bought it from time to time when she had an errand in Bogotá. An almost completed Swedish crossword. That's what she'd used the pencil on. She pushed out the chair next to her, gestured for him to sit.

"Soon. Wait a second."

The stairs to the second floor squeaked a little more every week. If he stood on the edge of them it was quieter. Cautious steps up to the first room. Rasmus, six years old. Lying on his stomach, and with both hands under his pillow, he'd slept like that since the very first night. Smooth, slow breaths. He was the more happy-go-lucky of the two, didn't worry as much as his older brother—this was just his reality, half of his life he'd been called Sebastian and spoken Spanish and been on the run. A light kiss on the cheek, Rasmus stirred a bit, mumbled something, then quickly returned to slow, even breaths. Next room. Hugo, eight years old. And he was dreaming, like his father. Sweating, nervously waving his arms, speaking out loud about something that was hard to make out, but with a voice that sounded hunted. Piet sat down on the narrow edge of the bed, put his hand to his son's forehead, stroking it in a way he knew helped. Hugo worried so much and hated moving and being given a new name, *I'm not a William*—no matter how patiently they explained that this was his name now, that they could never use Rasmus and Hugo because someone wanted to do them harm, *Mom, Dad, can't you see it doesn't fit*—no matter what he or Zofia said it didn't make an impact because their son refused to take it in. And at night, that's when it weighed on him most, when he felt most hunted, because that's exactly what they were.

Hoffmann stood up and went to the stairs, which creaked less on his way down. Rasmus. Hugo. He was at least allowed to *think* of them that way.

She filled her empty wineglass halfway, sat an empty one down in front of him, and filled it to the top. He sat down on the pushed-out kitchen chair, put his hand on top of hers.

"Room with at least one *B* in it. Seven letters. I have an *H* in the middle and an *E* at the end. I'm stuck."

He leaned in close. To her. And the crossword. She was the one who enjoyed them, spending a few hours not thinking about other things, and she was the one who was good at them—he was too restless, lacked the patience.

"Beehive."

But sometimes when she got stuck, she asked him to look at it with new eyes.

"Okay . . . *okay*, I see it now. A room and a *B*. That really was a bad one. But thanks." She smiled and filled five letters into five empty boxes. Then closed the newspaper. She caressed the hand that lay on top of hers and waited for him to start talking. It usually took a while.

"Today, Zofia . . ."

"Yes?"

She still loved him, of course. But on nights like these it was hard to know how they'd be able to stay together.

"Today. This morning. I killed a man. Another one."

A nine-year-long lie. A double life, parallel worlds. At home he'd been a husband and father, running a private security firm. And at the same time—he'd been a man immersed in the criminal world, while also risking his life every day on an undercover assignment. It was a greater betrayal than if he'd been with another woman. There were lies inside lies and no matter how you approached it, how could you really take it all in? Another woman would have been easier, she would have existed, seen, understood, hated, given Zofia a clear reason to leave.

She'd chosen not to leave him. And a life with two parallel worlds continued.

"One gunshot."

She had demanded the truth. To always be given the truth. Nevertheless, sometimes she wished she didn't have to hear it.

"In the forehead. Between the eyebrows."

Sometimes she wanted it even more. The past. Her weekdays picking up her kids at preschool or soccer practice. Watching them run off somewhere when he got home, not coming inside for dinner when he called. None of that existed now because *they* didn't exist.

"And then . . . Johnny became El Mestizo, again."

She knew what he was doing. And that it was for them.

"Young men, Zofia. Boys. Ten years older than our own. He shot them in the neck, in the back, because he could."

She knew that her husband came across death in his work. Sometimes even contributed to it. Directly when he was protecting those who killed. Indirectly when he protected the drug that kills.

"Five people. Just today. In one place. Do you understand?"

And she had tried to tell herself that if he hadn't done it, someone else would have. That didn't work anymore.

"Does it make any difference?"

"What do you mean?"

"If you shoot a man . . . where was it you said . . . between the eyebrows, or if Sánchez shoots four in the neck?"

"I do it to survive. So we can survive."

"They all end up just as dead."

Maybe her voice sounded harsh. But it wasn't him she was angry with.

"We have to leave, Piet. Go back home. This isn't working anymore."

"To life in prison? A life without each other?"

"To something else! Something that's not death."

Piet tried to drink the wine. White, rather sweet. Something in his throat wouldn't let him swallow.

"It's going to change you, Piet. It already has. Every time we sit here and talk about people who are no longer breathing, you become a little less of the man I love. Killing someone changes you, you'd have to change in order to stand it. In order to continue. Piet . . . you have empathy, you care about things. For real. You can cry, laugh. Genuine feelings. I love that! That's you! But for how long? How many shots, how many breaths, before it runs out?"

"I—"

"Piet, listen to me. I have thought about this. If you're doing it so that we can remain together. And if that makes you not you anymore, into another version of you I don't want to be with—then what's the point, right? I'd rather visit you every day in a Swedish prison than think of that ugly, cold, dark void that is even more isolated."

He put down his wineglass, pushed it across the table as far as he could, to the other side. He had tried several times now—but still couldn't swallow. "I love you, Zofia. You know that."

Going home. A life sentence if the Swedish authorities found him there. A death sentence from the Polish mafia if they found him. Staying meant putting off the inevitable. And at the same time. He was sweating even though it was cool, his heart racing even though he was sitting still.

"I love Rasmus. I love Hugo. You know that, Zofia. And it has nothing to do with anybody else's life. Or death."

"Yes. It does. I decided, we decided, this was the better option. But if that's no longer the case, Piet? If it's worse? If every time you kill someone part of you dies as well? Part of us?"

She took his hand again, both his hands, and they sat like that for a long while before walking up the creaking stairs. Passing Rasmus's room, he still lay on his stomach, not moving, past Hugo's room, he mumbled something and tossed and turned, and continued on to their bedroom. And held each other hard as they made love like they usually did.

A CUP OF coffee. Hoffmann grabbed the mug as soon as the hot droplets passed through the machine, drank up, and placed it back on the plastic grille to be filled again. He stood in the middle of a large windowless subterranean room, which was currently deserted. Despite the silence, it still reeked of alcohol and money and women just a few hours after closing time. On the empty dance floor next to the empty stage. On the empty tables in the empty sofas and empty chairs. Behind the empty counter, where he was finishing his second cup of coffee.

La Casa Heaven—the large club in the basement under the hotel. The eighty young, lingerie-clad women who worked here for most of the day—one hundred and twenty from Thursday to Sunday—were tasked with making sure newly arrived guests were assigned a table and served two drinks, the minimum cost to sit down. And every afternoon and evening and night and dawn after customers emptied their glasses, the women would smile and take their hands and lead them up the rickety stairs.

Hoffmann opened the fridge under the counter and pulled out an ice-cold bottle. Strong coffee followed by bubbling mineral water—his body slowly waking up this morning too. He sat down at a nearby table and leaned back on the soft sofa. A musty dining room, ballroom, meeting place. And above it, three floors of small rooms—bed, vanity, bathroom with shower. Johnny made his money in two ways. First, the alcohol. Then the room rentals. Cali's only brothel whose owner guaranteed protection without requiring a percentage of customer fees. A commercial practice that provoked anger from his rivals as soon as he entered the area—identical brothels lining both sides of the street—to hand out his business cards. *Things going well for you here? How much you earning, for real, little one? My name is Johnny, but they call me El Mestizo and I own that place over there. Come by sometime, I don't take commission—booze and rent goes to me, fuck money goes to you.* He sounded proud when he told how the young women had flocked from other brothels, even from other cities, begging for permission to sell their bodies here.

Hoffmann shrank slightly into the empty silence. There was so much he no longer understood. Like female bodies for sale. Like the fact that he'd killed someone, again. Like the fact that Zofia had decided they had to go home again.

To what? To what he could never actually live with?

"Coffee?"

Johnny. That's who he was here at the brothel. Soon, when they left this place, he'd become El Mestizo again.

"There's some in the pot behind the counter."

"Fresh?"

"I just brewed it."

Powerful, heavy. But fluid in his movements. His black braid hung down over his red shirt, which in turn hung down like a caftan over the green military slacks out of whose side pockets bulged a knife, an extra magazine, and a box of cut coca leaves. He poured two full cups and carried them over to a table that was always kept vacant and clean, and where Hoffmann was sitting now—the owner's table.

"You awake yet, Peter?"

"Soon."

"Good work yesterday."

Johnny pushed one cup of coffee across the table. It was down here, in the musty darkness, that Hoffmann's boss—and unwitting guarantor of continued infiltration—felt most comfortable. That restlessness that could quickly turn to irritation or anger was just as much El Mestizo's companion as Hoffmann, and it was least on display here during the hours between the last customer of the night and the first deliveries of the day.

"You hear that? I appreciate what you do." His laughter was a low chuckle and didn't really fit that huge body. "Damn, if I don't almost trust you!"

Johnny's brothel is in its twelfth year—started as part of a collection from one of the guerrilla's permanent customers, a small mob boss in Jamundí who hadn't paid up in time for the fifty kilos he'd received and sold. The usual warning—*I'll kill the youngest member of your family, then the second-youngest, and so on until you've done right by us*—had been ineffective. Only on the third visit when El Mestizo lost his patience, put the barrel of a gun to the head of the debtor's six-year-old son, was the final payment made. But by then he was no longer content with the initial sum—he wanted interest, decided he wanted one of the brothels that formed a part of the debtor's local empire. The one where they sat drinking coffee right now. It was the sole purpose of the demand for interest. For reasons Hoffmann had never been told. El Mestizo had reached an agreement with the guerrillas. He would run the brothel himself—it was the kind of business no one had any interest in being linked to anyway—and give them 25 percent of the profits. And the top boss had said yes. Not because of the money, but because he realized what was driving El Mestizo and why this particular brothel in Cali was so important to him.

"And Maria? How is she, Peter? You're taking good care of her?"

Zofia. Who had never made herself more clear. Time to go home. No matter the consequences.

I'd rather visit you every day in a Swedish prison than think of that ugly, cold, dark void that is even more isolated.

They'd held each other close, until he awakened from the peace he found with her—and with a stiff arm around her body.

"I'm taking care of her. Always will."

Johnny nodded, satisfied with the answer. Again not understanding what it meant, how that affected him—all the things that played into *I trust you.*

"This."

A large pink envelope in Johnny's hand.

"Got it yesterday. Thought you might want to see it." He turned it upside down, was about to empty the contents onto the table, when someone shouted down from the stairs that led to the first floor.

"The car is here!"

The last swig from the coffee cup. The envelope slid into one of the side pockets of his pants.

"We'll deal with that later." Johnny stood up, walked toward the stairs and loading dock in the rear of the hotel. Once a week a car arrived from Buenaventura's harbor with smuggled liquor. The main source of income—the two glasses of alcohol every customer had to purchase at an exorbitant price before he could buy a girl. The sales value over a day when every four-ounce glass cost twenty-five US dollars added up to more than thirty thousand. Twenty times what he paid now. Johnny looked over the handcarts of packed bottles, counting them, and took out a tight roll of hundred-dollar bills encircled by a rubber band.

"Down here. And you better be damn careful."

Three hours. Then the doors would open again. The smell would intensify, becoming more pungent with lust.

"And the whiskey, I want you to put that over here."

The two dockworkers were done, were rolling their empty handcarts toward the exit and the delivery truck, when Johnny waved Hoffmann over. It was time to head out for the first collection of the day.

"But first I think we should go buy a moped. What do you say to that, Peter? A red one with white stripes and a soft, oval seat."

They took one of the jeeps today and didn't drive far before El Mestizo stopped for the first time. An industrial area near Cali's northern exit. There it stood, unpacked and ready to go. Red with white stripes. They helped to lift it up and tie it onto the flatbed of the jeep. The next stop was at a small, neat house that lay halfway to Palmira in a neighborhood where quite a few police officers lived. This particular policeman was young—Hoffmann guessed around thirty—and was pushing a lawnmower around a tiny, greenish-brown lawn.

"I heard from a little birdie that your Leandro is about to start school." El Mestizo made sure to squeeze the young policeman's hand just long enough. "My God, it seems like just a minute since I bought him a tricycle. That was red and white, if I remember correctly?"

The proud papa smiled. "You remember right. They grow up fast."

"In that case . . . you'll need one of these now, right?" El Mestizo motioned to the proud papa to accompany him to the back of the jeep. "Because you're going to need to drive your boy to school."

The two of them lifted down the moped, whose red and white paint glowed in the burning sunshine.

As they continued their journey, Hoffmann turned around in the passenger seat and watched the government employee roll his new moped toward the garage, his hand caressing its long, soft saddle. One of the many who received a fixed salary from his other employer, the PRC. And who every other month would be rewarded with some little gift to remind him that those who give should also receive—this young police officer's task was to warn them of any raid on the brothel—as long as you serve us, we serve you.

"It's like giving a dog a treat when he brings you the right shoe."

"Excuse me?"

"Has that ever occurred to you, Peter? That they're like dogs. And a dog has to keep getting his treats if you want him to fetch your shoes. No treats—no fetching."

El Mestizo always sounded like that. They all sounded like that. Profiteers. Hoffmann exhaled slowly. *We* sound like that.

We, the drug traffickers, who are both inside and outside the PRC, we always marginalize and mock accomplices and buyers—profiteers who look down on the ones we profit from. It was the same everywhere, in Stockholm where he'd worked, but considerably worse here, as if the more we earn from the drug trade, the more contemptuous we have to be toward drug users—the weak.

"But you have to handle it with style, Peter. They should never have to ask for help—you offer it. A moped? I could see you thought it was ridiculous. You've been here a while now, but you still don't understand. And you're in good company—there are those who've grown up in it who don't understand fully. They don't see the whole picture when it comes to that red and white moped. It makes me think of the general and the airport. One of the groups there, Peter—you've met a few of that crew, but this one took care of smuggling from the airport long before you came—paid a general six thousand US dollars to avoid customs when they sent their cocaine to the US. It worked well for a few years. But eventually the general noticed all the shit this gang was buying—jewelry with huge fucking diamonds, tons of Porsches, big fucking houses, and even estates with horses and winemaking. And one day he told them, *You run around showing off your flashy lifestyle, and I only get a paltry six thousand, so from now on, I want ten.*"

The red and white moped and the police officer tightly holding its handlebars disappeared behind the curve of the road, and Hoffmann turned back around again, toward the mountains looming in the distance, which was where they were headed.

"The leader of the smugglers just laughed, cocky as hell. *Listen you fucking soldier,* he said, *you got what you're going to get.* But the general had made up his mind, turned to his men. *Handcuff him.* Only then did the smuggler understand. *Okay, okay, we'll pay.* Now it was the general's turn to laugh. *Too late, asshole. I don't give a shit about you. I'll be doing business with somebody else.* Shit, Peter, they put them away and threw the book at them. They even took the houses their families lived in. And they got twenty-five years in prison. All of them. You understand? If things are going well for you, your contacts need to get a little bit of payback, so they feel like your success is helping them. They should never have to ask for more money. If they're happy with you, they'll protect you. They'll keep you out of prison to keep delivering drugs and making even more money."

"Like yesterday?"

"Yesterday?"

"The dead ones."

"That was different."

"How?"

"That's why I'm in charge in this car. Because you don't know these things."

The sign said two hundred and thirty kilometers to Medellín. And Hoffmann still didn't demand any answers. Because it was pointless. And because they drove out for these collections a couple of times a week, all over Colombia, and it was usually with three, maybe four hours of driving ahead of them that El Mestizo would provide any necessary background. Never earlier—in El Mestizo's world owning information meant owning power and control, the confidence that comes from knowing what others don't know, a sort of mental life jacket. But no later either—in order to ensure Hoffmann's full protection El Mestizo had come to realize that a certain amount of prep time was necessary. They'd just passed Cartago when he started to describe Prez Rodriguez—no children, unmarried, thirty-eight years old. Twelve of them at La Picota for drug smuggling, a special prison in Bogotá. Rodriguez had belonged to the Medellín cartel, caught and took the fall—had protected others but hadn't received any damned help while serving time, not money nor food nor whores. So when he got out, he'd offered his services to their competitor, the PRC. Now he owed them three accounts, seventy kilos. A small-time dealer, but right was right, this was about their reputation.

A white plaster house. Bars on several of its windows. On the short sides of the house red bricks that hadn't been laid straight. A few simple cars parked just outside and some kids playing down the street, a cluster of telephone lines a few meters above their heads, like long, untuned guitar strings. Central Medellín near the end of Calle 3 Sur and the intersection of Carrera 52. A staircase marked number 17. A tiny, filthy elevator that El Mestizo walked past—he always avoided them, climbing the stairs resolutely, because then he was in charge, no machine was going to decide if he got stuck somewhere. Hoffmann followed him, counting the steps, eighteen between each floor, seventy-two to the fourth floor, and the door with RODRIGUEZ engraved on a gold-plated metal plaque.

The doorbell was a small, round, black button that didn't work. El Mestizo, who stood in front of Piet, knocked instead. Several times. Until they both heard steps. Hardly light, not much of a bounce, more like shuffling. Someone who was tired, or perhaps sick or old. The latter. A man with long, thin, silver-gray hair opened the door hesitantly, peering out through a narrow slit. A pair of glasses with taped-up frames hung from a twisted band over his bare chest. Hoffmann guessed he was seventy-five. The same age his father would have been. With a voice that was unexpectedly powerful.

"What do you want?"

El Mestizo grabbed hold of the edge of the door and tore it open. The older man came along with it into the stairwell. "We're looking for Prez Rodriguez."

"He doesn't live here. I live here. Alone."

"And who the hell are you?"

"Luis Rodriguez."

"If he doesn't live here, then why do the tax authorities disagree?"

"And why exactly do you think it's my job to keep track of what the tax authority records say?" The elderly man used his long, skinny arms to try to pull the door shut. El Mestizo held tight and took a step closer.

"Rodriguez. It's on your fucking mailbox. It's your job to keep track because it's your fucking son who bears your name!"

"Listen, *if* I did have a son, then it would be none of your goddamn business what I named him."

Hoffmann didn't smile, not outwardly anyway. The old man was doing his job. As a parent. He was protecting his son. Which a parent does no matter how old that son is.

"You got that, you Indian bastard?"

"This is the way it is. This son, who you named and who you think that I should forget about, has now been warned through *you* that he has exactly three days to pay up what he owes. And this, papi, is his only warning."

Luis Rodriguez took a step forward too. Stood very close to El Mestizo. Frail and well into retirement, but with the same attitude he probably had when he was young and strong.

"Are you standing at my door threatening my family?"

"Yes."

There were no more steps to take. So Luis Rodriguez just stared. Those watery eyes, now covered with a film, had probably once been sharp, penetrating.

"If you hurt my family, you Indian bastard, I'll kill yours."

Hoffmann was still smiling, on the inside. It was . . . well, sweet. And real. Somewhere inside of that hissing, spitting, fighting man, he saw his own father, whom he missed.

"Three days. Are you aware, old man, while you stand there calling me names, what the consequences of not paying your debt to the PRC are? You can be goddamn sure your son is. That's why he's not here. That's why he took off and left you to face the consequences." El Mestizo let go of the door, turned, started to leave. Then he stopped on the third step and turned around again. "Luis?"

"Yes?"

"You shouldn't have threatened me."

Back in the car, behind the wheel and headed down Carrera 52 toward Medellín city, it was as if nothing had happened. Even though El Mestizo's life had just been threatened. Because that's just how it goes, part of everyday life, rarely leaving any traces.

"A petty dealer. Next time we pass by, if the son still owes us, we might as well kill one of them, simple enough, no one will mourn them. But this thing with his old bosses at the cartel, well, that complicates things, Peter. You realize that, right? There are competing operations in this region. If this plan is to be executed, we can't be seen to be involved—we'd be starting a war. The last time we did that, we won eventually—but it cost us thirty-six employees. I'll find another way this time."

Hoffmann sat in the passenger seat, looking out at drab houses, any of which might contain Prez and Luis Rodriguez. And he knew what *another way* looked like. He hated it. The only time he'd spoken openly about what he thought of El Mestizo's world, the only time the discussion got close to raised voices and fists, the only time he chose to jeopardize his undercover mission, was when he couldn't stand to swallow and spit out this life.

Teatro Metropolitano. They had arrived. It was there, outside the main entrance, that El Mestizo usually stopped when they had business in Medellín—and where they parted ways. Therefore, the rest of Hoffmann's employer's journey was unclear. After a couple of visits—with Hoffmann insisting he was responsible for protection and wasn't even supposed to leave his side—El Mestizo let it be known that he would be at Carrera 7 in a hospital called Clínica Medellín. That—but no more. And they always met again outside the theater exactly two hours later. Piet, as the protector, knew where, but not what, why, had never received any answers, and eventually quit asking. And Hoffmann had found the perfect way to utilize his free time.

That's when he usually met Lucia Mendez, the meetings that were his one and only true mission.

Their meeting places always had at least two entrances and two exits on two different streets. And they arrived at different times. They took place in empty apartments that were under renovation, plastic covering every piece of furniture. They'd sit down at someone's kitchen table, drink someone else's coffee. No matter if they met in Medellín, Cali, or Bogotá. The same principle as the meetings he'd had with Erik Wilson, his handler in Stockholm.

Scaffolding in the stairwell. Paint, rollers, toolboxes, and men in identical caps and jeans. Hoffmann nodded and started to zigzag past them up a stairwell enclosed by plastic. A glance out the window at the terrace that marked the first floor, he knew she had come from that direction, crossed the courtyard and in through the rear staircase, gone all the way up to the attic that connected this building to the other one, and down these stairs.

Third floor. ORTEGA on the door. Same last name at every meeting place. He rang the doorbell, listened to the drilling taking place somewhere on the property. One more ring. And he caught a shadow observing him through the peephole.

She opened the door. Dark, curly hair, eyes that had the kind of seriousness he looked for in someone before almost trusting them. "Come in. It's just as messy as usual."

Lucia Mendez, special agent in charge of both of the DEA's Colombia offices. El Mestizo had informed Hoffmann late last night that they'd be headed to Medellín for a collection and a hospital visit, and Hoffmann had contacted her in turn, as they'd agreed, and left the branch in Cartagena. He could never say exactly when, because El Mestizo always withheld when and how until they were on their way, and so she had to be in place for a few hours already—it was the same at every one of their twenty-eight meetings over the last two and a half years.

They walked through a dusty hallway, continued on to the kitchen, and she pulled plastic off the table and chairs while he unwrapped the cupboards and found a jar of instant coffee and peeled more plastic off the stove. Poured water into a saucepan and lit a flame that flickered blue and red. Just like in Stockholm—Erik had pulled off the plastic, and he'd put on the coffee.

"Lucia."

"Paula."

Wilson had given them Piet's codename in Sweden and the DEA had decided to continue using it. So he was Paula in this room. El Sueco to El Mestizo and the guerrillas. Peter Haraldsson to his neighbors in Cali. Piet Hoffmann inside. Lies, truth, it was difficult to know where the line stood, to even know if there was a line.

She put a couple of porcelain cups between them on the table, smiled. "How's it going?"

"Just a regular day." He liked her quite a bit. Two and a half years of service and no contact with Sweden and Erik, no contact with the US and Masterson, who recruited him, so Lucia Mendez, by definition, was his only colleague. Sounding board. Security. She wasn't Erik, who'd had nine years, but on her way.

"And Zofia?"

"Fine, as usual."

She'd been trained, like Erik, at a base called FLETC located in Glynco, Georgia. And you could tell. Like Erik, she did her best to form emotional ties with him, get close to him, get him to risk his life for her every day, for just a shard of information. He hadn't realized it with Erik. He'd been young and naive and grateful to be accepted with open arms after serving time in prison. He could see through it now. The manipulation followed the same pattern. But it didn't bother him. This time he was the one in need, in need of work in order to survive.

"And Rasmus? Hugo?"

"Both good."

She was the one who helped Zofia find a job as an English teacher in Cali. She'd arranged protection for the boys when he'd feared retaliation. Arranged protection for his family when he exposed them to danger—they'd almost been shot up once, in his car, they'd all been sitting there just moments before, and the vehicle shortly after looked like a colander, a childish thought, but that's exactly what occurred to him as blood flowed from his right shoulder and the windows, doors, and roof were covered with black holes. And—when a man going by the name of El Sueco was wanted by the police for attempted murder and extortion, and bribes were not enough to make it go away, she was the one who made charges disappear, twice.

The water was boiling now, and he filled the cups to the brim.

"I don't know how it tastes. But it has to be better than the coffee of our mutual friends, which is mixed with another, much stronger powder." They drank. About half a cup each. And then it was time.

"Here." From one breast pocket he pulled out the GPS receiver and placed it on the table in front of her. She read the decimal degrees on the display,

57.308326, 15.1241899

and scribbled down the coordinates of the place he'd visited yesterday—latitude and longitude in code—on a fresh white page in a small notebook. They would give her the location of a PRC-controlled cocaine kitchen in the Amazon jungle when she ran those numbers through the converter back in her office in Bogotá.

"Lucia—no sooner than eight weeks. Okay?"

"Four weeks is what we've agreed on. That's when we'll strike."

"Last time you waited exactly four weeks. This time you need to wait at least eight."

"In eight weeks the kitchen, the drug factory, will be gone."

"This cocina, it's central to the operation in that region. And it's so remote, so lavish—rest assured it will be there for a while."

"You're sure?"

"No. But it's a risk we have to take in order to avoid any appearance of a pattern related to my visits."

An incubation period. Which had to vary. In order to minimize the risk that Hoffmann's information—which provided the entire foundation for a strike by the US authorities—could be linked to a certain Peter Haraldsson, who the PRC were paying to protect that very same cocaine kitchen.

"You've got the place. And time. But I have to give you a warning as well."

She looked at him, expectantly.

"This cocina, Lucia . . . it's not like the others. It's bigger, the biggest I've been to. It has a whole other level of defense—heavier weaponry, skilled soldiers—ones I helped train. You have to be prepared, more manpower, more firepower. Otherwise, you'll be the ones left lying in that jungle."

Afterward they draped the plastic back over the cabinets, tables, chairs, washed up the two porcelain cups, changed the name on the door from ORTEGA back to SILVA—as if they'd never been there.

He was supposed to leave first, take the northern exit she'd entered by. He hugged her good-bye, that's how they'd always said good-bye, and it would feel wrong and weird to suddenly stretch out a hand instead. He'd made it out the door and halfway across the landing, when she caught up with him and grabbed his arm.

"The phone?"

His other breast pocket. He pulled it out while she took another one out of the inside pocket of her blazer. The same system as when he worked in Sweden. That phone received calls from a single number. Sent calls to a single number. Two burner phones that only called each other, two anonymous subscribers that could never be traced.

"It's been a month. Time to change."

She had put a paper bag on the wrapped hat shelf in the hall and grabbed it now and took out a new phone.

"If you could give me your old one."

He did so and took the new one. With a single preprogrammed number.

"From now on, use this one instead. And—we'll see you at the fourth if we meet in Bogotá, or the second if it's Medellín, or the first if it's Cartagena."

Hoffmann passed by more construction workers as he made his way down the stairwell than he did on the way up, they were bolting together metal scaffolding that blocked off large parts of the space, and his clothes were covered with a layer of dust and paint chips by the time he stepped out the front door.

SPEAKER CROUSE STOOD in the corner of the barracks' yard with his weight resting on his right leg. Standing for too long always made his left hip ache, and he was worried that someone might notice. He didn't know why, after all he was a middle-aged man, and like other middle-aged men he walked around in a body that life was gradually dismantling. Maybe vanity. Maybe it was the fear of revealing weakness, a politician who didn't radiate power got no voters, no votes, no missions. He stayed in motion, getting up and down from his chair at the conference table during long meetings, preferring to stroll during interviews, and when he had no choice, like at the lectern, he'd found his own solution—memorize what he was going to say and then lean forward on one elbow where others kept their papers, then the pain ceased and no one saw.

A gentle drizzle was delivering its first drops—part of an eternal cycle that carried water the way he moved—up, down, all around. So fragile that the crackling-dry gravel continued to rise like smoke as the twenty-man squad moved in formation in front of him—left right left—the captain's monotone shouts over the megaphone—left right left—black marching boots and uniformed arms whose gestures and movements were an exaggerated theater. Because that's what it was. Spectacle, performance, because their spiritual father was watching them, the Crouse Force, from just a couple of marching steps away. Drills that were repeated ad nauseam. Crouse turned around, glancing up at the elegant officers' club on the top floor of the building from which he'd just come. They usually insisted on inviting him up there, on the other side of that beautiful panoramic window, he was supposed to be impressed by the incorruptibles, convinced that the money he worked so hard to get mattered, was making some impact, building something new. But he'd never liked the red carpet and silver cutlery of the officers' club. He preferred standing alone without the colonel, who he himself had carefully appointed, looking over his shoulder, without any of the other officers either, without Roberts scanning the area, concerned for his safety.

He breathed in deeply, felt almost calm. Here. Of all places. In the corner of the courtyard, surrounded by eight bunker-like buildings, which housed the one hundred and fifty incorruptible soldiers that made up Camp Justice. A completely ridiculous name. But the Colombian politicians who'd made this possible had been so proud when they christened it with that name that Crouse let it be, and today, a few years later, was almost accustomed to it.

Stillness. Despite the fact that Combat Platoon 1—policing and reconnaissance—were now marching side by side, shouting out those drills, right turn and halt, which he loathed. He stared into the smoke of gravel dust swirling around them like a smokescreen and his mind wandered to other images—a murder streamed live via satellite followed by mass killings, bodies buried by a cleanup crew for a few pesos more. He usually argued that evil didn't exist—that it was constructed to explain behaviors we didn't understand. But when life was reduced to money, people paid to bury other people, he realized he might be wrong—evil might really exist. The whole evening, night, morning, he was flooded by these evil images, which could only be replaced by good ones. By people who couldn't be bought. His fourth trip here, and it was only now that he understood that feelings won't let reason and thought in until the strong were neutralized. There, in the corner of a barracks' courtyard, the images changed again. Pushed away by contrasting images, the scene in front of him and the resistance it implied, to take on the drug world and dismantle it piece by piece—those bastards were never going to win, and if they did they'd lose so much in the process victory would be meaningless.

Incorruptible. That's what they were, the ones who were marching. Recruited after a long selection process from various professions—policemen, soldiers, paramilitary, customs officers, prison guards, and the occasional psychologist, or teacher, or political scientist—their most important attribute, besides performing well in combat, was that they were not for sale.

It had started a few hours earlier, as soon as they landed at El Dorado International. Those images of the newly dug graves started to waver as soon as the pilot parked the plane on the runway. It really did work to come here, to visit the regiment, which stood in what used to be one of the few remaining green spaces in the center of Bogotá—a triangle framed by Carrera 60 in the southeast and Calle 53 in the northeast and Calle 25 in the west—knowing that he would soon see coca plantations burned to the ground or warehouses filled with chemicals explode or closely monitored storage facilities, filled with several tons of cocaine packaged and ready to be smuggled out the next day, taken over and seized. Images that replaced the filthy, disgusting ugliness and gave him the kind of serenity he only felt when he thought of his daughter as a child, back when he still believed she'd die after her parents, like she should have.

"Right, left, right left right!"

A courtyard of incorruptibles. It had been a long and winding ride here from the day he'd decided to find a way to survive while Liz was slowly disappearing. When he needed something solid to hold on to, to keep from falling apart. A contrast as much as a crutch. And his need for it grew stronger with the realization that no matter how loudly he screamed, he was never going to get it into her head to stop killing herself. He'd realized he had access to a tool that other parents of children battling addiction did not. Power. He could meet with experts, very clever people, and surround himself with them. He had the power to change things. Even though his political rivals initially tried to use Liz *against* him. Politics. Throw shit and try to avoid getting hit by any shit yourself. But then it all flipped. He'd done the opposite of what they expected—went public with all of it, didn't deny a thing, didn't hide or neglect it. Revealed everything about a daughter who didn't want to live. About the Crouse project, which was in its early stages. And his private hell ironically became a professional asset—his credibility and passion were never questioned—America's war against drugs became Speaker of the House Crouse's war against drugs.

"Right . . . turn!"

The Crouse Room at the NGA. It was there that it all began. Spy satellites deployed all around the world in order to gain control over production, supply, the behavior of the drug profiteers. But that feeling of just watching, without being able to participate or intervene, had paradoxically increased. The sharper the satellite images became, the closer they got, the more obvious it became that they were little more than spectators. Because almost all drug production took place in extremely corrupt countries, the project staff could raise the alarm as much as they wanted and still nothing happened. The intelligence gathered in the Crouse Room made no impact beyond its doors. Then, after a few years of ineffectual satellite reconnaissance, the Crouse Force was born. Honest police forces that would be trained and positioned near markets where a culture of bribery protected the drug barons. And they would start with the biggest of them all, Colombia.

"Company . . . halt!"

An agreement was made with the Colombian government, and one hundred and fifty-five candidates were taken to the United States for training in advanced techniques for narcotics policing, all at the US government's expense. Their task was to destroy the means of production and prevent deliveries. Future members of the Crouse Force were given very high salaries in order to stave off corruption—ten times a Colombian policeman's salary. And because it worked so well here, it exerted pressure on other drug-producing states to create similar forces.

"At ease!"

The soldiers shook off the dirt, adjusted their equipment, went back to where they were before.

He'd seen this exercise several times before—the same movements against imaginary enemies—both here and in the United States, an illusion meant to convince. *But it wasn't enough.* At night, those hellish images pushed their way back inside, invading his bed, they . . . he glanced up at the panoramic window. They were still standing there: Colonel Victor Navarro and his subordinate officers. Speaker Crouse started to rush toward the slightly narrower, higher building that housed the officers' headquarters at the heart of the compound. The stone stairs echoed as he climbed up the slightly wider staircase, his hand on the soft, wooden railing that tickled his palm. He almost ran into the officers' club over the red carpet, rounding a serving cart bearing beautiful, hand-painted glasses and heavy, well-stocked bottles, passed by a line of officers, didn't stop until he reached the window and the back of the regimental commander whose eyes were on the courtyard Crouse had just left.

"Navarro?"

The colonel turned in surprise toward the panting Crouse.

"Sir?"

"That stuff down there, in the courtyard, that's fine. If you like that sort of thing. I don't. I like results. And I don't want to watch any more marches."

Combat Platoon 1 had performed their theatrics, only a thin veil of dust was left, and everything seemed so clear from up here.

"The results of all those exercises, all that training and education. The latest crackdown—that's what I want to see! The consequences of the marching!"

"Sir, that's not really advisable."

"I'll decide what's advisable."

"Enemy territory, sir. It's absolutely impossible to guarantee your safety if we take you there. We're talking about the jungle. The world of terrorist guerrillas. And they know it much better than we do. I *cannot* recommend that you go out there."

After the performance came lunch—they wandered around the courtyard, sauntered toward the dining room, laughing and smoking, their imaginary enemy sure to stay away until everyone had been fed.

"The latest crackdown—what was it?" Crouse didn't raise his voice—that rarely had the same impact—instead he stepped closer, stared into the colonel's eyes.

"A cocina. A cocaine kitchen."

"Where?"

"At the edge of the Serranía de la Macarena National Park. Around where the Río Guaviare changes into the Río Guayabero. Not quite the Amazon, but still very remote, an area where the rain forest meets the savannah."

"Distance?"

"Two hundred and eighty kilometers south of Bogotá."

"Travel time?"

"Four or five hours. By car."

"Good. Take me there."

Until now Roberts had been standing as usual. Right next to Crouse but not interrupting. But now he did just that, interrupted. Two steps forward, covering his mouth with his hand as he whispered into Crouse's ear. "Sir, could you step aside with me for a moment? I'd like to speak with you."

"I know what you're going to say. The same thing you said yesterday after I watched people rolled into a mass grave. And the thing about graves—the people in them will never go home to their families. Those we saw yesterday, Roberts, on the computer screens, buried for drugs . . . every single one of them has someone who misses them. And I can't just keep watching that on a screen."

"Sir, I have to insist. Can you come with me?" Roberts nodded toward a corner of the grandiose room, behind Navarro's desk, in front of a wall hung with two crossed bayonets.

"Sir, we talked about it yesterday. And I explained to you I didn't have time to get the security detail I needed together. And you promised me, sir, that under *those* conditions you would stay confined to the garrison area. On such short notice, we won't even be able to get the planes we need to do the necessary radio jamming. The jungle has ears, sir, and those who are listening report what they hear."

"I also remember saying that if that's what there is, that's what you have. One hour, Roberts. Then we head out. I'm damn tired of drills and uniforms marching in unison. I want to see this fight against death with my own eyes."

Roberts was standing in front of a very powerful man, who also happened to be his boss, and this was usually as far as he went with his arguments. He had come to understand the authority of Crouse's grief and guilt. But not now. This didn't feel good. He had to make himself understood.

"Tim, dammit!" He had never called the speaker by his first name. And certainly never sworn at him. Now he whispered again with his back to Navarro.

"Listen to me—this is the same area where they just found a mass grave filled with two thousand unidentified bodies. And last weekend in this region, Meta, there were twenty-eight deaths reported in the drug war. That's just what we know of—fifteen beheaded on a sidewalk in La Macarena, eight riddled with bullets in a taxi, five mutilated in a car." Roberts grabbed his employer, pulling on the bulletproof vest he'd made Crouse wear, despite his protests. "I gave this to you before we stepped off the plane. This was enough for the airport, for the trip here, and inside this regiment's walls. But you can put on ten more of these and it won't make a difference. Out there, this—" Now he pulled on the vest again, a bit harder, and Crouse's shirt as well. "—this crap is no more than makeup that gives you a false sense of security. My God, Tim, you might as well take it off right now if you don't understand that! What you seem to have made up your mind about, you're doing for your own sake. If we head out there, you're risking not just your own life—you're risking other people's lives!"

Speaker Crouse looked at him, aware that this man, who was willing to sacrifice his own life for him, meant well. But still his bodyguard was speaking only half-truths. He wasn't allowing for the fact that that same weekend the Crouse Force had apprehended Andrés Julio Ramos, supreme leader of the drug cartel Xetas, in another part of Colombia. That's what the Crouse Model was about: apprehending, wiping out the biggest parasites, and now Ramos was accused of murder, torture, and money laundering. We get them. Step by step. But every time they bust somebody, there were other groups ready to fight to fill the power vacuum left behind. We have to do it again. And again. Until nobody is left to fight.

"Roberts, nobody knows what we'll find out there. And it's your job to protect me from it. That's what you're getting paid for. I assume you plan to continue doing your job."

"I . . ."

"And don't ever call me Tim again."

There was a rumble outside the panoramic window drowning out further conversation. Four tanks had rolled into the courtyard for the next performance and the crystal and china rattled.

Crouse waited while it petered out, then shouted toward the officers. "Victor?"

Victor Navarro turned around. "Sir?"

"One hour."

The colonel, commander of this regiment, had a self-assured and powerful way of moving, shaped by the kind of gravel down in the barrack's courtyard.

"In one hour . . . what, sir?"

"We depart. From here."

Frank Roberts held on tight to the wooden handle of the machete while using it to hack away at the lianas and thick branches that stood in front of him like an organic curtain—he wanted a clear view while he worked, he was limited enough as it was by the irritating moisture that was creeping along his back and gathering in a puddle beneath the holster on his shoulder. He'd already left his blazer in the front seat, but it didn't matter—the oppressive heat, the buzzing insects, the complete stupidity of standing out here exposed to every kind of risk scrambled every square inch of his brain, making it difficult to think clearly.

An abandoned guerrilla camp. Located somewhere inside the area of the Serranía de la Macarena National Park, surrounded by the rainforest.

They wandered among trash strewn about as if on the outskirts of a shanty town: slashed tires, rusty gas cans, empty food containers, beer cans, pieces of cloth hanging between overgrown trees, and that godforsaken mud that lurked in the grass, which your shoes slid on and sank into. A place where no one lived anymore, a place humanity had abandoned.

Roberts looked around. The military had formed one ring sixty meters out with the cocina at its center—like the protective skin of a human body—and with four trucks and one armored vehicle, and fifteen Colombian soldiers deployed in between, everything that Roberts could gather and vouch for at such short notice. Inside that was a smaller ring, twenty-five meters from the center, like a ribcage—fourteen Colombian special police. Then the third and innermost ring, woven around the heart, Speaker Crouse and Colonel Navarro inside the cocina—twelve American security agents from the Diplomatic Security Service for hand-to-hand combat.

They were more than an hour from La Macarena, the nearest sizeable town. More than two hours to the nearest major city. A long, long way from any other soldiers or police officers, from any additional protection or support.

The tall grass had been trampled into the mud, and a slight breeze wafted for a moment across his forehead and cheeks. Roberts passed through three layers of protection and reached the cocina at the center, positioned himself between the benches and plastic barrels and glass containers and low vats of galvanized sheet metal, just behind Crouse, who stood listening to Navarro.

"The latest crackdown, sir—just as you requested. Three weeks ago. We used the expertise of all seven platoons. Combat Platoon 1—

Colombian police specially trained to lead a crackdown within the legal process, including arrests, detentions, investigations—started reconnaissance of our objective, based on information from a DEA informant. One week before the crackdown. The sixth cocina we've taken down based on information from the same informant! According to reports, he's infiltrated deep into the PRC, to the inner circle."

A flock of brightly colored parrots flew away in terror in the distance, chirping and chattering, a red, yellow, and green swarm against a clear blue sky, and one of the captains took a few steps forward and whispered "big cat" into Crouse's ear.

"Combat Platoon 2, liaison—combat soldiers like all the others, but with special training in communications—placed at base station for retrieval and linkage to satellite images, while Combat Platoon 7, air—trained for deployment by helicopter and small aircraft—conducted overflights and documented the site with both regular and infrared cameras."

Crouse took a lap around the simple building, knocked on the metal ceiling, kicked the dirt floor. It didn't look like much. But this was the source. The root. This was where the long chain began. What a fucking centennial—manufacturing and transportation and sales made possible by corrupt police and military officers, and customs and justice officials who protected the wrong side. A trillion dollars a year—the cocaine trade's sales when a measly 5 percent of the product was seized, while 95 percent reached consumers. Figures illustrating the problem and the solution—educate and spend more than the other side. They might not destroy it today. But tomorrow. In a generation, maybe two, maybe three.

"Sir, this way." Navarro gestured toward a straggly path, they headed down it, with Crouse ducking the cut off lianas and split branches. The jungle shrank around every cavity, making green walls and a roof for the eternal darkness. At the end of the path they reached the river, beautiful and very wide. Crouse guessed it was at least three hundred feet across, but it could just as easily be double that. On the other side of the water stood a high plateau, completely dry in the burning sun, and behind that the sky above an even greener roof.

"Combat Platoon 4, marines—trained to operate in small and large boats, dive and conduct underwater attacks, stop and force underwater vehicles to surface—they launched twenty kilometers to the north in a motorized rubber raft, five soldiers on board, and headed downstream, this way." Colonel Navarro took a step and kicked a few round stones at the river's edge, a muffled splash as the glistening surface was pierced and became blurry. "They disembarked five kilometers upstream, hid the raft, and then floated the rest of the way fully equipped for battle. They did the last five hundred meters underwater and continued on to the riverbed, to here, where we're standing now. They went ashore at dusk and cut off the most obvious escape route."

Another path back, an older one, and they fought against overgrown squares of ants in motion and the godforsaken spheres of flies and mosquitoes around their heads, which made it hard to see. Crouse stumbled a couple of times as he stepped over the thick carcasses of trees that were slowly being bleached by the sun. They approached the *cocina* from the back, zigzagged around other trees—around Brazil nuts fifty meters high—and Crouse couldn't help but go up to them, run his hand over their powerful trunks, and then he continued on, stepping back into the abandoned cocaine kitchen, toward the colonel's low voice, hovering between a bass and baritone.

"This whole area, everything around us, was booby trapped. We knew that from our DEA informant. So our offensive was launched by Combat Platoon 6, explosives—trained to do more than blow things up from the air, they've developed explosives that generate so much heat that large quantities of cocaine simply burn up. Sometimes it's more about elimination than securing evidence. The platoon located and neutralized all the mines—you can still see the craters out there, it made a hell of a lot of noise. And then, with the mines gone, they attacked. We went in full force. Until all camp personnel were captured or killed."

Crouse's gaze had followed where Navarro pointed to the cocaine kitchen door, toward the mines that were no longer there, and when he turned back he was struck by something for the first time. Twenty suitcases. All made from identical, brown leather. Stacked in a corner.

"You think they travel a lot?"

Navarro had seen what caught Crouse's attention. "Something like that. There have been similar piles in a couple of other cocinas we've taken out. Suitcases in the middle of the jungle? We still don't know why they're lying here. Can't be for the transportation of drugs, they're too small, we're talking about deliveries that weigh several tons."

The colonel lifted up one of them, opened it. Completely empty. "We let the dogs go through them. Nothing. No trace of cocaine."

A few burners, which could be found in just about any camping kitchen, stood next to a couple of big tin pots filled with a sticky mass—three weeks earlier it had been on its way to becoming cocaine when an enemy attack interrupted the process and it was now coated with a layer of dead insects, dust, sand, mold. A somewhat looser batter was bubbling in a cast-iron pot to the right. Crouse waited for the next bubble to burst. When it did, he was met by a distinct smell, or rather a stench. It had fermented. That's what it smelled like, overly fermented beer or some sort of mash he might have forgotten in his dorm room way back when he used to brew moonshine in an old bucket out of stale bread, apples, and water.

"Sir? May I continue?" Navarro gestured toward the exit, that's where they were headed. Crouse was one step behind, Roberts right after him. "Everyone in the camp was captured. Or killed. Two platoons are still at work. Platoon 3, the canine unit—their dogs are trained in warning and tracking corpses and explosives and can detect cocaine and other substances used in its manufacture. And Platoon 5, chemistry, which analyzes all the ingredients used in drug manufacture—it's thanks to their efforts that we've been able to track the cocaine all around the world."

Navarro had waded through the mud toward the intensely green high grass and halted when he reached a dark rectangle amid that lushness. He seemed proud, maybe even stretched a bit. "Here. This is where we burned up all the shit. Cocaine in every phase of being processed. Quite a bit of basuco and some finished product, too, right into that blaze. Nearly a ton in total. We saved just a few plastic bags, some samples for our chemists. And over here, if you follow me . . ."

Then he stopped. Suddenly. Midstep. Listening to something.

Soon Crouse heard it too.

A motor. Several of them. Cars? Maybe trucks? Not yet visible, but going down the same muddy path they'd arrived by, he was sure of it. And then more engine noise. From the river. Boats, also more than one.

The tension was palpable.

"Sir, this is not good."

The special police and soldiers started shouting orders in Spanish. Crouse made out *load*, and what might have been *rocket launcher.* He saw Colonel Navarro pull his gun from his right hip and run over to one of the trucks, felt Roberts grab him by the shoulders.

"Somebody's seen us, sir!" Roberts's breath was hot on the skin of his neck. "Our water route is blocked—you heard those boat engines. Our land route is blocked—you can hear those cars clearly now. We have to go back, sir, into the cocina!"

Roberts pulled his employer backward into the cocaine kitchen and pushed him down on the dirt floor behind one of the benches, the spot with the least amount of visibility, then sat in front of him like a human shield.

That was when they heard the echo of the first shots. And then more shots. And louder. The machine-gun fire mixed with the explosions. *What's not supposed to happen is happening.*

Crouse twisted to the side, beyond Roberts's wide body, trying to look outside. And he saw. How everything had turned white. Like the barracks courtyard earlier. Thick, compact smoke surrounded them, the cocina, and what was outside.

"Head for the exit!"

But this was not a drill. This was for real.

"Now!"

The white smoke absorbed all sound. Explosions and gunshots were drowned in that softness; Roberts's voice was weak even though he was screaming.

"Crawl, sir, it could be toxic!" The bodyguard crawled and scooted forward over the dirt floor, and Crouse tried to follow suit, his eyes fixed on the dirty soles of Roberts's shoes. Crouse pressed his light-colored suit into the mud, crouching, each new breath brought even more smoke into his throat and lungs, and he coughed and coughed until he finally threw up. He couldn't go on. The cough penetrated deeper as the vomit sapped his spirit, the smoke was so thick he couldn't see anything. Except for an angry red laser beam searching around anxiously in front of him, finding the silhouette of Roberts's head. Which shattered.

Everything was completely silent as strange, excitable gloved hands grabbed his arms, pulled him, pushed him forward. As the wall of smoke became a dancing fog, a floating veil that slowly thinned out. As young people wearing gas masks and camouflaged uniforms dragged the dead through the tall grass, as if they'd been out hunting and were gathering all their quarry into a single pile. As they tore into him, held him, making sure he really saw who lay there in front of him on the ground. Colonel Navarro. On his stomach. In the middle of that black rectangle where they'd burned the drugs—Navarro had never reached the protection of the truck. It took a moment for Crouse to see the rest. The ground *beneath* Navarro, which showed clearly through the large hole between the colonel's shoulders.

And complete silence as someone forced his arms into zip ties, which cut deep into the skin around his wrists, and someone else placed a black blindfold around his head and tied it tightly.

A flatbed truck. He could tell that much. He felt it. He sat down with his back against the raised edge of the platform and at every unexpected turn, every bump, every brake, he was knocked with new pain.

Crouse still couldn't see or hear. It was dark, silent. The blindfold had been followed by earmuffs, which muffled sound. Yet he understood, could interpret. He'd waited, tied up in the grass, and could make out the insistent stench of gasoline as they set fire to one vehicle at a time, felt the vibration of violent explosions from four trucks and a tank that had stood in the outer ring of his protection and two larger cars and six motorcycles that DSS agents traveled in, and the car he and Navarro came in, which had been rebuilt and strengthened until it looked more like a small tank.

The attackers, likely guerrillas, had known the precise moment that a vehicle, armored to withstand bombs and drive over mines, would become useless because the person it was meant to protect had left it, exposing himself.

Nobody knows what we'll find out there. That's what he always thought, how he'd decided to look at life. How he'd answered every time someone in charge of his security explained how his everyday life had to be further curtailed. Now he knew.

The platform edge shook, pounding against his spine, the uneven road was full of holes and slippery. But he had no idea where he was. Other than in the jungle, in the terrible heat and humidity, which drained him. He had been sitting like this for several hours, he was also sure of that, despite the pain from his tailbone and left shoulder, which made it hard to think, keep track of time.

The attackers, murderers, kidnappers had left forty bodies in a pile. Set fire to the vehicles. And then . . . filmed everything. Cámara, película, televisión. The last thing they let him hear before they cut him off from the outside world. Filmed? Why? Had they filmed all of it? The attack? A face being blown apart?

A sharp turn, his neck and the back of his head hit the cab, and the next time it was an elbow, a nasty, awful shock through his body, which he hadn't felt for a long time.

He wasn't alone. Far from it. He could sense them breathing, several people surrounded him. And they were armed, the weapon of the person sitting closest to him bumped against his hip and thigh, and he wondered if it was intentional, so that he'd know better than to try anything.

They'd taken the lives of the others. But not his. They'd allowed him to live. Why had they spared him but not Roberts?

No head. That's what he'd seen. His bodyguard's skull split open, his body collapsed.

You were right. This is my fault.

"Señor?" A woman's voice, sharp and nasal, she kicked him, the tip of her boot against his chest, pulled one of the muffs from his ears. "Muchas horas."

Strident laughter. Several of them in unison, he was supposed to hear it. Then she let him put his earmuff back on, and it was silent again.

Many hours. But to what?

PART TWO

STOCKHOLM. AFTERNOON. AND a gentle September rain.

Ewert Grens didn't notice any of it. He walked the short distance to the car in the parking lot, crammed between walls of empty, stacked shipping containers. Värta Port, tons of traffic and people in motion. On their way to or from Finland, Estonia, Latvia, Poland, one doorway of the capital's transportation system. He didn't notice the light drops falling on him, his focus was on the plastic bag he was carrying in his hand, and it meant more to him than any of his surroundings. The temporary premises of the wine auction, that was where he'd been, purchasing rarities he'd otherwise only be able to bid on online—two bottles of Moulin Touchais 1982, which he always purchased at this time of year. A large and important collection, so the entire cellar had been moved out to this location for an old-fashioned auction, where buyers would have the opportunity to see and touch. He'd paid the standard 2,350 kronor, for the first bottle. The next, with identical contents, had gone for 3,000—the suit who'd lost the first bid to Grens had waved his paddle more frequently. It turned into a contest for the sake of prestige, as sometimes happens at that sort of auction. Overpriced, Grens realized that, but he didn't give a shit about the connoisseur's smile, nobody else understood the actual value of these bottles. He bid on a third bottle that he didn't need. Just to mess with him. Pushed up the price until it was a good deal more expensive than the other two—and the moment the suit triumphantly bid the highest, looking pleased with himself, it had been Ewert Grens's turn to smile.

He climbed into the car and placed the plastic bag with two bottles inside it carefully in the passenger seat. He backed out of the parking lot, between confused travelers, and headed toward Gärdet and Östermalm and the city.

Fancy bottles. Even though alcohol no longer interested him, not the taste nor the effect. Drunkenness was an illusion for cowards who needed a deceptive world to face themselves. Then there were those who thought wine auctions were too expensive for a policeman's salary. But this was no expense, that was what they didn't understand. This made him richer. Besides, the only other expenses he had were the coffee machine in the hallway and the occasional Mazarin tart from the vending machine.

Now he noticed it. The rain shining in the occasional glimmers of sunshine, he put on the windshield wipers and folded down the sun roof.

Sometimes the wine tasted slightly of cork, the bottles were old and time had had its way. That didn't bother him in the least. One glass for him from one bottle, and one glass for Anni from the other, then he poured out the rest. That was exactly how much they'd drunk that night. A seven-minute ceremony at the Swedish embassy in Paris—an embassy official as wedding officiant and two porters as witnesses—and then the Loire Valley and the guesthouse that looked like something on a postcard.

He was on his way to her, as always on this day. But he made a detour through the city, over Tegelbacken toward Kungsholmen, where he'd stop by the Kronoberg police station and retrieve the cooler from his office—the wine had to be kept between eight and ten degrees Celsius. And on top of the cooler lay the two peaches in a small bowl.

Moulin Touchais and peaches. He remembered only a portion of the wedding dinner. Lobster soup as an appetizer, and he'd refused to let go of Anni's hand, he hadn't known you could hold another person in that way. A main course while he slowly drowned—constantly looking at her, into her, knowing that he would never again feel alone. Mostly he remembered dessert, how they giggled at how improbable it was that they'd really just gotten married and drank sweet dessert wine, which the guesthouse proprietor proudly explained came from the region, and which you were supposed to drink with flambé peaches, because peaches apparently brought out the taste, enhanced the scent of honey and almonds. Grens still had no idea after all these years if that was true, he couldn't tell the difference, but he always made sure to bring two peaches.

The traffic light outside City Hall turned yellow, and he stopped. The car behind him, a taxi that had been following a little too close, slowed to avoid a collision and honked irritably and without interruption until the light turned green. On another day Grens might have stepped out of his car, pulled open the door, and demanded to know what the hell the taxi driver thought he was doing. But not on this day. Not on his way to her.

They always drank that exact wine, exact same vintage, on their wedding anniversary. First, when she was still healthy, and they lived together. Then after she'd entered the nursing home, he brought in those unopened bottles, sat in her institutional room and held her hand while they toasted. Anni had smiled and taken a sip as best she could when he brought the glass to her mouth. He'd been sure she recognized the taste, that it awakened something inside her. The doctors had said what they always said, that it was impossible, but they'd never stopped him from letting her have a drink, and he knew something they didn't—that her hand felt different inside his on those days. Every year the wine got more expensive and harder to find, until finally only available at auctions.

He glanced at the bottles as he turned right onto the street Norr Mälarstrand. They lay beside him in a plastic bag, clinking a little in time to the music—Siw Malmkvist and *Lyckans ost*. It had taken him a long time to find a functioning tape deck for his car. He turned up the volume and sang loudly in chorus with Siw, out the partially rolled-down windows.

Suddenly the taxi that had been honking behind him veered out into oncoming traffic in a furious attempt to pass him. And the driver realized too late that a traffic island with a high curb was up ahead. The taxi driver increased his speed a little more and squeezed into Grens's lane just before hitting the island—forcing Grens to hit the brakes. Everything inside the car continued forward, crashing against the window and ceiling and doors.

Silence. Slanting across the road. He looked around—he'd heard right. A sound that drowned out tires screeching on the asphalt. Bottles shattering.

The plastic bag had hit in the center of the dashboard and expensive wine was now dripping onto a floor mat covered with large shards of glass. The taxi drove on without checking to see if there'd been any consequences for his fellow commuters. Grens started the car again, sped up, and caught up with the taxi near Rålambshov Park. Now it was his turn to trail too closely and honk persistently. Until the cab driver tired of it and slammed on his brakes.

It was inevitable. Grens drove straight into him. And both felt and heard the two vehicles buckle as metal met metal.

"You old, fucking bastard . . ." The cab driver, a middle-aged man in a blue taxi uniform with a glowering, red face, jumped out of his car, shouting at Grens. ". . . Why the hell did you stop at that yellow—and honk at me now!"

Grens yelled back through his rolled-down window. "Because you drive like a fucking cabbie bastard!"

They were in the middle of the road, not very far from each other. If Grens were to step out of his car, they'd collide. Again.

"Fucking asshole! I've been driving taxis in this city for twenty-two years, and the surest way to make me laugh is for a fucking amateur to try to tell me how to drive!"

More honking. But it wasn't from Grens or the taxi driver this time—behind them two cars had formed a queue, which was getting longer with every swear word.

"Listen . . . I've been a cop in this town for thirty-nine years and the surest way to make *me* laugh is to see some asshole cab driver lose his license." Grens was searching through the inside pocket of his jacket for the black leather case that held his police badge. He located the badge, held it up, waved it a little bit.

The taxi driver walked over, put one hand on the roof of the car and one hand on the sideview mirror, glaring at the plastic card with the word *police* written on it. "Cop? I could have bought something like that online. Get the hell out of here before I get really mad and do something I might regret."

The cab driver was outside Grens's car door, waiting, when he started showily sniffing the air and leaned forward, following the smell that was streaming out through the open windows. "What the hell . . . I smell booze! You're really fucked now!"

Grens shook his head angrily and shifted his heavy body slightly, lifting up the leaking plastic bag, pulling out a shard of glass that ripped the air between them to pieces. But the taxi driver never saw that, he was already gone—loping hastily back to his own car, then pushing in the two buttons on either side of his radio in order to place a call.

"Four-three-one-nine has been hit by an extremely drunk and aggressive driver."

At one of Taxi Stockholm's switchboards there was now a flashing red light on the ceiling and a sign in front of the operator that said EMERGENCY.

"Please call for police assistance as fast as possible! I'm on Norr Mälarstrand, near the west side of Rålambshov Park." Then he jumped out of the car again and against a backdrop of honking vehicles, shouted in triumph. "Ha! Now you're gonna catch hell, you bastard! Are you a drunk, or what?"

Grens sat in the driver's seat, the wet bag in his hand. "You've just ruined my visit with my wife."

"I don't give a shit about your wife!"

Before Grens managed to stand up, before he could roar, *nobody says that about Anni,* he saw a new taxi approaching at high speed, coming to a stop in front of the two stationary vehicles and blocking the roadway. A ruddy, freckled man jumped out. In one hand he held a baton. He looked around and then joined his colleague. Grens waited while they spoke to each other, almost debating. They apparently came to some decision, and the first one pointed and the second one raised his baton and started to walk. Toward him.

"You hear me, wino? This is what we're going to do—you step out of that car. You're in no shape to drive. And we're gonna have a little talk." He hit the baton against his palm, repeatedly, a smacking sound, like a whip against unprotected skin.

Grens had no intention of escalating the situation. But he didn't carry a baton with him, and if he left the driver's seat without a weapon there was a high probability that Freckles would use his. But sitting here was no real option either. He had only one choice—use a weapon that was more powerful than his attacker's. He unbuttoned the shoulder holster hanging diagonally across his shirt and took out his gun, put a bullet in the chamber. "I don't think so, cabbie. I'll wait here until *my* colleagues arrive. Moreover, if I were you I'd be sure to put that tiny baton of yours away real quick. Otherwise, I might think you're trying to threaten me."

"And if not—what the hell are you gonna do about it? Run to the liquor store and buy a bottle of consolation? Get out of there, you stupid fuck!" He slammed his baton hard against the roof of the car. Then again. And again. It was that sound that destroyed what remained of Grens's patience. He threw open the car door, knocking the driver onto the asphalt, then jumped with unexpected force out of the driver's seat and pointed his gun at the spitting, swearing man on the ground.

"Drop your baton!"

And suddenly it was as if everything froze.

"And turn over onto your stomach!" Complete silence. He heard it now. No honking anymore. "You do whatever the hell I say!" Grens cocked and aimed toward his legs.

Until the driver, mumbling, reluctantly turned over. "Fucking hell . . . a man like you should stay off the booze."

Traffic stood still, a line of cars all the way to City Hall, as the sirens echoed between the buildings and the rotating blue lights reflected against the plastered facades.

"Here they come, cabbie. My backup. They'll pick you and your friend up."

The police car used all four lanes of the road, winding its way through vehicles and curious onlookers. Two younger colleagues in uniform. Grens guessed they were cadets. They opened their doors simultaneously and stepped out with guns held high.

"Drop your gun!"

Grens looked at them, didn't recognize them. And they looked at him, didn't recognize him either. "I'm a police officer—and I've arrested this man." Grens made sure they were able to see his weapon, kept it pointed at the man on the ground. If they were to misunderstand the situation, get the idea that he was aiming at them, they'd do what so many of his younger colleagues might do—shoot first and ask questions later.

"Watch out!" The taxi driver had turned his head, lifted himself a bit, as he screamed. "He's wasted and armed!"

"Put the gun down and get on the ground—face down!"

"I'm Grens, with City Police, I—"

"Drop the gun or I'll shoot!"

They don't know who I am. I won't shoot them. But they will shoot at me.

Grens was as careful as before to make sure his colleagues could see exactly what he was up to as he emptied the chamber of the gun and let the magazine fall to the ground onto the cab driver. Then he took the cylinder out and emptied the bullet there. It bounced off the face of the cab driver and onto his shoulder. Then Grens got down onto his sore leg and gently placed his service weapon on the ground. "Everything according to the rule book—which I've been following since before you were born."

"For the last time—get on the ground! Put your hands behind your back!"

"In that case, you can borrow *my* handcuffs. They're in the car, in the glove compartment, right next to where I just put *my* badge."

"Shut up and don't move!" The hard steel of handcuffs chafed around Grens's wrists. "Now you can get up again."

With his hands behind his back, that was no easy task for a man past his prime. His colleagues grabbed him by the upper arms, pulled him up in order to inspect him, patting Grens's jacket and pant legs, while speaking to the taxi driver still lying on the ground.

"Did you call this in?"

"No. The driver who did is standing over there."

The young cadet waved the other taxi driver over. "Can you come here?"

He didn't have to ask twice. The driver who'd sped past other cars just before a traffic island and then forced his way back into their lane, causing the other cars to brake in panic, now sped up again, jogging forward.

"You called this in?"

"Yes, this asshole—"

"What you reported seems to be true. The whole car stinks of alcohol."

The taxi driver's voice almost cracked with uncontrolled excitement as he turned to Grens. "What did I tell you, you fucking drunk!"

Ewert Grens hadn't said a word since they'd told him to lie down, it was as if all his energy had leaked out with the wine. But now it returned. "For fuck's sake! Those are—*were*—two bottles of 1982 Moulin Touchais, and they cost me five thousand three hundred and fifty kronor! So don't tell me it stinks!" He continued, turning to the young police officer. "And I haven't drunk a drop of them. Now, release me and deal with the men who are guilty of reckless driving and assault and *not* detective superintendents."

The other cadet, meanwhile, had opened the door to Grens's car, searched through the glove compartment, and, just as Grens claimed, found the handcuffs and a leather case containing his police badge. "Well, that seems to be true. According to this, he is a police officer."

"For thirty-nine years!"

He examined the plastic card, fingering the metal shield. "Grens. Ewert Grens? Is that your name?"

"That's none of your goddamn business."

A sigh, deep and theatrical, as the young officer took out his phone.

"Okay." And dialed a number that Grens tried to read without success. "If that's how you want it, then I won't give a damn who you are. Because nobody, and I mean nobody, talks to me like that. So now we're calling the top, *Superintendent*, no fucking special treatment."

Someone answered and Grens was close enough to hear an electronic voice.

"Welcome to the prosecutor's office."

"Can you put me through to the *chief* prosecutor?"

A few rings. Then a clear, substantial voice.

"Ågestam, City Prosecution."

It was hard to tell if the chief prosecutor was speaking unusually loudly, or if the cadet deliberately angled the phone so that everyone in the vicinity could hear. Whichever it was, it worked. Grens could hear. Every word.

"Paul Lindh, Södermalm police. Exactly fourteen minutes ago, we were located near Hornstull when we received an alarm from Taxi Stockholm. On site we have arrested a person who forced a taxi driver to the ground at gunpoint. He smells strongly of alcohol. According to his ID, which seems authentic, his name is Ewert Grens, and he's employed by the City Police. How should we handle this?" The cadet smiled at Grens, pointed to the handset, angled it up further.

"Did you say . . . Grens?"

"Yes."

"One moment."

That voice. Grens knew it well. He disliked quite a few people, but he detested only one man. That fucking voice. That voice, in cooperation with internal affairs, had interrogated him at least seven times and managed to get him suspended once—Grens's fist had gotten too close to a cabinet secretary at the Foreign Ministry who should not have contributed to the extradition of a condemned prisoner.

"He's been thoroughly documented by internal affairs. Possible drunk driving, did you say?"

"Yes."

"And use of a lethal weapon?"

"Yes."

"In that case . . . I think you better take him in to Kronoberg, and let him calm down in one of the cells on the seventh floor. I'll get back to you."

The police cadet hung up and put the cell phone into his pocket. "I suppose you heard that?" And seemed quite pleased when he looked at Grens. "So—if you'd go ahead and climb into the backseat of our car, nice and quiet, then everything will be fine. Or maybe you'd prefer I help you in? In a couple of hours, after you've sobered up on your cell bunk, then maybe we'll get ahold of your supervisor."

ERIK WILSON HAD tried to count the raindrops as they fell on the upper left half of the window. It worked at first. Until there were just too many drops to count, out of sync with the rattle of the window ledge, flowing together, so the outside world blurred, and his colleagues walking across the courtyard of the Kronoberg police station seemed coarse and clumsy, their movements difficult to interpret.

Not long ago he'd been the one walking out there, blurring together. One step ahead in a reality that just got shittier and more violent every year. Then everything changed. He'd become a superintendent. What a meaningless title. Head of the City Police's homicide unit. An appointment officers fought for. And it had probably been some kind of reward for excellent work and ambition. The youngest superintendent ever. He'd been as flattered as anyone would be and unable to refuse the honor, even though his whole body was screaming for him to do just that, *no, damn it, this is not you,* but prestige and status work that way sometimes—blinding us. Now he was locked up with those who didn't look out. Far from that reality—as a handler for confidential police informants—which had been his whole world, the sharp tip of the Swedish police force that penetrated furthest into organized crime. They were the ones who should be sitting in a prison, not him, a prisoner to the hierarchical bureaucracy of the police force.

The phone on his desk rang. It usually did. Five rings, eight, eleven. Then it stopped, someone gave up, hung up.

The raindrops on the window multiplied. A late summer rain. He'd just completed a final meeting with the National Police

Agency's weapons experts who were investigating the reluctance of some officers to use new ammunition called Gold Dot, which was intended to kill, rather than just stop, a criminal. Two hours of discussions about how strange it was to have to explain to police officers that the primary reason they carried weapons was to defend themselves. And soon he'd be sitting at another conference table with the politically elected head of the police board, top management's alibi to prove that society was given some say in police work. Then a hearing with the union. And deliberations with Occupational Safety. And talks with the personnel department.

The phone started ringing again. More times than before. He gave up, capitulated, as you do when you're locked up. "Yes?"

"Do you have a TV nearby?" English. An American accent.

"Yes."

"Turn it on. To CNN. In about four minutes and thirty seconds."

That voice. It had been a long time. One of the few he trusted. He remembered a café in the main building of FLETC in Georgia, one of those oppressively hot days when everybody in uniform sought out the air-conditioned hall—it was cramped, space was limited, and she nodded when he asked if he could share her table. After an uncomfortable silence, they started chatting, which in turn grew into a conversation about things you didn't usually talk about. He, who'd been invited along with a few other European colleagues and heads of various US law enforcement agencies, to receive further training in intelligence gathering, undercover operations, and witness protection. She, who was a career police officer, in a hurry to make her way up, in charge of the DEA's local office in Boston. He remembered the café and the immediate sense of closeness. Sometimes that happens. You know you've met someone who will continue to be in your life. And that just intensifies the feeling.

Sue Masterson.

If she was calling, it had to be about Paula. The only thing they shared nowadays. And he wondered if it was going to be a good or a bad call. If there'd been some kind of breakthrough after a years-long police operation. Or if everything had gone to hell.

He hurried out into the corridor, past Ewert Grens's empty office, past Sundkvist and Hermansson, into the small break room, which held two tables and a TV on a wheeled cart. Late lunch. The most likely time to find people in here, some having a hasty cup of coffee between their stacks of case files, others slowly dipping their cinnamon buns while longing to head home. But he had to watch this alone. He almost ran out of the break room, into the corridor.

There was also a TV in the meeting room at the end of the hall, that's where he was headed, and when he opened the door eleven faces turned toward him. There was only one unoccupied seat. The one he should have been sitting in, answering questions from the police commission.

The only thing he knew, come hell or high water, was that this was important. Sue Masterson was now the head of the DEA. She'd climbed all the way to the top. And she was the only one, besides himself and one American handler, who knew about the DEA's cooperation with an informant named Hoffmann, who had worked in Sweden under the code name Paula. You have to keep that kind of knowledge limited to a very narrow circle. Because if anyone near Paula were to learn who he really was—it would be tantamount to a death sentence. Which was what happened in Sweden. Which was how he'd become El Sueco in another world. This must be serious, because Sue had just made unlawful contact—the head of the DEA would not risk revealing anything if she didn't have to.

Wilson apologized to the members of the police commission and closed the door. Two minutes to transmission. He ran past the elevator to the stairs that had fifty-five steps—he counted them mechanically. And now his adrenaline, his internal gauge, which he used to like—a positive conversation would make the adrenaline laugh inside him, disguised as euphoria, a negative one would make pain flash violently—was turning to stress. It wanted to rush, rush, rush through his body, but had no focus, because he still didn't know what he was headed toward. He reached the ground floor and continued through new corridors and locked doors. The faster he moved, the slower it seemed to go. The County Communications

Center. He used his access card, opened the door to a large room. The heart of the police station. The floor filled with operators in front of a sea of computers, making decisions about life and death—this was where every emergency call in Stockholm County was sent and judged. He ran between the rows of desks to a much smaller room that resembled an aquarium, glass walls around only one fish, today's on-duty officer.

"The staff room? Is it available?"

"Yes."

"I need to borrow it for a few minutes. Okay?"

The officer looked up from yet another computer screen, even more lights moving around, blinking. "Come with me."

He was tall, much taller and considerably wider than Wilson—a man who spent too much time swimming in his little glass cage and not enough in the police station's gym—but his movements were unexpectedly agile, and he moved quickly toward a door in the corner of the hall.

"There's a meeting booked in here in half an hour."

"I'll be done by then."

The officer unlocked the door, Wilson thanked him and closed it behind him, turned on the fifty-inch TV hanging on the wall next to a clean whiteboard, and went over to the window to draw the blinds.

Barely a minute left. He flipped through SVT, TV4, BBC, Sky, until he found CNN and sat down on an uncomfortable office chair. The staff room. The crisis room. This was where they sat six weeks ago when a confrontation between the police and some rival gangs in the southern suburbs escalated into a war, four weeks ago when they told snipers to shoot the suicide bomber who'd entered one of Stockholm's biggest department stores during the Friday rush, two weeks ago when there was a mass escape from a high-security prison. A room for chaos. Battle. Emergency. Inferno. This time he was alone. But the feeling was the same. Anything could happen. It could all go to hell. Even though he had no idea what he was about to see on the screen in front of him.

A man. That's what he saw. Strait-laced, trustworthy. He looked just like every other talking head at CNN, as if they were all the same person just packaged in different clothes. Atlanta, Georgia. Erik had gone there on police business the first time he trained at FLETC, it wasn't far from the military base. A place that reminded him of where he sat now. In a crisis, in chaos and noise and under fire, something happened—employees stepped up, became more alert, sharp. A newsroom and a police station were different, but driven by the same forces. The darkness, which burned and damaged and killed, was their reason for being.

Now. The graphics above the reporter's shoulder changed—the image of a car crash. Above his hairline the words *BREAKING NEWS* spun, while another banner rotated in the opposite direction near the anchor's hands—*Speaker of the House of Representatives taken hostage*. Turn after turn, while the anchor tried to say something, impossible to make out.

"You see, Erik?" From inside his pocket her voice came over the phone again.

"Yes. But what . . . ?"

"Keep watching." Then Sue Masterson hung up, like before. A burner phone. That couldn't be tracked. *Keep watching—for what?*

There were two bottles of mineral water on the table. He opened one, drank greedily. The line of text below the studio reporter's hands kept spinning with the same intensity. The American speaker of the house had been kidnapped? Wilson wasn't sure he'd read that right, interpreted it correctly. Had the third most powerful politician in the United States, after the president and vice president, been taken prisoner? In that case—this was global news. Wilson knew that. But not what it had to do with him.

The proper-looking, trustworthy but indistinguishable anchorman cut to a feature. An excited, chattering voice spoke as a detailed map of Colombia gave way to another map of its border region near the Amazonian jungle, which gave way to images of burned-out vehicles.

The camera closed in on them, the images became more detailed. Destroyed trucks, cars, motorcycles. Outstretched blankets in the grass around them. Under those blankets—motionless bodies. Legs in suit trousers and black shoes sticking out from under the fabric, several of them. And legs in green military uniforms and heavy boots, several of them. Then legs in a dark-blue uniform with pointed boots, several of them. Wilson counted them unconsciously, as he had the steps just now. Twelve American security agents, fifteen Colombian soldiers, and fourteen Colombian special police.

A blaring voice spoke of the war on drugs. How it was led by Speaker Crouse. About a visit to a confiscated cocaine kitchen. About PRC guerrillas who had attacked, abducted Crouse, and then an hour ago, taken responsibility. And he slowly began to understand. Not what, not how, but who.

Colombia. Cocaine. Death.

Paula.

Back to the newscaster in the studio. *BREAKING NEWS* still written above his well-groomed head. But the text at the bottom of the screen had changed.

America declares a new War on Terror.

Then the next feature began—and Wilson opened the second bottle of mineral water. He was rarely thirsty, unlike Grens and his other colleagues who ran relay races between their offices and the coffee machine, but now the water streamed down his throat into his chest and stomach and down into some bottomless pit without rinsing him clean.

A new voice and the first image—the familiar lectern of the White House, which he'd seen in countless movies, and for a moment Wilson felt himself wavering on the border between fiction and reality, a kind of hope that perhaps, just maybe, this wasn't happening at all. But this *was* for real. It *was* reality. This was the actual president, not some movie version who'd step off the set, leave the studio, and go to some trailer to touch up his makeup for the next scene. He did what American presidents do when something serious has happened, looked straight into the camera as long as he could before pretending to look down at a piece of paper that didn't exist, before looking up again and continuing to read from the teleprompter. A practiced pause and a lowered voice and the words *the American people* just like always. To the right of the president stood the vice president and then his chief of staff, and at the furthest edge stood the director of the CIA. A demonstration of power. Seriousness. As far from fiction as you could get.

And now the American president said that an attack on one of America's most powerful elected officials was an attack on the United States. The United States does not negotiate with terrorists. The terrorist organization PRC, which had taken responsibility, was now an enemy of the United States. The war Timothy Crouse was waging on drug trafficking had now become the United States's war. They would now focus on destroying the PRC, that was how you won this sort of war. Destroy their organizational structure. Destroy the cocaine trade that funded them.

"Sue?" It was the first time he had called her.

"Wait. Soon." She hung up. Again. And Wilson stood alone in a darkened conference room—other than an annoying stream of light that flooded through the gap where one of the curtains didn't close tightly. He smoothed out the crease, driving away the outside world. What was happening now was for him alone, his fight, and it began three years ago when everything went to hell in a prison cell—it was his responsibility to keep the man he recruited, who against his better judgment he came to like and even care about, alive.

New images. The lectern at the White House was replaced on the screen by some kind of deck of cards. Some kind of list. Wilson stepped closer.

First a picture of a playing card with a red heart—the Ace of Hearts. But in the center of the card stood the word *Commander-in-chief*, and a face—a blurry image of a man in a large, green beret. A proud face with dark, penetrating eyes, and under that, his name: *Luis Alberto Torres*. And then his alias, *Jacob Mayo*.

The TV announcer explained that from today, this guerrilla leader would now be at the top of America's new Most Wanted list.

A list of thirteen individuals that the FBI and CIA considered the most powerful or dangerous members of the PRC. One by one, they appeared as figures on a deck of cards. The enemy would be taken—dead or alive.

The picture switched from the Ace of Hearts to the King of Hearts—second on the Most Wanted list, *Commander Bloque Amazon.* A young man with a broad scarf around his forehead and an unkempt beard, a passport photo of *Juan Mauricio Ramos*, alias *El Médico.* A new shift to the Queen of Hearts, *ideologue*, a woman in her forties, a black-and-white photo taken in a shadowy jungle. She was tall and thin, and according to the card her name was *Catalina Herrador Sierra*, alias *Mona Lisa.* Then the Jack of Hearts, title, *hitman,* with a square, indigenous face and a thick, beautiful braid, *Johnny Sánchez*, alias *El Mestizo.*

It made for dramatic television. They all looked dangerous. And the viewer knew that they were probably doomed to die. Wilson had seen this before. During the US invasion of Iraq. They'd used a deck of cards to illustrate the fifty most wanted members of Saddam Hussein's government. And images of the execution of the Ace of Spades, Saddam Hussein, were something that Wilson carried with him. The same pedagogy. The same strategy—define and dismantle your enemy's organization bit by bit.

The Jack of Hearts was followed by the Ten, Nine, then Eight of Hearts. The *Commander of the Bloque Cielo* became *Commander of the Bloque Juanita* became *responsible for weapons* and then *in charge of explosives and ammunition.* Everyone on that list was an outlaw from this point on. They had a price on their heads. A reward, dead or alive. A countdown. That's what it felt like. Toward something. He didn't know what. Until he did.

On the television screen the Seven of Hearts appeared. And what Erik Wilson felt was not fear, not terror, that couldn't encompass it. This was more like a sword plunging from the top of his head down through his chest into his abdomen. He had no children, no wife. Therefore, he'd never feared losing someone close, and as for losing himself, that had never bothered him, that day came when it came, old energy transformed into new energy. But now he felt it—the fear of losing someone he cared about, for real. He wanted to sit down. But couldn't, his legs wouldn't move. He wanted to stand up, that too was impossible, his legs couldn't bear the weight. He leaned against the conference table, was held up by it.

Seven of Hearts. Across the television screen, across most of the wall. And it felt like the playing card stayed there so much longer than the others. There was no photo, a black silhouette filled its center. Above it stood *Military Instructor/Bodyguard*, and under it an alias, the only name the US authorities knew: *El Sueco.*

And then, from the silhouette, moving and rather blurry images of an individual shot from above emerged. From a satellite, he was sure of it, a sequence showing a man getting out of a truck, a weapon in his hand, clear that he's protecting his freight. Wilson remembered meetings in empty apartments undergoing renovations between a handler and an informant. He remembered those life-and-death phone calls late at night, after Paula had infiltrated the upper echelons of the group and explained that it was time to strike, to eliminate.

You. El Sueco. Paula.

"What's going on?" The door had opened. The on-duty officer stood there looking at him.

"What do you mean?"

"I heard you scream, Erik."

He *had* screamed, could feel it in his throat. And he'd done it unconsciously.

"No. You must have heard wrong."

"If it wasn't you screaming, then who smashed that bottle?"

Wilson looked in the direction the on-duty officer was pointing. One of the mineral water bottles lay in front of him. In pieces. It must have been thrown against the wall, crushed, and fell to the floor, which was now covered with fine shards of glass that glittered in the light of the television. He'd thrown hard.

"I just wanted to check in. I'll leave you alone now." The officer looked at him, nodded, closed the door. And Wilson took deep slow breaths to try to regain his self-control.

Now he knew. Paula. On a kill list.

The adrenaline pumping through him now found its focus. What had expressed itself outwardly as a scream and a glass bottle thrown against a wall had inwardly turned to throbbing pain—a pressure on his chest, near the heart, a stabbing pain again and again somewhere in his gut. It wasn't fear. Not anger. It was everything—at the same time.

He stepped onto the glass, and it crackled. The remote control. He couldn't find it. Had he thrown that too? He searched along the black plastic edges of the TV for the small buttons, tried them one by one, and the sound rose, then a roaring image, and then something flashed on the right edge, and then, finally, that terrible newscaster voice, so severe and intrusive, dissolved. And there was silence, and stillness, until the phone rang again.

"Erik, I—"

"Why the hell is he on that list?"

"It *wasn't* a kill list when we put him on it six months ago. You know that. It only just became one."

That was how the police worked in Sweden. That was how it worked in the United States. An informant had to have a certain level of credibility in order to infiltrate a group, present themselves as a criminal in order to be accepted. In Sweden Erik Wilson, after recruiting Piet Hoffmann, had over several years put Hoffmann on various lists as a suspect for serious crimes, the Courts Administration records retrospectively gave him a more serious prison record, on the Swedish prison and probation records he became characterized as violent and psychopathic—all of it gradually fueling the myth of Piet Hoffmann until he was considered one of Sweden's most dangerous criminals. Falsifying information essential to the rule of law was part of this method.

And that's how the DEA had used the FBI's Most Wanted list, subcategory "Drugs," a list that identified the top players in the cocaine trade and was used by the Crouse Commission's so-called War on Drugs. That very same list was now being used to hunt down the PRC, newly categorized as a terrorist organization.

"We decided it was the simplest and quickest way. Hoffmann was able to infiltrate the PRC in eighteen months. He was just as good as you promised, maybe better. His intelligence was correct. It already stopped several deliveries and closed down a couple cocaine kitchens. None of our other informants had gotten nearly so close, gained that level of trust. But he needed to take a step beyond Sánchez, make his way further into the heart of the organization."

From his office in a Swedish police station, for lack of any other information, Wilson had often looked into a man called El Sueco—when he first came across the name on the FBI's website he knew implicitly. Number seven. On the Most Wanted list of the PRC's most dangerous individuals. Placed in the middle so as not to seem too conspicuous, but still flanked by other names that strengthened his status. When PRC's senior management saw how highly the FBI, and therefore the United States, valued him, he was able to gain more of their confidence and thus penetrate even further into the organization—he was the enemy, defined as an asset, a self-fulfilling prophecy that made him more important.

"I'm the only one, besides his American handler and you, Erik, who knows the truth. We couldn't risk anyone else knowing. So officially, according to that list, he is one of our most dangerous enemies. An absurd confirmation that we'd been doing a good job. Not even my bosses have a clue."

"Sue, if anyone understands, it's me. But what I don't understand is why, *why the hell*, you didn't inform anyone before this went public."

"Because I found out only moments before you did."

The informant's alias had been snuck onto the list of the PRC's thirteen most dangerous individuals. And it worked just as well as they'd planned. Until one of America's most powerful public servants was attacked, taken hostage, and abducted. Until this became a kill list.

"*I* chose to place him there, Erik. This is my responsibility."

It *was* her responsibility. Just like it was *his* responsibility when the same thing happened in Sweden.

"I've already booked a meeting with the chief of staff and the vice president. In three hours. I'll explain there's been a mistake. That someone who's working *for* us has accidentally been misidentified as the enemy. And meanwhile, Erik, you should go to the American embassy in Stockholm. I want to find out how much they know before the meeting."

"They?"

"The White House. The people who just decided Piet Hoffmann should die."

MANY HOURS. THAT was what she'd said.

Speaker of the House Timothy D. Crouse had no clue.

Shoulders, back, hips, tailbone. He had long since gone numb, didn't feel the pain. But he could tell that those around him were sitting on some kind of benches, that he was the only one forced to ride on the floor of the flatbed.

Every time they braked, every move of the steering wheel meant a sharp, clumsy blow against his muscles and bones, and the roads refused to hold up, several times they got stuck in the mud, and he could feel through the flatbed that the others had jumped down to push and shove the heavy truck forward.

He eventually floated into sleep, anxiously trying to keep a hold of his mind and consciousness, waking only when he heard, even through the earmuffs, a shrill, sharp laugh. Then he understood. One of the soldiers had stood astride him, and despite the potholes and sharp turns, kept his balance long enough to urinate all across Crouse's chest, neck, face, and hair. Someone else kicked him in the side, toward his chest, screamed *fucking wake up* in stumbling English, and someone else shouted *the bastard peed on himself*, and a third, a woman, *he's got on a suit, but he needs a diaper.* A discordant chorus of laughter in varying pitches, like the magpies near his house in Maryland when they dug into a loaf and started squawking loudly and one of them fled with the last bit of dry bread.

He fell asleep again, disjointed fragments of a sky, green leaves, sparkling sun. They stopped one more time, away from the mud. He'd tried to move his blindfold by pressing his forehead toward his collarbone, gotten a peek, and managed to identify a PRC outpost at the edge of the road. Then it went dark. No light penetrated. The jungle had a tightly laced canopy on top of walls made of trees that stretched eighty, ninety, a hundred feet or more into the sky.

They'd passed by a base camp, he was sure of it. When nobody was looking, he'd turned his head until his earmuffs slipped above his ears, and heard first *monte*, jungle, then *caletas*, huts. And then a peculiar sound, like the smacking of lips. He knew what it was, *churuquiada*, the signal the guerrillas had copied from monkeys, it was the sound they made when it was time for everyone in the camp to wake up.

The snorting, grumbling truck stopped. Again. But for real now, the engine was turned off, the doors of the cab thrown open. It felt like a jungle—the dampness, the scent. He reckoned he was probably still in Colombia.

Someone tore off his earmuffs, brusquely grabbed his upper arms, pulled him up from a prone position and pushed him down from the truck bed. He heard new voices, not as many as before, those who had pissed on him and cackled like magpies had been replaced by others who sounded somewhat older, hoarser, deeper. What he could hear was his reality, not the guerrilla terrorist's unreality. The hands on his arms moved to his back and shoved him down a muddy path, he fell down and hit his forehead and one leg hard, a sharp rock met his kneecap at full force.

And it occurred to him how much louder it was now that the truck had been turned off. The buzzing of thousands of insects created a deafening hum that entered his body, made his bones and sinews tremble. The chirping of hundreds of birds fluttering to and fro above their heads. And the monotonous cry of monkeys bouncing from clearing to clearing across the Amazon.

More hard shoves in the back. Until somebody stopped him, pressing their hands against his chest, then cutting off his blindfold so that it crumbled to the ground.

The muddy path had led him to the center of the camp. An armed guard stood in every corner. And huts, hovels really, were scattered around in some sort of pattern. Soldiers behind and in front of him, all dressed in camouflage and muddy rubber boots up to their knees, automatic weapons—what seemed to be AK-47s—hanging on their shoulders.

A temporary camp. That's what it felt like. One that could be quickly dismantled and rebuilt somewhere else.

The man poking his ring-adorned fingers into Crouse's chest was short and overweight. It was difficult to guess his age, anywhere from twenty-five to forty-five. As blank as all the other faces, a permanent film of sweat, but here multiple layers of old sweat were stacked under the new. The eyes dominated the face. They looked worried. But weren't. Someone *trying* to appear worried because he'd learned people responded positively to it.

"Señor Crouse. Or is it perhaps . . . Speaker Diaper? Welcome, my friend. My name is Maximiliano Cubero. Commander of the PRC's special front. But you can call me Commandant like all the other prisoners."

The voice was like the eyes. It sounded calm, friendly. As if he was *trying* to sound like that, had learned people liked calm, friendly voices.

Then he raised it, became more intense as he turned to the man right behind him, giving orders. To someone who, according to his insignia, who was second in command. And who, in turn, tried to sound like the commandant when he turned to the two men behind him, standing at strict attention. They both listened and then started walking toward a small wooden building with a tin roof, which, unlike the others, was closed on all sides with a narrow door of bamboo bars. The commandant prodded Crouse hard in his side with an elbow and pointed to it.

"The House of Representatives. We'll be calling the caleta that from now on. What do you say to that, Mr. Speaker?"

A cage. That's what it was. Nothing else. Crouse glimpsed a straw mattress on the floor, and next to it a plastic bowl. And there, he hadn't noticed at first, in a back corner of the cage sat a human being. A severely malnourished man with an unkempt beard and hair, the remains of a shirt in rags, a pair of dress pants cut off at the knees, held up with a thin rope around a sunken waist. The two guerrillas opened the lock and the jail door creaked, they stepped inside and pulled the man up with a hand under each armpit, dragged him out behind them.

"Have you met?" The commandant's eyes looked worried, his voice friendly. "If not, this is Señor Crouse from the United States. And this is Señor Clarke. Also from the United States! Isn't it lovely that the two of you could meet like this? I mean, since you're both traveling abroad?"

Clarke. A name Crouse recognized. One of the most prominent of the 254 Americans currently being held hostage by the PRC. They had in fact met at a celebration and subsequent press conference in DC. Four years ago. Maybe five. And he'd been here basically ever since, moving from one jungle encampment to another. When Crouse got closer to his face, he could make out vague traces of the man that used to exist.

"Good. Now that you've had the chance to get to know each other, it's time to say good-bye."

It was strange. Crouse had thought about it since the truck bed. He should be afraid. But he wasn't. Not yet. Furious! That's what he was.

The commandant nodded toward his second-in-command, who immediately shoved the emaciated prisoner in front of him onto one of the few patches of grass. He took a black blindfold out of his pocket, identical to the one Crouse had worn during the journey, and tied it over Clarke's eyes. The commandant strode over to him, and it was only now Crouse noticed that, unlike the others, the leader wore black boots with clinking spurs in the shape of stars with red stones sparkling on either side. On his right hip hung a revolver, he put it to Clarke's head, circled around to that thin face and pressed the barrel hard against his left temple. Now the troops started to shout in chorus. *Muerte. Dead.* In English too, just to be sure. The commandant held the revolver to Clarke's skull while he turned to Crouse, making sure the new prisoner watched him take care of the old prisoner. Watched while he pressed his finger to the trigger. Watched him shoot. *My reality, not this terrorist's unreality.* Blood and spinal fluid gushed out of the bullet hole, staining the commandant's uniform. And the troops laughed loudly, because that's what the commandant was expecting. And when Clarke fell—not headlong, as if the gritty, sore body couldn't decide if it should fall—it happened so slowly, as if through water, surrendering as all bodily functions shut down, and not even the will to live could turn them back on again.

"Next."

The second-in-command ran over to Crouse, eager to obey his commandant, shoved the speaker as he'd shoved Clarke toward the same little patch of grass. Crouse was forced to stand next to Clarke's body.

"Do you know the very best part of advancing within this organization, Speaker Diaper? Of becoming an officer? Maybe even of becoming . . . El Comandante? Of course. It feels good to get as far as I have, I won't deny it, and I like to feel good. But the best part, the very best, Speaker Diaper, is that it's *my* job to execute powerful Americans. In these parts, I'm the one who does it. So the others had to spare you, keep you alive, for my sake."

The commandant held up his gun, rubbed his index finger on its muzzle as if removing dirt, nodded toward his second-in-command to untie the black blindfold that had slipped down Clarke's lifeless face and move it to Crouse's, tie it around his eyes.

The world went black again. Just sounds and smells and vibrations as someone moved. And he heard it again. The troops howling. *Muerte.* And felt the round metal mouth of the gun pressed against his temple—and he had just enough time to think, right side not left, like Clarke—before it fired.

ERIK WILSON RAN. Out of the darkened meeting room in the County Communications Center, up the stairs, through the corridors of the police station, and toward an almost forgotten and rarely opened oblong closet in one corner of his office. Eight uniforms on hangers. It had been a long time. He hadn't even worn them on those formal occasions where it was expected. It just wasn't his style. Now he tore away the dry cleaner's plastic around the uniform hanging at the far back, threw it on, and ran out again. Past the closed door of the conference room, where he should be right now, and for a moment he wished he'd decided to go to that police commission meeting instead, that he'd never answered the telephone—then he'd still be unaware that his friend, his responsibility, might be legally assassinated at any moment. An outlaw. Again.

This door he opened. The SWAT team's room. Said hello as he passed by his busy colleagues and hurried on to the next room, toward external command. A large cabinet of keys stood open and he grabbed a set somewhere in the middle, was on his way out when the SWAT-team chief shouted.

"What the hell are you up to?"

"I'm borrowing one of your squad cars for a few hours."

"Listen—in *my* department, we ask first!"

Wilson had already been swallowed up by the dark corridor and entered the irritating fluorescents of the stairs. Uniform. The marked police car. He had less than three hours to gather the information Sue needed, so she could play her best card. Piet Hoffmann's card. The Seven of Hearts. And it was all about being taken seriously, sending the right signals, getting into a sealed embassy.

The short hill out of the garage and up toward the boom and the sentry box, he turned on the sirens and flashing blue lights and accelerated along Hantverkar Street.

The PRC. For decades these Colombian guerrillas had been kidnapping Americans, Scandinavians, Japanese, French. Lengthy negotiations, often lasting several years, people locked in cages in a jungle no outsiders could penetrate. But this was something else. Timothy D. Crouse. Speaker of the House. A very powerful person. The USA was going to be forced to act. And everything had changed.

Wilson zigzagged through a thick line of cars, drove on the sidewalk past City Hall, on a bike path past the government offices. He remembered how Paula's escape started right there, in these very corridors of power, during a meeting with both the minister of justice and a police chief who guaranteed total immunity and support for Paula's mission to infiltrate the Polish mafia in a high-security Swedish prison. Wilson fought down an infantile reflex to stretch a middle finger in the air at all the people who had made promises and betrayed them, who had sacrificed lives in order to preserve hierarchy. But they weren't worth it. And, besides, they'd already been handed their sentence—convicted in the decade's most high-profile trial—to sit in the very prison cells they'd left Hoffmann in to die. He kept shifting back and forth from sidewalk to street until he hit Gustav Adolf Square. There was no way forward there. Snorting, stressed out, carbon-belching cars formed a living wall. The beautiful roundabout that separated the state department from the opera, parliament, and royal palace, the very heart of the capital, was clogged and no siren or blue lights were enough to break through it. He checked the dashboard clock, waited a minute, waited one more. And then drove metal to metal, back, forth, along the side, forcing his way across the roundabout, bumping against flower boxes at the base of the statue of a king pointing out over his city. He increased his speed on the footpath through the Royal Garden and across the busiest street of bus traffic, which he never learned the name of, all the way to Nybroplan. There, in the middle of the small square, the phone rang again.

"Sue, I don't have time right now, I'm on the road and—"

"Sorry to disappoint you—this isn't Sue. I'm calling from Kronoberg jail. You're speaking with the chief."

A deep, harsh male voice, a heavy smoker, Wilson was sure of it.

"Then I'm the one who will have to disappoint you, since I don't have time to speak to Sue or some prison chief right now."

"Well, this very much concerns you. So you'd best listen to me, Wilson. I have a prisoner up here making quite a fucking scene in one of my cells. And I want you to *personally* come here and pick him up."

"And why the hell would I do that? I'm hanging up so—"

"Don't hang up. You're the one who needs to keep his eyes on his employees."

"Excuse me?"

"Your employees. The people the public is paying you to be responsible for. The people who should be out on the streets chasing down trouble. Instead of causing it themselves."

"What are you talking about?"

"So *now* you're listening?"

"Goddamn it!"

"I'm talking about our favorite detective—Ewert Grens. He's in cell five right now. He's been arrested."

Strand Road. The water at the very edge of the sea, beautiful no matter the season.

"I don't understand."

"According to the chief prosecutor Ågestam's written arrest order, Superintendent Grens was taken in on suspicion of illegal use of a firearm and disturbing the peace."

A red light at Djurgård Bridge, Wilson slowed down, passed by the line of cars, and continued toward the fancy neighborhood where embassies stood in each other's shadows.

"Give me a couple of hours. I'll deal with it. But until then he'll just have to sit there."

"He's making quite a ruckus."

"I don't have time right now."

"It's *my* staff who has to take care of him."

"If he doesn't settle down, tell him you have a message from me. Whisper that I think he'll look great in stripes."

Wilson had deliberately delayed turning off the siren, did it now as he parked in front of the sentry box and guards in uniforms with crew cuts, large patches on their shoulders and sleeves. They were protecting a small piece of the US in the middle of Sweden. He stayed in the car, they needed to wonder who he was, what an emergency vehicle was doing here, why a high-ranking Swedish police officer, who would soon step out, needed to be admitted without question, taking up time they didn't have. He counted the seconds, as he sat near all these small fortresses. Not far away the Italian flag waved, and next to that stood the German embassy, and then the British. On the other side of the road, streamers marked the entrance to SVT, Sweden's largest TV channel. And here, right outside the passenger-side window, stood sloping concrete ramps and a high steel fence, surveillance cameras, and loaded automatic weapons wielded by people who had an angry fuck-off attitude—it reminded him of the prisons he had to visit regularly for his job. Everything was different now. After 9/11. The whole world had been designated the enemy.

He opened the car door and knocked on the closed glass hatch. He wondered if he was still the person he used to be, if the Erik Wilson who'd once been an expert handler—the policeman who found people in order to use them, who could get them to like him, trust him, give him what he wanted—still existed inside the current version of Erik Wilson, the superintendent firmly enmeshed in the managerial bureaucracy, unable to move. If he still had it.

I know what they want to know. But how much do they know already?

He was pummeled with questions by the guards, but his answers flowed naturally, and he started to feel that rush again. And not just that, he no longer felt scared or in pain, this was exactly what he'd missed. A forbidden feeling. Someone he cared about was in danger. He should continue being upset, confused. But he was filled with energy, excitement, focus.

I feel alive again. Because your life is at risk.

The guard hung up the telephone on the inner wall of the sentry box, nodded slightly, opened the heavy iron gate—whoever he'd called, the answer had been yes. The first step. Wilson left security zone 1.

The embassy vestibule looked like the waiting room in a dentist's office—except the marines on guard duty and the cameras, which now seemed to be following only him. Security zone 2. A woman smiled and asked him to sit down while she inspected his police badge, just like the guards outside. She also explained to him that he would be meeting with a Mr. Jennings. After twenty minutes, Wilson knocked on the window of the smiling woman's office, asked how things were going, and was told it wouldn't be long. He sat back down. Another twenty minutes, another knock, another just a minute, and he sat down.

"Sorry for the delay."

One hour and seven minutes later.

"I'm sorry. I had to vet you."

Mr. Jennings. The same age as Wilson. Or, maybe not, maybe that was wishful thinking. The man, who had short hair, a mustache, and wore a gray blazer, was probably not even forty.

Another one of those closed security doors. Jennings opened it and led Wilson inside. Security zone 3. Some level of trust. A new sentry box with more cameras, more soldiers. Someone compared his face to the picture on his police ID for the third time. And then frisked him. Ran a curious hand scanner over his legs, arms, torso.

"You're cleared to go ahead."

A short hallway. A bare room with fluorescent lighting that made you look pale, bluish, almost sickly. A simple table sitting in its center, a pair of chairs. That was all.

"This was the only room we had free."

Sure it was.

This was the kind of room designed to place a visitor at a disadvantage, to show his lack of power. The kind of place he himself used when visiting Aspsås prison, when he first selected Piet Hoffmann as a possible informant and started to approach him and win his trust. Where he, step by step, pretended to be his best friend. That was how it worked. A handler becomes the informant's best friend, so that the informant continues to be willing to risk their life to uncover new information.

"Erik Carl Wilson."

Mr. Jennings didn't even look up as he opened a folder and flipped through the papers inside.

"Assistant at the Metropolitan Police in Uppsala for four years. Inspector at the Homicide Division in Gothenburg for seven years. Chief inspector for the CI handling unit in the regional intelligence office for five years, in charge of informants at City Police for four years. For the last two and a half years, head of the homicide unit."

"All that in an hour? Not bad."

"But, between us, that's not why I let you in—I'm not overly impressed by the Swedish police."

"Hey, just between us, neither am I. Right now, I've got a detective in lockup."

"On the other hand—you've done five residencies at FLETC. Our facility in Georgia for special police training. Recruitment, information gathering, witness protection, interrogation techniques."

That's where all of this started. It was the knowledge he gained there that helped him choose the prisoner Piet Hoffmann. It was how he knew to add a few crimes to Hoffmann's record, a couple of Kalashnikovs for some weapons charges. From there it had been easy to push for tougher restrictions—no parole, no contact with the outside world. Hoffmann, who had a wife and two small children on the outside, became desperate after just a few months without communication or human touch. He would have done anything to get out of there.

"The highest marks, Wilson. Best reviews. There aren't many who get that, not even among us Americans. I myself wasn't even close."

Hoffmann had been assigned the code name Paula. Had become Wilson's tool. Someone the Swedish police could use and throw away. That's how he and his colleagues who worked in undercover operations thought about it. Since it was forbidden to use a criminal as an assistant, even though they worked best—only a criminal can play criminal—they'd learned that once a Paula, a Pia, a Berit had been discovered by the group he'd infiltrated and was doomed and in need of immediate police protection, they had to deny all knowledge and let him die.

Tools. Resources. That was what you were supposed to be.

Sometimes things don't turn out quite like you expected. Sometimes we end up meaning more to each other than we intend to. And he still didn't know if it was a good or bad thing to feel this way about another human being, to care about someone so much.

"Okay. You've been approved, Wilson."

Jennings wore his suit jacket buttoned up. He was slim and when he leaned back in his uncomfortable wooden chair, his jacket tightened at his right hip. A gun holster. Armed, in here? A paper pusher?

"And now it's your turn to explain. What do you want?"

I want to know what you know.

"I saw the breaking news on CNN."

Without letting you know that I know what you want to know.

"About the new war on terror. Thirteen terrorists who are going to be hunted down. And one of them, the Seven of Hearts—they called him El Sueco. The Swede."

Mr. Jennings was still leaning back. But he was listening.

"You had pictures of them. All of them. Passport photos or mug shots or blurry images in the jungle. Except that one. Because you don't know who he is."

"Yes?"

A tightrope. He had to know. Without them knowing that he might know.

"If there is a person in the jungles of South America called El Sueco, who *might* be Swedish, then of course our not-so-impressive Swedish police force would be interested as well. Who is he? Can we identify him? Can we assist our American colleagues in their search?"

Mr. Jennings smiled. That ironic smile that US officials sometimes give to the representatives of inconsequential countries just south of the North Pole.

"And how exactly would *you* be able to assist *us*?"

Walking the tightrope. Winning trust. Without arousing suspicion. There'd been a time when he'd been damn good at that. Even the grades this civil servant had dug up proved that. But that was then. Maybe too long ago.

"One thing you should know, Jennings. When it comes to Sweden, there is no other democratic nation, anywhere, that has collected as much digital information about their citizens. Information that exists across many different systems. Many are open to the public. But there are others you might want access to that are closed. Inaccessible to unauthorized persons. So you need us—*if* El Sueco turns out to be Swedish. That useless Swedish police force has access to them."

Wilson tried to sound confident. But maybe he was rusty, exhausted.

"But maybe that's not something your bosses are interested in?"

The gun in its holster. It pushed more firmly against the blazer as the American officer leaned further back, as if it wanted to insert itself into the silence.

Maybe I went too far.

Wilson tried to read Jennings's face. It was square, much like the face of the indigenous-looking guerrilla on the hit list. But it was paler and lacked any braid to frame it. It was also completely neutral and impossible to interpret. Until the officer suddenly stood up. He had the folder with Erik Wilson's police record in hand, ready to go.

I went too far.

"Okay." Mr. Jennings looked at him: measuring, weighing, considering. And then he unbuttoned the blazer and took it off, baring what could only be seen in outline before—a black leather shoulder holster against a white, perfectly ironed shirt, as stark as a mourning band. Inside was a Glock 22, as black as its holster. A butt that would leave an imprinted pattern on any hands that squeezed too hard.

Then he seemed to make up his mind, hung his jacket over the chair. "I have to make a few calls."

Wilson hadn't noticed the door behind him, the same color as the wall. Now he did, as Jennings opened it and stepped into security zone 4, the heart of the embassy.

I didn't go too far.

Alone in a bare room, like a prison cell. He thought of Paula infiltrating his way into the prison. Exposed and abandoned. But still tricking them all. Only one man, besides Piet and Zofia, knew what happened and where he fled. Erik Wilson.

Since then they'd met four times a year. Gaira Café in Bogotá, Calle 96, between Carrera 13 and 13A. At 15:00 on the first week of every quarter. A meeting place where no one asked any questions and to which Wilson traveled at his own expense. That was when and where Piet had asked for his help, explaining how the money had dried up—it was expensive to be on the run, even more expensive with a family. Living costs, buying protection, paying off the authorities in a country where bribery was a way of life. That was how he'd come into contact with the PRC guerrillas who financed their operations with drugs. Hoffmann returned to the same business he'd had in Sweden: drugs, buying and selling them, passing them on to dealers, and his business grew. Until the night two of his most reliable dealers ended up on the wrong corner and were executed for it. And their drugs and money—his drugs and money—disappeared. The capital for two deliveries, and now he couldn't pay.

Representatives of the PRC knocked on his door, threatened to kill him and his family, but in the opposite order. His youngest son, Rasmus, first. His eldest son, Hugo, next. Then Zofia.

Hoffmann had defended himself and his family, taken out two guerrilla hit men. But what about the next time? And the next? He had no choice—he had to work off his debt, and when that was paid back, he stayed on to earn money. Six months later Wilson offered him an opportunity to double his income, introduced him to Sue Masterson at the DEA. *The best undercover informant I've ever known is hiding in South America. He has the confidence of the PRC and would be willing to inform for you. Use him. A perfect solution for both you and Hoffmann.* That was how he sold it. Piet Hoffmann needed more money, and the US authorities needed exactly that kind of informal agent. And that's how it turned out. The US authorities recruited Hoffmann to infiltrate the PRC, the organization responsible for a significant portion of the drugs flowing into their country.

"Coffee?"

Wilson hadn't heard a knock or a door opening. A very young man with a coffee tray.

"Thank you."

A thermos of coffee, a pitcher of milk, and small dry cookies with a chemical taste to them. He had been waiting for half an hour. He chewed and continued to wait.

Piet Hoffmann, who transformed into *Paula,* had now transformed again, to El Sueco. He was given a clear objective: get close to the PRC leadership—something Hoffmann started to do when a so-called El Mestizo realized how useful he could be. Slowly a conversation began, the initial hatred and suspicion transformed into trust. Piet Hoffmann was an expert at this, had done it several times before. The hit man and brothel owner had now, without suspecting his new mission—to expose, destroy from within—turned from employer to guarantor. After six months in El Mestizo's circle, Piet's duties were expanded, in addition to collection, he started protecting drug shipments and cocinas and training guerrillas. It was this confidence that his new employer wanted to take advantage of. And from his first day undercover Hoffmann's American handler—the DEA's equivalent to Erik Wilson—had been provided with tips for the best spot to intercept a delivery or tear down a cocaine factory in the process of being built.

"Excuse me. That took some time. Again." He had sweat stains on the back of his shirt and an open laptop in his hand. Jennings no longer wore an ironic smile. The phone call, to whoever it was, had resulted in the answer Wilson hoped for. "That news broadcast you and the rest of the world saw, those few seconds from a transport, came from this."

The embassy official ran his finger across the trackpad, clicked on an untitled icon with four files, opened three of them.

"Here's the film from the NGA's satellites above the Amazon. Somewhere in Colombia. But this—this is the unedited material." A total of two hundred and ten seconds, at times quite blurry and choppy. All shot from above.

First, a shipment of coca leaves and chemicals to a cocina guarded by soldiers, which *you and the rest of the world* have already seen. Then a river transport. Then a group of guerrillas in the border region near Venezuela being trained by the same man, and it was clear—from how he moved, gave orders—that he had advanced military training. Finally, more detailed images, again the same man, but now in the company of the hit man with the square face, and it was clear they were jointly guarding a shipment of weapons.

"All of these are from above—not enough for a facial recognition program to develop a basis for identification. Until we got permission to use this new British technology, which has resolution down to the centimeter. Then we found this."

The fourth file. Jennings clicked on it. The same sequence as before, the weapons transport. But now zoomed in on one of the men. On his head, something that could be a lizard tattoo. Then on his face. An image that broke down into gray squares as they zoomed in.

"We've had access to this for a few months. That's as close as the technology can take us."

The face recognition program mapped the contours of the face in squares. Vague lines became a nose and mouth. A person who didn't exist. El Sueco.

I see you. And they don't know. You don't know.

"What do you see?"

You're blurry. But I know you so well.

"Wilson? Do you know who that is?"

Jennings searched Wilson's face while Wilson avoided eye contact, pretending to look at the image again, as if he were truly trying to decipher it.

"No." He looked up, met a disappointed expression. "No, Jennings. I don't have any clue who that is."

A SHED WITH wooden walls and a tin roof. A narrow opening, bars of bamboo, for a door. A straw mattress in one corner, a bowl in another.

"Chontos."

In just a few hours he'd learned a new word. The large hole in the ground that you squatted over. A wooden plank above, and you shoveled mud onto the excrement. The only place he was alone, two slashed potato sacks hanging from a tree branch, but it was enough, a makeshift wall to keep the bastards away.

"Again?" The girl was probably no older than sixteen or seventeen. Around the age Liz had been when she disappeared. This girl's long hair was held back in a knot, and she wore a uniform, had a weapon slung diagonally across her chest. Her lips were painted. "It's nice."

"Excuse me?"

"Your new House of Representatives, Speaker Diaper. I mean, hardwood floors, even a bowl for food with no holes in it." She was speaking loudly. She obviously wanted the three teenage boys, automatic weapons thrown casually over thin shoulders, to hear. And they laughed. Not at her, but at the prisoner she was humiliating, who needed to be broken down.

"Okay then. Chontos. One more time." His jailer opened the gate with fingernails as red as her lipstick, aimed her gun at him, and walked behind him to the potato sackcloth. There she stopped, asking him every thirty seconds to hurry, telling him he had no more than five minutes.

He sat down over the hole, long since finished, but just looking for some quiet, trying to understand his mock execution. He hadn't closed his eyes. The metal was on his right temple, and Crouse had stared into the blackness, listening to the sound of the commandant's silver spurs as his index finger pressed the trigger. He hadn't thought of anything—just waited. Then the click drowned out all other sounds. He hadn't even realized that's what it was, a click. Not until the troops started howling with laughter—gurgling, hiccupping, chattering laughter that chased away the clouds of insects. A revolver loaded with a single bullet. Clarke's bullet, the prisoner who was never exchanged, because all negotiations with the US government ceased after their list of demands had been rejected.

But the fear caught up with him. He was going to die.

Without being able to control it, he actually did wet himself after that click, and the troops howled even louder, *Speaker Diaper*, they chanted, *Speaker Diaper*. But it didn't break him, didn't take what was inside. There was nothing in there to take. It was already in a grave in a field outside Washington.

"Okay, Speaker Diaper. You're done. No more chontos until tonight." The woman, the girl, was speaking for the benefit of the others again, who rewarded her by aping a man peeing on himself and walking with his legs wide apart, hands to their noses as if something smelled very bad.

Crouse was herded into his cage and the door padlocked behind him. He was sweating even more than before, his skin was shiny, and small drops rolled from his hairline down his forehead and cheeks and neck. And when the food came—a long ladle grabbed and then filled the dish—he had no idea what kind of fish was floating in what kind of broth. But he was sure that there were loose fish heads and eyes staring up at him.

THE BLUE-AND-WHITE POLICE car was standing where he left it. Just outside the glass sentry box with its uniformed guards. Erik Wilson nodded toward them, got in, and drove slowly to Strand Road and the city, while thinking about those gray squares. One centimeter resolution. A face he recognized. Because a man is so much more, a way of moving, an impression, that only those close to you recognize. He stopped at the red light at Djurgård Bridge—he was in no hurry. He had done what he set out to do, gained the trust he'd wanted to, got the answers he was searching for. He still had it, that skill he'd used in a former life to get criminals to trust him, to recruit them, turn them into sources or informants for a few paltry thousands a month in exchange for risking their lives every day.

"They don't know." He had called back, probably for the last time. Contact could be traced, and they'd already risked too much.

"Are you absolutely sure?"

"Sue, they don't know much more than what everybody could see on TV. His alias. And that he's working with protection and training."

At one end of the phone, Hamn Street. Crowded, noisy, messy. In the middle of the small country in northern Europe that people often confuse with Switzerland. At the other end of the line, DEA chief Sue Masterson was walking down Pennsylvania Avenue, toward 1600 and the gate to one of the world's most famous buildings.

"In twenty minutes I'm sitting down with Vice President Thompson, Chief of Staff Perry, FBI Chief Riley, and CIA Chief Eve. And I'm going to take care of our problem. I'm gonna explain everything, that El Sueco is in our employ, that he's working on our behalf, that he is our most valuable asset inside the PRC—that we managed to sneak him onto *our own* list of enemies. That we need him alive."

Wilson wove his way through road construction and honking buses, Hamn Street turned to Klaraberg Street and then the bridge toward Kungsholmen. While a woman he trusted proceeded toward what many considered the most powerful building in the world.

"What if it's like what happened here—the politicians responsible know but deny it?"

"It won't be like that."

"Sue—*if*?"

She was standing still now. He could hear it. Her breathing was stabilizing slowly.

"Then we have a huge problem."

Then complete silence. It seemed like lunchtime in DC should be louder. Wilson wondered if she was deliberately covering the microphone, and if so, why.

"I won't be able to use official channels. Or even unofficial. I'll have to block his handler—the only person besides us who knows his true mission."

There were plenty of parking spots on Berg Street near the southern entrance to police headquarters, which was unusual. It was quiet in Washington and empty here. It didn't seem right, that much he knew, and a feeling of uneasiness stole over him. A day when the world didn't make sense. He parked and went in—but not to the homicide unit and his office. He headed in the other direction—toward the jail. And the detective who was locked up there.

Just one guard. They trusted her. And the Secret Service officer in his black uniform with a golden badge on his chest and golden stripes on his pants was probably escorting her more out of politeness than suspicion.

This remarkable building, which she'd visited several times, whose walls and echoing floors seemed to be scrutinizing her and whose high ceilings seemed to press down—every time she walked through the hallways of the West Wing the feeling of being one of a chosen few washed over her. It was seductive. And dangerous. She apologized as they approached the open door, paused, took a slow, deep breath, and hid it far, far inside. If she gave in to that feeling in the room she was about to enter, then she'd already have lost.

She straightened her short blazer and pants. Civilian clothes. That was important. Only on her very first visit, before she had assumed her position at the DEA, did she wear a uniform. But she'd discovered that she got more done, was listened to more closely, when she dressed like this. The more she mirrored them outwardly, the greater her success.

The open door to the vice president's office meant that she was welcome, even though she'd insisted that overbooked calendars had to be rescheduled and planned meetings postponed. Ten minutes. That was what she'd been given. The Secret Service officer smiled and waved her in. Her earlier White House meetings took place in the chief of staff's office and consisted of constructive planning meetings on a chair next to the director of the Office of National Drug Control Policy. She'd never been in this room before.

"Welcome, Sue."

Vice President Thompson. A tall, middle-aged woman with blonde hair and glasses that evoked the fifties. She was sitting behind her oak desk, and she pointed to the only vacant chair. Sue Masterson looked around. A brief nod toward Chief of Staff Perry, never her enemy, who was sitting on a white sofa with overstuffed pillows, and a brief nod back. The other two, however, she had regularly fought with. In the blue chair, Marc Eve, director of the CIA, and in the green one, with his arms folded, sat William Riley, director of the FBI. She'd never met with them at the same time before.

"Coffee?"

"No, thanks."

But a glass of water from the pitcher that had a slice of lemon wedged on its edge. She poured, drank half. They waited for her to begin. And it was clear that everything about that newly published kill list had been decided right here, by these people. They looked exhausted. The kidnapping had been carried out in an isolated area of the jungle, and since everyone was dead except the kidnappers' target, they were the ones who chose when to talk or make demands. The kidnappers had waited hours, until midnight. And a few hours after that the people sitting around her now had gathered.

"The Seven of Hearts. El Sueco."

She looked at the big clock over the fireplace. 9:50 a.m. By ten, she had to be done. Had to make them understand.

"He's not one of the enemy. He's one of us."

Four individuals examined her, just as she was examining them. Three men, one woman. But it was as if they were all part of the same genderless body exuding the same genderless power.

"I'm talking about this kill list. It contains one of our own. Our best informant. We only placed him on the Most Wanted list to strengthen his status. If we, the enemy, defined him as dangerous, then our enemies would, too."

She wondered if she'd become like that. Someone who exuded genderless power. She had so few true friends to ask such a question—the number of close relationships she had shrank with each new appointment. It was as if her titles scared people off, even people she'd worked side by side with for a long time suddenly saw her differently when she became their boss.

"We've never had anyone get so far, never had anyone more capable. Based on information he's gathered, we've taken down at least seven cocaine kitchens and stopped fifteen big deliveries. He's the one who gave us our biggest achievement so far, a record seizure, fourteen tons of cocaine just outside Tumaco. The Navy and the police worked together to crack down on a lab not far from the port. We apprehended twenty-four people, destroyed all the equipment on site, seized nine boats used for transport."

Sky-blue carpet, ocean-blue wallpaper. A mirror with a gold frame, a chandelier that held white candles that had never been lit. Even the room itself seemed to exude a kind of stereotypical vision of power.

"So the kill list contains a mistake—and it has to be corrected. Now." She looked at them one by one. While they tried to take in what she was saying.

"Sue?" Chief of Staff Perry rearranged the pillows, as if he wanted to be free of them when he began to speak. "Are you absolutely sure about this?"

"Yes, I'm quite sure." She was glad he'd spoken first. No matter what he said, she knew that it would be based on analysis, not personal differences.

"Well, that complicates the day somewhat. We just finished a press conference that's been broadcast all over the world. It would be pretty hard to go out there and take back what we just said."

"Daniel—he's employed by us."

"He's a criminal who provides us with information."

"He's more like a public servant. In the service of the United States. Entitled to the same benefits, the same protection as the rest of us."

"Sue, an *employed* civil servant has a *contract*."

"But *we* were the ones who put him on the Most Wanted list! Because *we* thought that would help him gain even more of their confidence—so he'd be able to do better work. *For us.*"

"Confidence? Politics is about confidence. But political credibility is no stronger than its weakest link. The kill list we released during the invasion of Iraq, which we succeeded in getting international political support for, was about confidence. Now PRC guerrillas are terrorists—and the world agrees. But when we chose to upgrade from 'terrorist' to 'war on terror,' which includes the right to extrajudicial kills, we have to maintain international support, international confidence. And if it turns out that we're wrong on *one* particular, then *all* particulars will be challenged, our credibility, our entire operation—and without international trust we won't succeed."

"If he's employed by us, he's also our responsibility!" Masterson wasn't shouting, not yet, but her voice had risen a bit above the recommended conversational tone.

"Excuse me?" The crossed arms and legs in the green chair unwound, eager to interfere. "Correct me if I've misunderstood this, but *you* were the one who snuck this name onto our list?"

Unlike Perry, William Riley had never liked her. The director of the FBI had even publicly opposed her appointment as head of the DEA, but he'd been disregarded. Her qualifications and competence had been more than enough, and she'd never really understood if he disliked her personally or was just opposed to female executives.

"Yes, but if you'll let me explain—"

"Without informing the FBI—the authority in charge of the list?"

She looked at the fireplace and the large clock hanging above it—still ticking loudly. "Yes."

"Then I guess he's *your* responsibility, right? *Your* problem?"

Five till ten. She'd used up half her time.

"The identity of an informant, especially a criminal, should only be known by a bare minimum. You know that's how it works, Riley. Planting false information in public records. Because being detected would be a death sentence. And each new individual who knows the identity of an informant increases that risk. That's how we've always done this, and how we'll continue to do this. And you'll continue to be grateful for it."

"This dilemma, if I may call it that, isn't about our methods. It's about politics."

"And morality. But maybe that's the same thing in this room?" Sue Masterson turned to the chief of staff, seeking his support. He didn't say anything. But he was frustrated, that much was clear. His ears were flushed red and wiggled slightly.

"So who is he?" Now it was the blue armchair. Marc Eve, the CIA director. And he smiled wryly while he waited for her response.

"As I tried to explain, he's *our* informant, one of *us*."

He knew when he asked the question that he wasn't going to get an answer. Now he scrutinized her with a piercing, unreadable gaze. She'd met eyes like those before, and she knew better than to give in. It was just as common among leaders in the police force as it was in top members of drug syndicates—a lot of power in a limited world. They were the most dangerous. Especially when they were fed half-truths, like now. Lack of empathy combined with the wielding of power, decisions reduced to their intellectual and rational aspects.

"I asked *who* he is. What's his name? Where does he come from?"

"I don't know his real identity. I don't have his complete personal data—that was part of the agreement with his contact person. What I know is that he's called El Sueco, and he's from somewhere in northern Europe."

"He's not a US citizen?" Now Marc Eve smiled for real. "Then there's no problem."

He looked around, triumphantly.

Sue looked around, worriedly.

A jury was deliberating on a death sentence. On a killing. Despite the fact that this jury already knew the accused was innocent.

"What is it you don't understand? We pay him—a branch of the federal government. He works for our government!" Her water glass was empty. The lemon slice on its way down the side. She filled it again, emptied it.

Morality and politics. They were *not* the same thing.

"And this . . . this is the fucking White House! Surely we can't be considering condemning an innocent man to death!" She had raised her voice again. She had thrown a curse word at the snooty walls, and it echoed around and around. Until the only one in the room who had yet to speak, Vice President Thompson, captured it.

"Sue?" A soft voice. That struck hard. "We're going to have to ask you to leave. We need to discuss this. And we'll call you again when we're done."

Every time, a new face.

Erik Wilson nodded toward the civilian guard who he'd never seen before, patiently held up his police badge until he got the nod back, and headed to the elevator, pressed the button for the seventh floor.

There had been a time when they loved each other. He still loved her, in a way. But it wasn't love that clouded his judgment. There was no one in the world he had more confidence in than Sue Masterson. Analytical, structured, strategic. Much better than he ever was or could be.

So he should relax. Nevertheless, his whole body felt uneasy, no matter how tight his control on his breathing.

"Your business here?" A voice above him in the elevator. He leaned closer to the microphone.

"Superintendent Wilson, on his way to relieve you."

A slightly too long pause. An audible sigh. Someone was definitely relieved.

The seventh floor. And he lingered without stepping out. He suddenly realized where his uneasiness was coming from, why it buzzed around his head nipping, sapping, spitting out all of his energy. He trusted her implicitly—as a police officer. But this was about more than just police work. This was politics. And he'd been caught up in something like this already—Swedish politicians who sentenced Piet Hoffmann to death on the basis of the false records they had access to. And when they were informed of their mistake, were told Hoffmann was paid by the Swedish police and not their enemy. And then, *despite* that, they let a false death sentence stand to maintain their power.

He stepped out of the elevator, a guards' station with another civilian employee inside sitting behind a rolled-up window. And now he heard a very familiar voice. It was quiet, still far away, but there was no doubt. As he approached, the strain from the intercom increased, the loud monologue of a man in a tiny cell trying to call attention to himself.

"Now get in here, as fast as hell, and unlock this door!"

The guard, a young man with kind eyes, shrugged resignedly.

"Do you hear what I'm saying! Fucking guard!"

"Yes. I hear what you're saying. I've heard everything you've said."

"So unlock this goddamn door!"

"I *can't* do that. I explained that to you, Superintendent."

"Unlock it!"

"I'm not the one you need to talk to, sir. The arrest order was written by Chief Prosecutor Ågestam. He's the one who decides when we should let you go. As you know, Superintendent."

"The chief prosecutor is *also* a magnificent ass! And that is neither libel nor defamation. It's the truth!"

The intercom wasn't entirely new, a model that had seen better days, and, apparently, its volume control sat on one side. Wilson noticed the guard turning it down.

"So he's been like that for several hours."

"I'm sure he could keep it up quite a bit longer."

"He's been asking for a breathalyzer, but it's too late to matter now."

He handed over his badge again, and the guard examined it quickly, stood up almost immediately, and opened the door to the jail. Wilson followed him, passed the rows of locked doors, a place where the dust seemed more oppressive than elsewhere. Cell 5. A man was screaming inside and kicking the few fixtures there were.

Wilson nodded at the young guard, who started to walk away—waited until he was alone before pulling open the small hatch in the middle of the door. The opening was positioned near eye level, and he found himself staring at the wide back of a blazer. Ewert Grens's back. In the civilian clothes he'd been allowed to keep. Out of fear of his screaming and threats? Or out of respect for a superior? Or because not even the staff at the jail believed him guilty of what he was accused of?

"Do you want to come out?"

The blazer back turned and became two black eyes. "Open up!"

"Because if you want that, you need to calm down."

"Wilson, for fuck's sake . . ."

There was a clear click as Wilson pushed down the hatch. A muffled sound. He sat down on a little three-legged stool that stood outside the cell. One minute. Two. Two and a half. Until it was completely silent behind that locked door. Then he opened the hatch again.

"Okay?"

"Okay."

"Good. Wait a second."

Wilson motioned toward the guard station, gesturing as if he had an imaginary key in his hand, and the guard soon headed toward him with a huge bundle of keys, as if he were in a hurry, as if he wanted to be sure that the detective who found the whole world incompetent wouldn't have time to repent and start yelling again.

A deep, metallic sigh as the heavy lock turned. A crumpled blazer. And large stains on it. The clear remains of wine on a man who, to Wilson's knowledge, never drank alcohol. Equally wrinkled and stained trousers. And the little hair left on Grens's head sprawled in every direction.

They walked side by side through the corridor, the air unreasonably dusty, maybe because neither spoke. Passing one, two, three, four locked cell doors. Until Grens stopped abruptly.

"What the hell are you wearing?"

"Ewert, I think I'm the one who should be asking you that."

"Still . . . a uniform?"

"I'm a police officer. And sometimes it's a matter of life and death."

They looked at each other. And maybe Grens realized that the seriousness in his boss's face was real, and no more explanation would be forthcoming at that moment, because that would require more strength than he had. For whatever reason, he kept walking without asking, stretching his stiff neck and sore right leg as they wandered through a large building that was part of the compound that formed the epicenter for Swedish police work. Three doors with keys, three with keycards. Both men lost in their own thoughts. Until they reached the homicide unit. Until Ewert Grens's office, where they separated.

"I assume you'll come by later to see me, Ewert, and explain what this afternoon was all about. How it is you ended up chewing out prison guards in a wine-soaked suit. But for now, just try to take it easy."

Grens had already disappeared into his office. No thank-yous, no excuses. The old stereo in his bookshelf crackled as he turned on a tape he'd recorded himself, where Siw Malmkvist sang a song in Swedish, and Connie Francis followed it with the original in English. Wilson stood there until "Tunna skivor" was replaced by "Everybody's Somebody's Fool" and he realized the detective had no intention of turning around.

"Ewert—I just got you out of jail. You're my responsibility. So now, for once in your life, do as I say."

The cheerful, hopeful, '60s voices escorted him down the hallway as he continued walking toward his own office, but when he reached the coffee machine the music changed to something electronic, monotone. His cell phone. His entire jacket pocket vibrated arrhythmically, urgently.

"Yes?"

"They wouldn't back down." Sue. Speaking with a voice he'd never heard. "They insist on keeping the kill list as is."

Her matter-of-factness. Her fearlessness, confidence. All gone.

"Hoffmann is still the Seven of Hearts."

"Damn it, Sue . . . you're sending him to his death!"

"If anyone's aware of that it's me."

"One of your own!"

"I've gone as far as I could trying to explain that. They painted themselves into a corner. And plan to stay there."

Now it was Siw Malmkvist again, in Swedish. And she sang from Grens's office in that old-fashioned way: happily, chirpily. Wilson understood for a moment why Grens sought out that simplicity, to avoid everything else.

"So now, Sue, it's fine to execute your employees for doing their jobs?"

He waited. For an answer that wasn't forthcoming. It was as if she'd hung up.

"This is how it is. So listen closely, Erik. I, in my role as the director of the DEA, will no longer be allowed to concern myself with this matter. At all. Even this conversation is a crime. If I did continue with this, it would, according to the people I just met with—and I'm quoting now—'be unilaterally perceived and interpreted as if the director of the DEA were deliberately working against the best interests of the United States of America.' I was also informed that, under such circumstances, first I would be dismissed, then prosecuted."

Even her breathing was less self-assured.

He listened to it, expectantly.

"He's sentenced to death, and neither I nor his handler can contact him or assist him in any way. But just because we can't, doesn't mean someone else can't. Right, Erik?"

He held the phone in his hand. But no voice, no breath beyond electronic silence. She'd hung up.

But someone else can.

The bastards had not backed down. Just like the Swedish politicians had not backed down.

Right, Erik?

She had spoken directly to him. Encouraging him.

There were only three people, besides Piet Hoffmann and his wife, who knew of his escape from a Swedish jail and that he was still alive. And two of them could no longer practice their profession without reprisal.

He stood in the middle of a corridor next to a humming coffee machine. If he listened closely, there were so many other sounds. Sixties music layered over a woman speaking loudly into the phone in the office opposite, and, farther away, people laughing on their way out of a meeting, easing the tension as you do when you stand up and can stop being serious for a moment. He turned around, toward the coffee machine, and squeezed out two cups, black.

There were only three who knew. Soon there would be four.

SKY-BLUE CARPET, OCEAN-BLUE wallpaper. A room that was meant to exude stillness, awareness, intellect. They'd made the decision jointly and convinced each other that it was the right one. Now they all stood up. Vice President Thompson behind her desk, FBI Director Riley and CIA Director Eve from their armchairs, Chief of Staff Perry from the sofa, while taking a last swig from his coffee mug.

Riley got to the closed door first, pushed down the handle, and opened it. Then regretted it.

"Can we trust her?" He closed it again, turned around. "Can we trust Masterson?"

Perry put down his coffee with so much force the flawless table whined.

"Can we trust *you*, Bill? Sue Masterson was appointed by the president. Just like you. And we choose to trust those we appoint."

The last drops of coffee had splashed onto the surface of the table, and the chief of staff wiped them away with the crumbly napkin of the dessert tray before continuing.

"We've explained to Sue that she should have nothing more to do with this case. And she understands that."

Riley smiled, or maybe it was a sneer. "Are you absolutely sure of that?"

First Riley's voice from one direction, followed by Vice President Thompson's voice from the other.

"Are you absolutely sure it's just a personal feeling that Bill is expressing? And not an actual risk? Because we can't afford any questions later, from anybody. Not about any tiny mistakes, like one of our top law enforcement officials putting one of our own on a Most Wanted list for strategic reasons. An individual they recruited, as the DEA so often does, from the criminal world. And that she did so *without* informing her superiors." She wondered what the Secretary of State would have said about all this if she were in town. She was on a diplomatic mission to China, wouldn't return until next week. It couldn't be helped. Better to deal with this themselves, keep it within this room.

She was now looking only at Perry. "You said it yourself, Daniel. Confidence gives us the support we need. Leaves us free to act."

No one heard it at first. A knock drowned out somewhere beneath the golden chandelier. The next time it was louder, more insistent. Riley, who was closest, opened the door. A young man was waiting outside, the Secret Service officer who previously escorted them here.

"This is for Chief of Staff Perry. It's important."

A white envelope. He handed it to the FBI director, who passed it to the sofa. The chief of staff looked at the vice president, who nodded. Perry slit open the envelope.

A single document. A photo. A man he recognized. A man he knew, but who looked very different from when he'd last seen him in these hallways just a few days ago. Speaker Crouse. Trapped in a cage.

ERIK WILSON HAD just heard music coming through an open door. But now, when he returned, it was closed. Grens had closed it in the short time Wilson spent on his way to and from the coffee machine, trying to indicate he wanted to be left alone. It was difficult to knock with two full plastic cups in hand, so he kicked lightly with the tip of his shoe on the bottom edge of the door, twice.

"We need to talk, Ewert."

"You told me I was supposed to explain it to you later. And I will. Later."

"I'm not interested in how you ended up in a jail right now. We need to talk about something else entirely. And it's a goddamn hurry."

Wilson stared at the closed door. No nameplate, no information whatsoever. Grens had refused to put up a new sign, objected to doing what every other office dweller did, for reasons he himself had probably already forgotten.

"Just a minute. Almost ready."

He'd been allowed to do as he pleased. It wasn't that important anyway. And Wilson had long since stopped waging pointless battles. He could hear the closet door opening inside, the same squeak in every office. Then complete silence. The coffee cups were burning his palms, and he put them down on the floor in front of the threshold. And waited in the dark corridor. It felt nice to do nothing, think nothing.

"You can come in now."

Wilson picked up the two cups and bent forward, pressing down on the handle with his elbow. The wine-stained suit lay in a pile on the floor. Next to it stood Grens. Also in uniform. It was on the tight side.

"I didn't have anything else." The superintendent pointed to the closet in the corner that probably contained additional uniforms even smaller than this one, from a time when there wasn't quite so much of Ewert Grens.

Wilson handed over one of the cups, and thin steam rose from it in the desk lamplight. Two men who never wore uniforms sat across from each other, wearing just that. And both realized how little it takes to see, and be perceived, differently. Two people who knew each other, but not really.

"Okay. What did you want?"

"Can I borrow your computer?"

Grens shoved his computer across the desk and turned the screen toward the visitor's chair, while Wilson fished his wallet out of the inside pocket of his jacket. With thumb and forefinger against the coin pocket, he edged out the flash drive he'd received from Jennings, pushed it gently into the computer, and clicked on the file called Seven of Hearts.

"Come here, please." He waited until Grens was standing beside him. "I want you to look at this."

Wilson moved the cursor toward the timeline, clicked again, making sure that it was the right sequence. The perspective from above. Slightly blurry images. But it was clear that we were in a jungle. That we were following a truck transport that was often obscured by the thick foliage of the trees. The truck approached a broad river, parked right next to the beach, and two people jumped out. They started unloading, stacking boxes onto a waiting barge. Until the flatbed was empty, and the two climbed on board.

"What the hell is this?"

"Just watch."

"I've already lost too much of my work day to a jail cell. So if you'll excuse me—I have a lot to do and absolutely none of it concerns your nature film."

"Keep watching."

The timeline again. The two men in the jungle were now riding the barge down a winding river. And Grens stared at the screen as he'd been asked—it had been easier to reach him than usual. Grens was listening in a different way. No arrogance, distance. It could be from the shame of having been locked up. But probably not. More likely it was the uniforms, Erik Wilson was almost sure of it. Not because there were more lines on Wilson's shoulders, Grens had never paid attention to such things. It was more that their personal differences had been erased—the personal was just no longer in the way. Maybe he should wear a uniform more often, at least in this office.

Now. A rapid zooming in toward one of the men on the barge. A vague outline of a body in gray squares. As close as they could get.

And Wilson searched Grens's face, which was gradually becoming more interested, focused. He'd had the same expression back then.

Three years ago—the hostage drama that a trapped Piet Hoffmann, facing death, had staged at Aspsås prison. Back then Grens had watched another monitor, and after much anguish, ordered the marksman to fire at the hostage taker. It was the first death Ewert Grens had commanded.

"That last bit? I want to see it one more time."

Wilson moved the cursor along the timeline, the sequence started again at the same point—zooming in on the barge. On the man moving on it.

Grens leaned closer. Toward someone who seemed . . . familiar. He could almost make out a tattoo on the shaved head. Shaped like a large, meandering snake, or maybe some kind of lizard. There'd been no tattoo on the head back then, Grens was sure that was new. And of course the clothing was very different. And he was leaner. And yet. The way he moved. The one thing you couldn't change.

"What the hell is this?"

"You recognize him?"

Grens hurried over to his bookcase, ran his forefinger along the backs of binders, pulled out one of them. At the very back was a plastic pocket and in it a CD.

"I studied him, Wilson. His movements. Hour after hour, day after day. That's the way movements are, they're etched in, and without you knowing it they take up their own damn space in your consciousness. I'd know this man anywhere."

Wilson watched as Ewert's face turned a deep red. The man who'd given the order for a fatal shot—and who only later realized that he'd made that call based on an incorrect premise. Unaware that Piet Hoffmann was in the service of the police. And that he, Ewert Grens, had been reduced to a useful idiot so others could get away with legally protected murder. And that's why he'd stormed into Wilson's office, screaming about hidden agendas, about truth and lies, in this very same corridor.

And now—he'd probably shout again. Because Piet Hoffmann was alive. Because Erik Wilson had known and hadn't informed him. Let Grens believe he was responsible for the death of an innocent man. But instead he seemed strangely calm, and his voice lacked that icy phrasing he was so good at.

"Paula. Piet Hoffmann. I knew he was alive. Just like you. The whole time." Grens coaxed the CD from its plastic pocket and wiped it with a quiet whistle, then came a barely audible humming as he cleaned away the messy fingerprints crowded on the reflective surface, finally he poked it into the side of the computer.

Wilson never looked away from his face. It had changed from unwilling to focused.

I knew he was alive. The whole time.

And now it was unreadable.

"This is a copy of the surveillance tape recorded by the central guard station camera at Aspsås prison. The week after Piet Hoffmann had, well, died there. Let me show you the fourth day." Grens had stopped whistling and humming, and his whole face tightened, lips as well as cheeks, as he pulled the cursor along the timeline for four days, four nights. And stopped at 20:06. "Do you know how many murders I have investigated, Wilson?"

They both saw it on the screen. A man with very short hair in a guard uniform was approaching. He stared up at the camera for a little too long as he walked out. Making sure that when these images were examined later you'd have time to see who it was.

"I've investigated two hundred and twenty-seven murders. Out of those, five are unsolved. And seven are solved but the perp remains free. But that man you saw there, Wilson—that's the murderer I wake up every morning glad to know I never caught."

Grens let the sequence continue, and the camera now followed the disguised man through the gate in the wall, toward a beautiful evening and freedom. "When I found this, realized he'd deceived me, us—well, I chose to keep it to myself."

Two men in uniform. On the same side of a desk. They regarded each other in silence.

Wilson had thought that only three people knew. But for three long years, there had been a fourth.

"Thank you." He searched Grens's gaze. Waiting. Until he got a nod, discreet but still there. Which meant *you did your job, I did mine, and that's how it works sometimes.* "Then I want us to do the same thing again, Ewert."

"Do what?"

"Make sure he survives."

IT WAS NOT a good photograph. Badly lit, not quite in focus. Despite that, it was still the most heinous image Chief of Staff Perry had ever encountered. Bars. A cage. And a man behind those bars, inside that cage. Timothy D. Crouse. Speaker of the House of Representatives—and part of the same power structure that everyone in this room belonged to. But the picture stripped that away, completely. He might as well have been naked.

"The IP address was traced to an Internet café in Bogotá. It's at the bottom there, an investigator at the NGA has written it out by hand, just below the photo's timestamp."

They all moved in closer, scrutinizing that same image. Or maybe not quite the same. They were struck by different details, as viewers are. One noticed how dark it was, late at night, and wondered if the photographer had deliberately kept him awake in order to increase the menace of the setting. Someone else was struck by the clay that surrounded the cage, brown mud covered with shoe prints. Yet another noted that Crouse was wearing extremely dirty clothes, maybe even the same suit he'd had on a couple of days earlier in the corridor outside this very room.

Thoughts like shadows. But that's how it worked. Focusing on the minor to protect yourself from the unthinkable. Like now, reflecting on how a suit and a jungle didn't really seem to go together.

And last, probably because it was noted at the top of the document, in the same sprawling handwriting as before, they saw how the NGA investigator had written that the picture had been addressed to the president and sent to the White House's public email address.

"What's that? Is it . . . ?" Chief of Staff Perry pointed to the cage floor. There was a thin straw mattress rolled out behind Crouse, but that was not his aim, he was pointing to the round bit of plastic that stood next to it. It looked like a bowl. "And it's half full. Some stew. Potatoes? And something else?"

A cage. A plastic bowl on the floor. To deprive a person of his dignity, treat him like an animal.

On the left near the edge, placed in that same brown sludge, a part of another cage was visible, and someone was sitting inside it, on the floor with her back against him, probably a woman. On the right edge, almost as if it had been arranged, they could just make out a weapon balanced on four metal feet in the mud.

"A Russian bazooka." The CIA director leaned closer, changed his glasses. "An RPG-29 Vampire. You could take down a tank with it. Hezbollah took out several Israeli tanks with it during the Lebanon war. A demonstration of power, in its simplest form."

"A cage. A rocket launcher. But no demands." Chief Perry focused on the man they all knew. He must have been instructed to stand in the foreground, holding on tightly to the bamboo bars of his cage. "I don't get it. Do any of you? Sending us this picture, but not a single demand?"

Crouse's fingers looked like they were cramping as they seized onto those sticks, holding him upright. A bottomless, blank stare. And the camera's harsh flash struck his face and turned his otherwise deeply tanned skin almost completely white.

Perry sat down on the sofa he'd just left, put the photo in the middle of the coffee table, pushed it away a bit, as if trying to avoid those fearful, pleading eyes. Vice President Thompson sat down next to him, pulled the photo closer, and studied it quietly for a long time.

"We've put out a kill list of the thirteen names who are ultimately responsible for this, the leaders of a terrorist organization." She held it close as if she were speaking directly to it, to her colleague who stood there and wanted to go home. "Everyone on that list will be eliminated, one name at a time. And no half-criminal European is going to jeopardize that."

She nodded toward the picture, toward Crouse.

"Crossed off, one name at a time."

EWERT GRENS HAD stood up, started pacing the room nervously. Soon he put a cassette into the tape deck like he always did when he was seeking equilibrium, "Tunna Skivor." Siw singing the same version, every time. He sat down, compared the surveillance video of a man walking out of a prison with the satellite recording of man stepping onto a barge in a jungle. Silent. Until now.

"So this is how he earns his living." Grens was often ironic, even cynical and malicious. This comment could have been interpreted in that way. But his face, his eyes, said something else, Erik Wilson was sure of it.

"Yes. That's how he supported himself. Until a half hour ago. When his employers chose to terminate his service."

Now it was Wilson's turn to approach the bookcase, the shelf above the ancient tape deck. He pulled out one of the books there—voluminous, heavy. A world atlas. He leafed through it, started from the back as he so often did, and noted the cardboard pocket and library card, the kind that existed before. He pulled it out, turned it, read.

Stockholm Public Library.
DUE: October 18, 1989.

And he smiled, glancing at the detective, who smiled back.

"Statute of limitations, Wilson. Right?"

Without answering, Wilson moved Grens's coffee cup, telephone, desk lamp, and his pile of ongoing investigations, making room for the bulky book, and continued flipping until he found what he was looking for on page 218. A large map of South America. He grabbed a red marker from the desk organizer and marked a couple of boundaries. A square, or rhombus rather, at the top left corner, the Caribbean on one side and the Pacific on the other.

"Ewert, what do you know about Colombia?"

"Best coffee in the world. Meant to be drunk black. None of that milky bullshit."

Wilson smiled, like before, the room had been missing that irony and cynicism for a moment. "Okay. Do you know anything else?"

"Beautiful, warm climate. But extremely corrupt. Violent. Powerful drug cartels. One of the few places I've decided never to visit—even though ninety-nine percent of the population is nice as can be."

Wilson turned the map toward Grens, ran his finger along the red line. "And yet that's where you're headed."

Grens didn't even look at the open page, spoke softly, almost whispering. "Almost everything we investigate in this fucking building—do you realize that, Wilson? Almost all of our investigations are related to drugs? To the products produced right there, in Colombia."

"Gaira Café, Ewert."

"One hundred thousand drug offenses a year in just our small country. Doubles every ten years. And I'm only talking about *drug* crimes. Not about the robbery, theft, burglary that happens in order to get money to buy the shit. Nor the violence that comes from defending drug turfs or recovering debts. Drugs, Wilson, are driving crime. They're behind everything we do. The cost, the total cost of Swedish drug use approaches thirty billion kronor a year—health care, social services, illness, premature death. That sort of thing. In addition, you've got all your smashed-up shop windows and broken doors and police and legal costs and all other health-care interventions caused by shootings or serious assault or . . . Wilson, drugs don't just drive all crime, they drive our entire society! When you think about it, do people even want it to end? When so many make their living from the consequences?"

"Gaira Café in Bogotá." Wilson flipped forward in the never-returned world atlas, found a city map, pointed until Grens gave in and looked down. "Calle 96, between Carrera 13 and 13A."

"If you say so."

"You'll meet the man sauntering through your surveillance video there. The same man who's switching from a truck to a barge in mine. You'll get the exact time when your plane lands at El Dorado International."

Grens didn't respond. But didn't protest either. He seemed to sink into the map, lines and squares representing another reality.

"I can't go myself. I wish I could—but it's impossible. *If* I were caught, the investigation would connect me with the person in the US who hired Hoffmann. And she'd lose both her job and her future."

The older detective stood up for a second time, turned up the volume on "Tweedle Dee," an annoyingly happy and catchy jingle that sounded more '50s than '60s.

"Listen to me, Ewert. You are probably—and I might as well be completely honest now—the person in this building *least* suited to this particular mission. And that's unfortunate. But—you can't be traced to her. And you know him. And that's what this is all about—you're the only one, besides me, he'd trust. You were the one he entrusted a brown envelope of evidence to just a few hours after his prison escape." Wilson looked at his colleague, who seemed to be listening as much to the music as to his boss. "Your task, Ewert, is to seek out and assist Hoffmann. Adapt to the situation and possibilities. You'll get the entire background after you've packed up and retrieved your passport."

A few final notes and the chorus had finally subsided.

"I want to see him here, Ewert, alive."

"Sorry. I don't have a passport. Never done much traveling."

"We can take care of that."

Silence. The tape had ended. And Grens didn't put on another one.

"I take it this is an order, Wilson?"

"No. This is not an order. You'll have no authority there. And no protection."

The burly police officer, who felt so safe in this office, with its shabby corduroy sofa and music from another time, now looked at his boss and shrugged. "You make it sound so tempting."

"And absolutely no one, regardless of the circumstances, can confirm your assignment."

"Just like any criminal informant." Grens smiled again.

"You have to leave now. Immediately. This is urgent. When Americans do these kinds of things, when they reach out for broad support and turn things into a question of international politics, history shows they strike fast. I'm convinced they already have their first target ready to go."

A VIDEO GAME. He would never get used to the fact that it looked like that. Or felt like that. At any moment, it seemed like his mother's voice might call out from downstairs, *food.* His mother never gave up until he stopped, pressed pause, hurried down the stairs, and silently ate something fried and cleared his dish, then rushed up again to his room and desk and a game in a different world.

Steve Sabrinsky held the joystick lightly while searching across the computer's two screens. It still felt like a video game. And that's how he tried to think of it, like the games played in the crowded room of his boyhood home, as if firing missiles at a human were something he was racking up points for, and that when this was over, he would be able to press restart. The whole world reset again, and nothing would have happened.

But it didn't work like that. This game was serious. The dead would remain dead.

He drank half a cup of green tea and half a Coca-Cola in a room some ship designer had crammed in below deck by one of the staircases. Just a few square meters left over on the drawing, which an architect discovered just before they started building and scribbled down *in this tiny room someone will sit at a desk taking people's lives from them.* And that's exactly what he did. It was cramped, but there was enough space for the desk, the two computer screens, and a chair.

"Sabrinsky?"

"Yes, sir?"

"Our target has been localized. It's under surveillance."

And—room for the combat commander on this aircraft carrier, who was standing just behind him, and who now leaned in closer as he handed over a piece of paper.

"Current GPS coordinates." Garlic. And coffee. That's what the commander's warm breath on his neck smelled like. "Activate the UCAV."

Steve Sabrinsky entered the real-world coordinates—beyond this video-game screen—which stood for a real house with a real family, then pressed the download button and waited for a light to illuminate, confirm.

USS *Liberty*. A real aircraft carrier: 365 meters long, 102,000 tons, 4,700 crew members. Separate takeoff and landing runways. A real combat commander behind him.

This was where he'd been headed for so long. This was what he'd been educated and trained for—getting his marching orders at midnight, leaving the 32nd Street Naval Station in San Diego and sailing the Pacific Ocean down the West Coast, past Mexico and Guatemala and El Salvador and Nicaragua and Costa Rica and Panama. All of it to reach this point. Eight nautical miles off the shores of Colombia. To trade the strident electronic air below deck for the caress of fresh sea air and to clearly see the outlines of Buenaventura.

He made sure the UCAV had a full tank, that the coordinates were entered correctly into the system, then started the engine and turned on the camera. And turned toward the commander, who nodded.

Steve Sabrinsky pressed one of the side buttons on the joystick. And the two-hundred-pound drone started rolling from one side of the ship's deck to the other. Until the numbers at the bottom of the screen confirmed it was going more than eighty-five kph. And at that moment, at the ship's edge, he pulled back the joystick and released the drone, let it take off, fly.

It was beautiful as it moved across the screen. On its way. Because he told it to.

Sabrinsky realized he had been holding his breath, and released it now, took another, deep breath.

It started to dip! More gas. More gas! Then climb again.

"Good. Leave it there. Five, maximum six meters above the water."

Almost no wind. No waves. This was going to work.

"Until it reaches Buenaventura. Then let it climb."

The target coordinates were in the top right of the screen. They matched. The drone was headed in the right direction. Height. Speed. Those figures were also consistent. And in the box below stood information on the armament—a rocket grenade with thermobaric charge. The kind they used on unprotected targets. When they were detonated, they generated a powerful wave that killed whoever the explosion might have missed.

"Distance to target?"

"Eight kilometers, sir."

"In here we don't use *sirs*. Understood?"

"Understood, si—understood."

"At the coast, climb to one hundred meters. Keep it away from buildings. The direction is Cali, according to the target coordinates. After contact with the target, climb another fifty meters. Then lock on target."

This was no longer a video game. This was his very first time. From game to real.

"Our objective has been confirmed to be inside the target. Now, Sabrinsky, lock on target."

"Locked on target. One hundred and fifteen seconds to detonation."

"Drift? Elevation?"

"Drift zero. Elevation one hundred and fifty meters and sinking."

From life to death.

"Unlock the charge."

"Charge unlocked. Fifty-seven seconds to detonation."

The large screen had a bull's-eye in the middle, or what looked like one anyway, rings nestled inside each other. In the innermost ring stood a house. As the drone came closer, and thus the camera, it became clear that someone was moving outside the house, probably three bodies, two small and one bigger.

Steve Sabrinsky rested his finger lightly on a button that would *abort*. The order could come at any moment.

"Ten seconds until detonation."

EWERT GRENS LIMPED a little more than usual with a bulky suitcase in his hand. Brown with an uneven, lumpy surface, the material was difficult to determine, maybe plastic, maybe leather on pasteboard. It had been in his storage space in the attic just like he remembered, as dusty as everything else up there. Not very elegant, not used much. They'd bought it together, back then. Or, Anni had bought one for each of them. And there was a stamp of the Eiffel Tower in one corner, which she'd pasted there on their first day in their hotel room. It had sat in storage since then.

"Ewert?" Sven Sundkvist sat behind his desk. His door stood open to the homicide unit corridor. Headphones on his close-cropped, blond head, and leaning forward slightly on his elbows. He usually sat just like that listening to and analyzing recordings of interrogations from before he became lead interrogator. Always so thorough. "You seem stressed."

"Yes." Grens continued walking, though usually he would have stopped, leaned against the doorframe, continued the conversation they'd been having for so many years, Grens didn't talk to many. Sven Sundkvist hurried over to the door and saw that Grens was trying to disappear down the corridor.

"Ewert, what are you up to?"

"I can't discuss it."

"A suitcase? Are you taking a—"

"Sorry, Sven, but this doesn't concern you."

The next door to open was Mariana Hermansson's. And she called after him.

"I heard you were inspecting the facilities at the Kronoberg jail! For several hours!"

Now he stopped, peeked inside. She was sitting just like Sven, at her desk, but not listening, watching a TV instead, a recording from a police lineup—men with numbers on their chests, being recorded by a camera on the other side of a one-way mirror. She had certainly seen it before and was watching again to make sure it was going to hold up in court. Sven there, Mariana here, both equally painstaking in their work. Grens was proud of them, in his own way.

"You surely couldn't have heard that. That kind of information is confidential. Surely the Swedish police wouldn't violate confidentiality or gossip about their colleagues. Right, Hermansson?"

"Seems like the detective violated it quite well himself when he was loudly proclaiming his colleagues incompetent."

"I don't have a clue what you're talking about. You can ask anyone in this corridor if I'm ever loud."

He smiled. She smiled. He got ready to go. She nodded to the suitcase.

"Going somewhere?"

"Yes."

"And?"

"That's not something I can discuss with you. But on my desk you'll find all my open cases where an arrest is imminent. I want you and Sven to take care of them while I'm gone."

"For how long, Ewert?" Like Sven, she was now calling after him. "Ewert!"

"I don't know yet. A week. Maybe two."

He didn't look back, just stepped into the elevator and stepped out again when he'd reached the ground floor exit toward Kungsholm Street. Erik Wilson was waiting for him there. He had his private car idling, ready to go. Grens threw the suitcase in the backseat, and they started driving through the rush hour traffic of a capital city. They took the bus lane. And took the dividing pavement when there was none. Once they left the inner city, he sped up.

"There." Grens pointed out through the passenger-side window. "That's where I was headed today."

The North Cemetery lay on the other side of the fence. And a person who had long meant everything to him.

"And I'm still on my way there." Two smashed bottles. He'd try again when he got home. "And the chief prosecutor is still a magnificent ass."

After that they sat in silence. Passed Helenelund, passed Sollentuna. As they approached Upplands Väsby, Wilson reached over Grens and opened the glove compartment.

"There at the back, Ewert, there's a plastic bag. Two telephones for emergencies only. One for communicating with Hoffmann. One for communicating with me. Each phone is for calls *from* a single number. Or calls *to* a single number." Two burner phones that only called each other. And if anyone were to get ahold of their phones, there would be no names, just an untraceable, unknown subscriber who made and received calls from an untraceable, unknown subscriber.

"Next to that is your emergency passport. Valid for two months. And it allows you entry to the United States, just to be sure." Grens pulled out something pink. *Emergency Passport.* Thinner than the regular kind. He opened it and saw a picture of himself, taken from his personnel file.

"And under that, in that plastic pocket, is everything else you need." Grens took that out too. First his flight information. Departure at 19:25. Layover and an overnight stay in London. Total flight time of twenty-six hours and twenty minutes. "You land in Bogotá tomorrow at sixteen ten. Local time."

Next document. A hotel reservation. "Estelar La Fontana. Room 555. Top floor. Extremely quiet. That's where I usually stay."

Then a map. Grens unfolded it. A city map of Bogotá, larger than the one in the world atlas and more detailed. Three large letters in red ink. An *A*—airport. An *H*—hotel. And a *P* between them.

"Paula. I still call him that. That's where you'll meet. Gaira Café, at fifteen hundred. I'll let you know the day."

Grens held the passport, the reservations, the map of the meeting place. “How long were you a handler?”

“Twelve years.”

“I can tell. You’ve still got it.”

Neither irony nor annoyance. Seriousness. That’s what Wilson heard in Ewert’s voice. It was the first time, he was sure of it, that he’d ever heard sincere praise coming from Ewert Grens. And it felt good.

“Yes. But then again, I usually recruit my colleagues from prison.”

They smiled, as they’d managed to do earlier today.

“Those final documents.” Wilson nodded at the glove box and Grens rooted around inside it, found five tightly packed A4 sheets in a separate plastic pouch. “I continued the logbook. Once I realized he was alive. You’re holding a copy of it.”

“And this time it’s . . . *everything*?”

Lies and truth in the same police corridor. Crimes hidden away in order to solve other crimes. Secret intelligence reports, which told what really happened—and falsified records that caused a detective superintendent to make the wrong call. That’s what had happened. And that’s why everything went to hell.

“Yes.” Erik Wilson slowed slightly, a truck was passing another truck, forcing the rest of the fast lane to slow down. Lost seconds in the race for a flight whose departure time was creeping ever closer. “Grens—I promise, no secrets.”

He’d never worked that way before. A handler’s first commandment—no information related to an informant can fall into unknown hands. But now he was doing the exact opposite. Inside that plastic pocket stood the name of the informant, the handler, the informant’s other contact; there were descriptions of strategy, meeting places, family situation, housing, appearance, distinctive marks—and a five-sided summary of two years spent infiltrating a guerrilla organization that had just been reclassified as a terrorist organization. During his time as an active handler, information like this had always been written down by hand and kept in a black binder. The code name followed by the date followed by a summary of that particular day's brief encounter in an apartment emptied for renovation in a property that could be accessed from two different addresses. Page by page, meeting by meeting. And attached to each logbook was an envelope that contained the informant's real name, sealed by the handler on the first day of the mission with a shiny red wax seal. A binder and an envelope that were kept in a safe by a responsible CHIS controller, behind a six-figure code and a heavy door.

This was contrary to all of his training and experience. But there were no other options. This was the only chance Piet Hoffmann had to survive.

"Read this on the plane to London. When you land at Heathrow, before going through security, go to the bathroom. Rip every piece of paper into the smallest possible pieces. And flush them down more than one toilet."

The exit for the airport. He turned right, drove the last bit at a significantly higher speed than was allowed.

"Pay everything with your own cash. I'll make sure you're compensated from the account for anonymous tips."

Grens dug into his inside jacket pocket—police badge, police identification, work phone. He put everything in the now empty glove compartment.

"You travel there as a tourist, and you step off the plane as a tourist. I'll repeat what I said earlier. No jurisdiction. No protection. No one here—regardless of the time or situation—can confirm your assignment."

Terminal 5. They had arrived. Grens got out, brown suitcase in hand. Wilson rolled down his window and held out another envelope.

"Five tickets. Home from Bogotá. All open."

The detective superintendent looked at his boss, then the envelope. He opened it. His own name appeared on the first. Peter Haraldsson on the next. Then Maria, Sebastian, and William Haraldsson.

"So that's what they're going by these days?"

Grens was more impressed than he'd like to admit. Wilson really had thought of everything—not a single hole or loose stitch in the fabric woven to protect the informant who was his responsibility. But he didn't have much imagination.

PH. Piet Hoffmann. Peter Haraldsson.

"He's coming back here, Ewert. Piet, Zofia, Hugo, Rasmus, they're all coming back to Sweden. Alive."

THE SCREEN HAD been turned off. But Steve Sabrinsky still sat in the tiny room. He should be happy, bubbling inside, laughing on the outside. This had been his goal for so long. This was for real. But it didn't feel like that at all. It felt empty. Maybe because it was for real. There was no *restart*. This day would never be coming back, just like that. He'd left video games behind and entered a world where living, breathing people walked around until they didn't anymore, because he'd blown them up.

There had been ten seconds left to detonation. He'd waited for a voice behind him to shout *abort*. But no one did. Ten seconds became five seconds, three seconds, one second, the display graphics had been so precise, so detailed as the drone released its armament and the target exploded.

"Sabrinsky."

Combat commander. He'd gone away for a while to the intelligence center, after *impact*.

"Yes, sir?"

"Sir? What did I say about that? That that's no good inside this room."

"I remember."

"Good. Because there's no sir in here." The commander put his hand on Sabrinsky's shoulder. It was heavy, warm, and squeezed hard as he spoke. "I want you to take a look at this."

He had three photographs in his other hand. He spread them across the narrow desk, between the keyboard and joystick. "A few minutes old. Taken by our scouts."

The first image. Black-and-white and angled from above. A house. Or what was a house until very recently. Now all that remained was a concrete foundation and burning, scattered rubble above it.

"You did it."

The next image had been zoomed out. And there were people lying on the ground, not far from the flames. Motionless.

"You took out the terrorists."

Sabrinsky ran his finger across the smooth surface of the paper. There was something that looked like . . . a small playground. Two swings that had spun and spun, lap after lap around a steel structure, until they got stuck at the top.

First an explosion. Then a wave blast.

In the third picture, he was brought in closer again. And it was easier to make sense and identify. He was sure now—the people on the ground were a woman and two children. But nowhere, no matter how closely he looked, could he find their target. Until he realized why. Their target had been inside a house, which didn't exist anymore.

ERIK WILSON WAS at a complete standstill near the exit to Arlanda, on his way back to Stockholm, waiting to get onto the E4 highway. Vehicle after vehicle as far as he could see. A traffic jam, here? Cars lined up for at least another kilometer, probably hundreds of them. And from his gut, through his chest, and into his neck—stress. Even though he didn't need it anymore. They'd made it. Grens was on his way to the departure gate—there was nothing more he could do right now. The adrenaline that had started pumping through him after he saw the news, racing through him when he was stuck in another traffic jam on his way to the US embassy, seemed impossible to turn off now. Maybe he didn't *want* to let go of the rush. So familiar, integral to who he was. The opposite of meetings and negotiations. And it wouldn't be going anywhere just yet. He knew that for sure. Not this evening, not tonight. His heart skipping a beat, sweating, those damn dreams where he was being chased. He used to, back when this was his life, take care of it with alcohol. But he wouldn't do that tonight. He no longer cared for the effects. It made him stubborn, almost aggressive, the adrenaline temporarily pushed aside only to show up the next morning with even greater force accompanied by apprehension, uneasiness, anxiety—and he had no desire to meet that gang again.

"Yes, this is the on-duty officer."

He'd entered the preprogrammed number, now put the phone's microphone to his mouth.

"Erik Wilson, from the homicide unit. I'm stuck in a traffic jam on my way to the city from Arlanda. Can you find out why?"

"One moment." Buzzing silence. A series of clicks. Eyes searching a computer screen. "A truck. Near Bredden. It's lying on its side after a collision. Obstructing all lanes."

"How long until they clear it?"

More noise. More buttons. "I'll look into it and get back to you."

Wilson sighed and waited, phone in hand. If he'd been in a patrol car, he could have put on the blue lights and passed by on the shoulder.

The tea he bought on his way out of the city was long since cold. Even the cardboard cup seemed chilly. He loosened it from the cup holder and drank what was left. It didn't help. He felt equally hunted, drums inside him rumbled out of step.

Thousands of people in the same traffic jam. Not one knowing why. A single person had made a bad decision, and it changed everyone else's night, maybe even their tomorrows, missed meetings were missed chances, expectations for change turned into the carbon dioxide emissions of idling cars.

He straightened up, stared out the window at nothing. A few drops of tea left, some throat lozenges, which lay in a rolled-up bag in the door compartment. Then the phone rang. The on-duty officer calling back with traffic information. That was fast.

"Yes?" Atmospheric disturbances. Electronic crackling. But no one spoke. "Yes, hello? Wilson here." Disturbances, crackling, still there. But there was something more. Breathing.

"Are you alone?"

A crack to the head. That's what it felt like. Something burst and out came a sea of relief. He'd never felt anything quite like it.

"Yes. I'm alone."

Not one phone call over all these years. They'd agreed on that. The risk was too high for something to be traced. But now, after a kill list, the road to life.

"I need your help, Erik, because the situation has changed."

They had a single point of contact. The place he'd urge Hoffmann to go to.

"I've been trying to get ahold of Sue Masterson and Lucia Mendez for four hours. Both of the numbers I have for them have been disconnected. I got my latest phone only thirty-six hours ago. I can't reach them."

Piet. Paula. El Sueco. Anyone listening to you now, intercepting our conversation, would think you sounded calm, matter-of-fact, almost bored. But I hear something else. Fear. A kind of fear I've never heard in your voice before.

A sharp, persistent scratching noise. And then, silence. The connection had been cut off.

Wilson had had no clue if Piet was aware of what was going on. If this afternoon's message had reached him—that he was officially marked for death. Now he knew Piet knew. The best informant he'd ever seen could prepare now, plan for his survival. And the sea of relief continued to overflow and fill the car.

His right hand vibrated. Wilson responded after a single ring. "It got disconnected. I—"

"They've already started, Erik. Just now, the first one. Commander Bloque Amazonas. His whole family."

"The King of Hearts."

"What?"

"That's what he's called. On the kill list."

"Was called."

Fear. Which only he could hear. It was clearer now. *His whole family.* A fear that had never been there before.

"You're in danger, Piet. But not immediate danger. That's not how this works. This isn't a regular war—it's a war against a terrorist organization and that kind of war is implemented slowly, systematically. One target at a time. The invasion of Iraq, fifty-two playing cards—it's been over ten years now. And they took them out one at a time, methodically. They're still doing it."

"Drones, Erik. That's what they used. What about next time? Missiles? Car bombs? Snipers? I can protect myself, you know that. But I can't protect Zofia, Rasmus, Hugo, while continuing to work with the PRC, Sánchez, this pretend life."

"You have to."

"This isn't just about my own safety!"

"If you suddenly disappear from the PRC, they'd know. If not immediately, very soon. Then they'd kill you. You. Zofia. Your kids."

A breath. Wilson listened, waiting, trying to guess where Hoffmann was, what he looked like, what kind of mission he was on.

"Erik, what the hell should I do? A kill list? What a fucking joke! You know, and Sue Masterson knows, and her superiors know, and they sure as hell—"

"In two days. Go to number one. The same time as always."

"Number one? You mean you're coming here?"

"The usual time, Piet."

In the distance, something was finally moving. A tow truck had reached the crash site on the shoulder of the highway, had taken hold of the truck and was pulling it away now, bit by bit. A predator tearing at its wounded prey. Soon, uniformed colleagues were waving through traffic, redirecting it to the left lane.

Then he felt nothing, in his chest. Nothing in his whole body. Whatever had broken, opened, gushed out—he'd run out of it. A fucking traffic jam—and a strange, insistent calm. He knew Piet was alive. Grens was on his way. He trusted them both, trusted their expertise. He'd done what he could, for now.

PART THREE

THE USUAL BOOTH, usual table—the owner's table. Ten o'clock in the morning and La Casa Heaven had just opened. There were fewer people than Johnny expected during the night, ninety-seven hostesses—that's what he called them on their employment papers—who sold 1,364 drinks, two compulsory drinks to everyone who visited the double beds with red velvet bedspreads on one of the hotel's other three floors. Now there were ten or so women ready to take on the day's first round of customers, already dressed according to their job description—black high heels and bright lacy underwear, nothing else. One of them served coffee to the owner's table with a smile, and Piet Hoffmann smiled back, because he too was an actor in this play, playing his part, speaking his lines to avoid any questions from his boss, both of them forced to endure this because neither had a choice. He met her gaze, those eyes tried to look happy but they weren't. She was probably no more than twenty years old, maybe younger, in the evening when she washed off all that makeup and took off that professional smile, all that was left was a little girl.

And that's just the sound they'd heard since they sat down. A little girl. From the still empty stage with its abandoned stripper pole, from the space behind the bar—the laughter rippled, as intensely as stubborn hiccups. Light, clattering footsteps. She came running now, winding her way through one of her father's offices. Alejandrina. Johnny's daughter. All the way up to the table and into Johnny's outstretched arms. He looked so happy, only she could reach him.

"Daddy? Daddy? You know what I want more than anything in the world?"

"No, sweetie, how should I know what you want more than anything in the world?"

He lifted her in his arms, caressed her cheeks with the back of his hand like always—then higher, Johnny held her straight up toward the ceiling, glanced at Hoffmann as if to show him how beautiful she was and Hoffmann nodded, she was indeed lovely.

"Daddy, I want to go swimming. In your pool."

Johnny smiled, caressed her cheeks again. "You're Daddy's little girl—but I have to work. With Uncle Peter."

"But I really, really, really wanna swim *now*!" She balanced one foot on each of his broad thighs, kissed his forehead, his hairline. She knew exactly what to do. "Please, please, Daddy?"

The first customers sat down by one of the tables in the otherwise desolate great hall and ordered their drinks. One of them downed both drinks, the other put them aside, never planning to touch them, instead signaling immediately by taking the young woman's hand—the one who'd served their table—and she smiled as professionally as before as she and her customer walked up the stairs with their arms around each other.

"Please? Come on? Favorite daddy?"

Johnny laughed and stretched his arms up in the air, as if giving up. "Alejandrina, you know what?"

"Noo . . . what, favorite daddy?"

"We're gonna go up to the roof. And go swimming." He walked toward the stairs with the girl in his arms. Hoffmann followed and ended up behind a new couple hand in hand, another hostess, also in her twenties, and her early-morning customer.

"Johnny?"

On their way up the stairs, they met a woman going down. Zaneta. Her smile was identical to Alejandrina's—mouth, eyes. So beautiful, so nice, after just a few times of meeting her, Hoffmann had the impression of a very easy person to like. Her husband embraced her, kissed her, then pointed to their daughter. "Somebody's decided we have to go swimming."

"But you were supposed to . . . Johnny, you wanted me to pick up . . ."

"Mommy—Daddy promised!" Her five-year-old eyes were indignant, looking at a father she could always control and a mother who occasionally she couldn't.

"There's always time for the pool. Right, my princesses?" Johnny placed their daughter on his shoulders and they continued up four more floors, used a key card to unlock the door that led to the roof. The little girl in charge jumped out of her clothes, and her mother didn't even have time to pick them up before the first splash.

"Daddy! Hurry!" The girl jumped up and down, up and down in water that smelled strongly of chlorine.

Johnny was wearing a black pinstriped suit, black shirt, black boots. He stripped off everything but his black socks—as if he were in such a hurry to please his daughter that he forgot them—and he rushed to the edge of the pool and stopped there with his arms pointing at the bouncing, excited five-year-old.

"What do you think . . . should I do the cannonball?"

"Cannonball, Daddy! Cannonball! A huge cannonball!"

And then he jumped. He jumped out and up, pulling his knees to his chest, locking his arms around his shins, clasping them tight with his hands. But he didn't exactly land, it was more like he plowed along the surface while a tsunami rained down on everyone in his vicinity, Hoffmann's pants ended up soaking wet, Zaneta's perfectly styled hair was plastered.

Piet Hoffmann sat down on a lounge chair that was as wet as his pants, but at least protected from the morning sun by an umbrella. Watched as a little girl happily splashed water onto her father, as her father splashed water back, as her mother lay down in another chair and watched as well.

Johnny. El Mestizo. A guerrilla since the day he turned twelve. And five years later sent abroad for further training. In order to become a perfect soldier. And once home, he worked his way up in the organization. To the top. To Julio Vargas and to a position as one of his two assistants, one of his two right hands. One hand, El Loco, took care of the business, and the other, El Mestizo, murdered people. When Vargas had been taken into custody and deported to the United States, he'd left behind a power vacuum and war broke out between the two. A violent and bloody war that took six hundred lives in a matter of a few months. El Mestizo's employees took just over two-thirds of them, four hundred, and lost two hundred of their own. In the final months, the police arrested the other right hand and locked him up, while El Mestizo was left free—the advantage of owning a few treasury friends on the presidential level.

Johnny swam to the edge of the pool and pulled himself up smoothly, water dripping off his big body, his wet socks making a *squish* every time they encountered the flagstones.

"Daddy, come back!"

Johnny sat down on the sun bed between Hoffmann and Zaneta, waved to his daughter. "Daddy has to go out now."

"Cannonball! Cannonball!"

"But Mommy is going to stay here—so you can swim some more."

He leaned back and worked on pulling off his wet socks, which at first refused to budge, then squeezed out the water.

"My darling . . . are you up here?"

A new voice, coming from the door. Yolanda—El Mestizo's *other* life partner, who spent her days in his other hacienda, which lay on the west side of Cali. Piet Hoffmann had never seen the two women in the same place at the same time before. Yolanda was young, not yet thirty, and she walked with a youthful, springy step that knew where it was headed. To Johnny. And she embraced him, sank down onto his wet lap, and got just as soaked as him, her dress, skin. They both laughed. Then she continued to the next chair, to Zaneta, and kissed her cheek.

"Zaneta, you get more beautiful every day. Johnny is lucky to have you."

And the slightly older woman did the same, kissed the younger.

"Yolanda, darling, Johnny is lucky to have you."

And then it was over. Hoffmann smiled. Nowhere else, only here. A hit man, brothel owner who swam in his socks with his child. His wife and mistress side by side on the pool deck. Johnny kissed Yolanda, kissed Zaneta, went to the edge of the pool and waved to Alejandrina, who swam toward him with the strokes of a beginner. He bent down and grabbed hold of her, fished her up, and kissed her on both cheeks, then on the tip of the nose.

"Daddy is coming home again tomorrow night."

"Cannonball, Daddy? One more time? Please!"

"Tomorrow. But here comes another cannonball!"

He held her tight, tossing her little body back and forth while she screamed, howled, but not out of fear, out of anticipation, until he released her, threw her a good way out and her plop became a small, short-lived fountain. He waited until she came to the surface, then waved to her, and threw her a kiss. She waved back, threw him a kiss.

The car was parked in front of the brothel by the post El Mestizo had put up to mark his private parking space. He drove, as usual, always in control. They'd passed the city limits by the time he began his short briefing on today's job.

"Or, rather, two jobs. First Libardo Toyas needs a little reminder. Then we're headed to a cage. Gonna try to help the man in that cage talk." El Mestizo looked pleased. Almost as pleased as at the pool. And he waited for follow-up questions. Even though he never shared any more information than was necessary.

"A cage? And you're gonna make the person inside it talk?"

"Yep. And this time I can go as far as I want. As long as I don't kill him."

Piet Hoffmann had trouble sitting still. He felt that worry that sometimes hunted him, wouldn't give until he knew what was awaiting him, what his next step should be.

A cage. A hostage. They'd done this several times before. But El Mestizo looked so happy, so proud, this wasn't your run-of-the mill torture session.

"Is it . . . him?"

Normally El Mestizo, with half a day to go, would have told him to shut up and wait. But he *wanted* to tell him. And after a few kilometers of silence he nodded slightly. "It's him."

Sometimes an already strange life got even stranger. Hoffmann was breathing in small, short bursts. The man who was the reason he'd been placed on a kill list. The man the whole world was talking about. That was where they were headed, they were going to visit him, speak to him later this afternoon.

And now he couldn't hold back anymore. What had throbbed and burned in his chest since he read his name on that kill list, since Sue Masterson and Lucia had cut him loose, since a drone had destroyed an entire family. He'd decided to wait until they were alone. Until swimming pools, daughters, wives, and mistresses were behind them. Until he realized the absurdity in the fact that every step he'd taken so far, every single action he'd carried out here, he'd done *for* the US government, which was now hunting him down.

El Mestizo hit the brakes. But he didn't curse, didn't even roll down the window and shout at an old man with a dog trying to herd his sheep across the road. Satisfied. That's what he was. Sure, he'd played with and held Alejandrina recently. He'd kissed both his wife and his mistress. But it was as if he refused to admit that their neighbor had bought an even bigger house in the neighborhood. The one they called La Muerte. Death.

"The drone attack."

"Peter, let's talk about something else. I'm not planning on playing the Americans' game."

"But you already are. I am too, and my family and your family as well. We have no choice. Just like the King of Hearts didn't have a choice. They turned him into a fucking playing card and killed him and his family! Joaquín, wasn't that his son's name?"

Piet Hoffmann glanced at El Mestizo, who'd given up on the shepherd and took his hands off the wheel while they stood still.

He pulled off the thin leather gloves he kept in the car, ran his bare hands through his hair and beard stubble.

"Joaquín. You liked the boy, right Johnny?"

Hoffmann followed those irritated hands as they made their way through long tresses, readjusting his beautiful purple hair tie with its elaborate silver threads. He had reacted. With anger, anxiety. That was good. El Mestizo had to feel the danger they were in, feel rather than intellectualize—that was how he handled all his emotions in order to avoid them. If he could feel the danger he and his family were in, he would act more quickly when attacked than if he continued to reason, to think this away.

The old man with the crooked back and shuffling feet had shooed his last sheep across the road, and El Mestizo grabbed the wheel again, put it in gear, and hit the gas.

"Yep. We need to be cautious. But, Peter, this changes nothing. We're always cautious. We're always in danger, somebody always wants a piece of us. But they made a mistake. They came here—to my jungle! My friends died because they weren't ready, but I'm ready! Nobody's sneaking up on me here! They can't affect our daily work, Peter. We have to be careful—but that damn well doesn't mean we have to hide."

Cartago. A city Hoffmann liked, lying on the road between Cali and Medellín. He sometimes came here on his days off with Zofia and the boys, shopping among the throng in the square, eating at a simple restaurant, stopping by the whitewashed cathedral with Hugo in one hand and Rasmus in the other, climbing the stairs that never seemed to end, standing in the tower together pretending to see across the Atlantic Ocean all the way to Sweden, all the way home.

Libardo Toyas lived in a hacienda east of the city. One of the very wealthy drug barons who sent large shipments to the United States. El Diablo, that's what he was called. But this visit to his estate was not about sales, or smuggling routes, or who needed to be bribed or why. This time the rich man had refused to pay, a one-ton shipment of cocaine and a debt that was growing with interest, and El Mestizo stressed as they slowed down and rolled up to the hacienda's wall that guerrilla leadership had been very clear about this mission—Toyas was only going to get one more warning, and it was their job to impress that upon him.

The iron gate had tightly placed bars with arrow-shaped tips stretching toward the sky, and the guard who stuck his head out of the guard station was wearing a cap and uniform in red. A single glance at El Mestizo, and he nodded in recognition, the gates unfolded backward, and they continued their journey into a courtyard that seemed to swallow the whole world. A work of art, that's what it was, this hacienda. White columns interspersed with shooting fountains, golden swimming pools sparkling next to snorting horses, neat rows of palm trees and fiery red flowers everywhere, on the marble floors, in clay pots, framing each new section. A fan-shaped stone staircase led to the main building, and more columns painted in a shiny black stood together with the railing and its round ivory knobs.

Libardo Toyas opened the door himself before they even got there. Horde of bodyguards absent, as usual, he was unlike so many of his colleagues and liked to show how confident he was of his own invulnerability. He was turning the tables for a negotiation—El Mestizo was an underling, an upstart, someone who did not have the cojones to touch one of the real drug barons. Piet Hoffmann said hello to the man, who looked more like the hero of an old Western every time he saw him—straight, dark hair, furrowed cheeks, the slightly curved nose, starkly white teeth, wrinkles at his eyes, even his suede jacket was adorned with a fringe of long, dangling pieces of fabric, as if they'd been cut up. Manolito. *High Chaparral*. That was the show.

"I told you last time. I don't have the money."

"One ton. A thousand kilos. That's what you owe."

"I don't have the fucking money because my wealth was confiscated when the boat docked in Miami. They were waiting for it. Headed straight for the tube. Somebody squealed. And so, my friend, I'm not paying."

Piet Hoffmann already knew from their last visit, Toyas's first warning, how this worked. That he—the man who would assist El Mestizo during this collection—was the one responsible for the confiscation three weeks ago of the container they were there to collect on. Now the same memories were flickering around them on the porch. While the dockworkers and harbor police had looked the other way, counting their bribes, Hoffmann had fastened a rope from a tube of a ton of plastic-wrapped cocaine to the bottom of the vessel, which was docked in Puerto de La Guairas. An hour later, it would weigh anchor and take a few days to cross the Caribbean, continuing up the Gulf of Mexico and the round tip of Florida, and then dock in Miami.

That was how smuggling operations worked—the seller was responsible for the first half of the trip to the port or airport or submarine. And the buyer's responsibility was the second half, beyond the border. This cargo had been protected by Hoffmann and his group of ten people all through Colombia and Venezuela. But twelve hours after the tube had been fastened to the ship, their mission complete, he, the informant, traveled alone to Bogotá, met with Lucia at number three, and provided her with all the details: the ship's name, its route, and how and where the container was kept. The DEA had plenty of time to prepare to crack down the moment the loading ramp was lowered.

"Toyas, you have plenty of fucking money. Many times that amount."

"Yes. But I don't have *that* money." The wealthy, arrogant man stood there smirking, convinced of his own importance and power. "I'm not paying for something just because you can't get a handle on a snitch."

"One ton. Today, in Colombia, that price is three thousand US dollars per kilo. Right? But you bought a lot. You always buy a lot. So you got a good price from us. Twenty-five hundred a kilo for the first five hundred, twenty-three hundred a kilo for the rest. So cut this shit out! We delivered. What happens after we deliver is not our problem—that's your problem. Your risk. And that was your last warning." El Mestizo swept his striped blazer sleeve toward Toyas, his home, the large courtyard inside, and whatever stood outside the walls. "You've been in business a long time. You've got your hacienda, your herd of horses that cost seventy, eighty thousand dollars apiece, you have your garages full of Ferraris and Rolls-Royces and . . . yes, a ton, that's a helluva lot of money—but you've got money!"

"It doesn't matter how much money I have, because you're not getting a single dollar. I don't owe you anything, because it's your fault the shipment got fucked up."

"Listen, Toyas, you can send your shit to the US or Chile or Argentina or wherever the fuck you want, that's your problem. You can send it to Spain. Or Gibraltar. I don't give a shit, you were given a price, you accepted it, you received your product here in Colombia. If you put it up your mother's cunt or your own ass, that's your problem, not mine."

"What exactly is it you don't understand? I'm not paying for something that's your responsibility—making sure there are no snitches among the producers, sellers, buyers, suppliers. This conversation is over." Toyas turned around and took the first steps back into his mansion. But El Mestizo grabbed his shoulder, his face red.

"You're fucking sick, man, you're a stupid bastard and you have only yourself to blame." And then—he started giggling. "This was going to be your last warning. But I changed my mind. There are no more warnings. I'm not coming back here in a week. I want the money now. Nothing else. I want it on that table. Otherwise, Toyas, you know what happens. I'll start with your youngest, and I'll work my way up. I never eat from the top down, I eat from the bottom up, until I get paid. The little girl. The other girl. The wife, mother, brother, cousin, friends, until you give me my fucking money."

Toyas tore loose from El Mestizo's hand and took a long stride forward.

"I've been doing business with the guerrillas for seven years. Never missed a payment. Johnny Sánchez, you stupid little mestizo half-breed, you stand here on my property, my veranda, with your European escort girl, and you threaten to kill *my children*? When you're the one with a traitor you can't control. A traitor who cost me my whole shipment! One thing I want to make very fucking clear to you—next time they send someone to me I want to make sure I'm talking to the brain and not the asshole."

El Mestizo's cheeks turned red now, and he giggled more loudly, more shrilly, an unpleasant sound. "Your daughter first. What's her name? Mirja? Is that right? Pretty name."

El Mestizo shoved Toyas forcefully against the doorframe and forced his way into a hall that was as big as a ballroom—long, wide, high ceilings. Toyas had no time to react. Not before El Mestizo started shouting, *Mirja*, and moved even farther into the heart of the hacienda, *little Mirja*. Toyas started running and screaming too, but with a completely different pitch and fury, *what the hell are you doing!* He understood now. Piet Hoffmann could see and hear it. *You leave my daughter alone!* And Piet had no choice but to follow along, do his job, protect El Mestizo. *Come here, little Mirja*. El Mestizo continued to shout with a terrifying voice, which sounded calm but had the exact opposite effect, whipping up dread. At first Toyas ran straight toward it, but then turned suddenly, headed into the kitchen to a large island, where he pulled a revolver from a drawer. *Mirja*. He cocked it and ran back toward that monstrous voice, *come here, little Mirja*, while Hoffmann drew his own weapon from his shoulder holster. *Drop your gun!* Aimed. *Drop your gun, now!* Shot. Through Toyas's arm and shoulder. And hurried over to the whimpering, kneeling drug baron. *You better lie still and keep your fucking mouth shut from now on!* And he shut it, his fucking mouth.

El Mestizo's last *Mirja*, and Toyas's last *leave her fucking alone*, and the echoing shot—everything died away. Piet Hoffmann caught sight of El Mestizo's back in the distance. Not once did he turn around after entering this unfamiliar, guarded home, so convinced was he that Hoffmann was protecting him.

Complete silence. Until a little girl came running, as scared as she was breathless.

"Daddy!" She came closer, her clear, fragile voice a few steps in front of her as she ran through one of the hacienda's many living rooms. "Daddy, Daddy . . . I heard loud noises, and I . . ."

Then she stopped. Her dark hair was held up in a ponytail, white sandals, green floral dress. And she tried to make sense of what she saw. At first there seemed to be a strange man squatting down, a wide and powerful man smiling at her. And behind that strange man, right at the kitchen door, her father was on his knees, and another strange man was aiming a real gun at him.

"Tiny, little Mirja . . . so that's what you look like?"

"My daddy!" She looked at the burly man saying her name in that artificial voice, stretching out both his arms so that she couldn't pass by. She sought a way around the giant squid arms and found a hole near the wall, but he was quicker, and there were arms in the way there, too, folded down like barriers at a railroad crossing.

"Hello, little Mirja . . . you can call me Uncle Johnny. Why don't you come over here? I won't bite." He folded up his arms and pointed at her. "We're gonna play a game, you and me."

"That's my daddy! I want my daddy!"

He'd never seen El Mestizo act like this. His way of moving, his voice, seemed to belong to another person. And he brought down his arms without warning again, snatched hold of the girl, lifted her up, and carried her. And held her close even when he put her down in front of the now hysterical Toyas, like a beautiful statue that he was trying to find the best place for.

"You fucker, you fucking pig, let go of my daughter!"

"Toyas, this isn't your last warning—it's your only warning. The money—*now*." And he pulled his revolver out of his holster, a .357 magnum, his favorite, and pressed it to the girl's forehead. "Now Mirja, we're gonna play a little game. You and me. You're gonna close your eyes. We're gonna have a little fun with your dad."

"I don't want to!"

"Just some fun. If you close your eyes."

"I want my daddy!"

El Mestizo was holding the child, who tried to break free, tearing at his arms with her nails.

"This time, Toyas, I'll shoot her right away. Now. And if you don't pay after that—I'll take your second youngest."

It didn't make sense. There was always a final warning. But El Mestizo's gaze, when Piet tried to meet it, slipped away.

"Johnny, what are you doing?"

El Mestizo didn't look at Hoffmann. He looked at Toyas. And at the girl.

"Dammit, Johnny!" Hoffmann was shouting now. "We agreed—no kids!"

"I do *my* job. You do *yours*." And then everything happened very fast.

El Mestizo shoved the girl a little more, she had to stand right in front of Toyas. He cocked the hammer of his gun. They all heard the double click, the cylinder rotating one notch to the right. A new location for the mouth of his gun, he moved it from her forehead to the top of her head, the pressure now came from above and the barrel sank into her hair.

The trigger back into firing position.

Toyas during this whole production continued screaming uncontrollably, words of fear and helplessness, and though unintelligible they said everything about a parent's despair.

"Toyas, fucking hell, you bawl a lot. Mirja, right?" He kicked at Toyas's shoulder to make sure he was watching. "She *had* a beautiful name."

The trigger, and now, all the way. The hammer hit the firing pin's back side.

But there was no bang of a bullet firing.

"Oh fuck . . . I must have forgotten to load my gun."

El Mestizo lowered his gun until it was caressing the girl's right cheek, then spun out the whole cylinder, pressed the ejector, and six cartridges fell to the floor. Hoffmann saw it, Toyas saw it. Five live shots. And one empty case. *That* was what stood in the firing position when he took aim. A previously fired and now harmless shot.

"The money. In one week. Otherwise I'll come back here. And I'll make sure my gun is loaded."

He released the girl and she ran over to her father, lay down beside him.

"Listen little Mirja. You know what?" El Mestizo switched to that voice again. "Next time I come back to you, if your daddy doesn't pay me, this revolver will be fully loaded . . . and then you won't exist anymore. Weird, huh?"

He caressed her cheeks with both hands and headed back to the hallway and entrance. Hoffmann stood there, looking at a girl, who was slightly younger than his two boys. Who lay next to her father, curled up in a ball.

THE THIN LEATHER gloves held on to the steering wheel lightly. He was driving too fast down highway 25, but they were late, and El Mestizo hadn't let up on the gas since their first stop just after La Estrella for a piss break behind the sun-bleached cactus and some tired mimosa bushes.

They'd traveled in silence. That wasn't unusual. But it *felt* unusual. It was the kind of silence that meant you didn't know what might happen.

"What the hell were you up to back there?"

The sort of silence that threatened to end everything for an informant whose cover couldn't be blown.

"Excuse me?"

The kind of silence he should just leave alone.

"We don't kill little children."

"I didn't kill her, Peter. I threatened to."

"And we don't threaten to. Not that way. It's not kids we're supposed to scare."

He'd never done this before. Openly questioned El Mestizo's methods. He'd confronted him before, but only when he had no choice, when confrontation was necessary for survival. He had never questioned his methods because it wasn't his job to question them.

"Sorry, Peter, that's the way we do it here. We use children when we do business. You still have a lot to learn."

You should record and expose, but not be exposed. Never, ever shift the focus to yourself, then he might see you, and if he sees you, really sees you, you might die.

"So explain to me, Johnny, again . . . what the hell was all that?"

The leather gloves tightened around the steering wheel, as El Mestizo slowed, stopped in the middle of the road, blocking the lane completely. The car behind them, a minivan, slowed abruptly, and the car behind that one, and a truck realized too late that the traffic had stopped and slid to the side of the road, half of its heavy metal frame ended up in the sparsely vegetated landscape. When he turned to Hoffmann, he seemed unconcerned about the cars piling up and honking behind them.

"You didn't do your job back there. You even defied me in front of a client. I let that pass! Your questions—I've answered them. But you keep on asking! Normally, this would be when I would kill you. But you've saved my life, Peter, several times."

He shifted gears from first to second and straight to fourth, as fast as before.

"That's the only reason I'm letting you live."

Hoffmann wasn't listening. He was thinking of a father. In an almost empty hall in his own brothel, lifting up his own five-year-old daughter just as he'd lifted up Toyas's daughter, caressing his daughter's cheeks just as he'd caressed Mirja's.

"What about Alejandrina?"

"What about her?"

"She's lovely."

El Mestizo stared straight ahead, but it was clear he was smiling. "She is."

"You've done a good job with her. The kind of daughter I'd be proud to have, if I didn't have my boys."

"Everything." The smile was still there. "She's everything."

Alcalá, a small town with a busy entrance (or was it an exit?), and then just open road again. Hoffmann tried to collect his thoughts, or was it El Mestizo's thoughts he was after, this ingrained behavior that snapped out sometimes and scared him more than the threat of violence and death. Behavior he didn't want to be part of, imitate, copy, the behavior of those without emotions—the kind of person he was not yet and now risked his life not to be.

"Mirja. She's everything, too. For Toyas."

El Mestizo lowered his voice, and neck, like always.

"I know what you're trying to do."

"He holds her, plays with her."

Jerky steering and the gear lever whined as El Mestizo drove past the gray wall that would lead them to Montenegro, a small tired town it was impossible to avoid.

"I'd strongly encourage you to stop talking."

"A daughter. Just like your daughter."

"That's enough, goddammit!" El Mestizo slammed on the brakes. Again. On a narrow street with a bombed-out droguería on one side and an empty heladería on the other. And pulled out his gun. Didn't turn off the safety, didn't aim. Just held it.

"Fuck. Fuck! I explained it to you. Didn't I? You saved my life. And that's why you're alive now!" He fingered the gun, put it in his lap, started the car again. "But we're even now. You've wasted your debt."

He increased his speed, a short interruption surrounded by the town and people and houses reverted back to endless countryside.

"And you won't be able to call it in the next time you need it."

ANOTHER LONG HOUR, silence inside the car and the countryside outside, if one of them had rolled down their window and let the wind in emptiness would have been traded for emptiness. It was then that El Mestizo for the fourth time—after another piss break and two stops to block traffic out of anger—slowed down and changed direction. Route 40 led to the back roads south of Ibagué, and to a helicopter hidden in a clearing among sprawling mahogany trees. Already staffed with a pilot who was ready to go. Traveling by air saved time in a country of long, monotonous distances—but it was a solution they rarely utilized. Neither the guerrillas nor El Mestizo, long distances by small aircraft didn't meet their security requirements—too easily tracked and detected by radar, or satellites, or even visually from the ground stations. A helicopter was a last resort. Like now. When they needed to be at their next assignment, a man in a cage deep in the jungle, in four hours and a car trip there would take them three times that long.

So now they hovered high above winding roads and small villages. And the occasional rich finca with lush, extensive orchards.

"Do you see that? And that? Really expensive properties that belong to the super wealthy." El Mestizo pointed through the glass wall toward the landscape unfurling far below. He looked happy, like this morning when he'd been swimming with his daughter. There were many versions of the man sitting on the seat next to Hoffmann—the giggling El Mestizo who pushed his gun into a little girl's hair, Johnny who trusted and talked to you, the father who swam with his socks on because his beloved daughter expected him to, the guerrilla who stopped in the middle of the road and threatened the life of his own bodyguard. Now he was cheerful, and Hoffmann didn't yet understand why. But he followed El Mestizo's arm and stated that he was right, the estates seemed to be amazing, endless properties.

"More drug barons. Like Toyas?"

"Toyas? Toyas, Peter?" El Mestizo tapped first on the pilot's seat, then on his back. "Turn off the intercom."

He waited while the pilot turned a small wheel in the middle of the dashboard.

"Like Toyas? Are you serious? Peter—I have as much property as that bastard. Even more! Twice as much! Two haciendas! Not bad for a half-breed, right?"

"And two wives."

He was just as excited, almost looked sneaky, it wasn't often he beamed like this.

"That's right—two wives! That coward Toyas, who can't protect his own children, doesn't have that. Fuck, they're probably not even his! A thousand dollars says that impotent bastard adopted them with his boyfriend."

Beautiful and endless estates were replaced by more jungle, the undulating forest and the Amazon tributaries branching into hundreds of pumping arteries.

"Two haciendas, Peter. And I have more cars than Toyas, more animals, more children. More in my bank accounts, both in Colombia and in Panama." He beamed happily, some kind of euphoria that had overflowed into talkativeness. El Mestizo had never spoken so openly before. A happiness that almost felt embarrassing, repulsive, but Hoffmann couldn't understand why.

"Soon, Peter. That cage we talked about? We're gonna help the man sitting in it talk. The one who refuses to do what they say. The same man who's responsible for that *kill list*, Peter—for your name and mine being on it. Responsible! That is exactly what he is! Joaquín—this is for you! And it'll be his fault if we lose more! As far as I like, Peter! As long as I don't kill him."

The euphoria felt embarrassing, repulsive. Hoffmann understood now. This was no ordinary torture session.

Hundreds of kilometers of dense jungle and no villages, no people. The distances were enormous. The kidnappers had situated Crouse's cage with care. Hoffmann closed his eyes, hovered. What if someone had told him about all this when he was growing up in a middle-class home in a suburb south of Stockholm? "Piet, listen now—one day you'll live in a country called Colombia, in South America—one day you'll be protecting contraband and the next a cocaine kitchen and the next flying over a jungle to torture some powerful American politician. And you'll do it because you have to, because you're on the run from a long prison sentence, and because you've been condemned to death by the Polish mob you infiltrated on behalf of the Swedish police, until those very same police abandoned you." If someone had told him that it would have made a good but hardly believable tale. You have to believe in a lie for it to become true.

The helicopter landed in tall grass at the edge of a tributary of the Río Vaupés. Wide, grand, brown and blue-green water that felt almost warm when you dipped your hand into it.

The boat pilot introduced himself as Cristobal, head of PRC-guerrilla waterborne transport in the department of Guaviare, and took them to a tree lying a bit out into the river. A boat was moored to it, a rope leading from the stern to its curved trunk and another rope from the bow leading to another fallen tree sticking up from the river bank, sprawling and tormented by sun and water. The boat had space for five fully equipped soldiers, a high-speed one-hundred-horsepower engine, and a flat bottom to land on rocky beaches without getting stuck. Hoffmann and El Mestizo climbed in, and Cristobal turned the ignition key, untied the ropes, and backed out into the stream, gliding westward, downstream. Hoffmann watched him. He was so proud, straight-backed as he maneuvered through the primeval forest in a camouflage uniform, a loaded Kalashnikov hanging off his back. Maybe a little older than the usual soldier. Hoffmann guessed they were around the same age, but it was difficult to tell, guerrilla life aged you prematurely. And it was fascinating to watch him pilot through the strong current—even though he held course, he reversed gears and controlled the boat's speed by sometimes increasing, sometimes cutting the gas completely in those places where whirlpools danced eagerly.

Mile after mile on the river, through vegetation and the animal chorus of sounds claiming this as their place, we live here, we rule, except for the blue sky and the ruthless sun. One hour of a winding, anxious journey until Hoffmann recognized the drone of the boat's engine as the pilot veered off toward the shore, shouting *stay in the boat* and waiting two seconds until giving it full throttle. They headed straight for the shore with the propeller halfway up from the water, gliding on top of what seemed neither river nor beach, a no man's land of thick reeds and leaves and the wayward branches of mangroves. All the way to the riverbed, and they felt the boat scrape the bottom—mud, rocks, the occasional log. They jumped out onto solid ground between four potrillos, canoes carved directly from balsa trees.

Cristobal went first, slashing with his machete at the branches that grasped them as they passed by. Foul-smelling. Swampy. Hot. Insects. Hellish humidity. And after a dawn rain the narrow path had turned to sticky mud. A few hundred meters and they arrived at the base camp. Always in similar places, extremely inaccessible and feared by both the Colombian regular army and the police, many of their own would die in any attack while the guerrillas could slip out and survive—this was their backyard.

On the edge of the camp they passed by a truck that had held twenty young guerrilla fighters, who were now sitting on the ground and leaning against their backpacks, waiting for something.

The boat pilot nodded toward the open space in front of them, the huts and tents framed a simple deck of planks, like a square in a city. "You can watch TV over there. Sometimes the reception's not bad." A small television set was tied to a branch, like in the camp at the cocaine kitchen.

Farther away, behind the huts, a new group of men appeared, similar to the soldiers sitting on the ground waiting for something. "Prisoners. The normal kind." Hoffmann counted twelve. Dirty and torn clothing, long hair and beards, chains around their necks. "They're not worth much. But they're good to have around for prisoner exchanges. Those ones are being moved to another camp."

That was why the soldiers had been transported here and now chained the prisoners neck to neck, linking them together, a train of hostages that would carry their little packs through the jungle—a straw mattress and whatever few personal belongings they'd had with them at their kidnapping several years earlier, and which despite daily visitations had yet to be confiscated.

Cristobal gestured with his machete toward the dense shrubbery—time to move on. Hoffmann had, during that brief stop, committed a sketch of the base camp to memory, its location and housing, and the lower hollow that sloped steeply down on the camp's right edge. The boat pilot's regular blows with his blade led them to a clearing and for a moment they escaped the canopy and were drowned in blue sky and followed the birds. Egrets, Hoffmann was sure of it. He counted every step. Two hundred, five hundred, twelve hundred equally long steps, ever darker, ever wetter. And then they were there. Campo Importante. A new detention center for only four prisoners, political hostages whose value was quite different from the thousands of Colombian soldiers and police officers scattered throughout the other jungle camps. The human resources for specific transactions. And if that kind of exchange were impossible, the guerrillas kept them, kept them for months or years, until it *became* possible. The most precious jewels locked in a safe, taken out occasionally to see how they shone, enjoying that possession, stashed until they were carried out or sold.

"I'm leaving you here." Cristobal was swallowed up by vegetation as suddenly as a short man appeared from it, a red bandanna wrapped twice around his head and jingling spurs on his muddy boots. Hoffmann wondered if he always wore them, or if it was in their honor.

"Welcome." His hand was limp, the man content to just offer it. "My name is Maximiliano Cubero—head of the PRC's special front. The others call me Commandant, but it would do me great honor if you were to address me by my first name." A handshake that didn't match the impression he intended to make.

"This is my camp. The soldiers you see have been selected by me, all very well trained and combat ready. PRC elite. And that is your assignment." He turned and pointed to a cage set up in the far corner of the camp.

The cage. So close. Hoffmann excused himself, walked through the camp while El Mestizo stayed with the commandant, passed by a row of young soldiers, many of them women recruited from Colombia's poorest neighborhoods, who chose this rather than a brothel. And he did exactly as he had at base camp, made a map in his head where no one could reach it, spacing out huts with sparse planks on the floor and walls of palm leaves and the doors of empty rice sacks. Until he was there. Worn, dirty, eyes that were exhausted—but it was still possible to recognize Speaker Crouse from the pictures in *El Espectador*. A powerful chain around his neck, connected to his wrists and ankles, and they tightened as he sat down directly on the floor and ate what was in his dish, the kind of bread that was just flour and water fried in oil.

It was only when Hoffmann got really close that he saw the rest. How the skin on his face and arms and hands was covered with uneven swellings, wide bruises, blotchy patches. They'd given him quite a beating. And then—the speaker's right foot. They'd pulled out all the toenails, left behind fleshy and pus-filled sores. That was why he was sitting on the floor. They'd already started, and failed at, the work that El Mestizo had been hastily summoned here to finish. The work he'd been so pleased about in the car and helicopter.

Hoffmann didn't yet know the real purpose of torture, what they wanted the speaker to say or do—what he was supposed to say or do by the time El Mestizo was finished with him. Just a few meters from a cage with bars of bamboo. And now the speaker heard him, looked up from his bowl, and his eyes—this man was tormented, but not broken.

Timothy D. Crouse dropped the bowl. Someone was standing near the cage. Someone new, not the soldier who guarded him nor the commandant who controlled him, this one didn't wear a uniform and his eyes weren't filled with contempt. Crouse tried to see who it was, but the pounding, irregular pulse from his right foot cut through his body like knives before and after each breath. Pointy, shiny knives that stabbed with rending blows, pouring down his neck and back and hips. That was where they started, the upper part of his body, hitting him with fists and canes.

The pain cut through his joints and muscles and nerves, but he withstood it. Again and again. But not the consequence of it—gradually losing the ability to think clearly, fighting against the daze, no longer feeling sharp or analytical. Which is who he was. That's why he couldn't place the man outside the cage. Even though it was someone he recognized. Someone he'd seen before. He was sure of it. That way of moving, not quite a young man but still physically fit. That tattoo on his head, a lizard, or maybe a snake, a green tail disappearing down his neck.

Crouse stretched out his right leg, angled it up, the pain didn't let go, but it lessened for a moment. And he made another attempt, looked at his visitor again, focused, trying to force himself to think. And then it occurred to him.

It's you. From the surveillance images on the large screen at the NGA. Your way of moving, the top of your head—what you can see from above on images that aren't captured with perfect clarity, the sum of thousands of hours of surveillance from spy satellites. The one the operators and investigators failed to identify. You, who work side by side with the violent man we managed to identify as Johnny Sánchez, or El Mestizo. You, who until now had no face. But now you do. I see you. I recognize you.

Piet Hoffmann met the speaker's eyes. At first they'd seemed muddy, unfocused, but now they were completely clear, with a bite and an edge that seemed to cut right through him. And he wanted to say something to them, lean forward against the bars and whisper, *Crouse, you don't know it, but we're on the same side, I was recruited by your countrymen, your employees, for your project, to infiltrate the very people who hold you captive, hurt you.* But he couldn't. The soldier posted as a guard right outside the barred opening was too close. If she were to hear, see, suspect, it would all be over.

Maybe later. If I can get close without them seeing me. Then I'll tell you.

"Speaker Diaper."

Crouse's eyes changed. They looked tormented. But there was something else, something just as strong. Hate.

"You're a very important person to us, Speaker Diaper."

The commandant. And El Mestizo. They'd placed themselves on either side of Hoffmann and were looking into the cage, at the person sitting on the floor with a chain around his neck.

"That's why these nice gentlemen have traveled all this way for you. All the way from the big city. In order to talk to you. Since you don't want to talk to us."

The American didn't withdraw further into the cage, didn't try to escape into one of its corners—away from the man with the rattling spurs. But he didn't reply either, he sat still and stared at them even though he knew what was coming, why they were here.

"You see? He's not much for conversation."

Then he seemed to change his mind, managed with great pain to get up on his hands and knees, his face turning red, his jaws cramping, his eyes tearing up. He pushed himself up from the floorboards, yanked his upper body up and grabbed onto two of the bars, pulling himself the rest of the way.

He stood a few meters away, carefully balancing his weight on both feet, even the one without toenails. And then he turned around, meeting his visitors with his back straight.

The guards—who'd mentioned several times how honored they were to be chosen for what was indisputably the most important task a PRC guerrilla could be chosen for, protecting this asset at any cost, seeing to it that it remained in the possession of the PRC—had all withdrawn. Not because they had been ordered to do so, but gradually. Every step El Mestizo had taken during the torture of Speaker Crouse *they* had taken one step back. And now, when they couldn't get any farther away, they turned their faces, one of them even covered his ears.

Someone had beaten him up with their fists the day before, *to no avail*, a soldier in his twenties had proudly demonstrated his skills at El Mestizo's request, intense shadowboxing and a few high kicks against a tree that was supposed to represent Crouse's chest. Someone had whipped him this morning, *to no avail*, and El Mestizo had demanded to know where and how—a professional has to prepare in order to continue working from the same level. The canes had been bloody and coarse at one end and the American's back, buttocks, and thighs had a pronounced pattern of red, swollen lines. The young guard that had been assigned the task—her hair in two braids and pale-red lipstick on her smile, she'd even curtsied to them—had tried to write out PRC with violent lashes in angular letters that reminded Hoffmann of the amateur graffiti of the Stockholm suburbs, young boys with spray cans repeating the name of their gang on wall after wall. Then someone, *to no avail*, pulled out the toenails from his right foot with a pair of pincers; the commandant had shown them how at El Mestizo's request and admitted that he himself—assisted by his second in command who held down Crouse's legs—had been the one to do it. He'd clenched his hands and moved them back and forth between himself and Hoffmann to demonstrate how, even let out a short howl to mimic the prisoner's, and the guerrilla soldiers in the camp had looked at one another and laughed once they were completely confident that the others would too, and that laughter was what the commandant expected.

Now they would get their results.

Piet Hoffmann walked with El Mestizo to the cage but stopped short—only the torturer and the doctor would go through the cage door. And he did as he used to, tried to find an approach, forced himself to think about the very first time, back when all of this was just tall tales. About isolated cases of torture in the city. And about how he—although it hadn't been his business back then either—had insisted on making it his own, wanted to demonstrate, to prove that he could be relied upon. It had been during his first months of service, when he was just another one of El Mestizo's men. He'd tired of fighting with their *you're a European, you are nothing.* It didn't help to tell them that he'd spent time behind bars, already shot two people besides the ones he'd shot in Colombia. Death is easy, they'd blustered, what's hard is killing slowly.

Hoffmann had since learned El Mestizo's methodology. After beatings with fists and canes and pulled-out toenails came electricity. That's why two of the young soldiers were now heaving a frame made from four welded-together iron bars into the cage. Two square meters, it just barely made it inside lying on its long side, almost hit the ceiling as they angled it. They removed two floorboards and exposed the soil below—to improve conductivity—and from it a line of four iron bars, fifteen centimeters long, all pointed upward. They fit perfectly in the four holes drilled in the bottom of the iron frame. The contraption was slipped onto the bars and held steady in the middle of the cage.

At El Mestizo's request, the young female guard cut the string that held Crouse's dress pants up, pulled them and his underwear toward his ankles. The two soldiers, after mounting the iron frame, now pushed the prisoner toward it, unlocked the chains around his wrists, and attached his arms to the frame instead. His hands were placed over his head and ten meters of copper wire was wound several times around his right wrist and the iron bar, then across the frame to his left wrist and another iron bar, diagonally down to where it was wound several times around his right ankle, and then several more times around the left ankle.

Always electricity. And always starting with the *entire* body. Hoffmann pretended to watch, because that's what he was supposed to do. But he looked to the right of it, if he concentrated his gaze there, the rest went out of focus, became the blurry movements of blurry people.

He'd continued to participate in torture in the city, even volunteered to build credibility. Usually that meant shooting the indebted person's body in various places. Sometimes it meant cutting. But he'd never really felt the screams in his gut and his chest, never been pushed that far. They usually went out to the Río Cali, and it felt more like going to the dump to drop off trash. Shoot a bit, cut a bit, maybe do something to one of their eyes. They'd screamed, but never like in the jungle. Never like Crouse.

From the bag that El Mestizo had ordered this morning, which had now been carried into the cramped cage, he pulled out two cables, like jumper cables for a car, but thicker. The red cable he connected with the clip to the iron frame, plus, and the black one, minus, around the big toe of the speaker's battered, nail-less foot. Then he stretched out both the red and the black until they reached the gas generator the two soldiers brought in. He yanked the pull cord a few times and the generator started chugging, a noise similar to a lawnmower or an old boat engine. The other end of the red cable was connected to the positive pole of the generator and the other end of the black cable to the ground terminal, and he held them like that for exactly two seconds. The iron frame flashed and sizzled and electricity arced out from Crouse's body. His head fell against his chest and his cries transformed to gasps while his muscles cramped.

This is when the doctor interrupted the torture—just like El Mestizo had instructed him to. This one was unusually young, even for a PRC doctor, recruited at the end of his second semester at medical school—they were rarely more educated than that. An instrument. That's what he was. Whose purpose was to patch up and whisper, *Why are you silent, my friend, that madman is crazy and will continue torturing—speak now in front of the camera as they ask you to.* His job was to keep the hostage alive, to be tender, to play the good cop, *But you, why should you have to go through this, cooperate now, he'll never give up.*

The young man held up a stethoscope that coiled out from his hand and to Crouse's chest, listened to his lungs and heart. "Did you let the current run through his whole body?" And subsequently examined one foot, smoke rose from where the clamp had closed its jaws around the skin. "Which way?"

"Yes, from his toes and up through his arms."

The young doctor wasn't a particularly good actor, overreacting as he breathed in the smell of burning flesh and delivering his rehearsed lines to El Mestizo as if reading them from cue cards. "His heartbeat is a bit irregular."

"So?"

"You can keep going if you turn down the amps a bit. That is, if you don't want his heart to stop; if you want to keep him alive."

El Mestizo turned toward Crouse, with exaggerated, theatrical gestures. "You heard him, Mr. Speaker? In that case, we should probably move the cables. You won't be producing much sperm after this, but you'll live a bit longer."

He loosened one end of the red cable, the one attached to the iron frame, and held it out.

"Mr. Speaker? Maybe you'd like to talk a little?"

Crouse's motionless head still against his chest, loosely hanging, saliva ran from the sides of his mouth.

"Well, then, Mr. Speaker. It's up to you. Keep on making bad decisions."

El Mestizo slowly moved the red cable toward Crouse's body, toward the lower, naked portion. And then, hellish screams exploded from the wooden cage and reverberated through the jungle as the cable touched his testicles for the first time, screams that continued and got louder. No matter how much Hoffmann concentrated on looking to the right, he couldn't help but hear everything.

El Mestizo had wandered around the prison camp for almost ten minutes, seemingly without aim, from caleta to caleta, into them and around them and even up onto the roof of a couple of them. Even went to the large pit, dug when the camp was established to a depth of three meters according to regulation. At first glance it seemed like a grave, but when the stench hit you, it was clearly a toilet. Then on to the kitchen, to the laundry, and to the food storage. Then he returned to the cage, went back in looking happy, like a man returning from a long journey, who's found what he was looking for.

"Mr. Speaker?"

The copper wire around Crouse's wrists and ankles had been cut off and he had been released from the iron frame. But despite kicks and punches from the female guard, he refused to sit on the floor, exhausting whatever limited energy he had hidden deep in his chest as he held tight to the bars and leaned forward against them.

"So, more electricity would kill you. But you're not supposed to die. Until you talk."

El Mestizo held out his hands and showed his findings from his tour of the camp—on one of his palms rested a plastic pipe and on the other some rusty barbed wire.

"After electricity I usually prefer scalding water. Or waterboarding. But for you, I'll make an exception and move on to this."

He moved the plastic pipe and the barbed wire back and forth in front of Crouse's down-turned face, making sure that the prisoner really saw it.

"This method comes from Europe, which is where I first saw it. I found this pipe, a simple fifteen-centimeter PVC pipe, under the refrigerator in the kitchen. When I insert it into your anus and through your rectum, and it's sitting firmly in place, we move on to the barbed wire, an unusual variety I found on the roof of one of the cages. As you can see, Mr. Speaker, no tiny little barbs, but long narrow spikes, slightly bent, which cause a lot more damage."

He dragged the sharp spikes along Crouse's chin and cheek, the blood rushed down his neck onto his shirt collar, which was not particularly white anymore.

"Up to that point, you probably haven't felt much—I will cover the pipe with a thick ointment, like you would for any thermometer or prostate examination. But soon, with the insertion of that barbed wire, it will become uncomfortable."

El Mestizo wiped off the wet, bloody barbed wire spikes on one of Crouse's shirtsleeves.

"I will feed the barbed wire into the pipe, which at this point is in your rectum. That won't feel like much either, the plastic protects you quite nicely. And that's when I will ask you one more time if you'd like to recite the commandant's short script in front of that camera, or if you want me to continue. If you keep making bad decisions and don't say what we want you to say, it will become a bit rough for all of us. Then I will have to start pulling out the pipe, while keeping that barbed wire in place. And all those spikes, they will be laid bare inside your bowels, will perforate your intestinal walls as I pull it out. You will be ruined forever, Mr. Speaker. When we're done, when all this rusty barbed wire is back out, you will have to wear a bag on your stomach for the rest of your life, and you are going to scream and cry every time you empty the contents of your cut-up bowels."

The camera didn't look expensive, but it was the kind that could take both pictures and short video clips. The commandant filmed himself and Speaker Crouse sat on the cage floor while he spoke straight into it; he was completely out of energy and to stand up defiantly was no longer an option. He quietly read the handwritten note that someone had formulated in correct and academic English. Hoffmann wondered who had held the pen—no one in the camp spoke like that, the few that spoke any English at all had heavy accents and limited vocabularies.

Speaker Crouse had resigned, accepted, and given up immediately as the plastic pipe touched his skin. What they had demanded him to say wouldn't put anyone else in danger, it had never been about that—only about not letting those bastards win, or think that they'd won. But as the plastic pipe met his body and it became about him being damaged for life, he had raised his arms yelling "stop," turned around, and pointed at the tripod that carried the camera.

The first time. But it didn't feel like it used to. Usually it was this moment that transformed all the time, all the lies, all the fear to confirmation—the feeling of finally arriving, of having succeeded, perhaps even feeling a little bit pleased with his own cleverness. This time it wasn't like that. After two years, Hoffmann had reached the very core, the apex of the group he'd been paid to infiltrate—but it was too late.

Crouse had just finished recording a video that would be uploaded to the Internet tomorrow in the city, and the commandant was putting away the camera, when she stepped out of the only caleta they didn't have access to. Catalina Herrador Sierra, alias Mona Lisa. The Queen of Hearts. A tall, slender, beautiful woman in her forties. She wore the same uniform as the others, but with insignias Hoffmann had never seen. The third most powerful person in the PRC, elected to the PRC's highest governing body. The woman the media was describing as the ideologue. A meeting with one of the Shadows.

In the past, Hoffmann had only been allowed to follow El Mestizo to a certain point, and then stayed overnight with others who weren't approved to go all the way. The Shadows. That's what they were called, since only a few knew where they were or how to contact them: usually, like now, in some camp somewhere in the jungle.

The last time this happened was when he infiltrated the Polish mafia in Sweden and he'd been unexpectedly summoned to Warsaw. Like now, he'd penetrated deeply into the organization, but had yet to stand face to face with the absolute power. A taxi ride from the airport to Wojtek International's headquarters, to Zbigniew Boruc and Grzegorz Krzynówek, had changed everything and had been the result of many years of planning that first time around. He'd been introduced by his contact, Henryk—another man who trusted him without knowing he was encountering a lie—to the deputy CEO and the Roof, the ones who controlled the company from a black house in the district of Mokotów.

Now El Mestizo was Piet's contact person, the man he'd manipulated to get here, all the way to the Queen of Hearts. Her smile seemed genuine as she met El Mestizo and received the memory card of Crouse's monologue. She hugged him, a tight, heartfelt hug you'd give to someone you trust and who shares your values.

"And here he is . . . El Sueco. We've never met." She held out her hand to Hoffmann. "But war changes things. As do kill lists. And those of us on them have to choose to trust each other fully. Just like Johnny has chosen to trust you and vouch for you, fully."

And when Hoffmann took her firm hand, she took a step forward and hugged him too.

Just like Johnny has chosen to trust you and vouch for you, fully.

Hoffmann held the powerful woman in his arms and thought about how all first times have their own first time. El Mestizo, not yet Johnny, after a few months' acquaintance had decided that his new European employee would become his bodyguard. And Piet Hoffmann had never been so close to someone so dangerous who he also happened to like and who sincerely seemed to like him back. The first of the first times they had arrived at another one of these prison camps in the jungle, and El Mestizo had declared that he wanted them to take a walk, wanted to show him the surroundings. Hoffmann thought that a walk was just that. Until he realized it was the opposite, that he was the one being shown to the surroundings.

The whole camp had to see that the new guy was El Mestizo's friend, receive the message that from now on those who touched El Sueco were touching El Mestizo.

A confidence he would soon destroy. Because that cage right there in front of them, and the broken American politician sitting inside, was his and Zofia's and Rasmus's and Hugo's only way out.

THE JUNGLE AT night was an enchanted world. The sounds, the smells, the immense power of what man couldn't rule over—the animal kingdom. Mosquito nets that had been rolled up like hard little branches were unfurled and tied together with strings to fend off clusters of insects buzzing in the darkness, the birds flapped and screamed against the black sky, and suddenly it was cold, a cold as intense and oppressive as the heat of the day.

Piet Hoffmann, a few hours earlier, found his way to the caleta that was his until dawn, sank into a simple bed, not much more than a straw mattress and a sleeping mat—but didn't fall asleep. He was waiting. For the guards stationed at every corner of the camp to relax to the snoring of the rest, and for El Mestizo, who had repeatedly left his caleta for long talks on his satellite phone, to find peace. It had been impossible to make out what he was talking about, though his voice didn't sound like usual. El Mestizo strove to speak in a controlled, low-key manner no matter how dangerous or urgent a mission or situation was, but now he spoke in a loud, disoriented voice, oscillating between threat and despair.

Hoffmann left his lumpy bed and sat down by the upturned wooden box that served as a makeshift table. Took a pen from his vest pocket, used a piece of toilet paper as a notepad. And he started to write.

Coordinates

The plan. This was how it begins. This was what he had to do first. In a moment or two he could sneak out while the guards were looking the other away, and after El Mestizo had turned off his phone.

Low Earth Orbit

The next step of the plan. To force those bastards to delete a name from their list. To avoid certain death.

Time window

And then the next.

Cesium-137

And the next.

Prism bomb

And next.

Magnets sled

He folded the piece of paper, a square that became an even smaller square until it fit in the bottom of the leather holster of his knife. And went outside. The chill felt like an angry animal wrapped around his body. He moved straight toward the stench of the toilet pit, the first checkpoint, then diagonally to the right between Crouse's cage and the kitchen. The guard was sitting outside the grating with no clue that another human had just passed by his loaded automatic weapon. When he reached the second checkpoint—a nearly thirty-meter-tall sapucaia tree—and the narrow path that Cristobal had cleared with his machete, the darkness became compact. Black turned even more black. But to use a flashlight, or even a match, was unthinkable. Any light would cut like a living being through the dense greenery.

Six hundred and twelve steps. Then the clearing, the open area between the prison camp and the base camp, without any densely woven canopy. He stumbled across thick tree trunks and wandering root systems, felt thorns penetrating the fabric of his pants and stung his hands against a swaying bush, which reminded him of the nettles that grew along ditches in Sweden.

Then he did just as he had at the riverbed near the cocaine kitchen. He took out the GPS receiver from one of the pockets of his bulletproof vest, pushed *mark* and read the decimal degrees—the coordinates of his exact latitude and longitude recorded in code.

68.779812, 22.3529645

The type of information he collected when locating a cocina, a shipment, a warehouse. Then forwarded to his handler at the DEA.

But not this time. This particular row of numbers was for him—it was for opening the door of a cage, for a trade, a life for a life.

THERE'S AN ODD sound when a helicopter takes off from the dry grass of an abandoned meadow and returns to a cloudless sky. Dull, pulsating—a discomfort that takes hold in your chest as the air is cut to pieces by whipping blades. Hoffmann didn't really like helicopters. Illogically assembled metal and plastic that traversed large areas and suddenly came to rest, completely still, hundreds of meters in the air. But here, next to a roaring river in a wayward jungle with no roads, there were no other means of travel. Plus, you never, ever, show weakness. He'd thanked Cristobal the boatman and again hugged the Queen of Hearts, members of a company who wished each other luck, then jumped into flying machines headed in different directions.

El Sueco and El Mestizo landed where they parked the car the day before and were attacked by sultry, trapped air as they simultaneously opened the doors of the car for the next phase of their trip home. They drove several kilometers along dry, dusty gravel, which gradually turned into a thin layer of steaming asphalt, before either of them spoke.

"We're traveling through Medellín, Peter."

The anxiety in El Mestizo's voice, the one Piet Hoffmann never picked up before but could now discern again. *We're traveling through Medellín.* The same anxiety in his voice the night before, when El Mestizo had been convinced he couldn't be heard above the moisture of the Amazon and the anguished screams of prisoners.

"A thousand-kilometer detour, Johnny. Nineteen hours."

"Do you have a problem with that? You got someplace to be?"

Yes—I do have a fucking problem with that. Yes—I need time to go home and make sure my family is all right before I head to a meeting in a café in Bogotá with Erik Wilson, my former handler who set me up with the job of informing on you.

Everything he couldn't say. While El Mestizo clearly showed that he too didn't want to talk about *his* mission. In order not to obstruct—destroy—their relationship, to be able to continue gathering information for another, actual, employer, Hoffmann had long ago decided not to insist on explaining how hard it was to protect a man who wouldn't trust you.

As always, they stopped every couple hundred kilometers, to stretch their legs and change drivers. Or, they usually did. But about halfway there El Mestizo had fallen asleep. Heavily. Snoring loudly, sometimes with his head against Piet's shoulder. And Hoffmann—as he increased the speed to gain some time—realized what he'd already suspected: anxiety, like a faint breeze around each breath, was real. He'd never seen his employer sleep. Johnny Sánchez, over their two and a half years together, met each moment watchful, ready. Spying. At first Hoffmann had tried to rationalize it—El Mestizo was probably just exhausted, a person's screams affected him, too. Maybe he was carrying the horror of that torture around, though he never showed emotion except with his daughter. The sturdy man next to him, who had killed and tortured and injured and coerced so many times before, maybe he was reachable, affected after all? Or . . . maybe it was a lack of oxygen? The air that became more elusive with each kilometer they traveled up toward the city, which was spread out just beneath the sky?

Dusk fell slowly. Few passing vehicles, few villages. When Hoffmann rolled down the side window, silence forced itself in in the same way the heat forced itself out a few hours ago. He turned on the radio. La FM Bogotá 94.9. An angry discussion between two male politicians who refused to listen to each other, while ignoring whatever the female host had to say completely. W Radio 99.9.

More talk of nothing, but calmly, as if the speakers actually cared if what they said became meaningless, if no one listened.

He turned it off. Alone with El Mestizo's regular breaths in compact darkness. Anxiety that could not be rationalized no matter how much Piet tried. The inflection from last night had returned. And now he was asleep beside him. It was connected, he knew it, but didn't know how. Not yet.

Mile after mile. Evening became night. And the passenger woke up outside of Puerto Triunfo, where Route 45 turned into Route 60. With a start. Rubbing his eyes like a child. Asked, almost aggressively. "Where the hell are we?" Used to being on his guard. But suddenly he wasn't.

"We just passed La Esperanza."

The paper cup of coffee stood untouched in the plastic cupholder, and El Mestizo's thick braid rocked as he leaned against the headrest emptying out the now cold liquid, carefully crumpling it. He was trying to make sense of how his constant watchfulness had abandoned him. How he'd temporarily become someone else, someone who depended on someone else. Trapped in a car. And it made him furious, that insistent anger pounding against his temples as it did sometimes. He felt ashamed. For exposing himself.

"Stop."

"Here?"

"Stop, damn it!"

A dark, deserted road. More asphalt, more arid meadows.

"I'll drive from here." El Mestizo threw the car door open and pushed his heavy body out of the seat, long steps around the front of the vehicle and forceful movements as he pointed his finger at Hoffmann's face. "Now!"

A man who stood there challenging without knowing who he was pointing at. He provoked, felt it his right to offend, to marginalize. In another time, Hoffmann would have acted reflexively, responded with violence. Not anymore. Nine years undercover for the Swedish police—half his adult life as a criminal and an outlaw in the inner circles of organized crime—had forced him to develop impulse control, taught him to identify his goal, his purpose, and then make every action justify it.

That's why he didn't grab that finger and break it. He didn't pull his knife and stick it into the space between the third and fourth ribs. He kept his mouth shut. He stood up, nodded to the man he was here to protect and simultaneously betray, and walked obediently in the opposite direction around the car while a warm breeze fanned his sweaty back.

"Seat belt." El Mestizo had turned the ignition key and waited while Hoffmann buckled up and the infernal beeping stopped. His strong hands clutched the steering wheel as he pressed his foot on the gas, driving fast, too fast. He had exposed himself, let someone get close, an individual who could have overpowered him at any time while he slept, handed him over to the police, the military, the paramilitary. Killed him.

El Mestizo accelerated faster, faster. The car swayed turbulently as he rolled down the window and the air that flowed in took his breath. Trusting someone like this wasn't him. To trust was to risk. Risk betrayal.

"In the jungle no one can hear you cry." El Mestizo continued to speak to nobody at all. "My grandfather used to say that. 'In the jungle no one can hear you cry, so act like a man. Grab yourself down there, Johnny. Grab it! You have two balls, right?' It was Grandpa who took me to a brothel when I was ten."

It wasn't much of a conversation. They didn't even look at each other.

"You have kids, Peter."

The car swayed again, even more violently, as Sánchez, without warning and with a movement so imprinted it had become mechanical, pulled the revolver out of his holster.

"Two of them. You're a father. So you understand."

A single hand on the steering wheel as he raised the gun to his own forehead, brought his thumb against the hammer and pulled it back until he heard the click, pressed the metal muzzle on his fragile skin.

"A father, so you understand that before I had children, hell, I didn't even respect my own life! I could sit in a bar and play Russian roulette, put in two bullets and spin it like this and pull the trigger. *Bang! Bang!* And when we offed some motherfucker who hadn't paid, I never thought there was any time for talking, didn't give anybody a damn choice. I was the one who said, *Why don't we shoot his cunt of a wife or fucking kid right here in front of him, just so he understands.* Nowadays, I give them a choice, a warning. But back then, if they didn't . . . *bang bang*, Peter!"

The car sped out of control while those pretend shots rang out. He put the gun back in his holster. And pulled out a wad of green hundred-dollar bills from his jacket pocket, squeezed the sturdy rubber band that held it together.

"Dólares!" He waved it in front of himself, in front of the passenger seat. "It's all about money! Money, my dólares, is power, Peter! Money and violence . . . potencia!"

The road had been climbing steeply, now it sloped gently downward, but still at a high altitude, heavy breathing.

"Buy my gun permit. Bribe my policemen and soldiers and politicians. Know I can shoot a guy and pay four thousand dollars and go free."

The barrel against his forehead. The wad through the air. He didn't say anything else. Not until after passing the Medellín suburbs, approaching the city center, the end of the journey.

"Sure as hell, the goddamn money is everything." But now he spoke neither loudly or aggressively. His voice was soft, whispering, it was hard to hear what he said, even in the seat next to him. "You get it?"

Hoffmann, who wasn't sure he'd heard correctly—that the man who was at war with the whole world, who singlehandedly ensured hundreds of people were executed for some drug territory, had really said that—turned for the first time in a thousand-kilometer drive toward his employer, tried to catch his eyes. But the moment had passed. It had belonged to anxiety and sleep and was unlike anything else El Mestizo had ever said or done.

They drove through a city about twice the size of Stockholm—Hoffmann's home, which he missed every day—through streets that began in poverty and ended in wealth, where slums rubbed shoulders with abundance. A city he preferred to avoid. It had one of the world's highest murder rates. An area where many of his fellow Swedes or Scandinavians had been taken hostage in order to be used as payment when profits from the cocaine weren't enough. Medellín. This is where it all began, where it took shape. The original turf war. To own this place, the right to sell drugs right here.

The cartels in Cali, where he and his family now lived, were in a war with the cartels in Medellín. In the beginning, in that original turf war, it seemed to have been easier then. Clearer. Over time, it got messy. Now fifteen different groups fought one another, just here. The war over drug turf had spread like a disease, an epidemic, which broke out and broke down and found life in every part of the world, in every country and every town, big or small.

They parked by a square and stepped straight into a roiling crowd of people. Commerce in endless uneven rows of stands, then on into a mall, stacks of fresh fruit and vegetables, the smell of food cooking in small restaurants jostling with the man who made shiny jewelry and the woman who braided belts with fabric she dyed overnight. Hoffmann remembered visiting the Kivik Market in southern Sweden as a child, and the Haymarket in central Stockholm as an adult, the feeling of abundance, of the rituals of negotiating a price until both parties were satisfied but neither would admit it. But those markets had been neither so shabby, nor so cramped—every step meant another elbow in his side, another sweaty neck to stare into.

Mainly he was struck by the stench, which got worse the farther in they went. Fish that had probably been out too long. He'd been hungry when they arrived—that was gone now.

A hand pulled on his left arm, and he spun around. An older man wanted to sell him soft leather wallets. When he didn't dismiss him quickly enough, a woman who could have been the old man's wife pulled at his other arm and held out small baskets braided from bark. He tore himself loose and hurried as fast as possible through the narrow aisles, trying to keep watch over his employer. And then it came to an end.

When they had passed the very last stands, cauliflower and cabbage on one side and some kind of meat on the other, they arrived at a deserted asphalt surface. Wooden planks joined together into makeshift tables and chairs arranged on it. And twelve boys sitting there. The youngest were the same age as his own son, nine, maybe ten, and the oldest slightly older, thirteen, not more than fourteen. They had been waiting there without doing anything at all. Until all of them, at the same time, noticed El Mestizo.

The boys stood up, stretched, and started walking toward him. A couple of them, the older ones, carried handguns openly tucked into their pants, and Hoffmann rushed toward them while pulling his own from his shoulder holster. Until El Mestizo turned around and swept his arm in the air, the big braid swung as he motioned to both his bodyguard and the flock of boys to stop. They did. Hoffmann had five steps to go, the boys were in front of their wooden benches.

They stood there, stock-still, trying to look like adults. Skinny, a little pimply, some with a few solitary hairs like wilted stalks on their upper lips. They tried to catch El Mestizo's eyes, hoping to be chosen. Then he nodded, pointed to one who'd been sitting on the middle bench, a short boy with large round earrings of which he seemed proud—he'd carefully arranged his long hair behind his ears so as not to obscure them. He wore a black, slightly too big T-shirt and a worn pair of jeans. He was maybe twelve years old. Prepubescent, a voice with a trace of incipient change. A boy who looked like any other boy. Until he started moving. His way of walking, greeting, throwing his head back as he laughed—he moved and carried himself with a kind of straightforwardness, not cockiness, not calculated for position among his competitors. He didn't need to, his presence was commanding, and unlike any other twelve-year-old. And when he took the bundle El Mestizo held out, the towel with gun and bullets, he grabbed it without fear, but with the respect weapons deserve, the same straightforwardness, like someone who had received bundles like this many times before.

"Calle 3S. Close to Carrera 52. Staircase 17. Fourth floor. Rodriguez on the door."

The twelve-year-old listened attentively, no pen, no notebook, information that should be memorized, never able to be part of the chain of circumstantial evidence of an investigator or family member.

"He's got gray, thinning hair. A pair of glasses with red frames that hang down on a cord across his chest. Seventy-six years old. Luis Rodriguez, that's his name. It's important that you find that out. His name. Before."

No questions. No hesitation. Straight, confident with the bundle that filled his twelve-year-old arms—the mission to kill a father who, when they visited, protected his adult son in a way that moved Hoffmann. The old man had even threatened El Mestizo in his son's absence.

"And two bullets. In the clip."

The boy smiled, white and well-kept teeth. "I know. One in the chest. One in the forehead."

A contagious smile when he looked at Hoffmann for the first time and then back at El Mestizo. A thin arm with a firm hand, they greeted.

"Camilo. Sicario. Twenty-four times. I have worked with your friend for three years now." He held on for a long time and looked Piet in the eyes, straight into him. Eyes Hoffmann had met before. In Swedish prisons when serving time there. Bottomless eyes that have killed, that are prepared to kill again, where nothing lands, just falls into that endlessness.

"No dar papaya. Okay?" El Mestizo coaxed two hundred-dollar bills from the wad with the rubber band.

The little one smiled again, no unnecessary risks, he promised that every time. Then he left, the small, light body passed by fruit stands and restaurants and wandering people, the same direction Hoffmann himself and the man he was supposed to protect had just come from and would soon return to. He watched the twelve-year-old walk straight ahead through the crowd, without stepping aside one single time. But those he passed did.

"You know, Peter, nowadays he's one of the veterans—I can pay him before his mission. He does the job and he returns the gun. Uses two bullets every time. He did so from the first time I hired him."

They left the asphalt and just as the narrow aisle narrowed even further, veering sharply to the right, Hoffmann turned around, looked back at the boys still sitting, waiting, hoping the next mission would be theirs. They climbed in the car, El Mestizo behind the wheel again.

"We have one more errand."

Hoffmann glanced at the clock. He was down to barely twenty-four hours until the meeting with Wilson.

"Since we're in the area. While we wait for the gun. Clínica Medellín Carrera 7—not far from here."

Johnny's voice. The anxiety had returned. And Hoffmann was sure. That's why his employer had chosen this unannounced detour. This was their actual destination. Clínica Medellín. The hospital. Camilo-twenty-four-times was not their main mission—*that* was just something they did *while they were in the area.*

Anxiety. Over what? The El Mestizo Hoffmann had come to know, had worked with, worked for—that El Mestizo threatened, injured, killed without fear or remorse.

"My father was a john."

But this version of him was just Johnny, and when Johnny spoke as he did now, as he had a few hours earlier, then what he said came from deep, deep within.

"And my mother was a prostitute. A couple of times she tried to burn me up. You understand? Make me disappear. She poured a can of gas over me and lit it. Sometimes I thought she might apologize. But no. So others, those who do what we do, they showed me my life. And through all the sickness, in what we did yesterday and what we just did, they took care of me. You get it? It meant everything. So I did whatever the hell they wanted me to. More than they wanted. *Are you going to shoot that guy over there? If so, don't do it, I'll shoot him for you, because you give me hell when I wear the chain too visibly around my neck, or when I put the gun in the wrong place in the belt so I can't get to it quickly enough or when I forget that I'm overacting.* I killed for them. And I would do it again."

A city in motion. And they moved with it. Slamming on the brakes on two occasions to avoid ramming into the vehicle in front of them, honking at drivers who honked back, fending off bicycles and pedestrians who turned in a direction they assumed others wouldn't turn. And then they were there.

A large sign pointed to the hospital entrance and a wide parking lot sat in front of a twenty-story-high, milky-white house. Clean. That's what Hoffmann thought. An unblemished facade, as if someone had just unpacked, assembled, and raised it.

"My brothel in Cali. I grew up there. At my mother's work. I was born there. A Catholic priest birthed me in the bed where my mother worked. Room number eight. The empty room that no one can use. The same bed I was conceived in. But they changed the sheets. Sometimes she says, *I demanded that they change the bedding. So it would be clean when you arrived.*"

There were two parking spaces for the disabled in front of the milky-white house. El Mestizo parked between them, the front wheels in one of them and the back wheels in the other. He didn't usually do things like that. He was brutal, yes, but never obnoxious, never a bully. The power he possessed was so obvious he didn't need to be. Only those who are unsure of their position, their power, need to puff up more than necessary. Hoffmann didn't recognize this man, now compensating for a version of himself that might no longer exist.

There was an electrical cooler in the trunk, which had been plugged in and buzzing since Cali, since yesterday morning. Johnny had picked it up in the port of Buenaventura, onboard the same Mexican ship they bought the smuggled liquor for the brothel from every week. Johnny had made sure to carry it personally off the boat and was equally careful now as he bore it through the bright entrance hall of the Clínica Medellín, past the cafeteria, the information desk, and the small gift shop, all the way to the elevators.

Pushed the button for the eighteenth floor. A rapid ascent, one that grabbed hold in your stomach and for a moment it reminded Hoffmann of the feeling he used to get at the Gröna Lund amusement park in Stockholm, on the beautiful island of Djurgården, where he used to take Rasmus and Hugo, and their laughter would last all the way home.

It smelled intensely of a hospital. A single step out into the long corridor, and then that sickening odor Hoffmann would never get used to. It surrounded him as if to say, here hope lives next door to disease and death. Johnny didn't ask, didn't look around, he seemed to know exactly where they were going and expected his bodyguard to follow him. Past the rooms of tightly packed hospital beds. Tired, resigned eyes met his. Take me away, they said. Hoffmann saw it, felt it. They wanted to go home. They would never get used to this smell either.

He sped up until they were almost walking side by side. Then he caught sight of El Mestizo's face. And the anxiety was no longer there. It was so much more—almost fear in a man who didn't know fear.

The room was waiting for them at the end of the corridor. A single patient and plenty of space. A woman lay in the bed with metal wheels. Her eyes were closed, maybe she was sleeping. On her back, on crumpled sheets. She was sweating, sticky hair against her forehead and her cheeks, blotchy skin. El Mestizo opened the window and a warm breeze drifted in, fanning them. Hoffmann looked at the woman. It was hard to tell her age, but her appearance was rough. He knew that kind of skin, a woman who'd lived a hard life—he guessed she was around sixty. A tube connected her left arm to a plastic bag hanging from a rickety stand of the same metal as the bed, transporting one hesitant drop of liquid at a time. It wasn't nutrition, he could see that, some kind of medicine was being supplied to this dormant body.

The sticky hair was distinctly gray at its roots, below the dye. Her other arm showed clear marks of another kind of needle in its fold, further up there was an irregular pattern of scars from thin razors—she had once cut herself, again and again. The top of her hands looked the same as the bottom of her feet, hole after hole, hundreds of needle pricks that had become bluish pus-filled sores. A note on a string around her ankle and she could just as well have been in a morgue.

El Mestizo moved to her bed, searched for her hand, grabbed it. And she woke up. Or, maybe she had already been awake, and just opened her eyes. "Hi, Mom."

She blinked her eyes against the bright glare of the fluorescent ceiling lights. "Johnny."

A creaky voice, faint, as if it wouldn't hold up much longer. And then it did, held up, became clear as she raised it. "Where is my money?"

El Mestizo held her hand, now with both his hands, and nodded toward the open window, toward the sky. "Only God knows where *your* money is, Mom. But I assume you mean *my* money?"

The fragile patient had been still, like a newborn bird with no stability. Then she changed, sat up with a jerk, the tender arm became powerful as it pointed, as she screamed. "You dirty fucking pathetic half-breed—I want *my* money! Now!"

At the same time the door opened behind Hoffmann and a middle-aged man in a white coat came in. The plastic tag on his chest meant he was a doctor.

"Good morning." He greeted El Mestizo. They had obviously met before. He took the cooler. "We've stopped the acute infection I informed you of last night. It gave in a few hours ago."

The doctor spoke to El Mestizo, looked only at him—no eye contact at all with the woman sitting in the bed, red in her face, breathing rapidly. The white coat obviously didn't like his loud patient, he preferred communicating with the patient's son, the man who paid, and no one else.

"Given her general condition, it remains crucial that you continue to deliver the medicine promptly." The doctor nodded to El Mestizo and Hoffmann and disappeared out into the corridor with the cooler.

"Now you've got what you need—paid for with *my* money." El Mestizo looked at his mother, who was about to start yelling again, but forestalled her. "But you didn't get what you want."

He kissed her cheek and left. Hoffmann followed, one last look at the woman, who was definitely no longer reminiscent of a fragile newborn bird anymore. A white woman. So it must be El Mestizo's father who was indigenous.

Her sharp voice chased them through the closed door, curse words in Spanish, the same South American varieties Hoffmann had heard in the market without knowing what they meant, only the last one, which was his mother's version of go to hell.

They waited for the elevator that would take them eighteen floors down. And everything was so clear now. The anxiety. The heavy sleep. It hadn't been about a man who started to feel something when he injured another man, who couldn't stand the terrible screams of a tortured body in a dark jungle. It was this scream, his mother's contempt. This was it. They rode down. In silence. Until Hoffmann couldn't keep quiet anymore.

"Your mother?"

"Yes."

"She poured gas over you? And lit you? She threw you out when you were eleven and didn't want to have any contact with you?"

"Yes."

"And yet you give her . . . this?"

"It's my mother. She's my blood. Don't you understand things like that where you're from, Peter?"

The echoing entrance hall—wheelchairs along the walls and patients in white hospital gowns on their way for some fresh air or a visit to the café tables. They had started walking toward the exit when El Mestizo suddenly stopped.

"She lives in a little house that I bought for her. I come over regularly with the cooler, antiretroviral drugs for HIV that you can't get here. And I give her food. Not money to buy food—but food."

Hoffmann looked down, away, to indicate that he didn't need to know. But El Mestizo continued, he wanted to tell.

"I *could* give her a lot more—and she demands more, as you could see and hear—but I'm not going to help her do drugs or drink herself to death."

They continued through the entrance hall, and glass doors opened as they approached. Down here there was almost no wind. They had just reached the illegally parked car when an ambulance with flashing blue lights passed them on its way to the emergency room. El Mestizo kept the car keys in his pocket and hurried after. As the first of the two paramedics opened the back door to pull out a stretcher, he caught up and stood in their way, grabbed the paramedic's arm.

"What happened?"

"I can't tell you."

Before the paramedic had finished talking, El Mestizo had pulled out his wad of money, removed the rubber band, and released a hundred dollars.

"Again. What happened?"

The paramedic shrugged, leaned close. "Okay. I guess the guy can't hear you anyway." He nodded toward the stretcher and someone lying under a blanket, completely still. "A shooting."

"Is it serious?"

"Death's pretty serious."

"How was he shot?"

"Twice. Once in the chest, once in the forehead."

El Mestizo glanced at the stretcher, then at Hoffmann. Both of his errands were done.

HOFFMANN PARKED IN one of El Mestizo's parking spots in front of La Casa Heaven, dropped off his employer, and headed for his own car, which was waiting in the rear parking lot. He'd just started his car when El Mestizo popped up by the passenger-side door and leaned in. "Come with me."

"I really want to go see Maria. And the boys."

"A quick one. Coffee? A beer? A woman—completely free?"

El Mestizo was always demanding—his voice, eyes, their intensity—but this was different from his usual demands, where power was used to threaten, and if that threat was challenged, to kill. Now he was . . . happy, almost exhilarated, seeking out contact like he did when a job went well, and he wanted to relive it. It was as if he had no one to share that kind of joy with—that he was alone despite the eighty women waiting inside, treated like products, investments that generate returns.

"I'm sorry, Johnny. I promised Maria, and I need to go home." He started the car again, and only now, after driving away from El Mestizo's appeal and the row of brothels, did the stories really start to reach him. As long as he'd had El Mestizo next to him in the car or helicopter or guerrilla camp, he'd refused to listen, but now, completely alone, on his way home, he couldn't ignore them anymore. Not the story of the electricity and the barbed wire through a man in a cage—that kind of story was a part of his daily reality here, and the reason that Zofia had finally insisted they go home. The other ones. That very recent description of a pitch-black, gaping, relentless threat. The story of drones and a kill list, which despite Wilson and El Mestizo's assurances of a slow war, had taken just one day to eliminate its first name. The story of an exploding family. Of rubble, fire, smoke. The remains of a man and a wife and two children identified by dental records and DNA.

"Hey, it's me."

He shouldn't call from the car. But her voice. He needed it, needed the calm it gave him.

"You're alive."

Now it sounded brittle, about to break, no matter how hard she tried to hide it.

"I'm alive."

"Piet? We have to talk."

The whole day. He knew that, of course. She too had had to bear the death sentence that had been passed on him. On them. Without ever getting the chance to talk to each other privately, to bear this together. He wondered where she'd been when she saw the news, realized it was her husband who was doomed to die. He should have been with her, held her hand, because when they held each other, nothing else existed.

"Rasmus and Hugo, Zo. I'm picking them up."

He wondered how he sounded. He was aware that he should be more affected, it wasn't normal to react like this. His life was threatened, and he should feel fear or anger or be on the run. Probably all three. But this had been his life for so long. Children killed on assignment, shooting someone in the forehead, torture, people who buried other people for a few thousand dollars. He was just so jaded, or "damaged" as Zofia would say.

"You're the one person who shouldn't pick them up."

"Zo, I'm the only one who can make sure they stay safe between Señora Vega's and our home."

For the first year Zofia spent her days with the boys hidden in the house, teaching them herself. They'd learned Spanish together using an educational CD-ROM and some lesson plans, and pretty soon the boys were better than their mom and dad. They'd been forced to seek out a new solution. Zofia longed to live a fuller life, and Rasmus and Hugo needed someone who could provide knowledge beyond where hers ended. She got a job as an English teacher, and they hired a private teacher who passed the background check his handler Lucia Mendez ran. Señora Vega taught the brothers at her home, which Hoffmann kept secure using the same risk analysis—motive, intention, ability, time—that he would for any other protected property. Academically, his six-year-old and eight-year-old were advanced for their ages, thanks to the benefit of constant contact with a teacher, but socially the lack of proximity to other children was starting to be a problem. They were paying a high price for the life Piet forced them all to live.

"Okay. You pick them up. And then, Piet, we *have* to talk."

About what they couldn't talk about on the phone. About if they were going to die. If two little boys were also at risk because of their father's actions.

"Yes. Later. But first, Zofia—an ordinary evening. Just us four together. Dinner and TV and bedtime and . . ." He hung up. He hadn't been prepared. He never cried.

The entrance to the three-story building on Valle del Cauca. A well-kept building in the same comuna in which they lived, the white-and-yellow facade was newly cleaned.

He parked and got out, headed over to the beat-up Volkswagen Golf on the opposite side of the narrow street, and knocked on the dark tinted window of the driver's side. It took a few seconds before it was rolled down. He greeted the armed guard from the private security company Lucia had recommended, noted that the strap on top of the gun holster had been unsnapped, a reflex when someone approached the car. And Hoffmann immediately handed a small bag of dog treats to the Rottweiler with the expectant eyes in the backseat.

"Everything okay today, Zacarias?"

"Everything's okay, sir."

"Good. You can head home for the day. Send my regards to Palmira."

Hoffmann crossed the street again, taking in his surroundings, everything seemed normal. He pushed in the access code and checked, without being completely aware of it, that the surveillance cameras were in place and searching like they should. Three staircases, the apartment at the very top and farthest from the landing.

Rasmus opened the door, he usually did. "Daddy!"

He still gave his dad a hug, he didn't feel ashamed of him yet.

"What's that?"

Rasmus, in his arms now, pushed his soft childish fingers into a hole on the left side of his jacket, at approximately chest height. Hoffmann hadn't noticed the sooty tear until now—from one of the small flashes of electricity that danced around El Mestizo during the most intense part of the torture session.

"A hole. Because I . . . got stuck. On a big shrub with nasty thorns, you know, like you do sometimes."

The curious finger slid further into the hole, and soon more—three small fingers could fit inside, and Hoffmann gently removed the unwilling arm. He had to remember to throw out this jacket, replace it with a new one.

"Dad?" Now Hugo was here, a pair of headphones still above his ears. No hug. But his head held a bit to the side. "Can I drive home? Like last time, when Rasmus was sick and you picked up just me?"

On a closed-off and empty street. Hugo had seemed worried when his father suddenly swung off and maneuvered the car past a fence with warning signs on it. And he let out a loud belly laugh when he realized why.

"We're in a hurry today, Hugo. And in that case, I would also have to let Rasmus drive. Right?"

"He's too little."

"Hugo, sweetie? So are you."

Fourteen minutes, and they stopped at another house. This time, it was their own. He could see her through the window already, despite the distance, easy to read her face, trying to radiate calm, but fighting off panic. She hadn't slept, not since the last time they saw each other; it was that kind of face. She'd probably been waiting there for a while, and now she hurried out.

"My darlings."

Rasmus, a bear hug. Hugo, a reserved hug, he was a little ashamed of his mother too. So they held each other, husband and wife, and for a moment there was only this—an embrace, peace, security. And she thought of the day she'd decided to go with him, flee side by side, how she'd done so on one condition: from that moment on he had to tell her everything. No more endless lies. Which through the years changed in form and content, adapting to each new reality.

A whole evening. And they acted just as he'd wished. They didn't speak of the one thing they should be talking about—what was pushing against both their chests. An ordinary evening. Eat, play, nagging about homework, sitting in the living room together. And reading a story, Rasmus and Hugo on either side of the bed, eyes closed, and light snoring. There was only one moment when reality intruded on the ordinary. A loud, unexpected bang from upstairs, and he reacted instinctively and from intense anxiety, three quick strides up the stairs with gun in hand. And there stood Rasmus with a broken flowerpot. And a *Daddy, I'm sorry, I didn't mean to.* Like a gunshot, that's what a smashed pot sounds like, he knew that now.

She was sitting at the kitchen table when he crept downstairs from their two sleeping sons. An unsolved crossword in front of her, pen in hand, held in a lazy grip. A ballpoint pen—she usually preferred a pencil so she could erase and try again. And with the pen still capped.

This evening's crossword would remain unfinished. He kissed her cheek and took her hand. Waited.

She put down the pen and looked at him. "It's begun."

They both knew what this was about.

"And not just him. His whole family. Do you know that, Piet?"

"Yes. I know that."

She grabbed the remote control hidden in a fruit platter on the kitchen table and turned on the local news. Explicit images from a drone strike, generic pictures of the White House, and a slow-motion listing of names next to the symbols of playing cards. She changed the channel, to the national news on Señal Colombia.

The same images. CNN, BBC, Al Jazeera—the same. And the confusion on her face when he got home disappeared. Her eyes were clear and bright.

"You see? This is for real. It's going on right now, Piet." She didn't scream. A voice that was neither panicked nor angry, more calm, slow, almost over-enunciated. Objective. That was how it sounded. "They're searching for you. Us. They know you're called *El Sueco*, that your appearance is *Northern European*, someone on the news was even talking about your *Scandinavian* traits. That you could be Swedish, Danish, Norwegian, Icelandic. How long do you think it will take them to start being curious about a Peter Haraldsson who lives in Comuna 5 in Cali?"

She grabbed his hand and held it tightly. His three remaining fingers.

The hotel room in Frankfurt—the first stop on their flight from Sweden, the high-security prison, and the Polish mafia Piet had infiltrated. She'd held his hand then too, but felt only inflamed fingers. When he'd climbed out of the ventilation shaft after four days of hiding there, without even noticing it—so full of adrenaline—he'd cut his fingertips to the bone while loosening the metal frame. Zofia had realized that two of them were so mangled they'd never heal and would have to be amputated. She'd carefully stripped away all the dead tissue and washed and wrapped the rest in sterilized bandages, which she changed several times a day, while she forced him to take hefty doses of antibiotics. After eight days, when she was sure there was no infection, she gave him five morphine pills, cut off the extra bone—tried first with a boiled kitchen knife, but had to switch to a pair of pruning shears when she hit bone—then cleaned the surfaces and glued the extra skin together with Super Glue.

"I'm not staying here. Not in Colombia or South America. The boys aren't staying here either. No matter how friendly and kind the people are. Not when the people *you* meet threaten you with death."

"I can't go home. I've got a life sentence waiting for me there, Zo. I can't take it. We can't. It would mean abandoning you—my family."

"It's not negotiable." She emphasized every word, articulating them with painful slowness, as if their meaning should be weighed—like what she said was going to change the course of their lives. "At least life in prison means you'd be alive. Dying here, Piet, is just another way of abandoning your family."

"Zo, I—"

"When are they coming for us? If you won't leave, then we'll leave without you. Head home. For good."

"This is not that kind of war. It will take time for them to round us up one by one. And I'm the only one who they haven't identified."

He stroked her cheek. And she pulled away, a little.

"Zo? We have to take it one step at a time—and the first step is to increase our security. From now on, the boys can't go to Señora Vega. And you can't work at your school. And we can't live here. We've been visited here before and if the guerrillas can find us, others can too. Tomorrow, before dawn, we're leaving Los Guayacanes. We have to stay away until I can solve this."

To his safe house. In another part of Cali. An apartment in Comuna 6's poorest area that cost little to buy. Narrow streets with substandard housing, it lay directly on the riverbank in imminent risk of destruction, despite the ongoing construction of dikes. An apartment he'd designed every detail of in order to protect them from a level nine threat—as close to the security of the US president's residence as it was possible to get. And which they would now use for the first time.

"Piet, you don't understand—we're not going to live somewhere else. We're not going to keep running. We're going home."

"One week. Give me one week to solve this. I have a plan, Zofia. Trust me. I have a meeting tomorrow, which is the first step. Wilson. In Bogotá. Tomorrow, call in sick to work, tell Señora Vega the boys are sick. We don't need to pack or buy food. The only thing you need to do when you get there is to follow the guidelines I'm about to give you. And in case of an absolute emergency—use the weapons I've got stored there, which I know you've mastered."

A situation that should never—based on the apartment's design—occur. But he hoped it would make her feel a little more secure.

"I've already started my work, my plan. I promise you—we're going to survive."

"That's not what I want. Survival. Just like I said." Now she was screaming. "I said I want to *live*! And I want to do it with you and my kids!"

Her desperate cries penetrated and hurt him with the same force that they bounced off the walls of the house. He waited it out, held her.

"One week. Trapped." She glanced toward the floor, lowered her voice, almost whispering. "Then I'm not waiting anymore, Piet. Not even for you."

A DUTY MANAGER in the communications department begged forgiveness for calling the chief of staff at 2:27 a.m. Then she told him an e-mail containing an attachment had just been sent to the White House's public address. She had assessed it as needing to be dealt with immediately. A one-minute-and-forty-three-second film.

The investigator at the NGA established later that the sender had used another Internet cafe and another IP address than at first contact, but this one was also located in downtown Bogotá and had the president as its recipient.

A single continuous, unedited shot. The picture was steady—the photographer had probably placed a tripod in front of the locked cage door. Chief of Staff Perry and Vice President Thompson still lacked the strength to talk. When the film finally froze on what they realized was the last shot, they sat in silence in front of the computer screen placed on the low coffee table, quietly breathing in sync, waiting until one of them couldn't wait any longer and instead leaned over and moved the cursor back to the beginning and started the film over. Seven times. And new details emerged with each viewing.

They both recognized the straw mattress and red plastic bowl from the proof-of-life picture they'd received earlier. They didn't notice the chain around his neck, oddly enough, until midway through the second viewing—a dark shadow had obscured it where it blurred from the tip of the chin and down to the upper edge of the breast. On the fourth viewing the chief of staff noticed deep wounds had replaced toenails on Speaker Crouse's right foot. On the fifth they distinguished the swellings on his hands and arms from bruises and cuts in the skin. And during the seventh, they noticed on the floor of the cage a ground plate with electrical wiring, a torture method they'd heard of, but never seen the consequences of.

The picture had been silent, no demands. This was a film. With sound. And demands.

Chief of Staff Perry moved the cursor back one last time. Thirty-two seconds into the timeline. That was when Crouse grabbed the bamboo bars hard and in a quiet, almost whispering voice read some sort of sign that was being held up next to the camera lens, his tired eyes jumped up and down the rows of stilted, slightly bureaucratic English.

"I, Timothy D. Crouse, am doing fine. I have been treated well and with respect by my hosts."

Chief of Staff Perry and Vice President Thompson could feel the pain in almost every word that came out of their friend and colleague's mouth, even in the soft armchairs of this beautiful office in the White House, and by the end they knew those words by heart.

"Mr. President, I am alive—but for how long? That depends on you."

Tim Crouse was strong, stubborn—the type with a back that would never bend. But his skin bore the traces of violence. Arrhythmic muscle contractions in his arms, chest, thighs, had been caused by electrocution. His empty gaze testified to further torture. Step by step they must have broken him down.

"I therefore plead that the Crouse Force, which I myself initiated and created, be dismantled effective immediately, and that our imperialist aggressions and provocations against the Colombian people cease."

The Crouse Force. The effort to destroy the whole system of production in Colombia: blowing up cocaine kitchens, seizing shipments, capturing arms shipments, laying waste to warehouses, burning coca plantations. Crushing the very infrastructure of cocaine manufacturing.

"If you cooperate, I will continue to live, with my loved ones, just as you live with yours."

The only information included in the anonymous email informed them that Speaker Crouse's appeal, spoken on a camera by his own free will, would be distributed in full to media in the morning.

"It's very important that you act quickly, Mr. President. I await your reply."

Chief of Staff Perry stopped the film and turned off the computer. He couldn't bear the hissing sound of the hard drive. And he knew how the movie ended. With several detailed images of Crouse's face and body, the terrible injuries that neither he nor the vice president could stand to watch anymore.

They would do as they were told, act fast—the hostage takers would get their answer. The United States does not negotiate with terrorists. The hunt would not be abandoned—it would escalate.

Therefore, the White House would immediately begin preparing for the next attack, check another name off that list.

THE LAST TRIP.

The one you only make once. Just as clear, as special as the first, which you also only make once. Then there are the rest, all the others in between, the ones that just happen.

Bernhard Glen watched a blinking computer screen, on a fairly simple chair at a fairly simple table. Three floors down and surrounded by armored steel. The USS *Dwight D. Eisenhower*'s command center, the heart of this huge aircraft carrier, which, just like his own, was protected by what was around it, was sensitive, powerful, and kept him alive. A short distance away he glimpsed the back of Commander Norton, who was in the middle of a conversation with one of the operators; in another part of the room Lieutenant Commander Eriksen stood with a telephone in hand. Quiet, calm, even with eighteen people working in a confined space around the clock, even though in just one hundred and eighty seconds two keys would turn at the same time and open the cover on the firing button.

He'd been just twenty-two years old the first time—Operation Desert Storm and those strange months in the Persian Gulf. That's how it had seemed back then, not quite real, an excitement he no longer felt—maybe his advancing age or the realization that it was real people they were shooting at had gradually changed his experience. But he could still feel the hot, dry wind on his twenty-nine-year-old skin during Operation Southern Watch's no-fly zone over Iraq, or hear the Indian Ocean's roaring waves as they hunted al-Qaeda seven years later from Djibouti to Somalia.

It all went by so fast. A professional life framed by death. That was also why he finally received his specialist officer grade—assisting researchers and engineers who were developing hybrid weapons, merging the control systems of anti-aircraft missiles and cruise missiles. In order to shoot, and kill, with them, too.

"One hundred and twenty seconds—all set?"

Lieutenant Commander Eriksen broke the silence. And Bernhard Glen nodded.

"Ready, sir."

His very last journey began ninety-six hours earlier, when they received the go-ahead and left the Naval station in Norfolk, Virginia. They'd been upgraded to Code Orange forty-eight hours ago, when a group of Delta Force soldiers localized the Queen of Hearts and Ten of Hearts on a small property in the village of La Cuchilla. Gone to Code Red twenty-four hours ago, when a sniper fired a capsule onto the lawn of that property and the microchip embedded inside started to broadcast.

"Ninety seconds—status?"

"Homing device calibrated to the targeting systems. The location coordinates have been verified to the target coordinates. The firing codes are in place for both the launching pad and robot."

The Caribbean Sea. He'd been able to see the coast of Colombia from the deck, make out the outlines of a city called Cartagena. And now in his monitor—according to the numbers crowded at the bottom left corner it was just over 278 nautical miles away—their intended target.

Washington sent the USS *Liberty*—which remained off the Pacific coast of Colombia—for a drone strike. But the property where these two doomed people were located, according to the Delta Force investigators, was equipped with jamming equipment powerful enough to ward off that kind of attack. The solution was one of the cruise missiles he helped to develop—modified for both satellite control, visual control, and inertial navigation. And it was neither the destroyers, nor the corvettes, who would fire it—it was him, and he was going to do it from this ship.

"Sixty seconds."

The last trip. And then what? He'd never really thought about it, even though he knew he should.

"Forty-five seconds."

There wasn't much else. Teaching? He'd started receiving offers. And he'd tried it, that year when he thought stillness outside was the same as stillness inside, and so moved onto land and into the classroom. And that first attack—the one against the King of Hearts—had been carried out by Steve Sabrinsky, one of the men he trained, and perhaps he'd felt somewhat involved. One man firing his first shot, another firing his last.

No. Never going to do that again. He was sure of it. It wasn't the same. He'd finally learned that that had been *his* education. The calm outside of himself did not translate to calm on the inside, instead it meant even more anxiety.

"Thirty seconds."

The ammunition handlers had left the launch pad. The camera on the tip of the missile searched the sky. The twenty-four digit and letter firing code, which was to be fed into the battle computer.

"Fifteen seconds."

Mamie. The name of this newly christened cruise missile. Eisenhower's wife. He wasn't sure it was a good name.

"Ten seconds."

Bernhard Glen took a deep breath, trying to freeze this final moment and stay inside it. It was impossible—it pushed forward, pushed under.

"Five seconds."

And he didn't know it yet, but afterward he'd even miss the jargon he'd despised for so long, dismissed as adolescent and tragic. *Time to play some poker, Glen. Shuffle up and deal, Glen.*

"Four seconds, three . . ."

The jargon he'd also encounter right after this was over.

Well played, Glen—King of Hearts, and now the Queen of Hearts and Ten of Hearts.

". . . two, one . . ."

Two more, Glen, and you'll have a royal flush.

". . . fire."

NOT FAR NOW to Bogotá. He'd tried listening to music, but no matter what radio station he switched to the song seemed like a fake scream, an aggressive public display, and the melody an atonal sound loop with no harmony. He'd tried silence, but no matter how intensely he stared out the windshield trying to lose himself in nothingness, his wife's words drowned out everything.

One week. Trapped. Then I'm not waiting anymore, Piet. Not even for you.

He'd tied a black piece of cloth tightly around his head, hiding his tattoos just to be safe, but it was hot and itchy, so he loosened the knot on the neck. The only concrete piece of information they had on him was that lizard tattoo. From now on, he'd have to grow his hair back, looking like Piet Hoffmann was now less dangerous than looking like Peter Haraldsson.

All morning he'd made sure to listen to the news at the top of every hour, that's what he'd agreed to do with Zofia, that was how they had to live now—with constant updates. And when the clock struck eleven as he approached the city's outer ring of suburbs, it became even clearer. Suddenly the slow report was interrupted by a blaring voice announcing there'd been a missile attack. At least that's how he understood it. A missile and two dead people. He was sure of it now. That was followed by the official press release from the United States, which described a successful attack, and then a report about how the search for the remaining ten names on the kill list continued in what was now called the "Final War on Drugs."

The news report had just ended and the weather report started when the phone rang.

"Did you hear?"

Zofia. He loved her so.

"Yes."

"Next time, Piet, it—"

"I'm gonna fix this. I promise. We will survive. *And* live."

He parked like last time one block west of El Parque Metropolitano Tercer Milenio and crossed the large recreation area—ignored the impulse to step out on the basketball court and play for a moment, shrugged his shoulders at two people who thought he should have stopped their misdirected tennis ball—and walked back out onto the streets on the park's east side. The World Orbital Systems office, one of forty-seven branches located in various world capitals, was on the ground floor of a newly built office building that was focused on technology and information. The slightly overweight, mustachioed manager didn't recognize Hoffmann from his last visit—for research and prep—but his smile was just as friendly and he seemed to have plenty of time for explanations.

"We call these ones spy satellites. Because that's what they called them before. And, if I'm being honest, because that name sells." The store manager winked, as if he'd just revealed something that was just between them. "They orbit the Earth just like any other satellite. But closer. Low Earth Orbit. And so they have to rotate considerably faster—otherwise they'd just fall down. It takes less than an hour for one of our satellites to orbit."

And Hoffmann had nothing against that, he liked salesmen who understood you got people to buy by making them feel special, that it was all about confidence and affinity—that's what you did as an informant as well—so he winked back.

"How long will it take until my satellite's sent up? Until I can use it. If you get the coordinates from me, let's say, now?"

"I'd say five days."

"And if I want it up there today?"

"That's difficult."

"But possible? If I pay double?"

A personal satellite released by a rocket at an altitude of three hundred kilometers. Thirteen centimeters long and weighing seven hundred and fifty grams. And with a life expectancy of three months, more than he needed.

"In that case I'd say it is. Possible." The store manager slid his eyes over to his computer screen and seemed to find what he was looking for. "One satellite. Today . . . let's see . . . if I move one of the thirty customers who bought a place in the next launch, suddenly we have a hole. A free spot. And now we can put you there. What luck. You might as well take it." A new wink. "Then we just need the purpose."

"Video recording of the Earth's surface."

"And . . . officially?"

This skilled salesman was good at that too. Reading people who were purchasing private satellites in order to monitor someone or something—and offering them discretion.

"Write whatever you like."

"Measuring the Earth's magnetism? Testing electronic equipment? A relay station for amateur radio? Biological tests?"

"You pick."

The smiling salesman chose the first option. Measuring the Earth's magnetism.

"You know that there's space for you to load something into your satellite, up to two hundred grams?"

"I just need video. That's all."

Hoffmann paid twenty thousand US dollars—twice the usual price—but he was allowed to stay in the store and follow the launch on the manager's screen. While he made his way back through a park filled with children and teens playing football in central Bogotá, his private satellite made its way from a rocket launched from one of the many islands that made up the Kingdom of Tonga. He was going to keep working on what he'd promised Zofia—making sure they survived, lived. *In two days. Go to number one. The same time as always.* After that unannounced detour through Medellín, he still managed to make it in time, now all that remained was the short distance to a café with bamboo walls and green door.

To a meeting—though he didn't know it—with a man who once tried to kill him.

EWERT GRENS WASN'T quite sure he was in the right place. A strange little door painted with green frills by someone who had too much time on their hands and who'd overestimated their talent. Bamboo was hung like a second skin across the walls.

This was Gaira Café. Grens wondered how Wilson had ever found his way here. Not much lighting. Chairs built for smaller, younger bodies. But pleasant music and a friendly waiter, who brought him a tray with a small coffee cup next to a metal tub of raw sugar.

It tasted fantastic. Colombian coffee that hadn't traveled halfway around the globe. Almost as good as what came out of the machine in the homicide unit corridor in the police station in Stockholm. There wasn't much else that even came close.

He'd left Arlanda on a temporary passport for a twenty-six-hour trip. He'd lived a full life without really knowing what jet lag was. Now he did—after a night spent in that feverish zone between dreaming and wakefulness at the Hotel Estelar La Fontana. Top floor, overlooking the streets of Bogotá, which never seemed to sleep. A continent he'd never wanted to visit. A city he'd never imagined seeing. Life—despite all these years—was still hard to predict.

One more cup. And the coffee tasted better.

Thirty-eight years as a police officer, he hadn't had a clue—none of them did—that so much would change. That they'd end up investigating a completely different kind of crime. That over his professional life, the number of drug-related deaths would increase by seventeen times. Seventeen-hundred percent. And then keep increasing. They'd all been taught to deal with other driving forces. Criminality so strongly linked to drugs, to drug use, to drug profits.

The main industry of organized crime. One of the biggest industries of our age, annual sales of 2.25 trillion kronor and huge profit margins. The drugs he investigated in Stockholm had traveled as far as this wonderful coffee, *I'd like a third cup, thanks*, on a road lined with violence, blood, death. And when an organization had been built to smuggle drugs, it could just as well be used to smuggle women and weapons as well. And when that wasn't enough, when profits need to be further maximized, it formed the basis for the more mundane crimes: looting, blackmail, embezzlement. A different time. When drug organizations run society.

Grens stood up. He was deliberately early, unsure if he'd find his way through a capital city that was so different from the one he lived in. A walk with Wilson's map, marked with three large letters in red ink, then a long bus ride, then another walk. Different—but he liked the surroundings. Despite this mission. He felt lighter here, the streets and buildings weren't watching him in the same way, old patterns and emotions had stayed at home, or at least hadn't caught up with him yet.

He was about to sit opposite a man he'd never met. Someone he'd hunted, had been convinced he'd executed. But who'd tricked them all. Someone who had been dead and should be dead, but still walked the streets—what did that make him, a ghost?

He's coming back here, Ewert. Alive.

Wilson had handed him five airplane tickets at Terminal 5. One with his own name. The other four with the first names Peter, Maria, William, Sebastian—all with the last name Haraldsson.

No. He wasn't bringing him back. Not against his will. The only murder case Grens ever investigated where he was happy to see the murderer go free—felt gratitude that he'd failed to solve it. Because this murderer, like himself, had been used, exploited. To take him back against his will was not an option. The moment they landed on Swedish soil, they'd have to assume other roles. Hoffmann would become—according to both the Swedish government and organized crime—the perpetrator of a double murder. And he would become a detective superintendent. *If* he brought Piet

Hoffmann home, then Grens would have to arrest him, attempt to prosecute him, make sure he was locked up for a long time. Given a life sentence. And once inside he'd have to protect him from inmates who hated snitches. And that was the wrong ending to this story.

And that was when he stepped into the dark, cramped room. Jeans, black boots, hunting vest over a thin shirt with short sleeves. Despite the tan he seemed tired, had aged considerably over the years.

Grens noted how he automatically searched the premises, secured it. And only then did Grens see how he'd consciously changed his appearance, something about the nose and the chin, and when he took the black piece of fabric off his shaved head, he uncovered a large tattoo.

"You . . . of all people?"

"You are correct."

"I was expecting Wilson."

"That's not how it turned out." Ewert Grens nodded to the counter. "A coffee? It's delicious."

Piet Hoffmann lingered, as if trying to decide whether or not to stay. And then he did—pulled out the chair across the table from Grens. "No, thanks. But I'd gladly take an aguapanela."

The detective looked at the man he'd thought so much about, but only spoken to once, a brief conversation over the phone before he decided to shoot to kill.

"I can't even pronounce that. Is it legal?"

"Sugar cane pulp and warm water. I think a detective can drink it without risking breaking the law."

Grens took five steps to the serving counter and ordered the new drink as best he could. *Dos*. One each. When in Rome. And then he sat down again.

"I was supposed to murder you. That's what you wanted me to think. What I did think. Until I watched several days of prison surveillance footage. Back and forth. And then, suddenly, a wink in one of them."

A man dressed like a correctional officer in a blue uniform heading out of the central guard station stopped at the camera, looked straight into it, winked his right eye.

"That was for you."

"Why?"

"Because you'd been manipulated into taking that shot. And you were the one who had to live with it. I had no choice, I had to manipulate the police officer who was responsible for the shot, you. But I didn't think you should have to fucking bear that, afterward."

Hoffmann spoke quietly, with control. Despite the fact that every fiber of his being resisted reliving what happened back then. Those goddamn police chiefs who sacrificed him for their own power. And worst of all was that bastard Göransson, who'd betrayed them the most, who'd had the job Wilson had now, who promised to support the informant no matter what, then turned his back on him.

"I'd heard of you already, Grens. I knew you were investigating the shootings on Västmanna Street and asked Wilson, before I committed the crime of being locked up and infiltrating from inside the prison, I asked him why he, too, like Göransson, was so damn worried when you started snooping around."

Two steaming cups were put down on the table by a smiling waiter, lemon slices on their porcelain rims. What they called aguapanela. Grens examined it, hesitantly, and decided it just looked like regular tea.

"I thought I might as well try."

"A lot of vitamin C. Something to consider, Superintendent."

Grens sipped, swallowed. "And a lot of sugar."

"That's how we do it in Colombia."

A real mouthful. Then another.

"Stubborn. Searching for the truth for as long as it takes, even longer, when he senses from the outset that this might involve his colleagues. The kind of man who never gives up." Hoffmann looked at Grens. "That was how they described you."

It was hard to tell if the detective—who was old enough to be Piet's father—felt some sense of pride, but there almost seemed to be the flash of something like it in his eyes.

"The letter you received, Grens . . . you were supposed to know it could only come from me. And if you were as good as Wilson claimed you were, if you started thinking and poking, then I figured you'd find that wink. I duped you and the whole fucking police force. You needed to know that you'd guessed right. But if you never discovered it, if you *weren't* as good as they said, then you could just as well live with the guilt. And then you certainly wouldn't be sitting here now."

Hoffmann winked with his right eye, just as he had on the surveillance tape and to the satellite dealer just now. And at that moment one of the three phones he'd lined up next to his steaming cup started ringing. A gentle, quiet ring tone. Grens tried to read the lighted display from upside down. Rasmus.

"Unfortunately I have to take this. It's important."

Hoffmann moved some distance away, answered when he reached the green front door. One of his few rules—always respond if one of his sons called. No matter what he was doing. He answered every time. They should know he was always just a phone call away.

"Mommy is sad."

"Sad?"

"She doesn't want me to notice. But I do anyway, Daddy."

Hoffmann heard a voice that was small but self-possessed, that took on responsibilities that someone so little should never have to bear.

"Rasmus? Everything will be all right."

"What will be?"

"Whatever is making Mommy sad."

"But how?"

"I'll fix it. And then everything will be all right again."

The Swedish detective finished the last of his warm cup and seemed pleased when Hoffmann returned to the table. He must approve of the sweet drink.

"Rasmus?"

"My son."

"Sebastian Haraldsson?"

"That's him."

They looked at each other. Until Grens looked away, down at the table. "I never had any. Kids, that is. I guess sometimes it just turns out like that."

Hoffmann should maybe have answered. Said something. Anything. But he didn't. There was nothing to say. So they both sat in silence. Until Hoffmann couldn't stand it anymore.

"Sometimes things just happen. And you're forced to survive them. To live. Especially if there's a Rasmus. And to do that I need your help."

"That's why I'm here."

"And that's why tomorrow morning I need you to fly to Washington."

Hoffmann had a small black bag with him. Now he opened it, lifted out a laptop.

"And when you get there, head to Arlington. And don't leave until you meet a person named Sue Masterson."

He opened the screen toward Grens and clicked on one of the folders, waited while it opened.

"The DEA chief. One of three people who knows who I am. Erik Wilson—my handler in Sweden. Lucia Mendez—my handler here in Colombia. And Sue Masterson—the woman who recruited me."

"One of four."

Grens and Hoffmann exchanged a smile.

"Erik, I can't talk to. Lucia and Sue have cut me loose."

"But now there's me."

"Now there's you."

A single image now filled the computer screen. Very difficult to interpret. Lacking sharpness and resolution, it was far from perfect. It reminded Grens of images he'd seen in Wilson's office. The perspective was from above. A satellite perspective. Of greenery that might be a jungle.

"Survive. Live. In order to do that I'll have to negotiate with the people who want to kill me. And in order to negotiate, I have to have something to offer." Hoffmann pointed to the diffuse image. "So I'll negotiate with this."

Grens searched across the screen, still not really able to piece it together.

"You don't see it? There, that grayish blob in the middle of the green—it's the roof of a cage. And inside that cage is a human being."

Grens lingered on the image. The *moving* image, he could see that now, birds flew by, treetops swayed slowly.

"As in . . . the world's most sought-after man?"

"Exactly."

And now he could see. If you knew where to look. A small opening in a dense jungle. And the roof of a cage in the middle.

"I know where it is. I'm surveilling it from my own computer. With information from my own satellite."

A new cup of that sweetness was on the table without them even ordering it. Grens thanked the waiter and sipped on a drink he could get used to. "I don't even know how to pronounce the slush we're drinking. And I know even less about personal satellites."

Hoffmann drank some of that warmth, too. "You can get one of your own, Grens. Anybody can, at any time. Completely legal. Eight thousand dollars for seven hundred and fifty grams of satellite spinning in orbit above you. Not as fine-tuned as the others, this ten-centimeter resolution, but I don't need faces—just need to know that the camp is in the same place."

Grens stared at the picture for a long time. At the cage. At Hoffmann. "And?"

"Free the hostage. My life for the hostage's."

"And would you do that on your own?"

Always alone. Trust only yourself.

"No. With your help, Grens."

They looked at each other. Until Grens nodded. "My help? With what?"

"Sue Masterson."

"Our mutual friend instructed me in a . . . memo on all the who, where, and how, before I came here. In case. And then handed me the key to her—which I should only use if there was no other way."

"The key?" Hoffmann was waiting for him to continue. He didn't. "The key, Grens?"

"Wilson's *private* key."

Hoffmann turned the computer slightly, light streamed in through one of the café's small windows, and the screen flashed annoyingly. "I want to know the schedule for the orbit of these geostationary satellites. For a specific location. And it's you, Grens, who's going to find out."

Grens tapped his finger on the plastic screen and the image of a cage. "This?"

Hoffmann shook his head. "Those coordinates, Superintendent, are my life. And I'm not giving them to anyone. I'm looking for the timetable for a completely different site—and I want to know exactly when the black holes occur there. The windows. The gaps. When the satellites don't overlap. When they're not watching. If someone were to be at this place, I want to know the moment when they couldn't be seen from above. Furthermore . . ." He leaned forward, speaking more quietly, even though no one was listening. ". . . I want Masterson to put at my disposal eight highly skilled, trustworthy, incorruptible people with military backgrounds."

"Why?"

"To negotiate. Exchange my life for the hostage's."

"Where?"

"The less you know the better, Grens, believe me—for your own sake."

"If you want my help, I want the whole picture."

"You're not getting the whole picture."

"Listen . . . Paula? El Sueco? Haraldsson? Hoffmann? Call yourself whatever you want, I don't give a shit. But now it's like this. I once gave a command to kill you *because I didn't have the whole picture.* I don't plan on doing that again. So either you fill me in right now—or you're on your own."

Hoffmann leaned even farther forward. Two heads very close together. Grens could see the hesitation, eyes looking for a way out.

"This is what the operation looks like." The informant pulled out his knife and emptied out what was hidden in its leather holster. Two folded pieces of paper. The first, with something handwritten on it, he put back. The other he held out, smiling. "My only safe these days." He unfolded it across the table—written on old-fashioned typewriter, away from every Internet connection or search engine, never leave a trace.

xx.xx (Briefing Calamar.)
xx.xx (Departure ATV.)
xx.xx (Arrival river.)
xx.xx (Landing base camp.)
xx.xx (Arrival prison camp.)
xx.xx (Attack, break in.)
xx.xx (Arrival helicopter.)
xx.xx (Arrival Isla Tierra Bomba.)
xx.xx (Underwater.)
xx.xx (Arrival ship.)
xx.xx.xx–xx.xx.xx (Time window.)

Grens read, read again. And pushed it back. "That means nothing to me."

"The timeline, not yet specified, for an operation that needs to start as late as possible—in order to minimize exposure—and has to end in the ocean. The Caribbean."

"That's not enough."

"A site along Colombia's northern coastline, one mile from Cartagena. And a ship anchored there."

Grens looked into those eyes that had changed from doubt to determination. A ship? Cartagena? *My God.* It had been only a few hours since he'd stepped into all this.

In order to fend off the empty, ugly feeling of abandonment that so often attacked him in a hotel room, he'd lain down on his bed with remote control in hand, restlessly flipping through the television channels. And met the same image no matter where he stopped, on CNN or the BBC, and most explicitly of all on a local channel called El Tiempo. Black smoke, fire, devastation. *The Queen of Hearts, the Ten of Hearts.* Special broadcasts, excited voices from both local and international stations. *A royal flush.* And a building razed to the ground.

"A ship? As in a US aircraft carrier? As in the aircraft that just took down two of your friends? Who happened to be on the same kill list as you?"

"Yes."

So close to each other. Grens looked into eyes that had cheated death before.

"You said survive?"

"I said live."

There wasn't much left at the bottom of the cup, just concentrated sweetness. Hoffmann drank the last drops, stood up.

"Your tickets, Grens. And a few other things." A white envelope on the table. "Say hello to Sue for me."

He nodded at the detective he didn't really know but had chosen to trust, turned around, and walked toward the green door.

A FOUR-AND-A-HALF-HOUR FLIGHT, and for the first time in his life, Ewert Grens saw the US capital. A slow turn over Dulles International and the United Airlines pilot urged all passengers to return to their seats and fasten their seat belts.

The stewardesses had handed out fresh editions of the *New York Times* and the *Washington Post* at the beginning of their flight, and the Swedish detective had had ample time to read every story on the kidnapping of one of the nation's most powerful politicians—no real leads—as well as day-after reporting on the sneak attack on two of thirteen targets in what they were calling the Final War on Drugs.

This trip was becoming increasingly strange. Only hours ago Grens had sat in a dark café across from one of the only outsiders who knew the precise location this powerful politician was being held at—and furthermore, opposite one of ten remaining targets of this war.

The taxi driver waiting in a pre-ordered cab at the terminal spoke English with an even heavier accent than his passenger, and confusion arose when Grens after a rather jerky journey tried to pay cash, just as Wilson had instructed him, even though the driver explained he didn't have enough change. But taxi drivers were friendlier here, didn't call the chief prosecutor on you when they didn't get what they wanted, and Grens headed to a government building that was significantly less conspicuous than the many they'd already passed—as if it too were an informant, always blending in, acting without being seen. And on his way, he realized how much easier it was to breathe here, that the thin, high-elevation air in Bogotá had been replaced by something moist and oxygen rich.

Identity verification. Passing through a metal detector. Visitors' area. And then on to the information desk located in the large entrance hall.

"My name is Erik Wilson, and I wish to speak to Sue Masterson."

The friendly, smiling receptionist turned to her computer screen.

"Wilson, you said?"

"Erik Wilson."

"I don't see any appointments here."

"I'd like to see her anyway."

"I'm sorry, but it doesn't really work like that. I'm going to have to ask you to make a formal appointment with the DEA chief, just like everyone else."

"I don't have time. However, I do have information that Masterson wants. And *if* she doesn't want it, I'm pretty sure she'll want to make that decision for herself."

The receptionist smiled genially. But she'd started to glance toward the uniformed guards who formed a human avenue near the metal detector.

"Sir, I'll have to kindly ask you to leave—"

"She's going to want to meet me. If you call her and let her know *Erik Wilson* is looking for her. She'll probably rush right down those stairs."

"You think so?"

"I think so."

"Chief Masterson? I'm calling from the front desk. I sincerely apologize for interrupting you. But I have a person here with no appointment, who's demanding to see you. He won't take no for an answer—and I've now asked him to sit down and wait. His name is . . . one moment . . . Erik Wilson."

Sue Masterson rarely felt scared. As a child and as a teenager, yes, but she'd decided one day that enough was enough. Fear was a depressing and ugly companion, it limited life. And here, in this office, which despite several years as boss still seemed unnecessarily large and furnished with way too many expensive couches, she'd never felt anything even resembling fear. But now she felt it. This didn't make sense. It couldn't be true. Erik Wilson? They were never supposed to see each other again. She'd explained that! Erik had understood that! He must be aware that he was putting her in grave danger just by coming here, putting a loaded gun to her temple.

She opened up the building's surveillance cameras on her computer. There. A camera located above the front desk. Facing three simple chairs that made up a kind of provisional waiting room.

A single person. Someone she had never seen before. In his sixties, wearing a suit, a bulky man. And she understood even less. Only three people knew of her relationship with Erik Wilson. Her. Erik. And Piet Hoffmann. No one else. But now there seemed to be four.

Her immediate reaction, when fear has been replaced by anger, was to ask the guards to throw the bastard out. Until she realized that was no good. This might be Erik's way of making contact.

She read the display and camera. An older man. He didn't look particularly likable. But not very dangerous either. *Who the hell are you?*

"Okay." She had put the handset down, pressed the microphone against the desk. Now she picked it up again. "I'm coming down. Tell the guards to keep him under surveillance."

In an oblong cabinet in one corner of the room a rarely used uniform hung near a shoulder holster. A Colt .45, her personal weapon, she preferred it to the standard service weapon. She put it on under her jacket and took the elevator down to the main floor.

Ewert Grens didn't like these chairs. They weren't really meant for sitting. At least not for long. Hard sticks poked into the soft tissue of his back, and the angle of the seat pushed up on his spinal column.

He was just about to get up and stretch when she came walking toward him through the large entrance hall. A beautiful woman, dignified, eyes that shone with power, integrity, wit. She reminded him of another police officer who used to sit in his corridor—that's how Mariana Hermansson would have looked if she'd been the chief officer of an American police organization.

"Erik Wilson?"

He stood up, held out a hand, which she didn't take. "Thank you for—"

"You're not Erik Wilson."

"No, we both know I'm not." Grens leaned forward, lowered his voice. "And we both know who El Sueco is—and what kind of situation he's in."

They looked at each other. She revealed absolutely nothing. The whole world had learned of the code name El Sueco in the past few days, and an unannounced visitor turning up spouting that name didn't necessarily mean anything.

Grens had expected that, would have reacted the same way, and when he continued, it was even more quietly, almost a whisper. "However, in Sweden, at the City Police's Investigation Unit where Erik Wilson is my boss, we called him Paula."

No reaction. She not only looked competent, she was.

"You want more? Details that only someone here on behalf of Erik would know?"

She didn't answer, but saw through him in a way he'd rather avoid.

"His real name is Piet Hoffmann."

No answer.

"And he's generally considered dead."

No answer.

"So today he calls himself Haraldsson."

No change in expression. Grens was starting to like this woman quite a bit.

"Okay." He smiled. "Erik explained in writing how this would work. That if I ever needed to contact you, if I ever ended up standing opposite you in this very building, that you'd treat me exactly as you're treating me now. So he gave me a last resort. You know, the very last. I'm using it now."

Sue Masterson shifted her position. And the words *Atlanta, June 9, 2006,* ran through her head.

"He told me to say, and I quote now, Atlanta, June 9, 2006."

She looked at him the same way as before, neutral. Or rather, she *tried* to look at him that way. But didn't succeed completely. There was a flash in her eyes, quick, but anything but neutral.

Then she smiled, weakly. "I'd like to add that we were only engaged for a very short time." And whispered. "Saxby's Coffee, six o'clock. On Thirty-Fifth Street in Georgetown. Three blocks from the Potomac. I want a coffee, black, and a jelly doughnut."

She began walking toward the elevator, but turned around, speaking more loudly now. "I apologize in advance for this." Then she stretched one hand in the air, waved to some uniformed guards, four in total. "Please see this man out."

Grens had no time to react. They ran over to him, grabbed him, two held him tightly by his arms, while a third marched in front of him and a fourth marched behind. They pushed and pulled the visitor through the front door and down the stairs. One of them told him to go to hell, and another said that if he ever showed his face here again he'd be arrested, locked up, and tried in court.

A crowded, intimate café with a long bar the same color as freshly ground coffee, which forced patrons to sit so close together they could no longer see each other. The sort of place he himself would have chosen, easy to control, monitor. While he'd been waiting, he'd strolled through the beautiful neighborhood DC called Georgetown, and he felt like it was one of the few places that could compete with Svea Road in Stockholm. There was a picturesque peacefulness here that he ought to dislike, but actually enjoyed. Saxby's Coffee lay on the corner of O and Thirty-Fifth Street, and he considered, when they were done here, stepping out of the café and entering the building next door, going up the stairs and knocking on the first door to ask if they had a room for rent indefinitely. Bogotá yesterday, Washington today, and that same feeling—Grens, locked into his patterns and routines, suddenly needed to fly, taste, smell, see more of the world, before life had passed him by. Later, maybe when he was done with another life, Hoffmann's.

He checked the clock on the wall. Thirty-three minutes after the hour. She was late. Or, he realized, she was acting like a professional. Masterson was sitting somewhere making sure he was alone, that he could handle waiting without getting too stressed, as someone with a hidden agenda might. Then she came through the door. She'd made her assessment, and now she walked over to his table, toward a cup of coffee and a jelly doughnut.

"Your coffee got a little cold. Where were you sitting? When you were studying me, I mean? Did you discover anything abnormal?"

She nodded to the building across the street, which was as beautiful as the one they were sitting in now, wood with green shutters against white panels. "If I had, you would have already been arrested."

"The coffee's cold, but the doughnut you wanted is fine. My treat. Maybe I can avoid getting thrown out this time?"

She smiled, then turned serious. "We have to keep this short. A federal prosecutor would consider my participation in this conversation treasonous. Before we continue, I'd like a name."

"A name?"

"Your name."

The older man leaned forward. "Ewert Grens, detective superintendent. The rest of what I said at our last meeting was true—I work in the homicide unit in Stockholm, for the City Police, and Erik Wilson is my boss."

"Grens?"

"Yes."

"*You* gave the command to shoot Hoffmann? *You* are the police officer that both Erik and Hoffmann told me about?"

"Yes."

Sue Masterson examined him, seemed to look through him.

"Well, then, I understand better why a man of your age would head to Colombia and then here to act on behalf of Hoffmann. Ewert Grens. You're driven by the same engine as me."

I'm sitting here because it's my goddamn fault that Piet Hoffmann was forced to flee. You're sitting here because it's your damn fault that he's been forced to flee again. We're both here because guilt is a very powerful force.

At the airport in Bogotá, he'd bought a basic laptop that he kept in an equally basic shoulder bag. Now, he placed it on the table between them.

"The kill list. The one you couldn't get his name off of. Hoffmann has his own solution."

A flash drive in hand, which had been kept in the same envelope as the tickets to Washington. Grens poked it into the computer, opened the video file recorded by Hoffmann's satellite. The location coordinates had been edited away.

Masterson did exactly as Grens had one day earlier—stared at the image without being able to interpret it. "And this is . . . ?"

"A cage. You're looking at the top of it. And inside that cage sits the world's most wanted man."

Her eyes didn't leave the screen. "I don't understand."

"Hoffmann's private satellite. Don't ask me how. But he's monitoring the cage via computer."

Masterson stared deep into the picture, slowly beginning to make sense of it, looked neither at Grens nor anyone else in the site she'd so carefully secured.

"So that's Crouse?"

"According to Hoffmann. If you trust him."

She sat in silence. For a long time.

"Our mutual friend' solution, to get himself off that kill list. involves freeing the man inside that cage."

And she swallowed her forgotten doughnut in two bites while nodding, which meant he should proceed.

"Windows of time. Those gaps where the satellites can't cover every moment. Holes. Hoffmann wants to know when they occur and where. I'm going to be giving you some coordinates. And he wants to know without having to say why."

She looked at him in surprise. He understood what she was thinking.

"No, chief—*not those coordinates.* Not the cage—that's his life insurance, and he's not giving those up. This applies to another place. A spot in the Caribbean."

Grens handed her a handwritten note with the long rows of numbers. She looked at it without taking in what it really was; for the moment it was meaningless. However, what did matter was someone sitting in front of her claiming he was acting on behalf of a man who'd located the site of Crouse's captivity. Everything inside her was screaming—she should call for backup, take him in, here and now. But she didn't. It wouldn't help—he didn't know where the cage was. No matter how hard they squeezed Grens during interrogation, it wouldn't matter. The death sentence was her fault. But—if the line she was balancing on held, carried her all the way, she'd be able to discharge her debt, make sure the informant went free—the only person outside of the PRC guerrillas with any knowledge of where the Speaker of the House was right now.

"I have contacts at the NGA—the National Geospatial-Intelligence Agency. We cooperate on several projects. I can get an appointment for you with a person who'll give you what you want—the timetable for these satellite orbits. And who will understand that this meeting never took place. You, in turn, will have to prepare yourself for another cup of coffee here in exactly . . ." She looked at the clock ticking on the wall. ". . . three hours and seventeen minutes. Then you'll have a half hour—they don't close until ten."

She touched the piece of paper with the list of numbers on it. *Now I'm committing treason. In their eyes. Now I'm stepping over the line.* But surely helping two of your own can never be considered betraying your country? Giving them the chance to survive? And if she *didn't* do this? It would mean ensuring that Hoffmann—the only man who knew where Crouse was besides his kidnappers—took that knowledge with him to his grave.

"Detective Grens—are we done?"

"We're done as far as these timelines. He can figure out the holes himself from that, apparently."

Masterson had, without being aware of it, folded the handwritten note into smaller and smaller squares until it was impossible to fold anymore. Now she unfolded it again, handed it back. "Exactly what is he going to do?"

"I don't know."

She looked at him—he really didn't know. He too had *chosen* to trust Hoffmann.

"However, I know that he has another requirement."

"Another one?"

"He wants you, and only you, to vouch for eight battle-hardened and incorruptible men, one of whom should be a helicopter pilot with access to a vehicle. And in seventy-two hours he wants them in a town called Calamar, in a small church close to something called the Registraduría Municipal del Estado Civil. Fully equipped for movement over water as well as in the jungle, for night combat, for a raid. And he wants to be in command of them for the entire length of the operation, twelve hours."

Masterson had so far let her cold coffee stand. Now she drank, mostly to give herself something to do while she considered what the older man, who'd managed to win the trust of both Erik and Hoffmann, had just requested and for what purpose. And if she, the DEA chief, could handle it.

Eight incorruptibles in a country where corruption ruled. There was only one option. The Crouse Force. Soldiers trained by the DEA in the United States, their salaries paid by the DEA.

"And after that, Detective Grens? After I've contacted the head of the Crouse Force and asked him to assist a faceless, nameless undercover agent and regain the reputation he lost during the hostage attack? What *else* will the man you represent want?"

"A simple fishing boat. Moored at a pier just south of Caño de Loro on an island called Isla Tierra Bomba. And under a tarp on that fishing boat, four 12-gauge shotgun shells, loaded with the thinnest carbon fibers cut in ten two-meter-long pieces. And a waterproof MP3 player with a recording of a Russian submarine blowing air underwater and then after one minute of silence opening its torpedo hatches. And a small container with Cesium-137. *After that,* he's satisfied."

She observed him. They observed each other. Cesium-137—a radioactive substance. They both knew that—the meeting was over. Because if she didn't ask, she wouldn't receive any answer that forced her to say no.

They stood up simultaneously, while Grens searched his inside jacket pocket, for another small piece of paper with numbers on it. "My unregistered phone number. If you need to reach me. We have . . . shared interests."

She took it, then grabbed a pen from her bag and napkin from the table next to them, wrote down her own number, and handed it to Grens. She smiled. "Bowling, right?"

"What?"

"Bowling. Our shared interest."

Ewert Grens smiled too. "Just what I was thinking."

Same table. The same kind of coffee and doughnut, he thought he'd try one for himself now.

Grens had spent three hours wandering around a neighborhood he wouldn't mind living in, admiring Georgetown's lovely houses, drinking lemon-flavored mineral water in some hole in the wall, attempting an American accent—which he'd never dared before—with passersby and waiters and whoever happened to be standing next to him at the bar.

When he returned to the café for a second time this evening, the owner nodded in recognition and started to grind up some Colombian coffee beans before Grens even had time to order.

At exactly 9:30 p.m. a young man walked in. Khaki shorts and a white shirt, dark hair that was pasted with sweat to his forehead. He didn't check his surroundings, didn't search, he knew where he was going. Determined steps toward the table where an older, Swedish detective was drinking his evening coffee.

"You wanted to see me, sir."

"Sit down."

"I'd rather not be seen here with you, sir. I only came here to give you this."

Another flash drive on the table. Grens was getting used to it.

"If you don't sit, our meeting is going to look exactly like you don't want it to. I've ordered some damn good coffee. You don't need to drink it if you don't want to. But you need to sit here for fifteen minutes. Then you can go."

Sweat dripped from his forehead. His eyes. His way of moving. The young man was extremely scared.

"And no need for the sirs. We need to be able to talk to each other. So this can seem normal."

The young man sat down and stared down at the table, uncertain, vacillating.

"Talk. You have to. About whatever you want. And you'd better smile too."

Grens waited while the terrified man raised his eyes, collected himself.

"Eddy. I work as a satellite operator—at the National Geospatial-Intelligence Agency. The NGA. A lot of people confuse us with the NSA. I'm one of four responsible for surveilling Colombia."

"Good. Now drink your coffee." The detective superintendent pushed the tall mug, filled to the brim, across the table and closer to the young man, who was clearing his throat.

"From what I understood, Sue Masterson says this has to do with Speaker Crouse? That this could help Speaker Crouse? That one of the DEA's undercover agents needs data in their efforts to locate him?" The sweaty young man searched Grens's face, perhaps for the first time. Searching for confirmation. Grens nodded.

"Exactly."

"Speaker Crouse visits us often at the NGA. He sits next to me, takes part in the surveillance himself. He's the only one who really calls me Eddy. A good man. I'm doing this for his sake—giving information to a foreign national, risking my future." He didn't care about the coffee. But the flash drive—he held on to it tight. "This has everything you asked for. The number of satellites—level of classification: Top Secret. Time windows worldwide—level of classification: Cosmic Top Secret Atomal. The specific location of a single long window where the satellites don't overlap, starting at 00:37:01 going through 00:40:00. Exactly three minutes. I'm giving this to you now. Because Sue Masterson asked me to do it. And I trust her."

His knuckles had turned white as he looked at his wristwatch, and then decided to let go of the flash drive, leave it lying on the table.

"It's been fifteen minutes." The chair scraped violently on the floor as he stood up. "We never met." And then he left. Without turning around, and with steps just as determined as when he entered.

Grens waited until that sweaty back passed through the door and disappeared into the cool darkness of the Georgetown evening. Before he stretched his arm across the table and grabbed both the flash drive and the untouched coffee—it would be a pity to let something so delicious go to waste.

SIXTEEN CAMERAS PLACED throughout the stairwell, near the door, in the garage, and in a circle on the street with a radius of three hundred meters—all equipped with motion sensors. Nothing moved in light or darkness without being documented by those cameras. Piet Hoffmann quickly fast forwarded through the night's recordings. Nothing deviated from the norm. Made a copy to an external hard drive—in case he ever needed to look through it again.

So quiet. Alone in the temporary kitchen of a two-bedroom apartment. Zofia in one bedroom, the boys in another, both doors open, a chorus of heavy breathing in different tempos.

He got up with the dawn, the same ritual every morning since his visit to the hostage and to the coordinates programmed into a private satellite—it was getting lighter over the jungle, he could see the cage, and the rest of the prison camp that hid and guarded Speaker of the House Timothy D. Crouse. The icon at the top right side of the screen was dubbed CAGE. He double-clicked and input the twelve-keystroke password, numbers, uppercase and lowercase letters, a semicolon, in the middle of it all a few digital snow crystals. And when that was approved he pressed his right thumb against a new box, which was waiting for his print.

Two seconds. Then the program and the transmission opened.

From something gray was emerging the black—or actually deep green, but still in that faint light and with limited resolution the nuances were devoured and lost—and he began to see other newly awake people moving around down there, a day about to begin. It was impossible to understand who and why, but that wasn't his goal—he wanted to ensure that the thirteen-centimeter-long satellite kept capturing that yellow spot with a little black dot in it, that the cage that held the world's most talked-about man, a man a nation started a war for, and whose geographical location they did not know, was still standing. His ticket out still existed.

Hoffmann stretched his back and walked over to Zofia, so beautiful sleeping with open arms, safe despite the chaos. To the boys, both of whom were sleeping on their left side, but with their pillows and heads in different directions. One week. That was how long she promised to wait here. Under lockdown in the safe house he'd spent a couple of years turning into a fully monitored and secure bunker.

A kiss on Hugo's forehead and his eldest son woke up, mumbled something, then turned around and continued breathing slowly. A cup of coffee at the kitchen sink, and he returned to the computer screen, and to the camp now painted in brighter colors as the sun hurried up.

That's when his phone rang. His Colombian mobile phone, a single ring, and he responded immediately, because his family needed their sleep.

"Yes?"

"Peter? You're awake."

El Mestizo. His voice was full of energy. He was feeling good, almost beaming.

"I'll pick you up in twenty minutes. We have an assignment."

"What is it?"

"I'll tell you when we get there. Wear what you usually wear."

Standard equipment. Radom, hunting knife, Mini-Uzi.

"In nineteen minutes, Peter. Outside your house."

El Mestizo hung up. Nineteen minutes. That usually meant ten. Hoffmann rushed down the stairs with packed bag in hand, toward the garage and his car. At this time of day, no traffic, he should be able to make it.

Northeast Cali, just over four kilometers from the apartment in the poverty-stricken Comuna 6 to the middle-class neighborhood Los Guayacanes in Comuna 5. A truck blocked one intersection and forced him to back up several hundred meters, a few vegetable carts rolled into the middle of the street, but otherwise the streets were just as empty as he'd hoped. Eight minutes. And he was standing outside an empty house with its blinds rolled down, waiting.

He had a plan to continue living—and his former employers, who once waited for his information, were now waiting to take his life. But he *had* to keep going. To keep El Mestizo from becoming suspicious and turning into another life-threatening enemy. A little while longer. Until this was over. Until they could do what Zofia had demanded and what they both wanted, to get out of here.

"Morning, Peter." El Mestizo had stopped almost at his feet. And looked just as alert as his voice had sounded.

"Good morning." Hoffmann climbed into the car and waited for El Mestizo to start driving. But he didn't. He looked toward the house, pointed.

"It looks dark."

"They're sleeping."

"A teacher? And two young schoolboys?"

"A couple more hours. You forget how it is? I guess it's been a long time since you were in school, Johnny."

El Mestizo smiled, he was in that kind of mood, and started driving. A total of four times over their three-hour trip Hoffmann asked about their assignment, what and where, and every time was met by silence. Until he didn't have to ask anymore. Until they passed Cartago and approached an iron gate with a tight grid and arrow-shaped tips that pointed to the sky. Until they rolled into a courtyard with spraying fountains and fiery red flowers in clay pots on marble floors.

Then, while they sat in the car just a few steps from fan-shaped stone stairs and a railing with round ivory knobs, El Mestizo grabbed Hoffmann's arm, not hard, not threateningly, more like he wanted to create a moment of unusual and unexpected closeness.

"I know you don't like this. We might have to threaten that same kid today. If we do, Peter, we do it because we have to. Because her father made a decision. Because he chose not to pay. Do you understand?" El Mestizo's hand stayed there, just below Hoffmann's elbow. "Whatever we think, Peter, we gotta do what we gotta do. But it won't happen today. Toyas is as dumb as a post, but he loves his girl like I love my girl, and if he pays, the little girl keeps on playing. She's useful in a negotiation, and we'll go home with the money the guerrillas have already waited too long for."

"Only a negotation?"

"Yes."

Hoffmann knew, like last time, that he was going too far. That by questioning his boss he was risking his own safety. But sometimes you do what you have to do.

"And nothing is going to happen to the girl?"

El Mestizo lingered, as if he hadn't yet decided if he needed to draw a line.

"Peter, what's so hard to understand? Now listen to me—nothing is going to happen to the girl."

They got out. And at the same time the hacienda's massive door opened and the owner stepped out, a gun tucked inside his black, tight-fitting trousers, his arm in a sling, and this time an additional bodyguard just a few meters away. Not more, just one—an indication that this was someone who didn't think spilling blood was good for business.

"Señor Toyas? Good morning!" El Mestizo clapped and laughed as he walked toward the entrance, that giggle again. Hoffmann was careful to always position himself, like a human shield, between the man he was protecting and the bodyguard. All the way up to the veranda with its beautiful bulging plants and golden chairs and its shiny marble table. El Mestizo stopped a few steps from Toyas and didn't offer his hand, he wasn't invited.

"Your debt, Toyas. One ton of cocaine. I'm here to collect on it. Twenty-five-hundred dollars per kilo for the first half and twenty-three-hundred per kilo for the second. That comes to two million four-hundred thousand dollars. Plus some interest. So we'll say . . . two and a half million dollars, even?"

El Mestizo leaned closer and stared, just like he always did, into the debtor's eyes. Stared. But nothing. Because Toyas didn't meet his gaze. The man with the deep furrows in his cheeks and shiny white teeth stared hard everywhere except at El Mestizo. Not because he was afraid—but to show his contempt.

"I don't owe a fucking thing. As I explained to you the last time you were here. Right?"

"And I explained to you that it wasn't *my* problem. I don't give a shit if you hid the money in your father's scrotum or put it up your mother's pussy, it's still *your* fucking problem."

His long hair, bluntly cut, swayed along with the dangling fringe of the suede jacket. Libardo Toyas looked like he did last time. Argued like he did last time.

"One of your people squealed. What I ordered never reached its final destination. And like I said, I don't negotiate with the ass."

El Mestizo couldn't lean any closer. So he pushed his neck and chin forward, and because he was the significantly taller of the two, his breath soaked Toyas's forehead. And at the same time—just as fast, just as unexpectedly as usual—he pulled out his gun and pressed it against Toyas's right temple. "You ordered and bought through me. So you talk to and pay me."

Now he turned—his revolver still pressed against Toyas's temple—first to the bodyguard to show he'd better not try anything, then toward Hoffmann.

"Peter, you go get . . . ummm, what was her name again . . . Mirja. Little Mirja!" And then back to Toyas, his breath now on his cheeks, as El Mestizo bent down slightly. "And here's where we get to my little problem, Toyas. If I kill you, I get no money. So I have to solve this in another way—I have to kill your family. One member at a time."

Hoffmann stood there, motionless, remembering the last visit. A little girl, slightly younger than his boys, turning into a beautiful statue, a scene like a mock execution.

"Peter?" El Mestizo nodded toward the house.

It won't happen today. Toyas is as dumb as a post, but he loves his girl like I love my girl.

"Peter? Do it now!"

In the kitchen. That's where Hoffmann found her. She had climbed up on the kitchen island, was sitting there in a yellow dress overlooking the sink and stove. She'd pushed away the knives and cutting boards to make room for three meticulously dressed dolls—he wasn't quite sure but it looked like the dolls were baking something, rolling out dough.

If he pays, the little girl keeps on playing.

She never saw him coming, not until he'd slipped behind her and grabbed hold of her, lifting her and carrying her out of the kitchen. She protested, but less when he turned around and grabbed her three dolls. Then she didn't fight as much, and he didn't have to keep his hand as tightly across her mouth.

"Mirja?" El Mestizo stood exactly where Hoffmann had left him, on the veranda and with a gun pressed to Toyas's head. "Little Mirja, do you recognize your Uncle Johnny?"

Now she screamed. "Daddy!" Dropped her dolls, tore at Hoffmann's arms, sobbing.

El Mestizo reached for her with his free hand, toward Hoffmann, stroking her cheek.

"Toyas? What do you say? Pay? Or the girl?"

Libardo Toyas didn't answer. Or, he did—by spitting at El Mestizo, hitting his shoulder, that was his answer.

"Very well, Toyas. It's your decision. Peter? Drop the girl."

Hoffmann put her down gently on the floor, now a statue again. But a statue that moved, ran. Not away—as she should—but toward her father and his hand. Just as El Mestizo expected. And then everything happened fast—again. Suddenly he had his .357 Magnum against her forehead.

"Little Mirja. Do you remember this? You do? Good. Very good. Cuz now we're going to play a game again. You and me. Do you remember? You close your eyes, and we'll have a little fun with your daddy."

She looked at her father, her small head tilted gently upward. Libardo Toyas shook with rage and humiliation but nodded first toward his bodyguard to remain calm while his daughter was threatened, and then smiled as best he could at her. She smiled back weakly and did as she was told, her eyes closed.

"Toyas, you stupid fucking ass. Listen to me now! You should have paid up ten days ago. But you didn't. So I came here and gave you a final warning. And you didn't pay then either."

The little girl cried and Hoffmann wanted to lift her up in his arms again, carry her to the kitchen and to the games she'd been playing. He'd do that soon. When the debtor agreed to pay.

"You got to know how this works, Toyas."

El Mestizo did like last time, pulled the gun across the girl's head, stopped and sank it down into her hair.

"I've got my orders and you've got yours. Only you can stop this. *Now.*"

"So says a little half-breed?" The drug baron had Hoffmann's gun pointed at himself and his youngest daughter had a gun to her head, but he was so convinced that he was right, that he knew exactly where the line was, how this kind of extortion ritual worked. "A half-breed who stands there hiding behind his tiny, little European *chica compañera*?" A wide and narrow sneer on his very taut lips.

"Oh, yes, that's right—you didn't much like it when I called you that? Mestizo. Half-breed. The harvest of a white man's seed. But that's what you are! So shoot. Shoot for fuck's sake! We both know this is theater. That your leadership would never allow . . ."

Time froze.

Hoffmann knew immediately that this moment would continue on and on and on.

When El Mestizo shot.

When the bullet pierced her head.

When Toyas held her tight and she hung there in her father's hand like a little rag doll, lifeless.

HE COULDN'T REALLY remember. How he got here, what happened in the hours between seeing a little girl hanging like a doll in her father's arms, to this, a dirty staircase overlooking a marketplace where adults sold their wares: vegetables and fruit and fish and meat and bags and belts. And where children sold death.

Piet Hoffmann was sitting on that staircase. A cup of hot coffee in his hand. He'd been sitting there for a while now, watching the boys waiting at the wooden tables at the edge of the market. Their role in this society was simple, to be given a gun and an address, tools that lacked any human dignity—in this world all value derived from drugs and the money drugs made.

He probably remembered a few houses. And the white silhouette of a cathedral. And a sign that read CARTAGO. He remembered that, and he remembered the rag doll. And he—with those extinguished eyes surrounding him, pursuing him, demanding his attention—sank into the car and instead of driving them both to the south to Cali, he told El Mestizo he had an errand in Medellín. He was going to climb out and go find another car. And when he did, he drove the two hundred and fifty kilometers north. Here. To a strange place he'd only visited once before.

He looked at the boys, most were around the same age as his own boys, who they resembled and yet didn't at all. And he wondered how a man could be two people. How could the man who shot a little girl be the same man he and Zofia spent the afternoon with at one of his two haciendas—where El Mestizo lived with his slightly older woman. The hacienda lay west of Cali, and El Mestizo met them at the gate with Zaneta and their daughter—relaxed, humorous. He had acted lovingly, had seemed almost gentle when he dealt with his daughter and Hoffmann's boys. Vulnerable, soft. That love was no facade. He had kissed Rasmus's and Hugo's foreheads, lifted them up, suddenly took all three out into the sun for a little while, which turned into an hour then two hours, to the stables, that's where they'd gone, said hello to the horses while Piet and Zofia and Zaneta had talked and laughed and drank the dark Colombian rum Hoffmann had become so fond of. And when El Mestizo returned, the three children around him, he had seemed so happy. Hoffmann had never seen that in his eyes, not before or since. Genuine happiness.

And then that moment. That child hanging motionless in her father's arms.

The same man who had taken a child's life had treated his own child, and Hoffmann's children, and the children of the prostitutes in the brothel, with sincere affection. The same man had rebuilt one of the rooms in the brothel, took out the bed with red sheets and the cabinet filled with dildos and gagballs, and moved in a playpen, high chairs, boxes of toys intended only for children, and hired an older woman to take care of them and put aside money for a daycare in a brothel.

The same man.

His cup was empty. Hoffmann stood up and saw in one of the stalls at the edge of the market a kind of small restaurant, and on its only table, he was sure of it, stood a pot of coffee.

He walked over slowly. Getting closer to the waiting boys, who were sitting on the other side of the small restaurant. The children El Mestizo had worked with for almost twenty years. He must have seen hundreds pass through. A hundred dollars had become two hundred, but otherwise, the same mission. Provide one of them with a revolver. Show them which direction to point the gun. Wait while the task is performed. Much like you'd train a dog. And for the boys, Hoffmann knew it was so, that for them it all began right here, right now. Their career. Because soon they'd be working for those who were even bigger. Sicario. Assassin. I'll pay you—and you kill for me. Hoffmann took a cup of coffee, and it was as strong as he feared. Murderer. He was one himself. But there was a difference. Surely, there were murderers and then there were murderers? Another kind of murderer who shot people to survive? He'd done so. He'd killed inside that Swedish prison to survive. And he had killed here to survive. Was that right? Was a murderer always a murderer? Was Hoffmann just another version of the boys who got their two hundred dollars, who bought a gift for their mothers on the way home without ever thinking of the death itself? Was there any difference when Hoffmann killed because he had no choice? Did they have any choice? Had El Mestizo just moved the limits a little—a child, a woman, whoever else—until it was reduced to an assignment? Like these kids I'm staring at. When will I readjust *my* limit? How long have I been here if I too am prepared to shoot a girl holding her father's hand?

Home. We're on our way home.

Hoffmann had seen how El Mestizo kept track of all the boys he'd hired. His employer and mark drank a little too much one evening and opened up one of the safes in the brothel in order to proudly present the contents of his bank accounts, here and in Panama, then his more morbid accounts, explained what the code really meant. Page after page. First name. Last name. The number of shootings. The number of bullets used per shooting. And last, almost every time one kept going for several years, a death date.

Hoffmann put the empty cup down on the table, thanked the kind woman, and took a few steps out of the tight passageway in order to see better.

All of you sitting there waiting. In ten years, you'll be dead. According to the only statistic that exists. Three of you will be killed by the person you were supposed to kill. Two of you will be killed by someone avenging the death of a relative. Two of you will snort yourselves to death, two will overdose, three will die because you know too much, three will fall victim to police bullets meant to clear you off the streets. And those few of you who manage to live until your twentieth year—you'll die when the pride of being selected ends and the shame of completing your mission sets in. That's how it works. The drug trade, profit, opens the doors to the darkest rooms of humanity

He'd just started walking toward them again, this time he'd go all the way, when a woman got there before him. Well-dressed, long, dark hair put up carefully in a knot, mid-thirties. She stood out as she made her way through the aisles and between the crowded stalls, there was something about her way of moving through a crowd. Someone who had power. Hoffmann saw her approaching the boys. They flocked around her until she picked one of them, a tall kid with a baseball cap on backward, *bang bang, he shot me down*, and the others, disappointed, returned to their seats to continue waiting, *bang bang, I hit the ground.*

Hoffmann waited until she was finished, until both she and the recipient of her mission had disappeared. Then he approached. And stopped the pack before they had time to gather around him, pointed to one, beckoning him forward.

"Do you recognize me?"

"You're Mestizo's friend."

Hoffmann nodded toward the stairs he'd been sitting on, that's where they were had been, that's where they went. "Take a seat."

The twelve-year-old boy in the too-big T-shirt looked toward his colleagues and competitors and seemed surprised at how clearly you could see them from here.

"Camilo, right? And you're waiting for an assignment?"

"Every day. What do you have?"

Authority. Hoffmann recalled how he'd noticed that last time. This twelve-year-old boy—who was neither tall nor dangerous-looking—radiated a self-control that was similar to the woman he'd just seen, ruling over life.

"How many times have you . . . ?"

"Twenty-five, señor."

A dignity that was obvious. Nevertheless, he was stretching to make himself taller.

"So what's my mission? I'm fast, señor. And use two bullets." His right hand shaped like a gun, he raised it and fired it against his own chest and his own forehead.

"When you get paid. For a mission. What do you do with the money?"

"That's my business."

"If you want this mission, you'll answer."

Camilo, child and professional killer, observed Hoffmann as if sizing him up, then shrugged.

"One hundred to my mother. The rest in my tin box."

"And what's the money for?"

"Savings."

"Saving it? For what?"

"For later."

Hoffmann turned toward the market, which seethed with life, the opposite of this boy's daily life. *Saving it? For later? You're going to die soon, like you all do, don't you know that?*

"Okay. Here's your mission."

A tool that had a function. He was someone. For a moment. And his eyes shone as Hoffmann pulled a small stack of hundred-dollar bills out of his jacket.

"Your salary." Hoffmann held out two of them, and the boy took them with an outstretched hand, waiting for more.

"I need the gun."

"You're not getting one today."

"A pistol. That works just as well."

"Nothing."

Camilo looked at his employer, put his hands around his own neck and pretended to squeeze.

"Nothing? Should I . . . do you . . . should I kill with my hands?"

"No killing."

"I don't understand."

Hoffmann took two more hundred-dollar bills from the crumpled heap. "Your mission is to *not* shoot anyone today. You should go home now. And this time, you get paid double. You give your mother two hundred dollars. Put two hundred into your tin box. And don't come back here for a month."

"A month? I can't."

"That's what you're getting the money for. Paid double. To *not* shoot anyone for a month."

Camilo sat on the gritty landing staring into space, not at the crowds that were always there, nor did he hear the drone of voices that were always there. He'd just been offered four hundred dollars for doing nothing. An insane fortune in his world. He should have laughed, cheered, danced. But he didn't.

"Those ones over there—they're just beginners." He stood up from the stone steps, pointing to the benches and the side where Hoffmann knew the youngest sat. "And those ones . . ." He shifted his skinny arm slightly, pointed to some slightly older kids at the far end of the other side of the bench. ". . . they've shot a few. But I . . ." He pounded his hand into his own chest now. ". . . I am a sicario."

The little boy stood there pounding his own chest. The most rotten of rotten societies, and he was proud. It was about money. But also about something much bigger, confirmation. Identity. In his world, this child *was* a sicario. And now that was being taken away by offering him money to *not* kill. Hoffmann watched the boy weighing, considering this strange question. Could it be worth *more* to not take lives?

When the drug trade shows you its ugliest face. When a human life is worth a few hundred dollars and the executioners are ten, twelve years old. When profit is boiled down to child sicarios, this is a symptom of the blackest darkness.

"Okay." The thin boy nodded, reached out his hand, and took the money. "I'll stay home. For one month."

Then he left. Camilo, twenty-five.

How many will you kill before someone kills you?

And after he was swallowed by the throng of the market, becoming part of that drone, Hoffmann left too. Headed to his car. It was time to go home.

SUE MASTERSON WALKED straight into a wall of heat. Built of stagnant and clinging humidity. At this time of year she collided with it every time she passed by the uniformed guards and took her first step out the door after a long day of work at DEA headquarters. Life in Washington. All those hours indoors in cool, air-conditioned offices made you forget you were living in a subtropical climate. Sweat was already dripping from her hairline after just a few hundred feet. But she liked it. Or rather, she needed it, as if to illustrate that her hours of living under constant threat surrounded by those ever-present bodyguards were over now. Every day, no matter the season, she walked to and from her home on Reservoir Road in Georgetown, forty-five minutes very early in the morning and late in the afternoon in her own world, but simultaneously in the other one as well, time spent clearing her thoughts, breathing in chaos and breathing out peace.

She had just purchased her usual bottle of water in the corner store—run by a married couple who no longer cared if their quarrels and nagging took place in front of their customers—when her phone rang. Her *private* phone. An incoming call from a number she didn't recognize. No. Too soon. She'd barely started walking, wasn't even close to feeling like she was on her way. This was her personal time, and she put the phone back into the purse she hung over her shoulders like a knapsack. The phone rang again. The same number.

"Yes?" She sounded annoyed, she knew that. That was the point.

"Good afternoon, Sue."

But maybe the voice on the other end hadn't understood that. Or didn't care.

"Or should I say good evening? I don't know what's up or down anymore, I can't make sense of the time change. Or at least my body can't."

A man's voice. Not American.

"This is your friend from the café yesterday."

Grens. The Swedish detective.

"Good evening. I thought we were done talking. That you would already have left?"

"I changed my mind—yesterday was so nice. I'm sitting here again. Same place, same table. Saxby's Coffee, on Thirty-Fifth Street. I've been here most of the day. Or, to be frank, *all* day. They have a great breakfast. And a great lunch. Did you know that?"

"No. I didn't."

"The coffee. The doughnuts. Sue, you have no idea what you're missing."

"Did you call to go through their menu?"

The rattle of a porcelain cup on a porcelain plate. And someone who slurped and swallowed, unabashedly.

"I'd like to see you again. Buy you a cup of coffee."

Masterson continued walking through the wall of heat and moisture. He sounded sober. Heavily accented English, but she was sure she understood him correctly. "Sorry, detective. I'm headed home for a cold shower."

"In that case, can I ask you to consider going home just a little later today?"

Restless traffic. Red light. And her bottle of water was already empty.

"For the last time, Grens—"

"I'd really prefer if you came here, Sue. Bowling, you know."

"Bowling?"

"Our shared interest. We never really finished talking about it."

He was sitting in the same place, a cup of black coffee and a plate of crumbs from at least three kinds of pastries. In front of her chair sat a larger cup, and he'd placed a dish on top of it to keep the beverage from cooling. He even pulled out her chair.

"Here you go, madam."

She lingered, not completely comfortable sitting down yet. This was beginning to resemble a courtship. "I don't know, Detective Grens, maybe you misunderstood something, but just to be on the safe side, I'm happily single."

He gestured to the chair. And smiled at her, a little too long. "Sit down, Chief Masterson. I certainly understand why Erik Wilson fell for you, and I'm single too, and a real catch—a body like a twenty-year-old and the same clothes as yesterday—but this isn't about me or you. It's about our child."

The limping, overweight man waited patiently. "Also—I already fell in love with a colleague once, and it didn't turn out so well. So even though I am completely irresistible, I'm going to have to ask you to keep this professional."

He smiled again, and she sat down, lifted up the dish, and felt the heat rise. Half a cup. "Grens? I'm just as accustomed to meaningless interrogations as you. Just as tired of them. So . . . you wanted something? My shower awaits."

"Yes. I want you to do something for me. For our mutual friend."

"I already did yesterday—made sure he got those timing glitches. I've been working on it most of the day—the carbon fiber and submarine sounds, the eight soldiers didn't take long, but the Cesium-137 did. I've exposed myself to risks so great you couldn't possibly understand them. But now I'm done."

"One more thing."

She put down the cup she'd just lifted up.

"One more . . . what?"

"Something you have to do. For him to survive. So they *both* survive—the one in the jungle, too. Then you'll be finished."

Her gaze was sharp, intense, searching—the kind of look Anni used to get when he went too far. He missed it every day.

"In that case, Grens—why the hell didn't you mention it yesterday?"

He met that look. And it pierced him.

"Because I wanted you to become a part of this. You needed time to think and feel. Sleep on it. Wake up with it. If I said yesterday what I'm about to say now, and you protested and said no, then we never would have gotten as far as we did."

She was silent for a long time. "At least you're honest."

"When it's to my advantage."

The waiter had slipped up behind them without either of them noticing, now he cleared the plates and asked if they wanted anything else.

Grens nodded. "I want a coffee. Black like before. And a very small brownie."

"They all come in the same size."

"Then one of those." The detective superintendent winked at Masterson. "Body of a twenty-year-old. One pastry at a time."

Then he leaned across the table. "Our friend needs our help with one more thing. A formal arrangement with the White House."

"Arrangement?"

"He'll free the speaker and deliver him unharmed—and you remove his name from the kill list. In a signed document."

The sound of glass shattering as a tray fell to the floor, and a waiter turning red as he peeked out from the kitchen. Masterson's gaze had gone from sharp to ice cold. Just like Anni's when he'd taken things another step too far.

"And who exactly do you suggest present this proposal?"

"I assume that the head of the DEA has training in negotiation? She might be a good candidate for the job."

"This is not about negotiating with criminal elements."

"Then how would you describe the White House's treatment of Hoffmann?"

LATE EVENING. SHE'D been asked to wait patiently for a spot in their busy schedules. She'd passed the time walking home, taking a long shower, eating some food, and walking slowly here. Now Masterson entered the White House once more, walked over its echoing floors and under its high but weighty ceilings. And it was just like before, but this time there were *two* guards. Secret Service, black uniform with a golden badge on the chest, and new instructions—one guard in front of her and one behind, what had been courtesy was now open suspicion.

Survivor's guilt. That's what they called it—the guilt you feel when you've failed to save someone from dying, while you yourself survive. And which forced her to say yes to Superintendent Grens's unreasonable request, to book a meeting about the one thing she was emphatically instructed to stay away from.

Unlike on her last visit, the door to the vice president's office was now closed. Masterson knocked, received a *come in*, and nodded to the woman sitting behind the oak desk, whose red glasses, rather than hanging across her chest, now sat like two extra eyes on top of her head. The chief of staff was in the other corner of the white sofa and had shoved the overstuffed pillows onto the floor. But he was just as friendly as last time, greeting her with a quick wink.

"Vice President Thompson. Chief of Staff Perry. I appreciate you meeting with me on such short notice."

The fireplace was quiet, but something seemed to move in the large gold-framed mirror as she passed. Masterson wondered who, then realized it was her own shoulder. She stopped between the blue-and-green armchairs the directors of the CIA and FBI had sat in last time, waited to be asked to sit down.

"Chief Masterson?" The vice president's cheeks were as red as her neck as she spoke. "What part of 'cut off all contact with your informant if you want to keep your job' did you find so hard to understand?"

"I understood. And I did not contact him or allow him to contact me."

"That's not exactly what I understood from the request you made through my secretary. You said this was *critical to our operation in Colombia* and concerned *national security*."

Masterson continued to stand. They were not going to invite her to sit down. "However, I have received information via a third party."

"Isn't that the same thing?"

"It's not at all the same thing. That's precisely why you'll see that I haven't acted against your wishes" She paused. "I've been asked to share a proposal with you."

No one responded, no one said a word.

Masterson had difficulty facing both of them at the same time and decided to try to meet the vice president's fathomless gaze. "I'm here representing a person in Colombia who knows the exact location where Crouse is being held. This person wanted me to present this deal to you. And—if you agree to it—it would mean Crouse would be freed and his life would be spared."

"Our policy is clear on this subject. The US does not negotiate with criminals."

"And as *I've* said before, the individual I'm negotiating for was employed by us, paid by us, working for us." She took the flash drive from her trouser pocket, stepped forward, and put it in the middle of the vice president's desk. "I want you to look at this—it's the cage Crouse is sitting in right now. This person knows where it's hidden and how to free the speaker."

"Sorry, Sue. You're not going to convince either of us of that."

"He has the *exact* location. But in order to free Crouse, he wants a written agreement. When he's returned the speaker to us alive—he wants the Seven of Hearts crossed off the kill list. A life for a life."

"No." This time it was the chief of staff who answered. "Even if what you say is true—we explained this to you, Sue. International confidence."

"If the speaker, one of the world's most powerful people, is freed and credits US expertise publicly, that would *inspire* confidence."

"No." Now it was the vice president's turn. "Negotiating with a criminal is inconceivable, as is the idea that one man—alone—could locate and free a hostage, then escort him to safety."

"You know what he's capable of."

"What we know is what you've told us."

"He's the best informant I've worked with as DEA chief. He's infiltrated the furthest into the organization responsible for Crouse's kidnapping. And, according to him, he knows where the speaker is. But that's also his lifeline. He'll *never* reveal that without compensation. If he's taken off the kill list, he'll deliver the speaker. What have you got to lose? Besides face?"

Vice President Elena Thompson and Chief of Staff Daniel Perry walked side by side. Marched really—left legs forward, then right legs forward at the same time. It was unconscious. The hour was late, they were both tired, annoyed, and in a hurry to make their way through the hallway and down the stairs to the bottom floor. To the Situation Room. The most mythical room in the entire West Wing—not because of its appearance or size, it was no more than five thousand square feet when all its sections were combined, but because of the operations that had been initiated there, developed, worked through to their most minuscule details. It was still furnished with the conference table JFK had chosen. The only room at this time of day and with so little notice that had the right equipment and staff. Sue Masterson had been asked to wait in the vice president's office, and it was unclear if she should continue standing. No one had offered her a seat.

"Is the object still in place?"

The operator nodded hello and continued the slow, monotonous work he and his two other colleagues on the night shift were responsible for—observing the large screen on the wall across from the conference table's short side. "Yes, ma'am. The object is still there. Now we're waiting for the next one."

The plasma screen showed a satellite image of a city that despite the late hour was nowhere near going to bed. Every window in the hotel was lit. Brothels in a row. A street in a city called Cali. The next target in the Final War on Drugs. A building that belonged to a man called El Mestizo, who for the past twenty-four hours had been inside it. The Jack of Hearts. But it wasn't enough. They were now waiting for his constant companion and bodyguard, El Sueco, to get there too. The Seven of Hearts. Next time they crossed names off the kill list, it would be after yet another double attack.

"We know their pattern—this is where they usually meet. I'm pretty sure we're close now."

"And this?" The chief of staff pointed to another large screen. "Can we borrow it for a few minutes?"

"That's intended for Delta Force helmet cameras—but it won't be used until the strike."

"Good. Can you play this?" Perry handed the flash drive to the operator, who inserted it into a computer, turned on the screen, and handed over a remote control.

"Works just like your remote at home. Play is there, pause there, and the volume is this button."

A satellite image, just like the one on the other screen. But the difference was that this showed absolutely nothing. Masterson had talked about the jungle and the mud and the roof of a cage. What they saw, however, was some green and some brown and a shade of gray, and something that looked like a small yellow spot. Blurry, out of focus, and barely moving film that could be anything. For twenty-five minutes. No matter how many times they moved the cursor back and forth.

"Do you have a minute?" The vice president put her hand on the operator's shoulder. "Can you help us to try to interpret this video?"

The operator blushed. The vice president had just put her hand on his shoulder. "Absolutely, ma'am." He watched the screen silently for a minute, then another minute. "That . . . is a jungle, Madam Vice President. Recorded from a satellite."

"That much we figured out. But this?" Vice President Thompson pointed to a yellow spot roughly in the center of the picture. And then, in the center of the yellow spot, a darker stain. "What do you make of that?"

The operator enlarged the image with a magnifying tool. "Sorry, ma'am . . . can't help you much there, because the image is already enlarged as much as possible. That spot, the yellow one with the little black that you pointed out, the pixels break down immediately when I start working with it."

"But what do you see? You interpret images every day." Her hand still lay there on his shoulder.

"It could be, and now I'm guessing really, ma'am . . . a very small house. A hovel. Or a large stone." Then he leaned even closer to the big screen. "And it could be . . . this may sound a bit odd, but it could be—with a little imagination—a bamboo ceiling. And this could be the bamboo shaped like a grid. Or that might just be an optical illusion. From the pixelation."

"And the dark spot in the center of the yellow?"

"With a little, no, with a lot of imagination it could be a man. But like I said—you do end up with optical illusions when the picture quality is that bad. Or, maybe a condor sitting on a fallen rubber tree? Or some kind of large monkey standing on a stump? Or . . . well, you see what I mean."

"We do. It's a desperate lie. Thank you."

Thompson and Perry waited in silence while the operator moved his focus to the second screen, his main task—to monitor the next target, a brothel owned by the Jack of Hearts, patiently waiting for the arrival of the Seven of Hearts, the signal for a double-attack.

They spoke quietly to each other. "Sue Masterson has had contact with an individual we forbade her to contact."

They both knew it.

"And she's obviously prepared to say anything."

The DEA chief was done.

"She just lost her job."

The meaningless flash drive was back in the vice president's hand, and she was about to head back when Perry stopped her. "Wait. Sue Masterson has to be removed. And it pains me, Elena, you know that. I liked her, still like her. She has to go, but not yet. We have to keep things as peaceful as possible while we're in the middle of this—and that's the opposite of a former high-level official speaking out in anger. Media focus has to be maintained so we have public support for this operation."

His voice was even quieter now. "So now we go to her. Open the door and smile. Explain that we're going along with this—that we're prepared to negotiate. That if the Seven of Hearts—who we're now concerned about for entirely different reasons—can get ahold of Crouse and bring him all the way here, then they have their deal."

Perry nodded toward the screen that showed a street lined with brothels in western Cali. "That will be enough to keep her calm—she has no idea that we're about to liquidate him. And she'll never know how it happened. Just that one day he disappeared off her radar."

EWERT GRENS HAD stayed at Saxby's Coffee until the owner kindly asked him to drink up and go, because they were closing for the evening, and—he added with a wink—they were running low on sweets and Colombian coffee. Their new customer had gone through their supplies. Two streets away, on Thirty-Seventh, the detective found a bar and sat down at a table in the farthest corner. With his eyes on the room, he drank a bottle of water and ate an omelet with black olives and feta. Several customers in varying degrees of intoxication placed their empty glasses on his table and tried to initiate a conversation with the solitary guest, who was not one of the regulars—but they tired of it when he shrugged and spoke Swedish to them.

Besides that, it was just waiting. For an answer. After playing his last card in a hand that was all about hearts. His highest card. If Sue Masterson got a no from the White House, then there were no more solutions. Hoffmann would remain on a kill list that was getting methodically shorter day by day.

It was half an hour after midnight when he finally saw her through the large window, headed toward this ever darker, ever noisier room. She opened the door, searched among the tables, and approached his.

Grens tried to read her face. Neutral. Professional. She'd played her hand and revealed nothing. He wouldn't want to be interrogated by her. A man's life hung in the balance, his survival dependent on what she was about to say.

He did the same. Waved at her, pulled out a vacant seat, revealed nothing. Despite the pressure in his chest, something wanted out. "A beer?"

"No, thanks."

"Something stronger?"

"I'm just here to give you an answer. Then I'm headed home."

He poured the last of his water into his own glass, drank half of it. "Well?"

Still neutral. If it had been a negative answer, she might be drawing this out because it cost too much to communicate it. If it was positive, she was dragging this out because she could. "Come on!"

"Grens?"

"Yes?"

"You just got your clearance."

"In writing?"

"The proposal was accepted in full. Verbally. That's how formal agreements work in that kind of place. Crouse's life for Hoffmann's life."

Grens wanted to hug her, rose with his arms outstretched before thinking better of it. She'd already confused his eagerness with courtship once. He sat back and raised his glass in a kind of toast and explained that from now on he and Hoffmann promised to leave her alone. He waited while she walked toward the exit and entered the Washington night, then waved for the check and made a call from a phone he only used to communicate with a single subscriber.

They had their go-ahead. Hoffmann had his yes. He would be allowed to live.

PIET HOFFMANN FOLDED up the phone. Grens and Masterson had done their part. Now he had to do his.

He left his car in the garage near the temporary housing in Comuna 6, started walking the first lap around the block in the darkness. He always did at least one lap in each direction to make sure everything was as quiet as it seemed.

He should be happier, should be rejoicing silently. He had his yes. A life for a life. But this agreement, which meant everything to him just a day or two earlier, wasn't enough anymore.

A rag doll lay in the way.

First lap done. He changed direction, cutting through the darkness of a poor neighborhood with no street lighting. He followed the cameras' three-hundred-meter radius, the extended perimeter. And on the second lap he took note of two vehicles he hadn't seen there before, a car and a pickup, checked their registrations via his phone and continued walking when he saw that the owners had lived in this area for a long time. On his way to the front door, he stopped in front of camera 14, the one that sat a little higher up surveying the greater part of the entrance, and adjusted it a few degrees to the right, minimizing a blind spot he'd just discovered where the path to the garbage room crossed the path to what could be bicycle storage, but was mostly used to store old furniture and piles of worn tires.

Three flights up to an apartment as dark as night. They were asleep. He loved listening to them breathe. They were alive. They had no idea what it looked like when a little girl didn't quite fall to the ground because her father held on to her, desperately, without understanding.

He wanted to sit down at the kitchen table, try to understand. How he had to stick to his plan. The one that would give him and his family a chance. And which became even clearer the moment El Mestizo ended a child's life as part of an economic negotiation.

But there was no energy. He had always, always found the strength, but where was it? Here, among the ones he loved, he could let go of that vigilance, that constant searching, and he'd felt it as soon as he opened the door—when he deflated, shriveled, became nothing once the tension pushing him forward dissolved, his whole body lacking solidity. He slipped and lost his balance twice over the short distance to the bedroom, hit his elbow and forehead hard on the door frame, and fell into bed with his clothes on, huddled close to her warm, naked body, and fell asleep as soon as he put his arm around her.

And dreamed. About someone arguing about money who ended up with a big hole between his eyebrows, buried deep in a pit. About a child hired to take a life. About the hellish screams of a man as he tried to escape electricity and barbed wire. *And they all came back.* To him. They pursued him, hunted him. So he shot at them. Again. And again. Stabbed them with a knife, stabbed, stabbed, and they fell, but got up again, and continued running straight for him. He beat and beat, stabbed and slashed, they fell and got up, and he couldn't run anymore, his legs didn't work, and he slipped and lay on the ground as they got closer.

He woke up several times. Sweaty, with the sheets in a pile at his feet. The last time he fell asleep, he was with a rag doll—and she looked at him, talked to him, even though she had no head.

"Piet? Honey?"

He was awakened by Zofia sitting beside him on the bed, pulling on his arm. And crying. Because of the way he'd been screaming. And he held her and asked her to lie down again, told her it was nothing, just a nightmare, no more. He lay quietly next to her, his arm on her hip, until he was absolutely sure that she'd fallen asleep, rocked by her slow breaths.

He kissed her and walked into the dark kitchen—dawn light was still a long way off—turned on the lamp above the stove, since its light was the weakest.

It was late at night, and in sleep it had been able to reach him, grab hold of him. When he could no longer defend himself. Sometimes he dreamed about those first shootings in Colombia, mostly of the man and the woman he killed in the brothel during the first month of his employment, something he later realized was a test. Occasionally, he dreamed of the two inmates he shot at the Aspsås prison in Sweden in order to survive. But they were never like this.

He sat down at the kitchen table in front of a newspaper and spread out the crossword. She'd brought it with her from their house, which—like this cramped apartment—she'd never seen as their home, but still tried to relate to. The same crossword, which the other night had been unsolved, was now half complete, filled in with pencil.

She had clung to her father's arm, lifeless. And he had refused to let go of her, because if he did, he was letting go of her life.

Toyas made his living selling cocaine, he was supposed to pay. El Mestizo made his living protecting cocaine, he was the one who shot. But also the so-called El Sueco made his living this way, and even received a salary from *two* bosses due to cocaine. That was why he loaded the cargo into that vessel and then made sure it was seized. That was why he went into the hacienda's kitchen and fetched a five-year-old girl.

He created the conditions for that shot. He didn't shoot. But he didn't stop it either.

Hoffmann had gone past a limit and knew it would haunt his dreams for as long as he lived. That was his punishment. Every time he abandoned himself to sleep at night, he would be inviting her in, and she would hang there trying to reach him.

The handwritten piece of paper remained where he'd hidden it on his way out of the jungle chill—folded in the bottom of the leather holster of his knife, next to a typed note. He looked through the lines he'd already crossed off. ~~*Coordinates. Low Earth Orbit. Time window. Cesium-137.*~~ And those he still had to solve. *Prism bomb. Magnets sled.* And then he wrote a new line at the very bottom, where there was still a little room left.

Suitcase.

Zofia was right. They had to get out of here.

DAWN. AND THEY were still asleep. The ones who meant everything to him. Zofia. Hugo. Rasmus. Nothing, there was nothing without them. And he—he existed only through them.

They slept, but he couldn't. Thinking about a plan stood in his way.

The bedroom door creaked, bare feet over the creaking floor. Zofia. Her sleep-warm arms around him, two kisses on the neck. "What are you doing?"

"I'm thinking."

"At this hour?"

"I have to go soon." He took hold of her hands, kissed each of them twice. "You gave me a week, Zofia. I've spent two of those days. And I need a couple more. But when I get back, my death sentence will be over."

It wasn't far to his first stop. Half an hour in the car to one of Cali's southern suburbs, a bit past Jamundí. Alone in the car, with no armor, no protection, here his thoughts were what they were. The truth. The truth was that he wasn't nearly so sure of his ability to solve this as he tried to make Zofia believe. Did she believe him? He wasn't sure. Probably not. She knew him better than he did himself, could read in his voice and movements what he himself wasn't even aware of. But she said nothing, showed nothing, understood as well as he did that sharing her anxiety was useless right now.

He stopped near a small industrial building on a carelessly paved plot. A printing company, until recently filing for bankruptcy. This was how these mobila labs were placed, a few months' rent in a temporarily vacant premises, while the owner looked for a new tenant. This version of Carlos, the name all chemists shared, Hoffmann had met twice before, but never here, his base for the last month, and for only one more month, when operations would be moved again to a similar facility in Medellín. Constantly requested, one of the few in Colombia who converted cocaine into an odor-free product in the shape of suitcases.

Hoffmann knocked on the door. It would take a few minutes for the chemist to check all the cameras and decide whether or not to let in his guest.

They greeted each other, not warmly, they didn't know each other—just a simple handshake. He looked sharp, wore suits under his white coat, spoke carefully with an attempt at Madrid Spanish—he'd gotten the idea that Europe was somehow better, finer. And as he showed Hoffmann in, he smacked his lips self-importantly, an imitation of someone fancy, expensive.

An industrial building with basically just the one large room hidden behind pulled-down blinds. There was rough, winding pipe all over, which used to transport water to the printing machines, but was now dormant and sealed off—in some places in Colombia water was a commodity that attracted thieves. Therefore, a row of filled water jugs had been set up next to rows of rusty gas bottles and blue chemical containers. They marked a path to the gas stove, which was placed on a simple wooden board and two wooden trestles.

The bag lay completely finished in the only other room, a kitchenette converted to a drying room. A roaring, singing fan blowing cold air.

"Three kilos. Just as ordered."

"Pure cocaine?"

"As clean as I've seen."

"How much?"

"Ninety-four, ninety-six."

Which you actually called 100 percent. Because that was as pure as it got. He'd visited labs all across Colombia and never been shown anything more than ninety-six. And if he compared it with the severely diluted version he'd sold on the Swedish streets, it was in another universe of quality. The content of a gram becomes more and more diluted the closer you get to the street level, and at the same time—more and more expensive. Three kilos in the form of a brown leather suitcase identical to those he'd seen in the jungle.

Hoffmann held out the all-important envelope. "Your fee."

"And you know how to convert it?"

"Yes."

"Be very, very careful. Otherwise you'll burn it. And then it ends up useless. There's no reversing it. Then you've ruined it."

As he returned to the car and put the shiny suitcase in the trunk, he counted. Kilos, percent, euros, grams, kronor. On the streets of Sweden they bought and sold 30 percent cocaine. From three kilos of 96 percent you'd get at least nine kilograms blended. Seventy-five euros per gram meant 75,000 euros per kilo, so nearly 6.3 million kronor in that suitcase.

EL MESTIZO'S PRIVATE parking spot had been converted a few years ago into two spots—one spot, slightly larger, for the brothel owner himself, harboring his black Mercedes G-Wagen, and one for the man the owner knew as Peter Haraldsson. Hoffmann parked there and got out, careful to making sure the trunk of his car was locked, and that he bore no traces of the cocaine lab in an industrial building that he'd just visited. Sometimes the distinctive odor of permanganate and sulfuric acid crept into textiles and lingered, the process of either killing it or bringing it back to life, disappearing a thick paste into leather or conjuring it from leather, and you could end up revealing more than you wanted to. So on his way here, he'd stopped at the small motel, changed clothes, and showered. If El Mestizo were to figure out his right-hand man was planning a journey, hopefully it wouldn't be through any carelessness on Piet's part.

Hoffmann took a deep breath at the entrance, about to enter the morning meeting in the brothel's large hall, where they always began their work—and today had to feel just like any other day. Because he assumed it was El Mestizo he needed to worry about, El Mestizo who was the first obstacle he'd have to overcome tomorrow in order to implement his plan. Hoffmann opened the front door but stopped again, turned around, and then turned once more, trying to shake off the odd feeling of being watched.

He had no idea that was exactly what was happening.

The lone operator in the White House Situation Room leaned closer to the big plasma screen on the wall on the conference table's short side.

There. The car was parked. The man had left it. *That was him*. Their second target, which they'd been patiently waiting for. The two terrorists were often together, traveled together or separately to the same places, and therefore were a good prospect for a double attack.

He dialed the number he'd been instructed to call. "Sir? I think it's time. The companion just arrived."

A stifled yawn. The operator looked at the clock—a monotonous twelve-hour shift was just ending. And he'd been watching that screen and the building in the middle of it for almost every moment of that shift. A satellite image linked and encrypted a few miles away by another operator in what they called the Crouse Room at the NGA, an image that was forwarded here, to a room that held much more power for further analysis and decision-making. A picture of a street with a line of brothels. The next target. He'd guarded it every moment with one exception—late last night when the vice president and chief of staff suddenly showed up, asking how things were going, and if he could help them use a second screen, which wasn't needed until the actual attack. Not needed until now.

He grabbed the remote and turned on the second screen and was met by a collage of images assembled from cameras worn on the helmets of four Delta Force soldiers. All of whom were stationed in the brothel on the other side of the street.

Morning in the brothel's main hall. A calm that appeared only during the hours between the night's last and the morning's first customers. At least on the surface.

But inside the two people about to meet over a coffee at the owner's table, there was churning, thumping, aggressive anxiety. It was most evident in El Mestizo. Not because today was the day when all the security officers on his payroll were allowed their free monthly visits to the brothel and they sometimes got a little too intrusive and prying. That didn't bother him at all. The anxiety was there because in the past few days, he'd come to suspect a change in his right-hand man without really being able to put his finger on it, what others might call paranoia was for him healthy suspicion, and he'd felt, had known, since that fucking kill list went public that Peter had been affected and, though he couldn't yet articulate it, was now on his way somewhere. And so he did what he always did when paranoia took hold—he ran around with a wet cleaning rag in hand, rubbing down the bar, wiping the tables, arranging the chairs. He'd even vacuumed the entire expanse of the floor—because he, though not necessarily the brothel, needed it.

The entrance door opened, and Hoffmann walked down the stairs, through the great hall, and sat down at the owner's table, in the chair that had almost become his own, said hello without receiving an answer. He recognized the mood. Johnny for some reason was as anxious as him. And because Johnny wouldn't talk about it, never did until it was too late, there was no choice but to wait it out—Hoffmann had learned it was pointless to nag, stress, this was just how his boss worked, cleaning up and arranging were his way of trying to relax and thereby getting at the root of what was bothering him. And at the moment, it was for the best. It gave Hoffmann more time to hide his own anxieties—which had to do with a suitcase, and a detective negotiating for his life, and making sure all of it happened without this man, who he'd finally come to hate, noticing.

Then Johnny came over. With sweeping arm movements, he swung his square body over to the owner's table. Set his coffee opposite Hoffmann, drank, and hissed in irritation afterward, the chair legs squeaked as he forcefully pushed it backward.

"Cold as ice. I'm gonna get more. You may as well look at this while I do." El Mestizo pulled a pink envelope out of the loose front pocket of his blazer. "Do you remember the other day? Before we went to Medellín and Rodriguez? I'd just received this, was about to show you. When the liquor delivery interrupted us."

He took out a handful of photographs, which he placed in a semicircle on the table before heading to the polished bar and coffee machine behind it. He returned with a hot cup and downed it in a single gulp, staring at Piet Hoffmann with his head sunk and his eyes hooded. "And, yes, I forgot about it afterward. But with everything that's happened since then, I thought you might like to see. How things went down. In fucking Amsterdam."

It was as if El Mestizo was trying to ease the tension they both felt. Bring them together. By talking about the shared triumph portrayed in these five photographs. Enlarged, in color, and of decent quality.

It took a moment to interpret them. A floor, that was easy enough to see. And there were people lying on it, all on their backs. A different person in each image.

It got worse. All of them were missing a head. And also, arms. And their leather vests lay on the floor, but a bit away. Like paper dolls. Hoffmann's first thought. He remembered his little sister, how she used to play with little cutout paper figures, which came in the weeklies their mother subscribed to. Bodies and clothing that could be joined to make whole people.

There *were* heads and arms. When he looked through the pictures. Placed on the other side of those sprawling leather vests—HELLS ANGELS HOLLAND on the back and AMSTERDAM on the left breast—that's where the rest of the body parts lay, neatly lined up. The magnification revealed straight, professional cuts. Each severed head had an entrance wound through the temple and an exit wound through the back of the head.

"So it wasn't you. Or anyone else here." Laughter. That low-voiced chuckle.

El Mestizo studied the photographs, one by one, holding them close.

A motorcycle club in a European capital. Good customers, a long business relationship. Until a few months ago. Until three hundred kilos were sent with the usual routine—divided into three containers aboard three ships with three different ports as destinations. Rotterdam, Amsterdam, and Ostend in Belgium. Until the message. Until the Dutch contact person phoned up El Mestizo himself.

"The load is gone. All containers are missing."

"What the hell are you—"

"And no cargo, no payment."

El Mestizo hadn't laughed then. His anger had turned to fury and then to hate, as he started his own extensive investigation to figure out who should die.

And soon received an answer: Everything *had* been loaded on board. Three hundred kilos of cocaine *had* been packed into wooden boxes—just like every delivery. The contents and seal *had* verified that the boxes contained Arabica beans managed in collaboration with FNC, the National Federation of Coffee Growers of Colombia—just like every delivery.

"You pay. Or you die."

Another conversation with his contact. Who turned on him.

"So you want us to pay for three hundred kilos that never existed?"

"That's your problem."

"Then you're screwing us."

"My responsibility ends when I load the product, and it's left Colombian territory. You know that as well as I do. You have two weeks!"

El Mestizo had deepened his investigation—assuming now that one of his own had talked too much.

The cargo never arrived! And he hunted. *Some bastard's been talking!* And he threatened. *Who the fuck sold us out?* And he threatened to kill. *Who the hell knew about this—who doesn't want to live anymore?*

Three sea captains. Seven members of the PRC. And his right-hand man, El Sueco. That's who knew.

His paranoia escalated. For the first time in more than two years, he'd even questioned Hoffmann—who answered him as usual, with certainty and calm—the furthest thing from what he actually felt. He bore another secret much heavier than a missing cargo of three hundred kilos of cocaine.

"Peter . . . El Sueco . . . I don't know who the fuck you are anymore!"

"I'm the man who's got your back, the man you've chosen to trust, the man whose hands you put your life in."

He'd learned already. That a lie can't hold up against doubt. That he had to be who he wasn't, and fully. That you can only sell a lie if it's got enough truth in it.

"Yes, Peter. You stand there. But are you my friend—or my enemy?"

"If you think it's me . . ."

"It is you, you motherfucker, you've fucked me? Right? Right!"

Only a criminal can play a criminal.

". . . If you think that . . . shoot me." He met El Mestizo's eyes, thoughts, threats, hate. Outwardly strong, inwardly filled with doubt—if he really sees through me, if he digs beyond that lousy shipment, it's over. The life of an informant. To be unmasked is to die.

Then everything changed. The questions gave a different answer. A German Interpol police officer high up on the PRC's European payroll found out the police in Frankfurt had seized a large quantity of cocaine in a criminal lab that matched the samples El Mestizo sent, the synthetic DNA that the PRC's chemists inserted into each batch—its own unique DNA profile—so the shipment had left the ship and was there, on the other side of the Atlantic. The cargo had arrived.

El Mestizo contacted the leader of the bike gang. Who acted.

The execution of five rogue members—the photographs scattered across the owner's table showing headless and armless bodies—were a clear message about how much the gang valued their business relationship. While the German Interpol police officer received his bonus—his son's university education was financed. Not because it was of equal value to the information, but because it was crucial to know who you could trust in this business. And not trust.

"What do you say, Peter?" El Mestizo smiled. The anxiety seemed gone. Replaced by self-control, which felt good. "I want you to look closely at those pictures again, Peter, while I finish cleaning up here. And then I want you to tell me what you think." Back to the bar, back to polishing.

Now he was moving the drinking glasses from the sink to the rack dangling from the ceiling. And because he was a bit farther away, Piet almost shouted the question. "Think? About what?"

"About what happens to the people who betray me."

Chief of Staff Perry put his cell phone back into the inside pocket of his blazer, preparing to rush through the long corridors of power.

"Sir? I think it's time. The companion has just arrived."

It was time to strike two more from the list. But first, a brief stop at his desk, while looking around the office he was so fond of.

The day he stepped into the White House to begin his job as chief of staff, as the president's eyes and ears, was also his first time here, ever. He'd never met the people who worked here regardless of an election's outcome. Just like when he moved to DC—the first time he crossed a state border was in a moving van he drove from Denver through an America he still hadn't had time to discover.

A room with high ceilings, wooden floors, functional furniture. Clarity. And he had learned to appreciate that clarity. He'd be able to value its opposite.

He searched along the bookshelf-lined walls. To have the world at his disposal, be embraced by it, understand how he influenced it. Bookshelves—but no books. There were, however, plenty of folders of varying thicknesses, in bright colors, files, and piles of loose paper, all of it organized by paper size from right to left, estimates, bundles of national and international newspapers, more bundles of trade magazines, and, finally, the long line of storage boxes for digital copies, CDs, DVDs, flash drives—he was careful to copy each day's work before going home, constantly worried that electronics would fail and thoughts disappear.

Always know more than everyone else. Always make sure that others know he's the adviser with the answers they lack.

In the center of the middle shelf, he stored what was going on right now, so he'd see it when he sat down at his desk. Right now there were thirteen binders. Red hearts on each one. Under every heart—a symbol and a number. He pulled out two of them. The fourth and fifth targets: Jack of Hearts and Seven of Hearts.

The binders rested against one forearm as he walked out into the hallway, and it felt like he was carrying something much heavier than a few documents—a duality, he knew one of those targets shouldn't die. *A political decision. Nothing more.*

Perry passed other rooms that held power before arriving at the elevator and sliding the plastic ID card with his picture on it that gave full access to the White House. Less than eight years had passed—but the man staring into the camera looked so much younger than him.

The basement. He'd arrived. The last narrow hall that led to the Situation Room, and there they were—the vice president and director of the CIA on one side of JFK's table, the FBI director and a new face he'd never seen before on the other.

Perry offered the newcomer his hand. A man in his forties, in uniform. But he didn't look like they usually did, he was a little too short, his hair a bit too long—the authority was in his eyes, voice, and a hand, which deliberately didn't squeeze too hard.

"Welcome. I'm Daniel Perry, chief of staff."

"Thank you. I recognize you. Michael Cook—Delta Force commander."

"The front line in our fight against terrorism."

"That's our mission."

"When did you arrive?"

"First time . . . well, almost exactly twenty hours ago, when we positioned our squad. Since then I've alternated between the screens down here and some meetings in the area."

Perry already liked this man in uniform, who'd flown in from North Carolina and who wasn't even trying to pretend that this room, and what would soon be led from within it, was normal. "And Cook—any sleep?"

"Soon." The Delta Force commander smiled and turned toward the two huge screens on the wall. One showed a moving image from above, wide focus over a long row of hotel-like buildings—one had a flashing red arrow pointing at a swimming pool on a roof, currently empty. The same image—from a city called Cali in Colombia—which he'd seen yesterday while visiting this room with Vice President Thompson to look at a different satellite image for a different mission. Or the same, depending on how you looked at it. The second screen, the one they'd borrowed, was now divided into four equal fields—cameras mounted on helmets that were in constant motion, sequences that moved here and there. But you could see that all four were in a hotel—you occasionally glimpsed a double bed, a large mirror, a half-open door to a dull bathroom—and their cameras and thus their eyes were directed at the hotel across the street.

Perry checked the clock, which for lack of a better place was squeezed between the two screens.

08:51:10

Eight minutes and fifty seconds left.

Twenty-two bodies stuffed into the boss's office. Her office. And it wasn't built for it. With the window closed, the door closed, it got extremely stuffy. But this was the only place she trusted, which never leaked.

Sue Masterson stood in front of the wall facing the courtyard, which was covered by a full-color map of the United States, divided into twenty-one areas—the same number as her visitors. The twenty-one directors of the DEA's domestic field divisions. In each field there were several marked sites. If someone, despite the heat, were to count them, they'd have added up to a hundred and nine sites, each representing a hub of one of America's most active drug distributors—white points marked factories for converting cocaine into crack, black dots wholesale warehouses, green dots key personnel, yellow spots shipping agents. It was on these sorts of days, in these meetings, that her work—which sometimes felt like rolling a stone up a hill just to watch it roll down again, and again and again—felt meaningful. Preparing to crack down on nineteen domestic hubs simultaneously—smashing the second part of the chain, the ones who picked up where the South American producers left off, crushing the distribution of a Mexican cartel. Days when it all felt worth it.

She never spoke with her colleagues about it. She and Erik had discussed it now and then, spoken of the forbidden, that it was exactly this that people like them lived for—how the criminality they lived to stop, because it killed, was a prerequisite for their own lives.

Twenty-one faces in front of her and all starting to fade in this airless room. She could see they wanted to stand up, find some fresh air, stretch their legs, maybe smoke a cigarette. She wouldn't let them. Not yet. She was aware of what they whispered about her in the hallways, but she'd gotten this far because she'd learned not to care—she simply put the same demands on others that she put on herself. And she wanted to go through this one more time.

Masterson wanted to break down all one hundred and nine crackdowns into a single mission, that they could go through together, from a scout's first observations to the final consequences of the arrests. She'd chosen the San Francisco division and a warehouse in Fresno as an example and was about to be sucked into a flow chart of one of the strike teams when the ringing began. Even though all phones were supposed to be turned off, her orders. And it continued—three rings, four, five. Until she realized it was coming from her own pocket. Her private phone.

"Yes?"

"Are you alone, ma'am?"

It took a moment to identify the voice, it was no one she knew, but the few times they'd talked on the phone there'd been that same tone of stress, fear.

"I'm a bit busy right now. I'll call you back in half an hour."

"Well, ma'am, that will be . . . too late."

She looked up at twenty pairs of eyes focused on her. "One moment." And lowered the phone. "I know you all want a break. You can take it now."

The scraping of chairs as they all quickly got up before she changed her mind—she waited until they were all out, and closed the door. Then she raised the receiver again. "Yes?"

"Ma'am . . . This is Eddy. You asked me two days ago to help you, for Speaker Crouse's sake, to give information to a non-American. And told me to keep you informed if I saw, or thought I saw, a certain person."

"I remember."

"I believe I did."

A man she'd only met in what they called the Crouse Room. An NGA operator who lived for his work among those monitors, which received images from cameras in the Colombian skies—the country that produced the cocaine they were currently preparing a crackdown on here in the United States.

"And?" She waited for his voice, which was even weaker now.

"For the last few hours, we've had our satellite trained on a property in Cali. A hotel, I believe. Or maybe . . . a brothel. On a street lined with other brothels. On orders directly from the White House—we've been passing on these images. To the Situation Room, to be specific, and to another operator who's sitting there on behalf of the vice president. And about thirty minutes ago, that's how long I had to search for your private number, I understood that this individual—which I believe to be the special individual you asked me to find—went into that particular property."

Stressed-out breathing from the other end of the line. She remembered how he looked and sounded after passing on classified information about satellite gaps to the Swedish detective, how, even though—like her—he was acting based on what he believed was right, in his case to secure Speaker Crouse's freedom, in her case to keep someone she was responsible for alive, he nevertheless was ripped apart a little bit more by each new sentence.

"And just now I got orders to pass on even more images to that same White House operator. Four of them. From helmets on Delta Force soldiers who are preparing an attack. My job is to receive and encrypt them. This means that I also see the unencrypted feed. And what I saw were images through a window just across the street from the . . . *same* building."

Masterson put down the phone on her desk, as she did when she needed to think. As if she needed distance, to be left alone.

"Are you still there?"

"I'm here."

"Just one more thing—when I check those four image sources, I also see a clock. Posted at the right edge. A countdown. Right now it's at . . . four minutes and twenty seconds."

She stared at the telephone, which demanded an answer—should she warn the informant who was her responsibility and risk the lives of American soldiers? If she interfered with life and death in this way, was she any better than that group in the Vice President's office?

"Hello? Ma'am?"

Cali. Brothel. Jack of Hearts.

"Thank you, Eddy . . ."

The Seven of Hearts.

". . . you absolutely did the right thing by calling me."

Still this morning's strange anxiety. Hoffmann sat there, alone, at the owner's table in the empty brothel. A third cup of coffee, a glass of water, and five photographs that were supposed to be summed up, otherwise only silence. While El Mestizo continued to polish and clean, right now he was down behind the bar unscrewing the spout from an empty beer keg and screwing it back onto a newly filled one. And then tested to make sure it worked by filling up a glass and tasting it.

"Ahhh, for fuck's sake!" He threw the contents into the sink. "That beer's not even fit for a bunch of johns! Tapir piss. That's what it tastes like. And *old* tapir piss at that! I'm gonna have a talk with the people who brought us that shit. Later." Then he went back over to the owner's table to get the answer he wanted before they headed out on their first collection.

"Well—have you thought it through, Peter? What do you think about those lovely photographs? About what happens to the people who betray me?"

"What do I think? White bodies seem like a good ending to the story."

Five photos. The brightly colored parts. That was what took the longest time to make out. Naked, dismembered, Dutch torsos glistening pure white. Skin covered with a thick layer of cocaine. The message: money is not important, but trust is essential.

"I almost lost my trust in you, Peter. And the whole time it was these handsome devils." El Mestizo pointed to the five pictures with an index finger that smelled like beer. "But if you deceive me. Let me down. If you ever do that."

It was never quite clear what El Mestizo meant when he looked like that, his head bowed down, his neck prominent, his eyes glowing, while his mouth smiled weakly. "If you ever lose perspective, loyalty. You see how it'll turn out, right?"

If he was serious. If this was a game. He probably didn't know himself.

El Mestizo gathered the five photographs, put them back in the envelope. And at that moment they both heard it. The phone. In Piet's vest pocket.

Johnny stared at it and at Piet—he did not like being interrupted. Not even by someone who had no idea they were interrupting.

Hoffmann let it ring. But the ringing didn't stop. He took it out, read the display. *Her?*

He closed his hand around it, encapsulating it, and it continued to vibrate against his palm. A cautious glance at Johnny—the only one who could never know who was calling.

The woman who . . . broke off contact?

The ringing, the buzzing increased his irritation and cut through the space between them like a cold, sleek icicle on its way down. He'd tried to contact her so many times the past few days, needed to talk to her, needed her help, trying to figure out how to handle being put on a kill list that he shouldn't be on—but he couldn't do it here, now, with El Mestizo.

Then silence, finally. Hoffmann let out a deep breath. He was about to put the phone back in his vest pocket—when it rang again. Her, again. Twelve rings. Until he had to. Had to answer it. "Yes?"

"You see who it is?"

Sue Masterson. It *was* her. Her voice brusque, forced.

"Yes."

"The White House will be making a visit to that brothel in exactly one minute and forty seconds. Four customers."

The Situation Room.

Perry looked around. Five occupied and eight empty chairs around an oblong conference table. Room for thirteen. As many as the deck of hearts they were eliminating one by one.

He kept meeting the vice president's gaze. Or, maybe *she* kept seeking out *his*, as if she wanted to share a curious meeting they'd had about images of a cage in a jungle, which only the two of them knew about. Sue Masterson's desperate lie to save the man about to die on this screen—a lie they'd both seen through.

Complete silence. Aside from a monotonous, hollow, electronic voice that belonged to the numbers at the bottom of the image, a voice that was counting down for the people in this room and for those who found themselves in a cramped hotel in Cali.

"Sixty seconds."

Clenched, focused faces watched the two big screens on the White House walls. The CIA director and the Delta Force commander seemed slightly more interested in the screen divided into four equal squares—cameras attached to four elite soldiers' helmets, who were waiting, impatient, ready to be released.

"Forty-five seconds."

The vice president and FBI director focused their attention on the second screen, which showed a street in Cali waking up, hotels, or what were supposed to look like hotels, lined up block after block. One of them was marked with a flashing, red arrow—it belonged to a man named Johnny Sánchez, who was called El Mestizo and now the Jack of Hearts.

"Thirty seconds."

They'd slowly closed in on him over the last few days. A hunt that ended in the surveillance of three addresses—two haciendas, one on the east side and one on the west side of Cali, and a brothel in the middle of the city. A brothel that, after further reconnaissance, became their main target—since it was mostly deserted between seven and ten every morning, while their objective was on site.

"Fifteen seconds."

They'd waited. For the man who was often found in the company of the Jack of Hearts—then they could strike two names off their list simultaneously.

And then just over half an hour ago, a male matching the vague description they had of the Seven of Hearts parked a car outside the brothel, vigilantly scanned his surroundings, and started walking toward the entrance.

"Five, four, three, two, one . . . now."

The powerful people sitting at that table were now concentrated completely on only one of the monitors—the four soldiers, each with his own camera, moving from one side of the street to the other, getting in position outside two windows on the ground level at the far end of the brothel. Two soldiers, two cameras, at each window.

And now everything happened at the same time, like a pair of gymnasts united in movement. The two frames at the top of the screen, helmet cameras whose wearers broke windows at the same time. The two frames at the bottom of the screen, helmet cameras whose wearers simultaneously dislodged stun grenades from their belts and pulled out the pins, threw them into the room.

A bright, white light temporarily knocked out the picture, causing it to go dark before recalibrating. A heavy, roaring bang temporarily knocked out sound, muted the microphone before readjusting. And then. Another forty-seven seconds. Until everything would be over.

Five pairs of eyes followed two identical films playing side by side. The same movements at the same time, even though the elite soldiers broke into the large room through two different windows. Uniformed arms using the butts of their automatic weapons to clear away the debris, the sound of broken glass landing on the floor inside, a quiet plunk against the bare walls, the soldiers preparing their weapons for a melee. The two synchronized gymnasts again—ten meters apart from each other in reality and a few centimeters on the screen—throwing a stun grenade, crouching, and jumping inside. Two images bouncing in parallel as they landed softly in a large hall where nobody who'd been inside would be able see after that bright light or hear after their eardrums shattered.

The two soldiers stood up, synchronously. Each took a step forward, synchronously. They were met by a green laser and a muffled bang, synchronously. And both fell, forward. In their own arc. Until each frame was completely still, each head against the floor, one turned left, and the other just as quietly, turned right.

Eleven seconds.

They'd been shot. Two frames frozen. Because two helmet cameras lay at floor level, motionless, facing nothing.

The people in suits in an underground room in Washington, DC, exchanged hasty glances. Fear. That was how they looked at each other, as if they were themselves lying there, dead.

Two moving frames left. At the bottom of the screen. The two soldiers who'd been waiting behind each group leader jumped in now and landed in the same hall. And did it just as synchronously.

They both looked over at the bodies lying in front of them and their cameras followed—even though five sets of eyes were in a room thousands of miles away around JFK's conference table, still the details were clear. The face of one of them had a bullet hole in his forehead, round and smooth-edged, red blood slowly leaking out his life, probably a shot fired by a standing shooter. The other one had been hit in the nose, and you could see the exit hole from his helmet, a shooter must have been lying down and aiming up diagonally, no visible liquid, it was probably pooling in his helmet. The two remaining soldiers looked up at the same time, stepped over the lifeless bodies, and entered the room from opposite directions.

But from that point on, they didn't move synchronously. One was slightly more hunched, and both cameras registered glimpses of what could be a wood floor and several tables with chairs, some sort of raised area that looked like a small stage.

Then the images changed. First, on the left, the soldier who'd advanced the farthest into the dark approached a bar and crouched, crept forward, and jumped over it, landed on the other side, and suddenly it was as if everything around him began to move . . . *up*. Tables, chairs, walls. Or, perhaps he was moving. Or falling, headlong, *down*.

Perry glanced uneasily at the others, who were doing the same thing as him—trying to interpret what they were watching.

It really was as if the helmet camera had fallen down, into a hole. Until it stopped, hit hard, a muted sound as it all ceased. A trapdoor. And one camera continued sending a single image—of a rough wall.

Twenty-six seconds.

Then there was a frame at the bottom right, the last one moving, changing. Making its way through a narrow aisle and along a stage with a polished stripper pole in the middle of it, approaching the booths and tables and chairs, escorted by the light mounted on the front of his weapon. Until something passed by in the image, from above, as if dropping over the camera. And then the sound of someone struggling for air, gurgling, something pressed against the larynx and throat, as the whole picture lifted and the last Delta Force soldier was slowly strangled.

They all responded differently. The CIA and FBI directors stared straight ahead, into the screen. Unreachable. The vice president's gaze was locked, too, but on the table, confused, looking for something to hold on to, trying to start over, or hang on tight. The major general from Delta Force stood up near the big screen, silent, he'd run there as soon as the first two men had fallen. He seemed as if he wanted to jump into the picture, into South America and Colombia and Cali and the brothel where the Jack of Hearts and the Seven of Hearts should have been killed. Jump in and help, complete the attack on his own.

Perry checked the clock between the two screens, *forty-seven seconds*, it said on four different images from four cameras. Everything was completely still. Resting against the floor, walls, ceiling. Images sent by cameras attached to heads that no longer moved. But then one of them did. One of the soldiers lying on his stomach with his head tilted obliquely to the side.

A pair of boots appeared, the kind guerrillas wear, at the edge of the image. They grew larger, got nearer. Then a deep male voice who lifted the lifeless head the camera was sitting on, the murmur of words that were impossible to interpret, and then . . . total black. The camera had been shut off. The chief of staff, FBI director, CIA director, vice president, major general—they'd all seen it. And understood when those boots appeared in the next image, determined steps toward a helmet camera filming the ceiling because its owner was lying on his back. The same voice, the same mumbling, and a face covered by a protective mask and wearing noise-canceling headphones looked into the camera—at *them*—just before the camera was shut off.

Hoffmann held a lifeless head in his hands, whispered *no, not him* just as he had when he examined the last one and shut off his camera. Twenty-five, twenty-eight, maybe thirty, it was hard to tell the age of an extinguished person. Two left. One in the hole under the trapdoor and one below the window, who El Mestizo strangled with a piece of rope—Hoffmann walked over to that body now, turned off the third camera, pulling down his mask, checking like before. And whispered *maybe . . . yes, yes . . . he'll work well enough.*

"What the hell are you talking about?" El Mestizo had been waiting in the darkness, now he reached the first body and started dragging it toward the open trapdoor in order to push it into the black hole in front of the bar. "Peter?"

"Mmm?"

"You're mumbling!"

"It wasn't important."

"Then shut up. You know they're dead, right?"

A dull thud as the next body hit the ground far below, two men now lay eight meters below that wooden floor. And El Mestizo hurried to the next, the one Hoffmann had just approved.

"Wait."

His employer wasn't waiting. He pulled and tore at the body, which was heavier than the last one, it seemed as if the blood and body fluids increased the friction against the floor.

"Hey, I told you to wait." Hoffmann ran the last few steps, grabbed hold of El Mestizo's shoulder. "I wanna hang on to that body."

His employer indicated he didn't like having any fucking hands put on his shoulders. And he didn't stop, kept dragging it toward that deep hole with focused energy.

"I'm just putting them down there for a day or so, we've got staff and customers coming soon, and El Cavo can't clean up until after closing time."

Hoffmann followed after him, his hand still on that wide shoulder and a little on that thick dark hair, and he pressed even harder—he'd never even touched El Mestizo before. "No. I want it just like it is. Whole."

El Mestizo stopped. Equally surprised by the strange request as by the hand that wouldn't release him. "Why?"

"I can't tell you."

There is always a first time. Even for doubt. They'd made it through the shipment disappearing in the Netherlands, those photographs they'd just looked at. The second time is worse. Because it reminds you of the first time.

"Why?"

"You have your secrets; I have mine."

El Mestizo scrutinized him with those critical eyes that so many around him avoided and feared. That kind of doubt that didn't end, but rather grew, nourished by what was left unconfirmed. Hoffmann had seen it up close. But only directed at others.

"Okay. Okay. But in that case . . ." Now he was the one El Mestizo was appraising. And despite the fact that he abandoned the lifeless body and threw up his arms, the doubt still danced between them. ". . . you, Peter, are responsible for getting rid of it."

"I will."

El Mestizo was already on his way to the other window to retrieve the last body, dragging, cursing as one arm got stuck in a houseplant in the middle of the room, pulled and coaxed at it until it came loose, nudged eighty-five kilos down the hole, listened for the thud, and closed the trapdoor. He stood there, silent, drying sweat from his forehead with the back of his sleeve. Then he drew his revolver from its holster, spinning the barrel, fingers accustomed to rolling death between their tips.

"Who called?" He bent down, grabbed hold of the ring, and opened the door again. And pointed the loaded weapon, steadily, at Hoffmann. "You and I were sitting here, Peter, looking at some photos of people in Holland who tried to betray me. And some elite

American soldiers are looking in on us. And you're . . . *tipped off*? Warned? What kind of fucking contacts do you have, anyway?"

They'd just been targeted for death, just like the others on that thirteen-name list. But the man standing on the floor of a brothel, pointing a gun at the one he'd just survived it all with, didn't think like that. He lived in violence, by violence. So used to people dying, to the fact that he too would die like that, that he thought that was the way life worked. But suspicion, paranoia, fear of being betrayed—those he had never really become accustomed to.

"Johnny, the gun—what the hell are you doing?"

"Somebody warned you! And I want to know who!"

Two and a half years at his side. It had been Hoffmann's job to protect this man, and he'd done such a good job that trust had slowly started to build.

This time he'd had just one minute and forty seconds. They'd grabbed the automatic weapons Hoffmann kept in a secret compartment he'd had built into the bar. They'd picked up the masks and noise-canceling headphones from a hidden compartment under the stage. They'd positioned themselves so they'd had a good view of the respective windows and looked away when the stun grenades exploded.

Two and a half years. And it didn't matter. Doubts easily hollowed out any painstakingly built trust.

"Who?"

"Why does it matter?"

"Who the fuck knew my brothel was about to be attacked by American soldiers?" El Mestizo cocked his gun. "Answer me, goddammit!"

Hoffmann hated him. He did. And knew exactly when all his sympathy for the man he was informing on had ceased. The moment he left a five-year-old girl hanging like a rag doll in her father's arms. So now, with a gun pointed at him, he felt so much more than fear. Frustration. That's what he felt. Amid all the hatred, whatever admiration was there had also shifted. El Mestizo didn't just like violence, didn't just work with it—he used it intelligently.

Capably. That was the best word Hoffmann could think of. They'd just fought for their lives, and he'd used one shot, one single shot, and killed the other with a noose. Terribly capable. And thus a formidable enemy.

"Johnny, they weren't warning *me*. Somebody warned *us*. That's what you pay for. And now you're threatening me for doing my job?"

"Just fucking answer me!" The cocked gun. The index finger on the trigger.

"I've respected your sources, Johnny, the ones you wanted to keep secret."

If I answer wrong. I'm sure of it. Johnny, who is now only El Mestizo, will fire that shot.

"And now I need you to respect mine. Do you have a problem with that?"

"Stop talking shit! *I want to know who!* Delta Force, that's the best they have! So whoever warned you is an American! A very powerful fucking American! And damn few high-ranking Americans know about secret Delta Force operations! That call, that information, means you're a snitch, a fucking informant!"

His index finger. Turning white. The slightest pull—the hammer would snap forward, the spark would unite, an explosion would propel the bullet.

"For the last time—*who*? Convince me of your loyalty, Peter! This was exactly what we were talking about over those Dutch photographs, this is how it ends for people I can't trust!"

Either he believes in me. And lowers the weapon. Or he thinks I am what I really am, an informant, a snitch, his most dangerous enemy, who he let get closer than anyone else ever had.

"Johnny, look at me. If that phone call—which saved *both* our lives—was tantamount to being exposed as an informant, why would I have warned you? I could have killed you. And handed myself over to them, the Americans, because I'm their man. Right?"

The finger. Whitening.

"Why, Johnny, why would I *choose* to take part in a gun battle that might end my own life—those weren't fucking pretend guns they came in here with—why would I *choose* to risk dying, why would I *choose* to take the lives of my own people?"

They looked at each other, very close, breaths met and mingled.

"And why, Johnny, would I be attacked by my own? Why would my own people put me on a kill list and then try to do just that, kill me?"

And they did it through this lie—a double lie.

"So my answer, Johnny, remains the same. You can point that at me as long as you want. You have your secrets, I have mine. I respect your confidential sources, you respect mine."

The finger lacked color. Until now. Its healthy red color rushed back. As he pressed even harder. All the way.

The shot ricocheted, echoed, cried out. El Mestizo had let off the shot right next to Piet's left ear, near the temple. And Hoffmann remained standing there because he had to. Even though his legs wanted to run. Or sink, or lie down.

"And my sources, Johnny, seem to be quite a bit better than yours. Right?"

Now the gun was cocked again, the click that meant the calm before the explosion.

"And that's why, Johnny . . ." As they scrutinized each other, while a lie was tested. ". . . we're standing here, alive."

Then he loosened his finger and lowered his weapon.

THE CAR JUST fit beneath the slanted red concrete stairs that constituted the first steps toward an unobtrusive entrance. A building like the apartment buildings in the Stockholm suburbs. Oblong concrete. Nine stories high. The kind of building he grew up in.

Hoffmann turned off the engine, waited in the driver's seat.

But this was no apartment building. He wasn't in Stockholm, not at home, where they wanted and needed to go. This was evening in Bogotá. And what reminded him of a Swedish apartment building was actually the Hospital Universitario San Ignacio.

During the last stretch, passing by Cerros de Monserrate and the side road between Circunvalar and Carrera 7, his passenger had started to move, sliding both down and to the side at each new turn. Hoffmann had eased up on the pedal, slowing until he was absolutely sure no one would be falling out of their seats. Now his companion was sitting there peacefully again. His hat tilted far down over his blue, puffy face. A beautiful silk scarf around his bruised neck. New clothes—a light suit over a white dress shirt had replaced his camouflage uniform—and quite a bit of alcohol had been splashed here and there. A very drunk man, sleeping deeply, on his way home after a night out. If the authorities were to stop him, ask to take a look in his car, the trunk would be the first place they'd go. A gentleman reeking of alcohol and clearly visible was therefore much less of a risk. Hoffmann loosened the thin nylon cord he'd fastened around his passenger's chest to keep him sitting up properly, then cut the wire he'd tied around his waist and knees—it was important to keep the legs from flapping back and forth, lifeless legs that had yet to develop rigor mortis were so unruly.

The digital clock on the far left of the dashboard didn't actually tick, of course. Yet he seemed to hear it anyway, monotonously counting down time he would never get back. Ten to eleven. He was early. And while he waited, his thoughts caught up with him.

I was one phone call away from death. Erik Wilson, Ewert Grens, El Mestizo—they all keep talking about a slow war. But the kill list is getting shorter every day, and this morning my name was supposed to be crossed off. I survived. And next time? If I find myself somewhere else and maybe with Zofia? With Rasmus, with Hugo?

Over there. The side entrance. It was opening now, a raspy squeaking sound came through the car's rolled-down window, and soon another, the scrape of a gurney with small wheels rolling sluggishly over uneven pavement.

"Benedicto."

He was wearing a porter's uniform, which was unusual. But he moved as slowly as usual, and smiled as widely. "Peter. It's been a while."

Peter Haraldsson had been here before, but only in the company of El Mestizo, after other late evenings when El Cavo had been too far away and bodies needed to disappear quickly. Hoffmann stepped out of the car and they shook hands, and Benedicto, his hand still in Hoffmann's, leaned forward and peered into the car.

"So my job got a ride here today?" The morgue attendant smiled as broadly as before, expecting a clever reply about death, some banter, that was how they usually talked over corpses neither of them cared about. That's how they managed their own fear—laughing at it, minimizing it.

"Sorry, not today, Benedicto."

The body in the passenger seat didn't mean anything to him, a man he'd never seen before, a voice he'd never heard. But it represented his own death. The one that had been scheduled and attempted just a few hours before, and which he was only now starting to absorb.

They'd decided he should die. So maybe to avoid it, he'd have to do just that. Again.

Benedicto rolled the gurney toward the car's passenger side, gleaming, rattling metal. Hoffmann grabbed the sitting body's shoulders, while the morgue attendant held his feet, and they both lifted, moved, then dropped it.

That could have been my body on that fucking gurney.

Covered by the dark patches of livor mortis, blood no longer circulating, just turning into black clumps. Joints stiffening, muscle tissue forever locked into place.

But you, who tried to take my life, are lying here instead.

They walked on either side of the gurney, steering it to the side entrance. Sometimes he envisioned his own death, Zofia's death, Rasmus's and Hugo's deaths, sometimes he tried to imagine it as a way of getting used to it, preparing for it, of dealing with his fears. That's how you protect yourself. His fear of death drove him, forcing him to act, function, survive.

A man who has everything to lose is at his most dangerous. Not the opposite, which was what many thought. A man without fear becomes careless, negligent, can be surprised, caught. Unlike the man who *can't* lose, who has everything to lose.

"El Mestizo?" Benedicto opened the hospital's side entrance, and they rolled the gurney through a gray, desolate corridor.

"He's not with me today."

"Give him my regards."

The gurney just barely fit into the elevator, two floors down, a small jerk as they stopped.

A new corridor, equally desolate, and a strong, distinctive smell as they opened the heavy door to the morgue. Education. That's what these donated bodies would be used for. Teaching materials to be dissected. Benedicto had once demonstrated for them, theatrically, how it happened—students begin with a finger, then a hand, then an arm, gradually facing death. The professors and medical students, without being aware of it, were helping out by maiming those who needed to disappear bit by bit.

White tiles on the walls. White tiles on the floor, but in slightly smaller squares. Cold fluorescent light coming from tubes on the ceiling. Stainless steel divided into rectangular compartments, room for three in each row, eighty by fifty centimeters, all numbered.

Thirty-nine refrigerators. Twenty-two occupied. Seventeen vacant—and it was one of those that Benedicto unlocked.

They held on tightly to each end as they moved the metal stand the body rested on from the gurney to compartment 31. Benedicto rolled it inside along long rails, locked the door, and tied a thin plastic cord around the handle, the identification documents were already completed.

It was around this time they usually started talking about compensation. Once the body was in place. Hoffmann pulled out a white envelope for the morgue attendant.

"This time I don't want it to disappear."

"Excuse me?"

"I want to keep him here. Whole. *In case* I have to pick him up again."

"Damn, Peter, you never mentioned that."

"I'm mentioning it now."

"That, my friend, will cost you a helluva lot more. It's one thing to roll out the wrong corpse for tomorrow's med students. But moving him around in here, from slot to slot, avoiding my colleagues . . . I'll have to come here every night. That's a two-hour bus ride."

Hoffmann didn't have much time. And besides, he realized the attendant's argument was reasonable. Benedicto wasn't one to squabble about money just because he could.

"A helluva lot more? Okay. You get everything that's in that envelope right now—the same as what you always get. And the same amount every week until I pick him up. Or until I tell you to get rid of it."

The short, slender man in the oversize white uniform held the envelope, flipped through it, as if weighing it in the air between them. Then stuffed it into a breast pocket with the hospital's blue logo on it. "Okay."

Afterward, there was just the smell. It followed him down the corridor, shadowed him closely as he exited into fresh air, sat down beside him in the motionless car. Hoffmann pushed an arm to his face and sank his nose into the shirt fabric. Yes, that's where it lingered. Embracing the cotton fibers of his clothes. The smell of death.

He turned the key, started the engine. But turned it off again. It had been a long day. He'd gone from a carefully prepared attack through the basement windows of a sleepy brothel to a locked refrigerator this evening in an empty morgue. But it had also taken care of the very last row on one of the two pieces of paper he kept folded at the bottom of his knife's leather holster.

The one written by hand on toilet paper. And which he unfolded now.

~~Coordinates~~
~~Low Earth Orbit~~
~~Time window~~
~~Cesium-137~~
Prism bomb
Magnets sled
~~Suitcase~~

Things were moving in the right direction—down the road that would lead them home, to living, to surviving. But there was room for one more item. In case conditions changed. A single word. If the direction of the road changed.

The pen was in the glove compartment. He wrote the word at the bottom.

Body

He knew, of course. Always alone. Trust only yourself.

HE HAD DRIVEN through the night, heading directly east from the morgue, southeast from Bogotá to the province of Guaviare, and the little town of Calamar. From the dead man who constituted his backup plan—if conditions changed—to the main plan, the rescue, the exchange of a life for a life with the US government.

And he hated the feeling, the loneliness, the darkness monotonously knocking against the window, refusing to leave him alone. It sucked the marrow out of him. It was the only thing he feared. Dying no longer frightened him, but living alone did.

"Hello."

"Hello."

He'd called her, of course. Woke her. He knew what she looked like groggily groping for the phone. And it never gave him a bad conscience—unlike him, she fell asleep the moment they finished talking, even when she was in a temporary shelter without any clear reference points. She was a rock.

"Where are you?"

"Far away."

"Where, Piet?"

"It's better that you don't know where. A place where I'm going to take back our lives."

Tonight she sounded harder. As she sometimes did in her very own way, Zofia-soft and Zofia-hard, at the same time.

"I hope you do. Because I love you, want to live with you, you know that. But you also know that even *if* you do, I'm still going. Do you really understand that, Piet? Even if you solve this, even if we *survive*, it won't affect my decision to go home."

"You promised to wait a week—I have four days."

"Yes. And I will. I'm waiting for you. But afterward, *if we survive*, we won't be sitting down together at the kitchen table again, hoping things will get better. If you succeed, the difference is that this time, the boys and I go home—with or without you."

After that they waited each other out, each with phone in hand, he in the car, she in bed. Silence for the next kilometer, then the next. Listening to each other breathing. Until she kissed the phone twice and hung up.

And by the time, much later, that he parked outside a quiet hotel in Calamar in order to get a few hours of sleep, that terrible loneliness was hunting him down more than ever.

PIET HOFFMANN HAD sat outside a university hospital last night working on one of two vital pieces of paper at the bottom of his leather holster. Now he unfolded the other one.

14:52 (Briefing Calamar.)
15:27 (Departure ATV.)
17:21 (Arrival river.)
18:31 (Landing base camp.)
19:21 (Arrival prison camp.)
19:25 (Attack, break in.)
20:31 (Arrival helicopter.)
23:16 (Arrival Isla Tierra Bomba.)
23:43 (Underwater.)
00:32 (Arrival ship.)
00:37:01–00:40:00 (Time window.)

The timeline for a rescue operation of a hostage that, when he'd shown it to Ewert Grens, had been marked with only xx.xx. But now he could time everything in relation to the very last entry, the time window. With as late a start, and as short intervals as possible. Less time meant less exposure, and that meant less risk that their operation would be discovered.

"Ready?"

They were in a church. Small, beautiful, and cool compared to the heat waiting outside—located on the small open space behind the Registraduría Municipal del Estado Civil, which had once been one of Calamar's most vibrant squares, but was now mostly home to rubble and homeless dogs.

"Ready."

He looked at seven black masks, who looked back at him, and synchronized their watches.

14:52 (Briefing Calamar.)

Nine hours and forty-five minutes until the goal. Until that gap in satellite surveillance. Which would determine everything and which all other times were based on. That was the precise time the final phase would begin—only then would the time window be closed long enough. The precise time at which he had to break the surface water. If he didn't make it, if he was a minute late, if his window had already closed, then his chance to exchange a life for a life would be over.

Through Grens, he'd asked Masterson for eight battle-trained incorruptibles—a helicopter pilot with access to a helicopter, and the seven standing in front of him right now in a place the outside world seemed to have forgotten, fully equipped for battle and capable of moving through water and night combat. And who were now listening to and memorizing his overview of Operación Obtener, Operation Recovery, as he broke it down into stages, minute by minute.

Hoffmann spoke, while thinking both of them and himself. He often did that. Stepped out of his body and observed and judged, while his mouth continued to formulate what his brain had already decided. Afterward, he was often unsure if he'd said what he thought he said, it happened so mechanically. But it always seemed to work, no one noticed anything, he'd managed to be both present and absent.

Now, as he briefed them on their advance from the river to base camp and then from base camp to the prison camp, the other half of his mind was busy with thoughts of how thin the line he was balancing on really was, how fragile the protection he'd built. *If you, who are standing across from me, were to overpower me now, roll up my mask—it would all be over.* Not much more than a meter away stood seven elite soldiers in the employ of the US government. The same government that had sentenced him to death. If they found out that the man who was about to lead them was also a person they were supposed to capture, dead or alive—it would all be over.

No identity. That was how Sue Masterson had presented him to the Crouse Force's newly appointed director, Navarro's successor. *One of our informants—who needs to remain faceless in order to survive—has located the hostage. The only outsider who knows where he is. And you will assist him.* She'd sold him with the nameless trust that was a precondition for all undercover operations. He was neither Hoffmann nor Haraldsson; he was a DEA informant whom she was responsible for and the informant's anonymity was crucial when identification meant the same as death, for him and for his family. The same conditions as for the members of the Crouse Force, who also wore black masks in public to remain anonymous, incorruptible—impossible to locate, threaten, influence. Anonymity as a starting point was therefore unremarkable, in fact quite the opposite. And as he approached the end of his detailed overview, the other Piet Hoffmann—the one who left his body and watched those seven elite soldiers and their leader from a distance—observed that they seemed to trust him, were willing to follow him in order to free the hostage. Without realizing that this was about exonerating himself, exchanging a cage for a crossed-out name on a kill list.

If they only knew.

15:27 (Departure ATV.)

Hoffmann checked the time. 15:26. One minute *ahead* of schedule, the pounding in his chest got quieter.

Without the helicopter pilot the transport vehicle had plenty of space on its flatbed for the seven kayaks and a RIB, which accommodated seven soldiers and their equipment. Everyone sat in silence, focused on the mission. A single sound penetrated—it came from the Crouse Force's Hawkeye plane, which, since their arrival, had been circling five thousand meters above them, radio-jamming the area around Calamar. Nobody in this city who discovered their presence would be able to warn the guerrillas—all telephones, all radio traffic, and data traffic would be wiped out until the mission was completed.

Hoffmann sat alone in the cab, accompanied only by the maps unfolded on the seat next to him. An hour's journey on what might generously be called a highway, twenty minutes on a much less navigable dirt road, half an hour through the jungle on no road at all. Until they reached a tributary of the Río Vaupes. Until they reached the next phase.

17:21 (Arrival river.)

He checked the time again. 17:25. Four minutes *behind* schedule.

Unbelievably hot. Unbelievably humid. Around their heads—restless, pressing clouds of sand flies, buzzing, buzzing, buzzing for blood. In front and behind them—rubber trees, sapucaia, Brazil nut trees, fig trees, mahogany, and everything else he had no name for that was part of the impenetrable vines and vegetation as thick as closed doors. He'd selected a small lagoon in the river as their starting point, that was where they loaded the large rubber boat with fluids—water in one of the twenty-five-liter cans and colada of Cuban espresso in the other. Then, the medical equipment—a first-aid kit enhanced with morphine, serum, tetanus vaccines, and blood thinners. This was also where they distributed the weapons, ammunition, and machetes before getting into their own battle kayaks.

A few seconds later they were pulled into the swiftly flowing water, fighting to keep balance as they were pushed downstream—the lungs of the Amazon and its bloodstream were transporting them deeper toward its heart. The world's largest river system connected by a thousand tributaries, which supported a whole ecosystem—and for the moment was manifested in those swarms of stinging flies that were then replaced by swarms of biting mosquitoes.

The green carpet on the horizon gradually shifted color as the sun went down. Hoffmann focused all of his strength on fighting and steering with the paddle—he had to keep the big rubber boat he had in tow from getting caught somewhere and pulling him down to his death with its weight. Down to the seven-meter-long anacondas. To the crocodiles and piranhas. To the candiru fish that everyone had stories about but no one had seen, who supposedly swam inside you when you peed in the water, hooked their barbs inside the penis or vagina, and remained there to consume your blood and tissue.

They'd been traveling for almost an hour when Hoffmann heard something behind him that sounded like a whip. He broke away from the current, slowed down, and searched for the source of the sound in the gloom. There. One kayak had collided with a tree trunk, or maybe a rock, and one of the anonymous members of the Crouse Force, who Hoffmann called Five, sat in the swirling water that was shooting like a fountain out of the hole in his sleek craft. While the kayak gave up and sank to the bottom, Five caught the lifeline attached to the rubber boat and blew air into his life-jacket. A couple of breaths, a few strokes, and the stream carried him closer to the rubber boat, then next to it. Hands around the edge, a jerk to bring over his upper body, a short break to gather new strength, a jerk—and his whole body was up. And when Piet Hoffmann gestured with his index finger and thumb from the kayak to ask *Everything okay?* Five stretched up a thumb from his new location in the towed rubber boat to answer in the affirmative.

18:31 (Landing base camp.)

About a kilometer later Hoffmann's GPS alarm went off—behind the next sharp bend in the river was the spot where he and El Mestizo had landed. All the remaining combat kayaks and the rubber boat left the wild, rushing current and headed silently toward the riverbank. When Hoffmann took his first step on solid ground, he also checked the time. 18:39. Another four minutes behind schedule. The incident with the sunken kayak. A total of eight minutes, and he couldn't afford to lose any more time—on the contrary, he had to gain some. The next stage was their move from the river, past the base camp, and on to the prison camp. They would have to move faster than anticipated.

They unloaded, moored the rubber boat to a winding root of one of those unidentifiable trees, and pushed out one kayak at a time into the rushing current. There they'd be captured by the swiftly moving water and in a few kilometers broken and sunk as the river narrowed and became shallower.

Hoffmann knew this place well. The same tiny space between two rocks where the camp staff washed, the same potrillos that he and El Mestizo jumped between when Cristobal brought them here to torture the man Piet had now returned to save. It had been light out then and was dark now. But he remembered every detail. How Cristobal had walked ahead of them with his machete for two hundred and twenty steps to base camp and how they continued without him.

They put on their combat gear and night-vision goggles, loaded their weapons, screwed on their silencers, divvied up the cables and medical equipment.

"Ready?" Hoffmann whispered. Nevertheless, his voice played around them in the humidity. And equally quiet voices answered and danced around too.

They walked slowly in a tight row along a well-beaten path, tripping on twisted roots, bumping into hanging vines. Until only fifty steps remained to base camp—and Hoffmann stopped. On his last visit he'd drawn a mental sketch of where the caletas and chontos stood, of the depression on the right side of the camp that formed its natural border. He also remembered where fifteen fully armed guerrillas and guards were placed, one in every corner of the approximately square camp area. Not especially well trained—young and dedicated, but with no expertise to match what he and his team had. They could easily win a battle here. But that would also be the end of the operation. It would mean discovery, a warning sent to the prison camp another twelve hundred paces away. He directed his men off the path, had them follow him straight into the vegetation, making a semicircle around the right side of the camp. With their machetes they created a new path in the direction of that depression, time-consuming, energy-draining work despite sixteen well-trained arms, and it had to be done in silence. As they reached the depression it went faster—far less concerned about sound spillage as a deep wall of vegetation encircled and isolated them. A good half-hour to move a few hundred meters. Until they reached the path again, now on the other side of the camp. Continued moving down the path until they paused halfway, the place he'd crept to in the middle of the night on his last visit in order to determine the exact coordinates, longitude and latitude—then he'd had no night-vision goggles and he stumbled and fell over the six hundred and twelve steps that separated the prison camp from the open glade they now stood in.

"I want everybody to drink at least half of what's left. Replenish your energy. Next time we stop, we do it for battle."

Water and colada from steel flasks, some stretched, some readjusted their weapons. Then they continued walking, approaching their objective, counting down the steps. Silently, stealthily, like hunters trying not to scare away their quarry.

19:21 (Arrival prison camp.)

He checked the time, like before. 19:32. Going around base camp had reduced their pace even more—now he was eleven minutes behind. Time he *had* to make up—this would all be in vain if he got to that gap one second too late. But he refused to feel stressed, the preparation and implementation of a rescue demanded a controlled calm, spontaneity and shortcuts were seldom the key to a successful mission.

They stopped on the trail with just twenty steps left, adjusted their radios, and put their earpieces in their right ears. While the members of the Crouse Force carefully crouched, crept, and wormed their way toward their assigned positions, Hoffmann snuck over to the tree he'd decided was *control mark two* on his last visit. A sapucaia tree with branches and thick leaf coverage a good way up its trunk. He quickly climbed two thirds of the way to the top, probably twenty meters, carrying his sniper rifle. From up there he'd have full control of the camp during the rescue. An overview of the twelve camp soldiers. Of Speaker Crouse's cage. From there, he would also be in control of communication between the rest of the group, no one would be allowed to speak until the operation was over and the hostage free, the seven soldiers would only respond by pressing the transmit button according to a predetermined code.

Hoffmann slid farther out on the tree branch. Now. He was in a good position, good view. His rifle mounted, firmly supported for any shot. A final adjustment to deal with the extreme heat and humidity—turning the sight screws one click to the right, TPR1.

Perfect. He was ready.

The first whispered command. "One to Two, are you in position?"

Two short clicks as an answer. Two was in place, seven meters inside the jungle with a clear view of the commandant's caleta.

"One to Three, are you in place?"

Three clicks from a small rise of five meters south of the chontos, the camp latrine.

"Four, confirm."

Four clicks from the most vulnerable position, as close to the prisoner's cage as they could get. Four would initiate the attack by neutralizing the cage's guard and then monitoring, defending, and freeing Crouse.

"Five, Six, Seven, Eight—confirm."

Eight clicks in Hoffmann's earpiece. Five, Six, Seven, and Eight were grouped behind the guerrilla soldiers' mess hall, or at least he thought of it that way, a regular caleta, which was used as a sort of gathering place.

"We are now ten and a half minutes behind schedule. Synchronize. Nineteen thirty-five and . . . zero. And don't forget—spare the commandant."

All were in place. Time for the countdown.

"Good luck. In thirty seconds."

Hoffmann, before climbing up, had taken off his night-vision goggles, which were useless for longer distances—now he pulled a pair of night-vision binoculars out of a leg pocket to orient himself in the camp and find the seven soldiers in position. Not even a trained sniper gaze could find any traces of them, much less see them.

"In twenty seconds."

He searched further, training the gun at one of the four places the Crouse Force members should be at. Nothing in his telescopic sight. Until he pressed the little red button just above the sight for the infrared camera and was suddenly staring at the yellowish-green outline of a man, motionless on his knees a few meters into the jungle, near the toilet.

He moved his sight again into the camp, the largest building, the mess hall. There, inside the thin cloth of the tent, the outline of five yellow-green figures. He'd hold the rifle right here.

"In ten seconds."

He closed his eyes and three deep, slow breaths passed through his nose.

"In five, four, three, two, one . . ."

19:25 (Attack, break in.)

The moment the sound of his own voice died away, he perceived two muffled shots just behind the hostage's cage—followed by four quick clicks in his earpiece. Four had taken out the cage's guard. Subsonic ammunition engineered for the silencer, whose residual noise would be soaked up by the wall of vegetation around them—taking out the prison camp without alerting base camp.

Eleven left.

In the rifle's infrared sight Hoffmann saw five figures in the dining room stand up, grab their weapons, and rush out through a door covered by cloth. And they all fell, one at a time, hit in the back by Five, Six, Seven, and Eight.

Six remaining.

He moved a small piece of a tree branch for better visibility. His rifle trained on the commandant's caleta. And there he was—running out, screaming.

"We're under attack! Set off the charges next to the cage!"

The commandant didn't get far—fell headlong to the ground as Two shot him in the right thigh and right arm, he was now unable to use his weapon, but he wasn't supposed to die yet.

Five and a half left.

Hoffmann picked up the night-vision telescope again—from now on all activity would be concentrated near Speaker Crouse's prison. This was where the two guards protecting the north corner ran, toward the cage, toward the tripwire, rigged to trigger a shell that in turn would trigger an antipersonnel mine—a combination of explosives set up to kill both the hostage and his rescuers in case of an attack. It shouldn't pay to take any of the PRC's property—the consequences should be death every time. The two camp guards suddenly stopped, raised their automatic rifles, pointing them toward the muddy area in front of the cage. About to shoot straight at the mine and trigger the explosion. But they slumped, lifelessly, before either could fire—Hoffmann's line of sight had been clear from the tree.

Three and a half left.

And it was clear through his night-vision telescope—they were sneaking up in a loosely formed group from the south side of the camp, slowly approaching the prisoner's cage. A muted bang—Three behind the latrine—and one of them, the taller one in the middle, hit. Two left, who promptly started retreating. Hoffmann could no longer follow them with night vision and readjusted—

again—to infrared, first directing his weapon at the commandant's caleta, which was empty, then toward the simpler sleeping caletas, also empty, and finally the mess hall, slowly sweeping along its walls.

There they were. That's where they'd retreated to.

Green-yellow contours inside the tent fabric. Floating ghosts in deep purple, convinced for the moment they were protected, undetectable.

Hoffmann breathed in, took aim, fired twice.

One half left.

And a new, sweeping motion through the camp's darkness while he counted up seven colored bodies, lives that exuded warmth, all exactly where they should be. Then the motionless bodies, dead but still exuding heat—eleven. Then, two more. Also yellow-green.

The commandant and Speaker Crouse.

No other heat sources. No more floating ghosts. Hoffmann adjusted his microphone, his voice in their earpieces.

"All eliminated."

As long as there were branches, he climbed meter by meter down; when the trunk became smooth, he let go and slid to the ground. A glance toward the cage.

Two was removing the tripwire, disarming the grenade and mine.

Four fired a single shot at the simple padlock that held the chain in place around the bamboo bars.

Not there, not yet. First he had to meet someone else. Someone who was proud of scarring a person for life, who laughed when he took away their dignity. Now he lay in the mud in the middle of the camp, bleeding and crawling.

Hoffmann grabbed his arm, the right one, the damaged one, and pulled him up from the ground to a kneeling position.

The commandant screamed in pain. Until Hoffmann's palm hit his cheek.

"No screaming. No one can hear you, because you don't exist. Okay?"

No answer. Just an intense, quiet whimpering as he dragged him through the camp in the direction of Crouse's cage. Hoffmann stopped regularly, kicked the commandant in the chest if his wailing got any louder.

"What did I say? No screaming."

Arrived at the cage. And it was open. The prisoner was on his way out, supported by Four and Five.

"You're safe now, Señor Crouse."

English, with a distinct Spanish accent. Crouse should see and hear a member of the Crouse Force. Questions risked turning into suspicion, and the group Hoffmann led, and was dependent on, had to continue to believe in the black mask hiding his face, not the death sentence, not the outlaw informant.

"We'll take you out of here, Señor Crouse. Home to your countrymen."

Dead people scattered about. Strangers with loaded weapons. However, Crouse didn't seem frightened. Confused, tired, dejected. But not afraid. A man who in a short time had been damaged so deeply and badly that he'd given up, accepted it.

Hoffmann loosened the leather holster that hung from his shoulder and across his chest, took out his gun, handed it to Crouse.

"Loaded, safety's off. And there, Señor Crouse, is the commandant."

Crouse looked at him, without making the slightest attempt to receive the gun. "I don't understand."

"We saved him. For you."

Timothy D. Crouse glanced at the man who'd been placed at his feet, who'd pretended to execute him, tortured him, reduced his life to nothing. "Why?"

"I know what he's done to you."

Crouse studied the commandant more thoroughly, listened to his moaning, lingered at the blood glued to fabric on his thigh, then at the wound on his upper arm, that blood seemed to have stayed inside his uniform, flowing down along his body. And shook his head slightly. "Thank you. But I'll pass."

Hoffmann put his gun back in its holster, snapped it, and bent down to the commandant. Toward two black pointy boots. Put his hands around the clanging, polished spurs shaped like stars with red and sparkling stones on either side. And gave a powerful jerk, the commandant screamed in pain, or maybe humiliation, and Hoffmann put the two spurs in Speaker Crouse's pocket.

"So later you know when in doubt—you were the one who won." He then untied the scarf from around the commandant's neck, tied it again around his open mouth and neck, then dragged him to the cage, threw him in, forced his hands and feet together with sharp ties. And shut the door, locked it with more cable ties. He'd be there for a while.

Three, Five, Seven, and Eight arrived from behind the latrine with a single, newly built, bamboo stretcher between them. Six gave Crouse a morphine injection in the buttocks through his thin pants, and they lifted him up.

They started walking back in the same direction they'd come, took turns carrying Crouse. At the clearing, they stopped short and Hoffmann assured them everything had gone exactly as planned. As they approached the base camp, they heard voices and the obligatory television suspended from a tree, a crackling sound. They slowly circled by on the newly cleared path, down in the depression to isolate any sounds until they got to the other side and continued down to the river. To the rubber boat, which they untied from gnarled roots before loading Crouse and themselves. Twenty minutes in thirty knots, against the current. And they had no choice, they had to start here, immediately. Engine noise would alert the base camp. But with the distance to the river, their lead, the boat's capacity—any pursuers would have a difficult time catching up.

20:31 (Arrival helicopter.)

He'd calculated a total sixty-six minutes for the attack, movement on foot, movement by boat. They'd carried out the plan in sixty-one. Five minutes gained, six minutes behind.

Hoffmann ran toward the helicopter and the pilot, while the seven soldiers sought out shelter in a grove of palms, behind trunks covered with sharp thorns—this was where they would wait until the helicopter returned to transport them back to the regiment, while Hoffmann made the rest of the journey alone.

First, he verified that he'd gotten everything on the list he'd sent to the new Crouse Force commander. Ticked off underwater sled and underwater scooter, continued on to the contents of one of the burlap sacks—lifted out and examined the underwater breathing mask, diving mask, the two air cylinders, can of grease, blood pressure cuff, the cone made of copper with a diameter of exactly four centimeters, and the plastic tube that was fifteen centimeters long. Then in the other burlap sack—a pack of C-4 plastic explosives, dry sack, the two powerful magnets, a fully automatic, sawed-off shotgun, tandem harness, a three-millimeter-thick neoprene suit, a diving computer the size of a wristwatch, and, finally, at the bottom of the sack, a buoyancy compensator.

Everything in place, except Crouse. Hoffmann held him tightly as they climbed on board, supported his body, which almost fell repeatedly, got him in place, and wrapped him, still conscious but drowsy from the morphine, in blankets between the two burlap sacks.

Then they lifted off and the pilot adjusted the helicopter's position in relation to the wind, steering toward the coordinates Hoffmann had keyed in. The pilot turned around to his temporary boss.

"Did I understand right—we're on our way to a small island, just off Colombia's northwestern coast?"

"Yes."

"In that case—flight time is two hours and forty-five minutes."

"That's what I expected."

23:16 (Arrival Isla Tierra Bomba.)

The view from the helicopter's window was beautiful—a gentle bay on the northwest side next to a white beach with plenty of distance to the buildings on the island's northern tip. They sank slowly toward the jetty, which stuck out a bit into the water forming a harbor for three small fishing boats. The pilot landed skillfully on a small, open patch of grass. The helicopter could take him no further. He'd have to deliver Crouse on his own and do so without being detected—deliberately revealing himself would be tantamount to asking for execution. The pilot and Hoffmann unloaded the equipment and carried it to a simple boat that looked like all the others, just as prearranged with Masterson via Grens. Under the tarp lay the rest of what he'd requested—the four shotgun cartridges loaded with carbon fibers, the waterproof MP3 player with prerecorded sounds of Russian submarines, a container of Cesium-137—which had been impossible to obtain through the Crouse Force's local channels.

Two hours and forty-one minutes. They'd gained four minutes—two minutes behind. While the helicopter took off, Hoffmann gathered Crouse, helped him climb into the boat. He seemed less affected as the morphine wore off, seemed to be gathering his thoughts again, not slurring quite as much as he spoke.

"Who . . . are you working for?"

"Soon, Señor Crouse. When you're safe. Then you'll get the answers to your questions."

"One more time. Who or what are you working for?"

This was good. Hoffmann smiled under his black mask. The speaker's injuries had compromised him physically, but not his sharpness, his intellect. That voice hadn't been crushed, it belonged to a revered politician, who was used to being listened to.

"The group of soldiers who liberated you, Mr. Speaker, is the group that bears your name. The Crouse Force."

The American tried to sit on the rail, but couldn't, so instead he leaned against it, his eyes turned toward Hoffmann, steady, demanding.

"The Crouse Force. Uh-huh. I don't know, but . . . have we met?"

"You've met every member of the Crouse Force."

"I didn't mean it like that. You seem . . . familiar. Not your voice, I don't know if I've heard it before, but the way you move. I feel like I've made your acquaintance at *more* than a superficial inspection."

Hoffmann had no time to chat. But he had to. Crouse couldn't doubt him, had to be convinced that only members of the Crouse

Force had freed him, in order to keep things flexible, no arguments or protests—only later would Crouse realize that the extra member who led the entire operation was one of the thirteen people his colleagues had labeled as their main enemy.

"You *will* understand, Señor Crouse. When it's time. All you need to know right now is that I'm on your side. I freed you to save your life. Your life is just as important to me as my own. My own depends on it."

Crouse held out a dirty, torn shirtsleeve, grabbing at Hoffmann's black mask. "And this?"

Hoffmann pulled his hand away, gently but firmly. "All according to the Crouse Force regulations. That you yourself helped to write."

"But *if* I would ask you to take it off?"

"When my mission ends."

The canteen hung off Hoffmann's hip, a few ounces of water left. He pulled off his leather glove, his left hand was missing two fingers, could see Crouse looking at it. Two capsules of Nembutal lay in his vest pocket, and he dropped them into the canteen and waited for them to dissolve.

"I want you to drink this, Mr. Speaker."

Crouse shook his head, his matted, wet hair pasted to his forehead and temples. "No."

"It will make you sleep. And that's important for the last phase of this rescue mission to work." Hoffmann held out the metal bottle. "You have to trust me now, Mr. Speaker. Both our lives depend on it."

Crouse drank after a moment. But reluctantly. Soon he was asleep, and when Hoffmann was absolutely sure of it, he pulled out a one-hour dose of Propofol and injected it into Crouse's arm. A very potent and dangerous anesthetic, so the dosage was weaker than would normally be recommended, but Crouse wouldn't be under the constant supervision of a professional, so better to minimize the risks. That was also why Hoffmann had shortened this part of the operation from two hours to one—difficult to implement in the time allocated, but necessary in order to give Crouse the greatest prospect for survival.

He lifted up one of the burlap sacks, took out the breathing mask along with the rebreather, threaded them over the sleeping Crouse's head, and hung them on his chest. And turned on the oxygen. The Rebreather 12 was the most advanced one he'd worked with, it allowed for deeper dives and longer endurance than its predecessors.

The transparent underwater sled reminded him of a glass coffin, and he carefully lubricated its rubber strips with the grease until the hatch sealed perfectly. Crouse hadn't been particularly large to begin with, and his time in the cage had taken off a few more kilos, so it was much easier than Hoffmann had imagined to carry him to the sled and lay him inside it.

With Crouse asleep inside the tow sled, Hoffmann had a few minutes to build the prism bomb. The sleeping pills and anesthetic had been stored in one of the breast pockets of his combat vest. In the other he had the detonator next to the small cone of copper he'd been searching for so long—until he happened across it in an antiques shop in Cartago that specialized in art and small sculptures. There it stood, on a cluttered shelf behind the counter, waiting for him, and it was just the right size. He molded a fairly thick, even layer of C-4 plastic explosive on the outside and pushed the fifteen-centimeter-long plastic tube around it—about three centimeters to cover the cone itself, and the remaining twelve being the distance needed to focus the blast before it reached its intended target—the optimal distance for the maximum explosive effect. Finally, he pushed the container of Cesium-137, into the copper cone, stuck it with a fingernail of sealant just below the tip of the cone, and stuffed it into the waterproof dry sack—together with the sawed-off, automatic shotgun, the custom-designed cartridges loaded with carbon fibers, and the two magnets.

Crouse was ready. The prism bomb was ready. Then his own equipment.

He undressed and covered his naked skin with a new, synthetic three-millimeter-thick neoprene suit. Considerably thinner than the diving suits he normally used, but this mission called for maximum mobility. And besides, for a person who'd trained in the cold waters of northern Europe, the Caribbean was warm enough no matter the season. Buoyancy compensator and the other rebreather over his own head, the straps around his waist and legs, and he felt supple despite the oxygen tube and lime container that cleansed the carbon dioxide, a prerequisite for being able to breathe in the gas mixture over and over again. Hung the dry sack over his right shoulder and put the diving computer on his wrist like a watch with a too-large display, which contained a clock, a compass, a GPS, a depth gauge, and an automatic dive logbook that warned you when it was time to go up.

The target was about ten meters below the surface. But the journey there was concentrated at two, maybe three, meters deep. The underwater scooter would therefore be able to pull both him and the sled with Crouse inside. A small round vessel with handles on each side and circular cover with fan blades. With enough batteries to run for two hours and a speed of about six knots, he would reach his target after a forty-five-minute journey.

A final check on the sedated American—his breathing was calm and regular. A blood pressure cuff around his arm to keep track of his vitals, he was sound asleep as the sled's transparent lid was closed.

And now. The moment Hoffmann needed to give to himself, no matter how urgent the time was. Sit completely still. As he did after climbing up on the railing. His ritual each time he'd been caught in circumstances like these.

Breathe in through your nose, exhale through your mouth. Visualize the mission. In through your nose, out through your mouth.

23:43 (Underwater.)

The target coordinates were already programmed into the computer. When he started it an arrow appeared on the display, pointing in the direction he should steer. He spat in his mask, rubbed the saliva on the glass, and placed it in front of his face. Oxygen on. The nozzle of the rebreather in place.

23:44. One minute behind, he had to make it up.

A firm grip on the underwater scooter as he leaned back, a soft splash as the body and the vehicle and the sled with Crouse inside fell into the water. He sank from the surface to a depth of two and a half meters, where he leveled out and started the underwater scooter at a constant cruising speed. And it worked just as he'd hoped, traveling in virtual silence—so quiet that he could hear the aircraft carrier and its convoy, the sound transmitted underwater from eight kilometers away.

00:13—after half an hour's journey—he stopped short, still at two and a half meters' depth, made sure that Crouse's blood pressure remained at 100/80. He then turned on the waterproof MP3 player and let it go, watched it sink as he listened to it perfectly reproduce the sound of a Russian submarine blowing air—the illusion of it preparing to open its torpedo hatches. Soon he perceived that just as the convoy's corvettes guarded the ship above the surface, submarines guarded it from beneath, and they now began to move toward the source of the sound. Toward a recording.

00:29—after forty-five minutes under water the dive computer on his arm started vibrating energetically, warning him that his target was now very close, just one hundred meters away. The USS *Dwight D. Eisenhower.* Confirmed by the muffled rumble of engines. Hoffmann dove seven meters farther down into the darkness, maneuvered the underwater scooter along the hull toward the bow and one of the reactors.

00:32 (Arrival ship.)

00:32:11.

Eleven seconds behind schedule—exactly four minutes and fifty seconds left until the satellite window opened.

After Hoffmann found his way to the ship's engines, he ignored the dive computer and relied on his analog compass—turbines were driven by magnets, so the needle of the compass was the easiest way to find them. It was there on the hull that he'd attach the prism bomb laced with radioactive Cesium-137.

He started the countdown on the preset timer for detonation at one hundred and eighty seconds. Enough time to get into position. To the place where he'd pull out the automatic sawed-off shotgun, loaded with four cartridges that contained ten pieces of carbon fiber thread each, and then, with that in hand, he'd change the water around him to air.

00:37:01—00:40:00 (Time window.)

00:36:46. Twenty seconds to detonation. Fifteen seconds to the window—when the satellites would cease to overlap for exactly three minutes, and when he would be invisible to an otherwise ever-watchful eye.

He'd made it.

The first thing he saw—00:37:01—as he broke the surface was what those on board called the island, or the tower, the heart of the ship, which held its captain and combat leader and a forest of antennas. It was also at that moment that he felt a detonation like a weak hissing ten meters beneath him. And soon the sirens started howling on deck. Soon an electronic voice started repeating *radiation leak, radiation leak,* over the speakers. Soon the crew was running toward their emergency stations in order to handle a radioactive leak that existed only in a newly assembled and detonated prism bomb.

A crew that was exhaustively and skillfully drilled—focused on the tasks at hand, none of them took any interest in looking at the antennas or for a fully automatic sawed-off shotgun. Hoffmann bobbed steadily on the water, cocked his gun, fired. Four shots. Bangs like whiplashes, but they were drowned out by the sound of sirens and alarms. And he watched as the strands of carbon fiber were wound like hookworms around both the parabolic antennas and transmitting antennas.

Communications knocked out.

He dropped the gun into the water, let it sink to the ocean floor. As long as those carbon fiber strands remained where they were, the aircraft carrier would have no access to radar, GPS, sonar—temporarily cut off from the world.

00:38:03.

One minute and fifty seconds left until his gap closed.

The crew might discover at any moment that there was no real radioactive leak. Might find those carbon fibers and reestablish the ship's communications and surveillance. From that moment, it would be impossible to return. Impossible to survive.

Hoffmann took the two incredibly powerful magnets out of the dry sack, ripped off their waterproof covers, and turned on the magnets' batteries. Now he pulled over the sled with the sleeping American inside, opened the Plexiglas cover, and saw that his breathing was steady and secure and would remain so for at least another fifteen or twenty minutes.

The first magnet would attach to the hull just above the water, that's where he would park—affix—the sled. The second magnet he pressed down between Crouse's legs inside the sled, closed the lid, and pushed it toward the magnet on the hull. It worked perfectly. The force of the interacting magnets snapped up the sled, it bobbed just as it should there in the shadow of the huge ship.

00:39:38.

Twenty-two seconds left until the satellite reopened its eyes.

Hoffmann grabbed the mouthpiece that hung loosely over his chest, brought it to his mouth, and blew out any residual water. The mask rested around his neck, and he adjusted it until it was sitting across the face. He turned on the scooter's engine and steered downward, under the surface, back to a depth of a couple meters.

He'd made it.

Three minutes. On the last occasion that time had been so crucial, it had been a matter of three seconds, so three minutes felt like an eternity.

Without the sled the journey to Isla Tierra Bomba would go much more quickly. And halfway there, when he was about the same distance from the aircraft carrier as the fishing boat, he'd surface in order to make a phone call to Sue Masterson, say three words—*exchange object moored*—and hang up. It would be her turn to call the chief of staff and vice president, who would have to fulfill their part of the bargain.

PART FOUR

THE WIDE AND deep porcelain cups were steaming with a hot drink that didn't look like much, still mostly reminiscent of plain tea. Aguapanela. Sugar cane pulp and water. It was here Ewert Grens had tasted it the very first time, the day after he landed in Colombia. Piet Hoffmann had persuaded him in that ill-lit corner table to try at least a sip. And he'd been hooked. Maybe didn't order it quite as often as coffee, but almost—and in his case *almost* meant a considerable amount.

Now he stood at the bar of the Gaira Café, exchanging pesos for a tray of steaming drinks. Sure, it tasted good. But that wasn't really why. It made him feel a little daring to venture so far beyond coffee, black. And now—well, this was a party! They had something to celebrate.

He carried the tray to one of the other corner tables, not spilling a drop despite the cups being filled up to the brim. And checked again before putting them down on the table—yes, from here, you could both see and hear the TV that hung from the ceiling on a metal arm. He pushed one cup across the table.

"Aguapanela. Like you like it. And on a day like this!"

Hoffmann looked at the cup without lifting it. "Thank you. That was thoughtful. But on a day like this, Grens, it's coffee I need."

A small sip before the detective rose again to fetch a new cup with different contents. He drank, as he studied a man who looked happy, in high spirits, but also extremely tired and worn—a generation younger but at this moment, in this place, they seemed the same age. Hoffmann was unshaven, his eyes red, and he'd almost collapsed into the hard and uncomfortable chair. He looked like a man who'd coordinated and carried out a precise attack to free the world's most high-profile hostage, all of it hinging on a narrow window of time that put one of the world's most modern aircraft carriers out of action, and then after delivering the hostage had gone back underwater and headed to his starting point on Isla Tierra Bomba. Then took a fishing boat to the mainland and from there drove seventeen hours through the night and day to arrive just before five o'clock in the afternoon, trudge through a wayward entrance of bamboo into a café in downtown Bogotá. The way a man looks after saving a life and knowing he'll soon get to keep his own.

"Coffee. Black. If you're more worried about the effect than the taste." Grens returned with two new cups and placed both in front of Hoffmann. "This should keep you awake until the TV program is over."

The detective raised one of his own cups—he also had two now, a lot of sugar and vitamin C—held it in front of himself and waited for Hoffmann to raise his. They nodded to each other in a silent toast. Celebrating. Soon they'd change the channel on that rickety TV on the wall and watch as the world received the news. The result of their collaboration.

Hoffmann felt the heat fill him, the new energy, but his hands also began to tremble, then shake—and the detective opposite him noticed it.

"An entire night in a car, Grens. With a bucket like this of black coffee. Straight to the central nervous system." He smiled, raised his cup for a new toast, and his hands trembled even more violently.

He missed her so much. Zofia. The boys. Soon. He would soon be done. *Almost* done. He'd delivered on his part of the agreement, but didn't dare go to the safe house yet, where his family was waiting for him—the people trying to kill him had found him at the brothel, and he didn't know how much they knew, how closely his movements had been mapped, what he could get away with before his name had been publicly deleted. My God, how he'd hurry, rush there as soon he got the green light! Immediately after the press conference from the White House that would announce the rescue and return of Speaker Timothy D. Crouse. They might even show him off in front of the cameras.

Hoffmann stretched up to the television, flipping through the channels until he found CNN. Just a few minutes to go. Right now, there was a news summary and images from a wildfire in California, which were exchanged for images of a plane crash off the west coast of Australia. He muted the sound, the smaller button to the left, images would do for now.

The detective leaned over the table. "And after this broadcast I can go home to my little office in Stockholm. You'll be crossed off the kill list. *Mission accomplished.*" As if wanting to ensure that no one heard him, even though they were completely alone now that the waiter disappeared into the kitchen. "But I have another mission. To ensure that the Haraldsson family comes home with me."

"We don't need to anymore. In just a minute, I'll no longer have a death sentence hanging over me. And I'm in no rush. Zofia wants us to go—but I can't go home to life in prison. Have you been in a prison, Grens?"

"Yes. I visit prisons all the time for my job. And have been for over thirty years. I've been in every single one."

"You visit a prison. And you leave. But you've never been trapped in seven square meters behind a locked steel door inside a seven-meter-high wall day after day, week after week, month after month. So you can't understand what it's like not to live your life—because that's how it is, you cease to live in there, you don't participate in time, it just disappears, gets used up, a long fucking wait."

Hoffmann glanced toward the television screen. Images from the Syrian civil war were exchanged for images of demonstrations against a summit of EU foreign ministers. A couple of minutes left.

"A life sentence, Grens? A whole lifetime of waiting? I can't do it. Won't. I would rather die here a little bit at a time. At least I'd still be living."

"And your wife? Does she feel the same?"

"I'm hoping that I can persuade her."

"A life sentence, you say? Or continue on here? What about a third option?" The detective was tense, excited—both because of what they were about to see on the TV and because of the idea he'd been turning over in his head for the last twenty-four hours. "I want to know the next major cocaine delivery to Sweden. Time, place, route."

"Why?"

"Because I'm a cop, and that's what cops do. Stop crimes."

Hoffmann wasn't overly interested. But he was listening.

"Like this: you give me a tip on the next delivery via England or Spain or . . . doesn't matter, as long as the final destination is Sweden. You're pretty good at that. With your tips, and if I address it to the right person, I'll find a solution. Even if that person protests, in the end he'll understand that he wins by not arguing. A solution that would mean you'd get a sentence—but a short one. Then you can be reunited with your wife, your children."

"Didn't you hear what I said? I can't go back to prison. And I'm never helping the Swedish or the American police ever again. It doesn't usually turn out so well for me—does it?"

"*Considerable ruthlessness,* it says in the penal code. I see several extenuating circumstances surrounding your conduct, which makes it far from ruthless. I will fix that. Am fixing it. But I need your tip in order to implement it. You'll simply have to trust me, Hoffmann. I'm neither a Swedish nor an American police officer—I'm Ewert Grens. And I keep my word."

Static slid across the screen like a run in a stocking. Hoffmann gently knocked the side of the TV and turned a couple of buttons. Until it suddenly disappeared and the picture became, if not perfect, at least fairly clear again.

"I won't be caged. I'd rather die. And I will make Zofia understand that—now that I'm off the kill list." He continued turning and pressing different buttons somewhat aimlessly. Until he found another frequency, a better picture. "I'm so fucking tired of everything. Do you understand, Grens? I turned my back on my life and gained another life, which turned its back on me. Used. That's not a good feeling. The police have gotten enough from me."

"Hoffmann, I—"

"Besides, I've got a death sentence, too. I'm a known snitch. The worst kind. There is no prison in Sweden where a snitch would be safe without protection. For the sake of the police, I went back into your fucking prison and they put me in isolation, didn't help, not even the hole. They proved they could reach me anywhere. That's why I'm here, don't you remember, Grens, you too sentenced me to death? I would need La Picota."

"La Picota?"

"It's a prison here in Bogotá. A special prison built for those they plan to move to the US. One of the world's ten most secure."

Grens was about to put his hand on Hoffmann's arm. But changed his mind. He was no good at that sort of thing.

"Listen. When you were serving time at Aspsås we had nine murders within the Swedish prison—and you were responsible for two of them. It's not like that anymore. There's a whole new section for prisoners whose lives are threatened. Because of what happened to you. Hoffman's Law, if you like. A lack of administrative responsibility and lack of cooperation between the authorities, that's what they called it. Since then we have not had any more murders inside those walls. In there, in that particular department, an inmate *is* truly protected from the rest of the population. And when you're released . . . there is no longer a threat! With the information you gave us—in cooperation with the Polish police—we took down the entire branch of the Polish mafia you infiltrated. Wojtek no longer exists. And can't threaten you anymore." He lowered his voice. "And another thing. In that particular section there are two more serving time who have also been threatened. Two senior police officials who were sentenced for using false information to manipulate me to . . . well, like you said, to shoot you."

The red eyes in Hoffmann's tired face gleamed, seemed to wake up. "Senior police officials like . . . the chief of police and Göransson?"

"Yes."

"And if I were to be given a reduced sentence in Sweden they'd put me in the same section?"

"Exactly."

Those eyes, suddenly very alert. Grens could guess what he was thinking. How Hoffmann must wish for a chance to meet the men who forced him to flee—how a meeting like that, without witnesses and on equal terms, though it might not compensate, would still mitigate some of these last three horrible years.

Now.

The newscast concluded. And a live press conference from the White House was announced.

"You'll simply have to trust me, Hoffmann. In ten minutes you'll be off that kill list. Then we'll begin your journey home."

Hoffmann shrugged his shoulders in a way that might mean "maybe" and turned the volume up on the TV, a bit tinny and muffled, but still audible.

A short intro. And then that same *BREAKING NEWS* banner across the top of the screen Grens had seen only a week ago—though it felt like a lifetime had passed—when Erik Wilson urged him to watch an American newscast in a Swedish police corridor. And simultaneously more text rotated in the opposite direction, with the reverse of last week's news—*Speaker of the House free after rescue operation.*

The exterior of the White House. And now inside the White House. And a podium. Grens recognized the president and the FBI and CIA directors. All of whom he'd expected would be there. And then someone else, a face he didn't recognize. At the far right of the screen stood a man in uniform, a highly decorated officer, as far as he could tell from the various medals and patches. As the camera zoomed in and showed each person's nameplate, Hoffmann stood up and walked closer. It landed on the man on the far right last. Someone named Michael Cook.

"Cook? Grens—who is that?"

Grens didn't have time to answer before the question became irrelevant. As the camera was adjusted to convey the small line *under* the name, partially obscured because Hoffmann was now so close to the television. But still legible, if Grens leaned to the side.

Delta Force Commander.

"Delta Force, Grens?" Hoffmann pounded his palm violently against the TV screen. "Grens, fuck! I've got a bad feeling about this!"

The detective watched as the man who would soon be freed from a death sentence slowly got closer to the television screen, as if he wanted to climb into it, be there on the podium, the first one to know.

"Hoffmann—I understand why you're nervous. But it will be over soon." Grens was as tall as his much younger fellow Swede, and when he put his hand on Hoffmann's shoulders to make him sit down, he did so gently, with more presence than force. "Relax and watch and listen. Not everything needs to be a battle, Hoffmann. Sometimes life is just good. And this—this is such a moment."

Hoffmann sank down slowly with Grens's hand on his shoulder, breathing in through his nose and squeezing the air out through taut lips, six times.

The camera focused on the president, who was clearly aware of his enormous audience, as he walked up to the microphone and grabbed the podium along its edges. He waited until all focus was on him, looked into television sets around the world, and slowly began a live speech about how he'd been awoken last night by a call from a voice he recognized, tired but present, and how relieved and proud he'd felt.

At this point he smiled, his eyes smiled too, and the press corps and his press advisers smiled along with him as he continued.

"That's what happens when you send the best. US Special Forces—Delta Force."

The camera now moved to the man in uniform. Major General Cook, who stayed silent, just nodding, inspiring confidence.

"It doesn't add up!" Hoffmann banged his hand on the table and overturned both the coffee mugs and slightly larger teacups. And when he stood up all signs of fatigue had vanished, he was as furious as Grens had ever seen anyone—except for himself.

And then he left. Toward the exit. Hoffmann's determined steps whipped the floor.

Meanwhile the TV image changed. From the president's face to a prerecorded feature in a helicopter, in the darkness, above an endless sea, with the muffled sound of a rotor blade. When the lens turned in toward the cabin, it revealed a man reclining on some sort of stretcher. Tormented, haunted, but at the same time a kind of peace in the depths of that gaze. Speaker Timothy D. Crouse.

"*Thank you.*" His voice was weak but composed. "*I'm alive. And will soon be back in the service of the American people—that's my mission. From the bottom of my heart, I'm so very grateful to my colleagues for their patient work, for the skills of the Crouse Force, and a special thank-you to the Delta Force member who found me and who led the mission to free me and bring me back to safety again.*"

The speaker closed his eyes, and the picture cut back to the White House and the press conference, whose focus had shifted from celebrating the rescue mission to images of the continued war to root out terrorism. And only when those ten names who still stood on the kill list were projected diagonally across the vice president's shoulder did Grens realize what Hoffmann had been aware of from the outset.

That the agreement they'd both negotiated had been betrayed. That the representatives of the world's most powerful democracy had changed history, to keep a bad decision from ever having to be revealed to the public. That their employee, the informant Piet Hoffmann, was still on the kill list of his employer. And they would continue hunting him until he was killed.

THIS AFTERNOON'S MEETING with Domenico José Peralta was crucial. And she succeeded. The final wording in a unique agreement that none of her predecessors ever came close to completing. Sue Masterson was rarely satisfied with herself or what she did, but just now she was—from the moment the head of the Policía Federal signed the bottom of that white paper and shook her hand, American and Mexican agents would be working together on both sides of the border. Both officially and undercover. With the joint forces they'd previously lacked, they could now identify, confiscate, and diminish the Mexican drug cartels. The Crouse Force targeted its expertise at production—this was focused on distribution.

Then she looked at the clock. Damn.

The press conference. Hoffmann's agreement—a life for a life. Which she'd negotiated just a few days earlier. She excused herself as she threw documents and pens into her briefcase and Peralta nodded, waved, and smiled, just as pleased.

She hurried, almost ran, out of the conference room on the second floor of the DEA. To the stairs. They were probably quickest. She climbed the three floors easily—she was so happy. Cocaine production's broad base would remain in Colombia, Bolivia, Peru, and Ecuador, that's why Hoffmann and other informants had been placed there—if you cut the throat it gets a lot harder to breathe. But now she'd started to cut another main artery—the geographical link between producer and consumer.

Fifth floor. Her office was seven doors away. The press conference had already started, but probably wasn't over yet.

The TV screen hung on the wall between the door and the bookcase. She pointed the remote and sat down at her desk, unsure if what was pounding fiercely in her chest was the unexpected run or the feeling of leaping joy caused by moving from one successfully completed agreement to another.

She was in luck. The press conference wasn't over. But most everything had been said. Maybe they'd even shown Crouse, he was supposed to be there, but she didn't see him. The image was now filled by an illustration of a kill list projected diagonally across the vice president's shoulder. Ten names.

Masterson counted again. Ten remaining names. There should have been nine. She leaned forward, trying to focus on the list as it slowly scrolled by. And there he was. The Seven of Hearts.

They'd made a mistake. Forgotten to take him off.

The list disappeared and the broadcast ended with a slow pan over the podium. And she remembered when Vice President Thompson and Chief of Staff Perry emerged from the Situation Room and returned with a flash drive and a promise. When she'd repeated that promise to Detective Grens in a dark little dive bar. When both, without having to say it, shared that same feeling, which is always most intense before you repay a debt.

"Yes?"

She'd called the vice president's private cell phone without being quite aware of it.

"Hello. This is Sue Masterson." And she realized that Thompson was of course still in the same room as the cameras, but a bit behind them and standing with the chief of staff, who was directing everything.

"Masterson? Wait a second."

She heard the vice president moving with phone in hand, the background noise subsided, it was almost quiet. She wondered which room she'd slipped into. "I'm watching TV."

"Yes, and?" She sounded normal. Neutral.

"And that image. The list. There's been a mistake. You forgot to cross off the Seven of Hearts."

"No."

"Well, I saw it just now on the news. And his name is still there."

"The list was correct."

It sounded as if a door opened and closed. As if the vice president might be switching to another room.

"We had an agreement."

"What agreement?"

"The agreement on . . . you know which fucking agreement . . . it stipulated that if the Seven of Hearts found, freed, and delivered Crouse, you would strike him from the kill list."

"Sue, I'm sorry but I really don't know what you're talking about—we made no agreement."

That voice. Just as neutral. And that's why it penetrated straight into her skull, like a sharp blade slicing her head in two.

"In your office . . . you were there, and Perry was there!"

A part of her refused to believe it—and part of her did, the part that raged, attacked, shrieked inside her.

"Are you quite sure? Which meeting are you talking about? I have no such records. And if I were to look into the White House visitor log I doubt anything of the kind would be there. At all."

She was moving again, it was clear because the murmur was getting closer.

"Look, Sue, I'm sorry, but I have to get back to the press conference. It turned out that one of our elite soldiers from Delta Force was able to locate, free, and deliver Speaker Crouse. So now we can focus on our continued pursuit of those responsible, who will pay with their lives, and just like before, I'll be leading the hunt."

IT WASN'T FAR from Gaira Café on Calle 96 to the Hospital Universitario San Ignacio in Carrera 7. Ten kilometers along Cerros de Monserrate, the lush green area that the inhabitants of the capital city used for recreation. But that's not where they headed, not yet. First stop was a small shop about halfway there, in the neighborhood called Chapinero.

The anger was gone. At least not the kind that was afflicting Ewert Grens at the moment—the superintendent sat in the passenger seat, swearing loudly, and now and then banged a fist against the defenseless dashboard. Piet Hoffmann felt nothing, because he couldn't allow himself to feel anything.

Always alone. Trust only yourself.

Action. That's how he survived. A choice between giving up or continuing on, and he continued on, always.

"Where are we going?"

"You'll see."

"Hoffmann, goddammit, if you want me to go with you, you have to explain!"

"Grens? It's not me you're angry at. And you know that. I need to work with you, not against you—I need your help. You will know everything there is to know. But right now we're in a fucking hurry."

He stopped in front of a graffiti-covered store with a too-narrow entrance and a sign that had once been lit, but was now content to faintly display the words SUPER DELI. Hoffmann asked Grens to wait in the car while he went in to the sparsely stocked deli.

"Cesar?"

A woman nodded toward the door behind the cash register.

"In there."

Hoffmann entered a room that was much bigger than the actual store. And there he was, in the back, sitting in a cluttered office with glass walls. Just like Hoffmann, he'd spent time behind bars, but Cesar's time had been much longer and harder.

"My friend, welcome, my world is yours."

They hugged each other as usual, though it had only been a couple of weeks since they'd last met—Hoffmann had needed a new Radom pistol and Cesar knew how to get ahold of one fast.

"And what can I do for you today?"

"I need your help solving a problem."

"Peter, I've been following the news all week—and I always help a brother. Especially one that pays as well as you. But this, damn . . . it's something else. When we start to talk about war, and about—"

"*That* I'll take care of myself. What you'd have to do is just a small part." Hoffmann pulled off the black cloth he'd had covering his head for the past few days. "This."

Cesar smiled as he surveyed the scalp, rather proud of the job he'd done on it. A rare subject matter that wasn't at all like the more aggressive ones he'd drawn using whatever primitive tools he could scrape together behind bars—it was a free, beautiful lizard with a thick, sparkling tail that disappeared down the neck. He'd never seen a tattoo that resembled it before, but Hoffmann had insisted, and it had taken him two nights to finish it, he'd drawn the whole of it freehand himself with no model.

"I recognized it even on those fuzzy video images they showed on the TV. And I realized they probably don't have much more than that on you. But removing it . . . that will be one hell of a job. And take quite a bit of fucking time."

"Cesar—you don't need to remove it. You need to make another one."

A few minutes later, the self-taught tattoo artist was waiting in the backseat of the car with his black tool bag in hand. Grens, who'd stayed in the passenger seat, turned around and greeted the man, who was in his forties, short but muscular. He reminded the detective of the lifers he'd known in Swedish prisons—not just in the way he moved, but something in his eyes, as if a feeling of confinement continued to slumber in those depths.

Hoffmann started driving, and Grens still had no idea why or where. What the hell were they up to? The only thing he knew for sure was that his mission—to ensure that Hoffmann's family made it home alive—had been badly compromised half an hour ago when a bunch of suits at a White House press conference had broken their promises.

"Hoffmann? I'm asking you again—where the hell are we headed?"

To the backup plan. Where we go if the conditions change. If the direction of the road changes.

Grens didn't have time to ask anything else. Hoffmann hit the brakes after taking a curve a little too fast, and stopped at a red concrete staircase in front of a nine-story building. Hospital Universitario San Ignacio. Bogotá's University Hospital. And out of one of its side entrances a young man in a white coat ran toward the car.

"Benedicto."

Hoffmann greeted him and waved to his two passengers to get out and follow along. Grens identified the smell as soon as they entered the hall, it wasn't difficult, after decades of walking into forensic centers and morgues his policeman's brain recognized any trace of those chemicals immediately. An elevator ride and four doors later they stood there. Stainless-steel refrigerators stacked in rows of three, each one the appropriate size and numbered. Harsh, almost blinding light bounced off the white tiles as the morgue attendant opened the compartment marked 31 and pulled out the two long rails that carried with them a metal stand and a motionless body.

"I'm relieved you're here now, Peter. Moving this around—I couldn't have managed much longer. I've saved it more than once from some knife-happy young medical students."

"A couple more days. Then you'll be rid of both of us." He nodded at the body and placed a brown envelope on its motionless chest. "This is for the time that's passed. When I come back for him, you'll get another envelope. And if I can borrow one of those smaller autopsy rooms for four, maybe five hours, while you wait outside with the door locked, you'll get one more—with just as much."

"Now?"

"Now, Benedicto."

It was easier to work on the body if you kept it on the gurney under one of the powerful lights in the middle of the autopsy room. Cesar started to shave off the dead man's hair, twisted and turned him to get to all of it, then opened his black bag and took out his needles, ink, and a tattoo machine, which looked new, that was both easy to transport and work with—far from his homemade tools in La Picota.

"Unused, sterile needles. Pointless. I mean, this customer isn't gonna be fussy about bacteria, is he?" Cesar smiled as he lowered the gurney—and thus the body—by pressing a foot on the pedal next to one of the front wheels. "It's good you waited a few days, Peter. Right afterward, it wouldn't have worked nearly so well. This corpse won't bleed at all—absolutely no one will notice it's been tattooed after death."

Then he raised it up slightly again, trying to find the best working position. "Maybe everyone should be dead when they get tattooed."

There was a side table—also stainless steel—at an arm's length from the gurney, this was where he lined up his various paint cans and made new mixtures in small bowls. "The decomposition process is already under way, and the skin will soon become wrinkled, gray, a completely different color. But I'm absolutely sure—these shades will work."

Grens, until now, had chosen to stand back. It was easier to study the signs of bleeding in the eyes with no one in the way.

"Who is he?"

"You don't wanna know."

"Just like I don't want to know who killed him?"

Hoffmann crouched down slightly. Cesar was considerably shorter, and it was important that the wax paper lay completely still on the corpse's head as the lizard's contours were copied. It was also a lot easier to avoid eye contact that way too, even though it didn't matter—the detective drew his own conclusions anyway.

"Well, I *have* figured out what you're up to, Hoffmann—and it won't work."

"It will work. The first thing they'll do, Grens, is to run his stats through the FBI's CODIS database. And they won't find shit there. This man *is*—unlike whatever we saw on TV just now—Delta Force. And therefore classified, and kept only in the Navy's own register. The various departments within the US keep each other in the dark. Just like in other countries. You may remember how it worked in Sweden when *you* tried to kill me? When you based your decision on what was in the police records? When the reality was something quite different within same police corridor."

Grens didn't need to answer. They were both well aware he remembered. The detective took the last step forward and put his hand—as usual when he was in a morgue—near the bottom of one lifeless leg, pushed a bit on it, as if wanting to wake up the dead man and get him to kick back.

He'd understood what this was about. And that the body in front of him didn't amount to a lot of evidence—height, weight, build. But it did match Hoffmann, that peculiar tattoo—which Cesar had copied from wax paper and then drew one needle prick at a time onto the dead man's head and down his neck—yes . . . maybe. Normally, it wouldn't suffice, not even as circumstantial evidence. But with a man who was as faceless as he was doomed, and a country that had to keep showing the public results—well, *it might work.*

When Cesar moved from the left side to the right, to have better access to what would become the lizard's eye, Hoffmann took his place. And opened the shoulder holster that hid his hunting knife.

He took hold of the dead man's left hand, pulled it closer, and began to cut at two of his fingers.

"You don't need to do that." Grens tapped Hoffmann on the shoulder.

"Yes, I do."

"They don't know about those fingers. If they did, they would have put it in the description. Specific characteristics are always used in investigations."

"Crouse knows."

"Crouse? It won't matter to him anymore."

"It will, Superintendent."

Hoffmann was careful to do exactly as Zofia had once done with his two fingers. When someone cuts off part of your body, you don't forget it, and he'd memorized every detail—it couldn't get much closer than that, couldn't get much stronger.

He cut gently into the skeleton with his knife until it gave in, hollowed out. From his vest pocket he took out a pair of pruning shears, the same tool she used, clipped parallel bone and tendons, a bit longer than what he really needed. He dissected loose skin until he was sure there was a little too much there—it could be lifted and folded over the stump—and finally glued the edges of the skin together with Super Glue.

In a normal amputation, the glue came loose when the healing process was complete, and the body let go of it. In this case, the healing would never happen since the person was dead. But if he glued carefully, no one would notice—a translucent surface that wasn't visible unless you really examined it closely.

Grens followed Hoffmann's unexpectedly deft movements. To height, weight, build, and a distinctive tattoo, you could now add bone damage to his left hand on identically mutilated fingers.

Hoffmann had not been granted his part of the deal after he'd delivered. So he had to take the next step—those who'd condemned him to death had to *believe* they'd managed to kill him. And therefore remove his name from the list. And because they didn't know his identity they had only watched him through blurry satellite images.

"You're right, Hoffmann. And when he's done with that fancy tattoo you might just succeed. But you've missed an important detail."

For the first time since they left the café and the press conference on a wavy television transmission, Hoffmann stopped. "Excuse me?"

"The fingerprint agreement. It didn't exist when you left Sweden. Now it does. The US's newly won right to have free access to the Swedish fingerprint database."

And when he stopped, he also encountered Grens's gaze. "What the hell are you talking about?"

"That just like the corpse, you have a few fingers left. So this won't work, because US law enforcement, through this agreement, can now simply look up fingerprints in our Swedish registers. My bosses clap their hands and talk about how important this tool is in the fight against crime. However, I'm quite sure that the investigators in the United States can get what they want without any Swede putting a stop to it, but it's not quite so fucking easy when we want something out of them."

Hoffmann painted on a little more glue and once again ran his fingertips over the area that needed to merge, to make sure it wouldn't be noticed. "It *will* work, Superintendent."

"Maybe you're right and the man lying here is not accessible in their registers. Just like you. Up to that point it works. But you're a convict, Hoffmann. And that's why you're in our Swedish criminal records. You'll spread your fingerprints and sooner or later they'll get ahold of them. And because they think you're Danish or Swedish or Norwegian or Icelandic, you, Hoffmann, will be identified as quickly as you cut off those fingers."

"I'm not spreading any fingerprints. And I'm not getting caught. So there won't be anything to compare it to. And, Grens, as soon as I'm found dead, no one will be looking for me."

Grens suddenly realized that Cesar had been standing beside them, working on the tattoo the whole time, and had heard everything. Grens nodded meaningfully toward the body and the tattoo artist, but Hoffmann didn't lower his voice.

"He doesn't understand Swedish. And not much English."

"Are you sure?"

"Yes. Completely sure. But it doesn't matter—Cesar's not stupid, he knows exactly what I'm up to. I trust him. Sometimes, Grens, you have to *choose* to trust someone, even though you can really only trust yourself. Damned if I don't almost trust you!"

Hoffmann smiled weakly, and Grens smiled weakly back. It felt good.

"So, Grens. Now we've come to why you're here."

Still as loud. Grens didn't feel entirely comfortable with that.

"You're the one who has to deliver me to the American Embassy."

"What?"

"Yes, now that I'm dead."

"Get them to let me in? Make them trust me?"

"Yes."

The bright light blinded Grens as he looked straight into it and moved closer to the body.

"I don't desecrate corpses."

"Grens . . . you tried to kill me once."

"Because I'm a cop. And I'm human—I made a mistake."

"And when you decided you had the right to do so, Grens, to kill me, then *your* moral right to judge how I survive ended. None of you have any fucking ethical mandate on that score anymore."

Grens pulled absently on both legs of the corpse. He was here to assist Hoffmann in his struggle to survive. And still furious at those who'd spat in the face of their agreement. He shrugged.

"You think it's possible?"

"Superintendent—I *know* it's possible."

The cell phone lay in one of the pockets of Grens's blazer. He took it out, turned it on, and moved a couple of steps backward. Until the whole body fit in the screen of the phone's camera.

"Very well, Hoffmann. Let's do this."

THE BROKEN NEON sign on the graffiti-covered stone wall was even more difficult to make out in the darkness. SUPER DELI. Ewert Grens rolled down the passenger-side window and glanced into the store—the same clerk still sat on her chair surrounded by half-empty shelves, and he wondered how it was possible to realistically hide the true nature of the business behind that door.

Hoffmann gave Cesar a warm hug at the front door, thanked him for his help, and offered him the envelope with the money they'd agreed on.

"No need." Cesar kindly pushed back Hoffmann's hand. "This time I should be paying you."

"Take it. Without you none of what I'm planning would be possible."

"You don't understand, Peter. Today I . . . hell, sometimes you just cross a limit. You live. Experience something. Inking up that corpse, I don't know, it's rare I feel this damn intoxicated when I'm stone-cold sober."

Hoffmann stubbornly held out the envelope. Until Cesar snatched it from his hand, folded it twice, and pushed it into the breast pocket of Hoffmann's vest.

"It was . . . well, interesting to work with skin that resembled the wax paper I put on your head. Out of pure fucking habit, I tried to wipe away the mess of blood that usually smears the paint—and it wasn't there, didn't bleed—the skin cracked and slid apart. I learned that Super Glue cleans and holds together so well. I promise, they won't see a thing."

A piece of the envelope stuck up, and Cesar pushed it down again, maybe a little harder, to be sure it would remain in Hoffmann's pocket. "And you, Peter, will need that cash for other things. Like getting out of here."

Hoffmann leaned closer. "You *will* take this envelope. Because you're going to help me with one more thing—a small bomb."

"A bomb?"

"Something to blow a car into the air."

They had both lowered their voices, to make sure Grens wouldn't hear.

"Like last time? Or do you have any special requests?"

"Self-timed explosive device with a remote switch. And also a vibration sensor, Cesar—that's important."

A few seconds of silence, a scrutinizing gaze at the older man still sitting in the car, then he nodded slowly with his dark eyes on Hoffmann. "Okay, my friend. In twelve hours. In the same place I always deliver your orders."

"Thank you."

Cesar lifted his black tool bag, ready to go. "Who, Peter?"

"It doesn't matter."

"Anyone I know?"

"Someone who turns angels to rag dolls."

Grens rolled up the window while the two hardened criminals discussed something on the pavement and ended by hugging again. The Swedish police officer smiled—apparently that was the same everywhere, the more hardened the criminal the more they hugged. Hoffmann drove slowly through a somewhat run-down neighborhood, and Grens's thoughts lingered on wax paper and tattoos and corpses. No matter how many years he worked, he still ran across new criminal methods. And no matter how fast they developed their policing, criminals always seemed to be a step ahead.

Darkened blocks replaced each other as the Chapinero neighborhood became the district of Fontibón, slightly nicer houses with broad fences in front of terraced entrances and staircases. The

Internet café didn't look like much standing next to—and completely overshadowed by—a large bingo hall, the entire property glittered Bingo Royale and the announcer's voice over a speaker charged through wide-open windows.

"Superintendent?"

Grens was halfway across the sidewalk when Hoffmann called to him from the driver's seat.

"One more thing."

Grens turned back and realized he was barely limping, his leg hadn't given him much pain for several days, and he almost missed it. Maybe it was the heat. Maybe the adrenaline, being responsible for a man who was literally fighting and running for his life.

"Your trip to Washington."

Washington. He'd never even visited the United States before this trip. And now he would head there for a second time in less than a week. Their options had finally boiled to one—only Sue Masterson had enough influence to vouch for him when he delivered the body of El Sueco. In order to get the US Embassy to let him in, believe in him—and in the corpse.

"How does it feel, Grens—you got this?"

Grens leaned in through the side window, and when he grabbed the door, he stood quite firmly. "Like I'd gladly meet Masterson again. Over a coffee. But I'm not so sure she wants to see me."

"Once you're done with this, Grens, and she's agreed to vouch for you, I want you to give her this." Hoffmann opened the glove compartment and pulled out an envelope that seemed like what he'd just tried to force on Cesar. And yet not at all. This one was sealed. With a red wax seal.

Red, round, and shiny with no stamp in the middle. It looked like the sealed envelopes the Swedish police used for their criminal informants and had likely used with Hoffmann, envelopes that were stored with a logbook and contained an informant's real name, sealed by the handler on the first day of a mission.

"What's this?"

"I know what you're thinking. But this has nothing to do with code names or real names. What you're holding, which no messenger can open undetected, is my absolute last tip. My parting gift to Masterson."

"Which holds what?"

"The time and location where they can pick up the pieces of one of the names on their list."

"*I* asked you for just this. You may remember that? For a tip. About a drug delivery. When we were waiting for that fucking press conference. I told you, you could go home. With your family. To Sweden. A short sentence in protective custody along with your favorite policemen. But maybe I was unclear? Or maybe you misunderstood one small detail—that in order to influence your situation in Sweden the tip has to be to the *Swedish* police. Not to American law enforcement."

"I remember. And I'm working on it. You'll get your tip, Grens. But this is something else entirely—it's personal—and it's meant for Masterson."

Grens took the envelope, fiddled a bit with the seal, and hid it in his inside jacket pocket. "If you say so."

"I do say so. Tomorrow then. See you outside the Hospital Universitario San Ignacio. And we'll unload some of the morgue's educational materials."

The car disappeared beyond the bingo hall's flashing neon sign, and Ewert Grens opened the door to an Internet café for the first time in his life. He paid for an hour at a computer and for a plastic cup of light liquid the café owner insisted on labeling coffee. And then he entered one of the few telephone numbers he knew by heart.

He was about to break his promise to leave no trace that could lead back to Erik Wilson and from there to Sue Masterson. But now, using his authority as a policeman was the only chance he had left to fulfill a greater promise—ensuring that Piet Hoffmann came home alive.

"Hello?"

Drowsy. Tired. Hoarse.

"Sven, it's me."

Someone who was lying down. Fumbling with the phone.

"Ewert?"

Someone who cleared his throat and rolled over on his side and whispered so as not to wake up the person lying next to him.

"You don't know how happy I am to hear your voice!"

Ewert Grens smiled, swallowed. And hoped that it wouldn't be audible over the phone. Sven Sundkvist, his closest colleague and the person in his life who'd put up with him the longest, might think he was touched. "And I was under the impression that you were pretty tired of it."

"Don't you understand, Ewert . . . you don't, do you, well— I've been worried. For real. You just disappeared. Wandered out of the station you've more or less lived in as long as I've known you—without a word—carrying a brown suitcase with an Eiffel Tower sticker in one corner."

Sven rolled out of bed now, bare feet against the cold floor, as he crept out of the bedroom he shared with his wife and down the wooden stairs to the darkness of their terraced home's first floor.

"It's the middle of the night, Ewert. You know that, right?"

"Night?"

Sundkvist knew that voice so well. Ewert sounded surprised, for real. And was perhaps just as surprised as his voice indicated. That's usually how it was. His boss wanted to talk—and as soon as it occurred to him to call, he did. Without considering the circumstances of the person he was calling. As you do when your own life lacks context, routine, family.

But this time he wasn't calling from the threadbare corduroy sofa in in the police station where he usually slept. The phone number. The sound quality. The background noise. He was somewhere else.

"So you hadn't thought of that? Okay, Ewert. A time difference. I guess I at least know you're a good distance from here. West? East? Will it soon be night or has night passed?"

"Sorry, Sven, but that's still none of your business." Grens brought the phone closer to his mouth, as usual when he was about to be serious. "Where are you?"

"In the kitchen. It's cold. We lower the heat at night."

"Then I want you to get dressed. Not because you're cold. But because I need you to drive into town. To the police station."

"Ewert?"

"How long will it take?"

"Please, Ewert, listen now—"

"How long?"

"Twenty-five minutes. There's no traffic now. Since it is the middle of the night."

"Good. When you get there, forward an email to the US Embassy in Bogotá—but do it from my email address. From the Police Authority in Stockholm. To a Jonathan Woods. Ask for a meeting. And attach a photo."

"A photograph?"

"Of a body."

"Ewert?"

"A corpse."

Sundkvist was no longer tiptoeing over the cold floor—he was sitting at the kitchen table with a glass of water. This wasn't good. He knew that, of course. When his stomach started burning like this, from his chest to his neck, tightening with each breath, he'd learned that meant *this* was something he'd rather not be a part of.

He hadn't seen his boss and friend for several days, and had been worried, thought more about Ewert than he dared admit to himself. Then suddenly Ewert got in contact with him. In the middle of the night. From a location Sven now realized was probably Bogotá, Colombia. And he did so with a picture of a dead man.

A reality that didn't quite hang together. Despite the fact that his thoughts turned in and out and back again, that damn corpse made no more sense now than when he started. Ewert Grens—in South America? It didn't fit. A man who spent his days between the police station in Kungsholmen and the apartment on Svea Road, a life that took place within a few square kilometers. If somebody had asked Sven just a few hours ago to guess the extent of Ewert's knowledge of the continent of South America, he would have wagered that his boss probably didn't even know where Colombia was located.

"Ewert—who is the dead person?"

"I can't tell you that."

"Who took the picture?"

"I can't tell you that."

"Who killed him?"

"I can't tell you that."

Sundkvist was a skilled interrogator. The City Police's best. But this time he wouldn't be getting any answers, because Grens was acting like all the criminals they'd interrogated or would interrogate—giving an answer that meant no comment, or an angry stare at the floor, or a simple fuck-you to the interrogator. Grens basically did all three at once.

"Okay, Ewert—then let's go back in time a bit, shall we? To the moment you ran past me in the hallway with your Eiffel Tower suitcase in hand. On the same day the news happened to be dominated by the kidnapping of an American politician and a new war on terror that focused on the global center of cocaine production. I didn't consider it at the time, of course. But now you want me to send a picture of a corpse to the US Embassy in . . . that very nation's capital city?"

"Finally."

"Ewert—what the hell is this about? Really?"

A dead man. And a detective's first instinct should be to investigate, seek answers. Ewert was doing the opposite. He was shutting down. Hiding something. Even from his closest associate. He'd done that only once before in the time Sven had served at his side—when two young women were transported to Sweden against their will and locked up in order to be bought by Swedish men. Back then

Grens had altered evidence, influenced the investigation, and risked his career to protect a man he cared for, felt responsible for. But in Colombia, on the other side of the Atlantic? In an official drug war? In that case—for whose sake? His own?

No. Not Ewert, he didn't work like that. Sundkvist was breathing very slowly. It simply didn't make *sense.*

"Sven?" An impatient, strained voice. "Sven, stop being so damn difficult! I don't have much time. I'm sending you a picture. When you get to the homicide unit, log on to the network from my office, using my login. And then send the email I'm asking you to send. I keep my ID card with my gun in the gun cabinet. And the key to the cabinet is under my tape deck."

The tape deck. Next to the photo of Siw and the cassette tapes, which were Ewert's everything. Where else would it be if not among the most important things in the room?

"Ewert? Answer me honestly now. No fucking *no comment* or *I can't tell you that.*"

"Sven . . ."

"Ewert—are you in danger?"

Grens hesitated. Too long. "No."

"Colombia? The American Embassy? A corpse? Can you guarantee, Ewert, that what you're asking me to do has nothing to do with you being in danger?"

"Yes, Sven. I can guarantee that. *I* am not in danger."

He'd answered. Without answering. *I am not in danger.* Someone else was in danger—someone he was prepared to take risks for.

"One more question. Ewert—is this an order?" The connection was bad and the distances extreme. Maybe that's what caused the silence that came rather than an answer. "Hello, did you hear me?"

"Sven, I . . ."

"Is this—an order?"

"No."

"Then I don't understand."

"Because all of this is for a case that doesn't exist—at all. You could search through every file and folder and report in the entire police station, and you still wouldn't find it. So I can't order you as your boss, Sven, not this time. But I can ask you to do this for me as my friend."

THE FLIGHT TOOK the same amount of time as before—four and a half hours. And just like before, he managed to make his way through every page of the complimentary *New York Times* and the *Washington Post* handed out by the flight attendant before the passengers were asked to sit down and fasten their seat belts for a slow approach to Dulles International. But the similarities between Ewert Grens's first journey to the American capital stopped as soon as he reached passport control. He was surrounded by three guards, taken out of a long queue, escorted to a dirty little hole that reminded him of the interrogation rooms he often worked in, and asked again and again to explain why he had no luggage, why he was planning to be on American soil for such a short time, so short he'd hardly have time to take a taxi into the city before he'd have to head back for check-in again.

Because he wouldn't need to. Because as soon as he passed through the perfume-scented and shiny tax-free boutiques, past the hall with the spinning baggage carriage, he was going to sit down at a table in a corner of a restaurant that served expensive airport food to stressed-out travelers mostly searching for the drinks menu. And he'd stay there—until he was finished talking to a woman who was already waiting for him.

"Thanks for coming out here. I don't have much time."

"Grens, neither do I. I especially don't have time for people who promised me I'd never have to meet them again."

"And I'll make the same promise this time."

Sue Masterson drank French mineral water. Grens asked for the same when the waiter passed. "But—we wouldn't be here if it wasn't for another promise, one you gave, that hasn't been kept."

She looked at him, and perhaps her eyes seemed slightly softer. Behind that hard exterior was probably someone who felt humiliated, heartbroken, and was looking for retribution. She wouldn't have met with him otherwise.

"Very well, Detective Grens, go ahead—one *last* time."

That hardness. He liked it.

"I asked you to come here, because for the first time since I applied to the police academy in the mid-seventies, I need a reference. I need an authority to vouch for me. You need to certify what an intelligent, reliable, analytical person I am."

She looked at him. Was he deliberately wasting her time? Was he mocking her? She decided that wasn't the case. The older man had the same facial expressions, the same way of holding himself as at their previous meetings. And the same jargon. She'd become familiar with it. And underneath that jargon was something quite serious.

"In about twenty-four hours you're going to get a phone call from the US Embassy in Bogotá. It will be to inform you that Piet Hoffmann is dead."

Her stomach. As if he'd punched her. As if he'd punched *through* her. And there was a hole there now.

"I don't understand . . . when . . ."

"Since Piet Hoffmann cut two fingers off a corpse with some pruning shears and tattooed its head to match his own."

The hole in her stomach. She slowly understood, and it disappeared. "Another joke like that and I'll leave. And now it's your turn, Grens, to answer my question. If you answer correctly, we continue."

"Okay."

"Was it a corpse from the beginning? Or did it become a corpse for Hoffmann's solution?"

An assurance. If a man's life had—again—been sacrificed to save another man's life.

"It *was* a corpse. A corpse that became a corpse when sixteen-hundred Pennsylvania Avenue sent him to make a corpse of

Hoffmann. So when your colleague at the International Narcotics and Law Enforcement Affairs Section in Bogotá calls, it will be to decide whether or not to look at that corpse. And he'll only do that if he believes the man sitting across from him. Me."

Masterson should have stood up and left. That's what she would have done if the same question had been put to her just a few weeks earlier. Back then, even considering a deception of the police authorities that constituted her whole life would have seemed like fraud to her. But now, there wasn't much left to lose.

"Okay, Grens . . ." She understood what Hoffmann was thinking. How someone else's death might mean his life. ". . . I'll vouch for you. If I know how."

Grens held out a two-sided document. "Here. An international drug project with the US and Europe as partners. The Inter-American Drug Abuse Control Commission. My suggestion is that we both participated in it. That's where we got to know each other. Through the meetings I've summarized there."

She took the handwritten notes and read through them quickly. "Do you believe in this, Grens?"

"In international drug operations?"

"That Hoffmann could be dead. That you can make them believe it."

"I believe that this is his very last chance. And you and I are obliged to do what we can to help him implement it."

She looked at him. Shrugged her shoulders. "Well then. I'll vouch for you. Say you're clever. Analytical. That we worked together." Then she got up, stretched a hand over the table, already on her way.

"Not yet." Grens pointed to her chair. "One more thing."

She chose to remain standing.

He pulled one more document out of his small briefcase. "This is Hoffmann's parting gift to you. A final good-bye. A tip about . . . somebody. Which I was clearly not supposed to know about."

She took it, ran two fingers gently over the wax seal. But she didn't look as happy, or even as interested, as Grens had expected. Despite the hardness, he thought she'd smile, at least a little. Every boss loved a tip.

"Sue?" He tried to reach her. In a tone that completely lacked any trace of teasing. This tone was serious. "Is something wrong? Besides the fact that we both got a very low blow from your friends at the White House?"

She smiled. "I'll take care of this envelope. Hoffmann's tips have always been exactly what he said they were. But it will also be the last thing I do in this position. Then it will be my turn to chase down references." She stuffed the envelope into her thin jacket's outer pocket.

"I wasn't just duped. I'm going to lose my job. It's not something anyone is talking about. But I know it—they never would have used a DEA chief like this if they planned on keeping them around, they've tried this with other police organizations that have bitten back pretty hard. I negotiated the only thing I wasn't supposed to. And lost."

Grens was not a man who ran around hugging people. But he felt like doing that now. For a moment she looked so small, vulnerable, despite all that strength.

"I understand fully what a risk you took by meeting me. Meeting Hoffmann through me. And maybe it's not much consolation. But I promise you. You will never have to do that again."

She smiled again, faintly. And pressed his outstretched hand for one second too long. "Now, when it doesn't matter anymore. When I could take whatever risks I want to. Like vouching for a particularly stubborn Swedish detective." And then she disappeared, through the restaurant, and then out of the airport.

Grens looked at the time, one hour until check-in, he had time to order again—replace the tasteless mineral water with a coffee and maybe one of those brownies.

HE'D CHOSEN A car with a large trunk. That was the only requirement. Enough space for a pale, rigid body.

They'd dressed the corpse in clothes from a secondhand shop, used but in good condition, high quality without being exclusive. Hoffmann studied his physical alter ego. The man Benedicto was pushing out of the Hospital Universitario San Ignacio's side entrance on a gurney seemed believable enough, could surely be the man millions of people all over the world had seen in blurry news clips.

"Thank you for your help. Here's your compensation." Hoffmann handed one final envelope to the morgue attendant, who'd been moving this cold, motionless body around to keep it intact.

"Anytime, Peter. You know that."

They shook hands and the metal wheels of the gurney whined as usual as Benedicto returned to the other bodies, the ones that *would* be sliced up for the educational benefit of medical students.

"And now, Superintendent, it's your turn."

Hoffmann grabbed the corpse's shoulders, Grens the legs. They lifted, pushed a little, lifted again—the dead man didn't quite fit, the trunk was difficult to get closed.

"Okay—now it's my turn." Grens had long since realized and accepted that he was not in control. That for a few strange days all he could do was follow, maybe try to understand a bit, but not much more than that. "But not until I get the tip we so desperately need and which you, Hoffmann, promised me."

Grens hadn't even finished the sentence before the informant, who always had his own agenda and timetable, held out a grocery store receipt. Told him to turn it over. On the back stood seven handwritten rows of tiny letters that Grens couldn't make out without his glasses.

"Place, time, route. Just like you asked. More than a ton of ninety-four percent grade cocaine headed to Sweden through England. But the information is *still* dependent on a condition: a short prison sentence."

"I told you. I'm not just some Swedish or American police officer. I keep my word."

They parted at the hospital driveway. Hoffmann took off in his own car, and Grens headed in the rental toward the US Embassy, from the eastern part of the capital, through the darkness of the city center, and to the west.

"Sven?" He'd dialed the same number as the previous night. Heard a voice that was equally drowsy and hoarse.

"Again? Ewert?"

"That's right. It's dear old Ewert. I bet you missed me."

The same groan, throat clearing, rolling out of bed with the phone to his ear.

"I did what you asked me to. I emailed the photograph. So I—"

"And you did it well. So well that I'm going to reward you with another job."

"Ewert . . . my reward is that I get to sleep. In peace."

"Soon. After you've written down what I'm about to tell you."

Something rustled. Sven Sundkvist had stood up, a pen and a notepad and pajamas, it was easy to imagine.

"Okay?"

"The biggest Swedish cocaine seizure ever."

"I'm not sure I follow."

"In thirty-six hours."

"One moment."

Grens heard a chair being pulled out, a sigh as Sven sank into it.

"Continue, Ewert."

"A freighter. Which originally departed from Venezuela, a port city on the Caribbean Sea, or the Atlantic—now I'm not entirely sure of the pronunciation but basically . . . Ka-ru-pano. Spelled with a *C* and with an accent over the *u*. Transporting cocaine to multiple destinations. Arriving today in Aberdeen in Scotland, officially carrying coffee beans, and planning to proceed to Cádiz in southern Spain. But it's the Aberdeen load that we are interested in. It's meant for two submarines. One headed to Denmark and Norway, one to Sweden and Finland."

A pencil. You could hear the scratch of the tip against rough paper.

"Did you say submarines?"

"Yes. Mini subs. Eighty percent of all the cocaine smuggled from South America to the United States is now transported underwater. It's the best way to smuggle it. You learn a hell of a lot down here, Sven. They've also seen even larger submarines headed in another direction—Europe. The risk of being lost in a storm or an accident is much greater than being caught. The ones I'm talking about go all the way from Scotland underwater. Filled with cocaine."

There was no longer any scratching. From the telephone line or from Sven's pencil.

"Where?"

"The east coast. The Stockholm archipelago. Near an island called Granholmen. I'll send the exact coordinates in an email from the Internet café."

His younger colleague was several thousand kilometers away in a land called Sweden, but you could hear him stand up, the scrape of the chair. Then those steps back to bed. His voice sounded hoarse as he lay down again.

"I'm hanging up now. It's the middle of the night here."

"Not yet. Tomorrow I want you to tell all of this to our favorite prosecutor. Every detail. Including the coordinates."

"Ågestam?"

"Yes."

Now Sven Sundkvist shifted position, probably to his side. "Why, Ewert?"

"I can't tell you. Yet."

Yes, on his side. That's how he lay. Definitely.

"You're telling me that this—and I know I'm tired—but you're telling me about the chance for a record seizure? And you want *him* of all people to take the credit for it? The man you like the *least* out of all of our colleagues?"

"Yes. Exactly."

"I don't understand."

"All you need to understand is that Ågestam has to take all the credit. The happier, the prouder he is, the better."

For the last part of the call, the car had been standing still. He was there. He glimpsed the roof of the US embassy just three hundred meters away. This is the spot where he was supposed to park, then take a taxi to his hotel, and it was here he'd return tomorrow to finish the work of securing Piet Hoffmann his last chance at survival.

THE US EMBASSY in Bogotá looked exactly like the US embassy in Stockholm. A high fence with guards on patrol, a red and white and blue flag fluttering in the breeze, light-colored buildings with flat roofs and on them stood giant round satellite dishes gaping at the sky with longing. It also felt the same. A particular kind of hostility and suspicion. The presumption that everyone was an enemy intent on destroying you until proven otherwise.

Ewert Grens was warm and flushed as he hurried up the gentle slope of the street on slightly aching legs and knocked on the window of the glass booth, the reception and entrance where Colombian service personnel were crowded in with elite American soldiers. He pushed his ID through the hatch, prepared for the same argument he had every time his investigations crossed into these small American kingdoms. But he didn't even have time to finish his prepared explanation because a man in a suit, a white shirt, and a blue tie with very short blond hair sticking up like one of those satellites was already waiting for him behind a wall of muscular men in uniform.

"Welcome. Jonathan Woods, director of the International Narcotics and Law Enforcement Affairs Section here at the embassy. Do you prefer English? Spanish? Portuguese?"

"Swedish."

Jonathan Woods had very white teeth, and he flashed them as he smiled broadly. "Well then, I'm sorry to say you'll have to make do with English—I never quite finished my Scandinavian studies."

They said little as they walked across the well-guarded courtyard. Grens counted the cameras, then the guards, and realized they were of basically equal number. Inside the building stood even more armed men, but dressed in civilian clothing. They climbed up the stairs to the second floor and entered an office with a view of the spiked iron gate he'd just walked through.

"Swedish police?" Woods waved his suit-clad arm toward a visitor's chair for Grens to sit down.

"Yes."

"Our background check confirmed that—thirty-nine years on the force, detective superintendent at the homicide unit in Stockholm in a unit called City Police. But we don't know why you're in Colombia."

The chair that had seemed so elegant was uncomfortable. Wooden slats pressed against his lower back. The upholstery chafed.

"I'm not at liberty to say."

The embassy official watched his visitor twisting in his seat trying to find a comfortable position, then asked him to wait a moment, came right back with another chair, or rather an armchair. Red velvet, rounded armrests, soft without being *too* soft. Grens nodded gratefully, sank down. It reminded him a bit of the corduroy sofa in his own office.

"You can't tell me anything, but you can send me pictures of a dead body, huh?"

"I can *show* you a body, too."

"And how do I know that it's the one we're looking for?"

"You don't know. But you can examine it. It's yours to do what you want with it."

"And what do you get out of it?"

"Nothing."

"Everyone always wants something."

They'd discussed the lie. Hoffmann had told him—a lie has to be true enough or it will be seen through.

"I ended up with a dead body on my hands."

The truth was both words and tone of voice, the movements of the eyes and the way of breathing. And Grens had told Hoffmann in turn that he, being twenty years his senior, had twenty years of experience on him when it came to lying.

"And if it's the body I suspect it is, then it will do you a lot more good than it will me."

"A Swedish detective in Colombia as a tourist. No official mission. But here he is running around with the corpse of one of the world's most wanted men."

"That pretty much sums it up."

"Grens? Is that how you pronounce it? I would guess you've conducted thousands of interrogations, heard from thousands of idiots. If you were sitting in my chair right now, would *you* believe your story?"

"No. But I can't tell you any more than what I have. Does it matter? You're looking for someone—and I may have him with me. If it turns out to be that person, you'll be a hero. If not, you've wasted a few minutes on a visitor who's not asking for anything. So if I was in your position, I'd stop asking questions. Get on the phone to a senior official and check to see if I'm a person who knows what he's talking about. And I'd start with your boss, Sue Masterson."

There are so many types of silences. Embarrassed. Forced. Uncomfortable. Threatening. Natural. Welcome. Pleasant. Comforting.

This silence was none of those things. It was a slow evaluation. And absolutely crucial. If the embassy official regarding him now, one Jonathan Woods with short, spiky blond hair, were to ask the stranger across from him to get up and leave, that would destroy Hoffmann's last hope. If, however, he continued to listen, to weigh, to make verification calls to DEA headquarters just outside Washington, there would be a small opening left for one family to survive.

"If you'll excuse me." Woods walked through the door and closed it ceremoniously behind him.

Grens remained in another kind of silence. A silence of waiting, anxiety, and lack of control. He leaned back in his easy chair, checked the clock ticking on the wall, and closed his eyes.

Twenty-seven minutes. Then the door opened just as ceremonially as it closed.

"It took a bit for me to get an answer."

Grens stretched unconsciously. "And?"

"Sue Masterson vouched for you. Apparently, you both worked in CICAD?"

"If you say so."

Jonathan Woods leaned forward, smiled. "It's that secret?"

"I promised Masterson not to talk to anyone about our joint work."

"With all due respect, the Inter-American Drug Abuse Control Commission sounds good, but I really don't believe in those kinds of international bureaucratic task forces. I would rather—"

"If you say so."

The embassy official regarded the Swedish detective claiming to be in Colombia as a tourist for a long time.

"Where is the body—*now*?"

"In a rental car. Three hundred meters down the street. In the trunk."

Woods moved to the window to a view of the embassy's iron gate and armed guards, as if hoping to see the vehicle they were talking about. "And when we open it—how do I know you don't have any other intentions? For example, what if it were to explode?"

"You don't know. But you've got an army at your disposal here that's pretty good at investigating those sorts of things."

They looked at each other again, in yet another kind of silence—quieter, cooler.

"Well then, are we done?"

Woods nodded. "I suppose so. I've called for someone to escort you out."

Grens had just stood up and started walking toward the door when Woods seemed to change his mind.

"Mr. Grens."

"Yes?"

"Now that I think about it—we're not really done here after all."

Ewert Grens had always had a face that hid how worried, how unsure, he might feel. He hoped that was the case now.

"I need one more thing from you. Before I can let you go."

The embassy official must have figured it out. Realized something. Seen he was facing a bluff.

"The car keys."

Woods didn't smile, but almost. And Grens felt his anxiety crashing down from his chest to slowly leak out the bottom of his stomach.

"Here." Grens held out his hand with the keys, and they said good-bye. When Woods opened the door, a young man was already waiting to escort their guest out of the building and off of US territory. The Swedish detective had taken his first steps when he again stopped, turned back, and this time he was the one with something to say. "By the way."

"Yes?"

"I'd appreciate it if you cleaned the inside of the car thoroughly. And fill up the gas tank before you return it. Apparently, they're sticklers about that."

A SHORT WALK. Hoffmann was waiting for Grens about a kilometer from the US Embassy. Grens was easily identifiable from a distance, the large body, the slight hobble, as his left leg compensated for the constant pain. They walked slowly down two blocks of well-preserved buildings—far enough for Grens to have time to give him all the details of how the dead man in the trunk was received, and thus confirm that there was at least one last chance. And when they parted, Hoffmann lingered in the intersection of two one-way streets and watched as the policeman he'd decided to trust—who'd just launched the most crucial phase of his plan for survival—left. And now it was up to Piet to finish the rest.

THAT FUCKING NEWS report.

The television had been on in the brothel bar, and El Mestizo was watching it distractedly while drinking a beer. It took him a while to understand what it was about, but gradually from someplace deep inside, his rage grew. A reporter spoke excitedly about authentic images being shown for the first time. The razor-sharp voice shouted out the revelation that another name had been crossed off the kill list. El Sueco. American politicians were holding a triumphant press conference to reveal the explicit photographs of a lifeless body. A team of prominent forensic experts had confirmed, *after comparing all external circumstances with the actual existing conditions and distinctive characteristics of the deceased*, that the identity of the individual known as the Seven of Hearts, who lacked both a face and a name, was *beyond any reasonable doubt a match for a man who had been found dead in Bogotá, likely strangled by a neck snare.*

Seen. Understood. Hated. After the last image had disappeared from the TV, his rage turned into a kind of panic, a dizziness he'd never felt, and he staggered up the brothel staircase to the first floor, to one of the rooms with large beds meant for selling sex.

It was as if everything around him became transparent. As if he were moving through a world without color. The fiery red carpet in the entrance hall, stained and rough where customers had spilled their drinks, the moss-green plants climbing out of their self-watering pots and up onto the trellis, the deep-blue sky that stood watch outside the brothel windows.

Everything was transparent. As if it no longer existed. Just like the trust he had—against his own principles—placed in another man, and now the man he'd chosen to let in and believe in also no longer existed.

And when he pulled his gun from its holster and shot at the first person he happened to meet in the corridor, then shot her again—even then everything remained transparent. His secretary, who had worked for him for twelve years, now lay on the floor of the brothel bleeding colorless blood.

It was the first time he'd found himself in such a world, and it was so much easier, moving without air resistance, as if he could walk straight through the customers who were now pressed against the walls and the young women who were crawling along the floor, while he continued firing his weapon at random.

Transparent.

He fucking knew what this was all about.

You or me. And I care more about me than about you, so I choose me.

El Mestizo yelled, screamed, pushed an armchair away, knocked over a couple of lamps, and kicked in a door—room 15, as good as any other. The woman lying naked on the bed, in front of a man who was getting dressed, saw her employer aiming his gun at him, shooting him twice in the chest. And she didn't understand why.

She didn't know that the man shooting wildly had just a minute ago seen someone betraying him in a news report, pretending to be dead, and that he would continue to shoot until the transparency had gone.

ERIK WILSON TURNED off the small fourteen-inch television on his desk.

Day after day with no information, and it had been hell. Then, no contact whatsoever. That was why he'd so enthusiastically cleared his calendar when Sven Sundkvist, Mariana Hermansson, and Lars Ågestam knocked on his door to discuss an upcoming raid on a cocaine shipment to Sweden. Because it had to be connected to Hoffmann in some way. That is why for the past several days, several times an hour, he'd turned on the TV and sought out the US news channels. It *could* be connected to Hoffmann. And that was why he now sat completely still in his office in the homicide unit of the Kronoberg police station, weeping.

Nothing would ever be connected to him again. Piet Hoffmann was dead.

The CNN report he'd just watched had said so—packaged and presented as today's big news in the fight against drugs. Another playing card had been ripped apart. The Seven of Hearts, the so-called El Sueco, had been killed.

Wilson tried to collect himself, tried to make sense of it. Had he understood correctly? Had the clips of Colombian coca plantations and cocaine kitchens really been followed by slow shots of the trunk of a car outside the US embassy in Bogotá? And did they really show that body?

Lying on its right side. That much he remembered. Facing the inside of the trunk, back to the camera. An image that felt arranged—they had twisted his right arm under his body to get the deceased into that position.

But then the camera zoomed closer. On the left hand were two mutilated fingers. On the top of the head was a black piece of cloth that they pulled off, uncovering a large tattoo—a lizard he recognized.

Hoffmann. Dead.

And even though he wept ever more quiet, gentle tears that lingered on his upper lip, which he removed with the tip of his tongue, still he continued to be emptied out from the inside.

THE WOMAN STANDING on the other side of the bar was naked from the waist up.

She pushed the bottle of beer toward El Mestizo, precisely as cold—never over five degrees Celsius—as he preferred it. This was his joint after all. The guests who came here, who consumed absurdly overpriced alcohol in exchange for access to young women and rooms, had no idea—they didn't mean a thing, they were only here because El Mestizo allowed them to be. Just as he'd allowed the man who betrayed him to be here.

Despite the serious tone of the news report, despite the convincing formulations and the tattoo, he'd seen through all of it immediately. The Seven of Hearts was not dead. He'd realized how that body, so very important to save, had been used. That was not Peter. But it was supposed to look like Peter.

And then after that the dead man had called. Said a single sentence. *Johnny, I bet you want to talk to me.* And hung up.

After that, Johnny had returned to the bar and asked Rosalita to turn off the television that played the same news reports on a loop. He'd closed his eyes, following his thoughts inward, remained still while they landed.

The man who'd gained his trust no longer existed. Not because he *was* dead, as the reporter claimed. But because he *must* die and *would*.

He waved her over, and she picked up another bottle of Aguila, made sure it was properly chilled, and pushed it across the counter like before. She was on her way to a new customer at the other end of the bar when he spoke.

"Stay here, Rosalita."

She did. Waiting. It was as if he were gathering his thoughts. Then he looked at her, pulling what he was about to say from deep inside.

"You need to learn something."

"Yes?"

"Never trust anyone."

"Excuse me?"

"That's just how it is, Rosalita. Do you hear me? You should never trust anyone." He waved his hand for her to go.

The beer didn't help. The truth was just as difficult to swallow. He'd learned never, never, never to trust anyone. One single rule. In his private life as well as at work. They'd spoken of it a bit, he and Peter, after they discovered they were alike. Peter was even the one who formulated what they both thought. *Trust only yourself.* And they'd laughed, two people who didn't trust a single motherfucker, how could they trust each other?

"Rosalita."

She'd better come back. He waved, she'd better *hurry* back.

"Something else? Should I . . . one more?" She looked at his bottle, still half full.

"What I said before, Rosalita."

"Before?"

"Do you? Do you trust someone, Rosalita?"

"I don't know if . . ."

"You can go again." For the second time, he waved her away. And traveled with his thoughts, inward, to the car he once fell asleep in. To the mother he'd chosen to reveal.

He shouldn't have done either. He shouldn't have invited anyone in. She'd been right.

Hoffmann tapped lightly on the bar, and Rosalita looked up. He smiled and waited until she smiled back and nodded to the owner's table, where El Mestizo now sat with a bottle of beer in front of him.

"The usual?"

"The usual, Rosalita."

She looked at him, knew very well what his usual was, both of them. When he was about to head to work with their mutual boss he wanted black coffee to stay alert, after they came back and he'd sit here talking with the boss he preferred Colombian rum to relax. Now she didn't know really. He wasn't dressed for work, but he seemed tense, as in the way he moved and watched her. Prepared. That's what he was. And when she combined his clothes with his behavior she decided to serve him coffee—and rum. He took the warm cup and the beautiful glass and nodded in thanks, she'd read him right. And then went over to the owner's table with his hands full.

"Johnny."

El Mestizo stared at him without answering. He had laid his gun on the table, and when Hoffmann got closer, he lifted it up, weighed it in his hand, pushed out the fully loaded chamber and spun it a couple of times before pushing it back in and putting the gun back on the table, careful to keep the muzzle pointed at his visitor.

"I had to. There was no other way."

El Mestizo stared at him, silent.

"Either I go home with my wife and sons, you know how much she wants that, or she'll leave me."

Not a movement. Not a word.

"And losing someone you're that close to, no man can risk that. Right, Johnny?"

Hoffmann closed one hand around the glass of rum, another around the cup of hot black coffee. Both still untouched.

The limit. Everything depended on that. To go near it, balance on it, but never go over it. Had he done so just now? Had he done so just by coming here?

But he had no choice. It wasn't the adult El Mestizo who had to be neutralized, it was the child, the betrayed El Mestizo who was dangerous—the El Mestizo who knew he was being abandoned, that the closeness he so rarely allowed had been taken advantage of. And if after finding out that Peter Haraldsson had been identified as the body El Mestizo finished off, El Mestizo would have analyzed and evaluated everything without contact, without explanation, then he would immediately put all of his resources to hunting down and killing Piet Hoffmann and his family. So instead Piet sought out El Mestizo to convince him they were still on the same side, that together they could fight back the next time they were attacked, that he would stand by El Mestizo to the end—and perhaps that would buy him the days he needed to get out of here.

"Yes. I understand that you're disappointed. And one day I will go home. To northern Europe. But not until this fucking kill list has come to an end. Not until I know that you too have gotten out unscathed. Until then, my friend, I will be at your side."

But maybe that wasn't the only reason for coming here—lying to gain time? Could there be another reason? Such as getting close enough to meet El Mestizo's eyes, see how the pain had dug its way inside a man who took the life of little angels and so must be deprived of his own—maybe it was because Hoffmann wanted this. He couldn't leave it alone. That feeling that he, who was now formally dead, would continue to live, while the man who sat in silence opposite him, formally still alive, would die—could that be it?

Manipulation. Revenge. Sometimes it gave you the same rush.

And when he left the brothel, much later, both the glass of rum and cup of coffee stood on the table, untouched. He'd never again need to maintain his focus before a job they'd do together, or sit down afterward and relax.

El Mestizo had ordered one more. Ice cold. And when Rosalita served it, he asked her to join him.

"Sit."

She did, hesitantly, at the very edge of the booth.

"Do you remember what I told you, Rosalita? Seven beers ago."

"No. Yes. What do you . . ."

"Never trust anyone. Rosalita. *Never.*"

She didn't understand. Why was she sitting here? At the owner's table? During all the years she'd worked for El Mestizo, she'd never seen him shake like this. She'd heard from Zaneta that he'd killed his secretary. He did things like that outside the brothel, she knew that, but he'd never shot anyone in here before. She should be afraid. She wasn't. Uneasiness, that was what she felt, his unpredictability had swirled around them, but she was sure he wouldn't hurt her, that it had passed now.

"Because if you trust someone, Rosalita, they will eventually leave you. Betray you."

Her boss took her hand, held it hard.

"And if someone disappears far, far away from you, you lose their loyalty."

Her hand. He pulled it closer, lifted it, rubbed it against his cheek.

"And somebody who you let get too close who's planning to be so far away—he might just talk, betray you, expose you."

He rubbed her soft hand against his cheek, back and forth, she felt the back of her hand grow warm and saw his skin turning red.

"And when somebody talks too much—they have to die. Did you know that, Rosalita?"

Then El Mestizo stood up suddenly, kissed each of her fingers lightly, and left. Headed toward the exit and his car. To the woman who had been right when she told him not to trust anyone. And toward the person who would take on the mission of putting an end to the man who betrayed him.

She'd been right. *She'd been right.* Even his father, a man he'd met on only two occasions, had been right. My son, he'd said the last time. You don't know what friendship is. But you'll understand when you end up in prison or in the hospital. Then you'll know where love exists. He understood what his father meant. As life went by, he had fewer and fewer friends. They took advantage of him. Stole from him, from what he was. And didn't give back when he needed it.

He remembered exactly when he'd made the decision. How he'd rambled through the morning, the day, the evening from communida to communida in Cali with Peter at his side, showing that the new guy from Sweden should be accepted, invited, was one of them from now on. He'd vouched for him and absolutely no one had misunderstood—the man I'm introducing to you now, you don't touch him.

Clínica Medellín's entrance hall was as bright and calm as he'd come to expect, and he stopped there at the small flower shop, pointed to a colorful bouquet, and tore away the paper as he rode the elevator to the eighteenth floor.

That fucking smell again. Disease. Death. Her death.

He counted even more beds than on his last visit. Now they stood in rows, and in two lines in the corridor.

But in the room at the end of corridor she was alone. Eyes closed, as usual. Yet somehow different. She was unconscious. And it gave her face a sort of peace. Her wrinkles weren't quite as sharp, her mouth not so ready to bite. He kissed her forehead, opened the window for some fresh air, moved the visitor's chair from the foot of the bed closer to her hands.

"Are you back already?" The female doctor, who he paid double to take care of a single patient, winced as she stepped in and realized that someone was inside the hospital room.

"She's worse. She needs her medicine."

"You left us enough anti-virals to last the next couple of weeks, as I told you on the phone. There are other reasons that she's doing worse."

"Other reasons?"

"Complications. No one dies of AIDS. It's the complications that get you. A yeast infection, a bad cold. Your mother is fighting pneumonia right now."

He looked at his mother. She was breathing with a peace she'd never had before, and it was contagious, he realized he too was breathing peacefully. And then he handed the cooler to the doctor, medicine for next month.

"I'd like to be alone with her for a little longer."

It was his money, his mother, so the doctor nodded and left.

He sought out her thin hand, stared into an emaciated face that changed slowly. If she smiled. If she pursed her lips and got angry. It didn't matter, she'd know he was there. He caressed the back of her hand, her cheek—and almost missed how that bird-thin woman used to transform into someone who screamed and hounded and demanded.

Her left arm was connected by tubes to a plastic bag of liquids, those reluctant drops pressed down, let go, and fell into her. Despite that, she seemed to be in pain. He felt it. And leaned against the stand, pressed the button to the infusion pump, several times, increasing her morphine. The drops now let go faster and were replaced more quickly by new ones.

The woman who taught him about trust was not going to end her life in pain. The woman who took trust from him, who taught him to never, ever, ever trust anyone.

You were right, Mother. If I open myself, let down my guard, I lose control. Or someone takes it away from me. Flies home to Europe with it.

He'd kissed her forehead again and left the room, the ward, the hospital. For the last time. Sometimes you just know, know it will soon be over.

A twenty-minute drive from Clínica Medellín to the other side of town, to the square that led into the dark, cramped aisles of La Galería. A throng, as always. People and voices mingling with the piles of fruit, fish, meat. All the way to the very last stalls of fish and melted ice at the edge of the market. There the boys sat on wooden benches, waiting and hoping. And when he arrived there he realized even the colors had come back. Everything could be seen and heard and tasted. A long journey from transparency.

El Mestizo stepped out onto the small forgotten square. And everything happened as it always did. Everyone stood up at the same time, rushed to him, stretched up for his attention.

That is, everyone except the boy he'd come to give this mission to. Camilo, who he'd hired so many times over the last few years, who El Mestizo had been employing since his very first mission. Now he sat there on the bench looking almost disinterested. El Mestizo stopped abruptly, waving away those who approached, and beckoning to the boy who loitered.

"Camilo?"

The lanky twelve-year-old waved back.

"Come here."

And he slowly cut his way through his disappointed peers.

"I have a job for you."

That smile. Which always followed an offer. It didn't come. And the boy looked down at the ground, when previously he always made eye contact.

El Mestizo didn't understand. The boy in front of him was usually so proud to call himself a sicario. He'd kill just to be able to kill. Now he stood here, in a place where such deals are made looking . . . sad.

"I'm not taking any jobs, señor. Not for a while."

"Two hundred dollars."

"I can't. I gave someone my word."

"So what are you doing here?"

"I want to be here. Always." Still no eye contact.

"So El Mestizo's best sicario is no longer the best? Maybe I need to pay you more."

"Afterward, señor, I'll work again."

"Four hundred dollars."

"Four hundred?"

"Yes. Because this is a very special and important mission. That's just for the first one. And you'll get four hundred more for each member of the family. His wife and two children, younger than you are. A total of one thousand six hundred US dollars for a single mission."

"One . . . thousand six hundred dollars . . . ?"

"Eight hundred now. Eight hundred when you come back."

El Mestizo held out two fists, unfurled them one at a time, revealed what lay in his left hand, then the right, and the boy stared at two genuine five-hundred-dollar bills and six genuine hundred-dollar bills.

Eight hundred for Mom. Eight hundred for his metal box. It wasn't often Camilo missed the what, how, and why. Now he felt . . . a bubbling in his chest, that was how it felt.

"Who?"

"My friend. Or he *was* my friend. Before he betrayed me."

"El Sueco?"

"El Sueco. And his wife. And his children. In that order."

Then the bubbling rose up to his head. Spun him around and around. Now during the time when he'd been paid to kill no one, he was being offered even more money to kill the one who'd paid him not to kill.

"That guy? Who usually comes here with you? Who protects you?"

"Not anymore."

A cautious nod. And finally he made eye contact. "Okay."

First, he wanted the money lying in the palm of one hand, it was important. Then he grabbed the ticket to a bus that left for Cali in two hours. Then the address. Then the gun, which came with eight cartridges, two for each person.

"The house you're going to will be dark and empty. It's been like that for the past few days. But all the furniture, all their belongings are still there. So they will have to go by there soon, because they're headed on a trip, and they'll need to retrieve their things. That's why we're in a bit of a hurry. So we can make sure you're there in time. To take care of them, one at a time."

The sadness remained, the sadness El Mestizo didn't understand, but the boy disappeared quickly with the gun, wrapped in a piece of cloth, along with the money—he was after all a sicario, a professional. El Mestizo waited until he was out of sight before turning back to the rest of the hopeful child hitmen. But now, he wanted the opposite—it wasn't experience he sought, it was a beginner. And he did as he usually did when he gave someone a mission for the very first time, waited to ask questions until they surrounded him.

"You've all done this before?"

They answered like they always did, all at the same time. "Sí!"

All of them except a boy who stood in the back. Who didn't raise his hand, or shout *five times* or *twelve times* or *twenty-two times.*

"What about you?"

"Never. Or . . . not yet."

"Well then, it's time. For your first. Today." El Mestizo peeled two hundred-dollar bills from a wad, then pulled a gun out of a sack-like bag along with a silencer and two cartridges. And a small photo.

"This. This is your mission."

The boy—El Mestizo guessed ten, maybe eleven years old—stared at the picture. "Him?"

"Him."

"But that's . . . I know him."

"Sometimes that happens. When you become a real sicario you're given a mission, and you shoot whoever that mission concerns."

The boy stared in confusion at the picture, turned it over, turned it back. The same face stared back at him. "I don't know . . . Camilo?"

"He's the mission. And you are a real sicario, right?"

The picture. The face. Two hundred dollars. The gun. Sicario.

"Yes. I am." He nodded. "A real sicario."

El Mestizo handed him a hundred-dollar bill and the weapon wrapped in cloth. "What's your name?"

"Donzel."

"Donzel? Good name. In about two hours, Donzel, Camilo will arrive by bus in Cali. And you're also headed to Cali. But you'll go with me, in my car. And when we get there I'm going to drop you off near a dark house. You'll watch the house, keeping hidden, so Camilo doesn't see you when he gets there. After Camilo goes in, wait. Until you hear the shots. Until he comes out, again, alone. It might happen fast or it might take a long time. You wait and wait, and when he comes out—then you finish your mission. With two shots, one to the head and one to the chest. Because sometimes it's important, Donzel, to erase your tracks."

El Mestizo was breathing slowly. Nothing was transparent. Everything had color.

IT SMELLED STRONGLY of tar. And something else. Maybe the remains of fish. Or, he imagined, it might be the metal buckets on the floor, the kind that used to transport fish, or the nets that hung so beautifully from the two long hooks on the wall—maybe what he saw around him reinforced a smell that wasn't really there.

A tiny fishing cottage on an almost uninhabited island in the Stockholm archipelago, located on a cliff that led down to the Granholmen dock. Detective Inspector Sven Sundkvist carefully stretched out one leg then the other, he'd been sitting uncomfortably for nearly three hours. Night-vision binoculars in hand, and a ghostly stillness out on the bay, black water in two-knot wind.

"Here, your turn. Still just as quiet."

He handed the binoculars to the man on his left—Chief Prosecutor Lars Ågestam, who was rocking back and forth on a simple wooden chair, and eagerly took over the task of staring out the window into the inky darkness. While the man on his right—a brigadier general he'd never met before and who led the special operation group, whose task it was to take care of any foreign submarines that might trespass on Swedish waters—sat there resolutely searching with a pair of his own night-vision binoculars just as he had since they got to the fishing cabin.

In the initial confusion both the police and military thought they'd be dealing with the kind of large submarines that had the technology and power to travel all the way from South America to Europe underwater, the sort the Spanish and Portuguese navies had been cracking down on more and more often in Cadiz, Faro, and

Gibraltar. Constructed of lightweight materials, cheaper and safer than traditional drug smuggling. But when Ewert Grens briefly described the itinerary in a second email—how the sub would be traveling from a Venezuelan ship anchored fifteen kilometers off Aberdeen—preparations were hastily adjusted. And as soon as Sundkvist arrived at the small island he'd started to relax—the brigadier general and his crew seemed to know exactly what they were doing.

According to Grens's information, the cocaine-packed submarine had gone underwater off the coast of Scotland and would cruise at a depth of thirty-five to forty meters through the North Sea with a heading set for Gothenburg, then they'd change course toward Öresund, passing between Sweden and Denmark, then around the southernmost tip of Sweden and enter the Baltic Sea, with their sights set on the Stockholm archipelago and the modest island of Södermöja. And then on to the much smaller Granholmen, which lay next to it. There, a bit out from Granholmen's dock, the depths measured seventy-nine meters, and it would be easy to unload cargo onto speedboats that would head directly to the streets of the capital.

"Sven, here, your turn again."

The prosecutor almost dropped the binoculars on the floor before Sven managed to grab hold of them. It wasn't often this mild-mannered detective inspector got annoyed, after all, he chose to put up with a person like Ewert Grens, but he was indeed annoyed right now. He still didn't understand why Ågestam, the man Grens hated most and who as recently as a few weeks ago had Grens locked up in jail, was sitting in this fishing cottage, why he would later be allowed to steal all the attention and adulation, all the credit he didn't deserve. It was a unique tip, a unique seizure based on information Detective Superintendent Grens had managed to secure on his own—he, and his collaborators, should get the credit.

"*Frigg* to base. The subjects are in motion."

The call over the brigadier general's radio cut through the fishing cottage, bouncing off its brittle walls. *Frigg*. One of the corvettes that lay near the Sollenkroka pier overseeing radar directed toward Kanholmsfjärden and two unknown motorboats, actually transport boats, that had been sitting still on open water for the last half hour.

"The subjects are in motion—headed for the target."

Now the two transport boats had started the next stage of their journey—headed for the decisive moment at Granholmen. The brigadier general brought the cordless radio close to his mouth.

"All units. Ready for combat." He then turned first to the detective inspector, then to the chief prosecutor. "When the objects reach their rendezvous point, the mini-submarine will empty its tanks and surface for unloading." He pointed into the darkness. With his whole hand. "That's when we strike. When the submarine has emptied its tanks completely."

Lars Ågestam smiled and his voice became shrill, as it so often did when powerful emotions took over. Whether he was angry, upset, scared, or filled with expectation, it sounded the same. "A record Swedish seizure! A Scandinavian record! It's not often you get to be part of that."

"Probably. Probably. But we're not there yet, sir. Since there is one reservation. *If* the submarine, if . . ." The brigadier general was careful to look at Ågestam as he spoke. ". . . it were to discover us and try to dive again, and if I were to determine that it had the capacity to harm my staff or equipment, I would give the order to sink it with anti-sub grenades."

"That must be avoided at all costs. We have to seize the goods. Catch them in the act!"

"Then the chief prosecutor would prefer that I shoot the crew instead—during the transfer?"

Ågestam waited, quietly.

"Because that's the only thing that would guarantee they don't disappear."

The brigadier general continued to examine Ågestam's now disappointed face. The prosecutor was certainly excited, so close to attaining publicity and praise. But he wasn't the sort to deny reality to reach for it.

"Good, sir. Then I know where we stand." Now the brigadier general lay his hand on Ågestam's thin shoulder, as if to take back that disappointment. "But—you can keep fairly calm. It's very unlikely to disappear. My people have this under control. It will most likely go as we planned."

And then he leaned in close, whispering, despite the fact that this tiny cottage didn't allow for secrets. "Between us, Ågestam—when you hear about a submarine hunt in our waters, it's usually a sub of this kind. When the prime minister and the supreme commander call a press conference and show off some blurry photographs and say *we can confirm that a small submarine has trespassed in Swedish waters*, and then, when the information is reported by those useful idiots, they add *analysts are unable to determine the nationality of the intruders and all information concerning the violation is top secret*. You follow? It's not the Russians, it's not espionage, but that's what we let the public believe, let them read between the lines, so they'll continue to say yes to defense spending. When really every time it's about drugs being transported, and the capital that generates."

The brigadier general adjusted his binoculars again, turned to the cottage's single window and the black bay outside.

A ripple on the water, perhaps fifty meters straight out off the dock. A bow wave. The mini submarine was here, just under the surface, waiting to meet the transport boats.

The brigadier general picked up his radio. "Prepare to board."

Sundkvist adjusted *his* binoculars' focus from the water to the land and the three squads—twelve men from Special Ops—who were leaving the protection of the wooded shore and hurrying toward the dock. And when they reached it they hoisted three black, well-camouflaged combat boats into the water.

He then handed the binoculars to Ågestam again. "You have to see this. They're ready."

Lars Ågestam was able to follow as the soldiers lay down in the boats four by four to wait. For the submarine to surface and take position. For the crackdown to be implemented.

The chief prosecutor again turned his binoculars toward the water, searching for the exact location of Grens's coordinates. Latitude 59.372905. Longitude 18.876421. Precisely where the submarine was supposed to surface, exactly where the transport boats would receive the plastic-wrapped Colombian cocaine, which they were responsible for shipping over that last stretch to Stockholm.

Stillness. Silence. Until that hum they'd all been waiting for. An almost tangible, thunderous buzz from the direction of Kanholmsfjärden. Increasing in intensity.

The two transport boats—now approaching Granholmen—suddenly stopped. The piercing sound faded and was replaced by a brilliant flash of light as both boats turned their headlights to the surface of the water. To the place where the mini-sub's turret was cutting the surface and opening its hatch.

"Launch operation . . ." The brigadier general's voice had changed in character, a shade more seriousness. ". . . now."

And then it all happened fast. The combat boats started their engines and drove at full speed from the dock toward the light. Toward the motor boats. *At* the boats.

Two of the three combat boats—with soldiers now strapped into safety harnesses—aimed straight for the transport boats, rammed them, and the armed and surprised crew was thrown violently against the deck and the railings. Soon the Special Ops soldiers were out of their harnesses, boarding, seizing control. Disarming them. Without having fired a single shot.

At the same time, the third combat boat steered toward the mini-submarine and was halfway there when the now open hatch exploded with the sound of machine-gun fire. A few seconds and a hundred shots. Then silence returned, as suddenly as it had been shattered. And Sundkvist tried to locate where that single shot, at the same time and with a different weapon, had originated from. Probably from behind him. From the woods.

A sniper. And that single bullet had knocked out one of two crewmen.

"Ten seconds!"

The voice was loud and piercing over open water and belonged to the soldier who sat at the front, in the bow, and who was the first to climb onto the submarine. He also thrust his weapon into the hatch.

"You've got ten seconds to surrender!"

It was difficult now to make out from land what exactly was happening, the reflection of the bright lights gleaming uneasily against the water hindered visibility.

"Five seconds!"

Sundkvist looked away after a while, it was so much easier to listen.

"Three, two, one . . ."

Then hushed voices, all at once. And Sundkvist turned his eyes back again to see that the bright lights were now still, and the transport boats out of the way. A man in his thirties, probably South American, climbed up the submarine's ladder and stepped out onto the deck with both hands in the air—and if his binoculars could have given him a close enough view, Sundkvist would have seen how the smuggler was bleeding from both ears. The shock wave. From the underwater mines. The eardrums always burst.

He handed the binoculars to Ågestam, and it looked as if the chief prosecutor was smiling. Flaming red cheeks, his blond bangs standing almost straight up, and even the occasional bead of sweat on his forehead—Sundkvist had never seen the prosecutor this excited.

"The seizure protocol?" His arms waved like batons when he was eager. "Sven, *you have* prepared it, right?"

Without waiting for a reply, he ran out of the small fishing cabin and into the darkness over the bare rocks toward the dock and the military boats that were returning with the mini-sub trailing a coarse rope. The captive was freezing as he was lifted, or rather pushed, onto the dock in handcuffs, and he looked as exhausted as you would be if you'd just spent several days far below sea level. Ågestam would question him later—but for now he continued just as eagerly toward the submarine flopping on the surface of the water like an upside-down whale. It wasn't that far from the somewhat high dock to the submarine, and he took a running jump. And fell. His shiny dress shoes slipped as he landed on the submarine's slippery surface, and he fell headlong into the icy water. Sundkvist had just reached the dock and threw himself onto his stomach. Ågestam thrust one hand into his and latched the other one onto the dock and heaved himself up slowly. The water streamed off his otherwise proper and dapper suit. But he didn't seem to mind. He said thanks for the help, stood up, and took aim at the submarine, jumping again. This time he made it all the way, grabbed hold of the turret and the open door, and fell down on his knees to peer into the hole toward the submarine's interior. Toward the cabin—so limited, so primitive, yet functional. Toward the cargo space—and one of the most astonishing sights the prosecutor had ever seen.

Rectangular, taped-up, plastic-wrapped packages. Stacked from floor to ceiling. Everywhere. Tightly packed.

"Plastic-wrapped small units. It's all here. The tip was correct!" He shouted, his shrill voice swallowed in part by the interior of the sub. "You hear that, Sven? One ton! A thousand kilos! That will never reach consumers. Because the load is hereby confiscated. And listen—after the seizure protocol I want this counted and photographed. Every single little package!"

Then he climbed down, sliding his wet, suit-clad body through the round hole. And Sundkvist called after him.

"Absolutely. Every single little package. A good tip, right? And in two days it will be followed by another good tip. A new giant seizure."

The chief prosecutor's head had just disappeared through the hole. But it popped up again. Head, eyes, and nose over the edge. "What do you mean, Sven?"

"At Arlanda airport. If you're there in two days, you'll get the next tip. I'll give you more details later." Sundkvist didn't say anything else. This was exactly what Grens had instructed him to reveal. And he did what the detective superintendent wanted—even though he didn't understand why. Then he left Ågestam and the mini-submarine and the dock, and headed a bit up the beach into the darkness, making sure he was out of earshot. He now needed to make one more call, also as directed by Grens.

Five rings. Then his supervisor's voice.

"This is Erik Wilson."

"It's Sven."

"Yes?"

"The crackdown I informed you about—it went as planned. The biggest ever in Sweden. But there was a small piece of information I left out. This tip came from a familiar source."

"Familiar source?"

"Yes. The tip came from within the organization. From someone who infiltrated almost all the way to the top on behalf of the American authorities."

Wilson cleared his throat, let out air from the bottom of his belly before he answered. As if he wanted to be sure that his voice would remain steady. "How do you know that?"

"Grens told me when he passed on the info. And he made it very clear that I was supposed to communicate to you that Haraldsson was doing his job excellently."

That voice. It wasn't so steady anymore. And Wilson wasn't trying to hide it. "You said *doing*? As in doing right now? As in . . . he's still alive?"

"Yes."

Sundkvist could hear the silence churning. Transforming from an inner chaos, to confusion, then to relief. As the inconceivable became conceivable.

"Grens wanted me to tell you this too. Those who are dead can be resurrected. Others have before him. And people believe. He hoped therefore that the commissioner would believe this too."

NIGHT. THREE THIRTY. The hour when the streets of Cali were at their most deserted, and which he'd been waiting for. Time for his final trip through a city that had never become anything more than a refuge.

Piet Hoffmann was sitting on one of the kitchen chairs with Zofia in his lap, close to him.

The final trip as in the final night as in the final hours.

He no longer apologized, she'd chosen to follow him to Frankfurt and start a new life together, and she never demanded his guilt or his gratitude in exchange—she wasn't like that, and they were in this together, trying to survive together.

"Home, Piet."

While the boys slept, they'd packed the three suitcases that they had with them here. Fragments of some kind of existence. Now, she kissed him lightly on the mouth, twice.

"Whatever home is now."

He didn't answer.

"Piet?" Two more kisses. "Piet? Hey, are you . . ."

"Home? That's wherever we are. Together."

She held him, tightly. He wanted to hold her back, with equal strength. He would when this night was over, when they were on their way.

"But I have no fucking clue what it is I'm headed home to. More than a promise."

She caressed his cheek, forehead, buried his face in her chest.

"I believe in that promise, Piet. When you've destroyed your reality like we've done, cut family ties, friendships, abandoned security, everything—then you have to believe in something. And I have decided to believe in a short prison sentence. Believe that the house we left, which Wilson says is still waiting for us, can become our home again. Because you, and I, and the children, we *have to* believe it."

He loved her so. Sometimes it was physically painful to leave her. As if she'd moved into his body and he had no choice but to carry her with him, inside him.

"Piet?" She put her hands on either side of his face, lifted it up, her eyes weren't accusatory, just worried. "What are you going to do?"

"Grab some things we left in the house. What little we want to take with us. A suitcase full of stuff."

"What *else* are you going to do?"

She knew him too well.

"Nothing."

"Piet?"

"One small errand on the way."

"What?"

"I can't say."

"That's not good enough for me." She looked at him. That look that could see inside him.

"I'm going to make sure a man who destroys little angels can't do it anymore."

He stood up and took one last look at the control panel and the continual gaze of sixteen cameras on the monitor. No unknown objects, no abnormal movements.

"I don't like you leaving here. Not tonight, Piet. We have so little time left. To risk it . . . there's nothing we need from that house. And no angel, no matter what you're up to, can be worth more than the two you're already responsible for."

One last kiss, *two* last kisses, then down the stairs, and out into the darkness. Warmer than usual, more humid, it was going to rain.

No one stood guard outside anymore, not on foot or in a car. That was how he'd arranged it, even though it put Zofia and the boys at risk. But when he'd weighed the alternatives, he'd decided it would be less dangerous to leave no traces.

Not much traffic. Just as he'd expected. The occasional car or moped, now and then a pedestrian. It was an easy drive, and he parked almost two blocks away, opened the trunk and took out a new, empty brown suitcase, which had been sitting there since the meeting at the industrial building outside Jamundí with a head chemist who could take away the smell.

His first errand. Their dark, abandoned house. Where he'd pack up a few belongings that he didn't want to leave behind, which needed to be inside the suitcase in case some customs agent decided to search it.

A few minutes' walk—he would never get used to how impenetrable the darkness was at night here—so little artificial lighting in comparison to the Stockholm he grew up and lived in. The house was just as dark. Hoffmann approached slowly, with full awareness of his surroundings, entering the small lawn from the direction of the parking lot—really the only way to approach since the back of the house was set against a high, ugly concrete wall. After exactly one and a half meters he stopped and took out a pencil-size flashlight, making sure to stand with his back to the house as he used the energetic ultraviolet light to search for the fluorescent thread. It wasn't there. He squatted down and looked at the ground. There it lay. In two parts—something or someone had stepped down on it. A dog? A cat? Children playing? Or an enemy who shouldn't be here?

Rapid but quiet steps to the front door, the key put gently into the lock, the handle pushed down. He listened. Nothing. The fan whistling from the toilet and the ticking of the clock on the dresser in the living room. He lit up the next checkpoint. The thin thread he'd strung up between the hallway and kitchen. It too was no longer intact—just like the one outside, it lay in two pieces at his feet.

Someone was, or had been, inside the house.

He sank down to the floor, crawled through the hall, and moved a rain jacket that hung from the rear shelf. A small cupboard was embedded behind it in the wall. He opened the door to a fifteen-by-fifteen-centimeter monitor, which displayed information from all of the house's thermal cameras. Four buttons at the bottom—one of them was flashing red. Upstairs. Rasmus's room.

Hoffmann pushed the button, choosing the image from that room. Pitch black, as it should be. Except there—at the bottom right corner.

A body, he was sure of it, radiating heat as red as the blinking light. And it looked as if it were lying on the floor, so it was difficult to determine whether it was large or small, animal or human.

He waited. Silence. One minute. Two minutes. Three minutes and thirty seconds. Then the red started to move. Stand up. A person, he could see that now. Short in stature. Headed out of Rasmus's room. Onto the next image, the infrared camera that captured the upper hall and the stairs. Toward the ground floor. Toward him.

Hoffmann loosened his knife from its shoulder holster, grasped the wooden handle, index finger lightly against the two-sided blade. A last look at the screen. The red figure, the person, was holding something in his hand—something shadowy that created a dark splotch.

At the moment the red on the screen reached the end of the stairs, Hoffmann attacked.

Two steps forward, left hand grabbing hold of the intruder's left shoulder and forcefully twisting his back to him, right hand on the intruder's neck ready to cut it.

Then he froze. This was not a full-grown man. He lacked the power, weight, ability to fight. This was wrong—he knew with certainty as soon as he felt an undeveloped Adam's apple.

He was about to cut the throat of a child.

"Drop the gun!" The knife pushed harder against the neck. "Drop the gun if you want to live!"

A dull thud as the gun fell to the floor. And a muffled bang as a shot went off and hit the wall in front of them.

Hoffmann held the intruder in a firm grip. It *was* a child. He turned on the hall light.

He saw who it was. But didn't understand. "What the hell . . . it's *you*!"

The adrenaline. Still pumping through him, his movements too powerful, too intense. If he hadn't . . . my boys would have woken up in a few hours to find out I was dead? And with me dead—would the child standing in front of him continue on to them and . . . that image, he hated it, screamed, shook the boy.

"Is this how you honor your agreements!" Slapping him hard on both cheeks, leaving the red marks of a palm. "So El Mestizo gave *you* the job to kill *me*!" He shook the child again, more slaps. "Answer me, goddammit!"

"Y . . . yes."

Hoffmann wasn't sure—but it might be that the child in front of him was scared. And if not afraid, at least stripped of his dignity. "Yes, what? Answer me—I can kill just as fucking easily as you!"

"Yes. I broke our contract because I got paid better *for* you than *by* you. Yes. El Mestizo gave me the assignment."

"And now . . . now you failed."

The thin body didn't try to tear itself loose, didn't fight back—the only power Camilo had lay on the floor, already fired. Hoffmann forced him down on his stomach for a more thorough search. In one pocket he had a stiletto, and in a sheath on his back a short sword of the sort that children ordered from Japan and called tantō. Hoffmann threw both of them to the other side of the room.

"And those who fail El Mestizo expose him to danger." Hoffmann stretched his right leg toward the gun and grabbed it with his foot, used his free hand to empty the magazine, seven cartridges left—it had originally been eight.

My whole family.

He pulled up the boy, no more than fifty kilos, threw the undeveloped body to the floor again. The boy slid a bit farther away, turned around, looked at him. And his fury vanished.

A child—who took the lives of other people. But nevertheless a child.

"And anyone who exposes El Mestizo to danger is putting themselves in a lot of fucking danger as well."

A child, who had curled up as if to protect himself, who couldn't know that his fury was gone.

"You . . . you're . . . gonna kill me?"

"Not me. I'm no danger to you now. Camilo—you've failed, and El Mestizo is going to kill you."

Hoffmann walked over to the boy, who raised his arms to protect himself, just skin and bone as armor. But the hit never came. Hoffmann grabbed him, lifted him, put him on the floor. He took a small stack of dollar bills out of his pocket.

"Now, go straight to the bus station. But don't go back to Medellín. Doesn't matter where you go—but not there, you hear that. You take the first bus you find and don't get off until the last station. And when you get there, stay there, and thank the Blessed Mother you're still alive."

Donzel had been sitting on the park bench waiting. For a long, long time. But he had a mission. His very first.

He kept watch with a good view of the house, just as El Mestizo had instructed him. And just as El Mestizo said, a man eventually arrived—tall, agile, with some kind of cloth covering his head and neck—Donzel was sure of it despite the darkness. It was the right man.

And just like El Mestizo also said, he soon heard a shot. Dull, fired with a silencer, but still clear.

And then, finally, just as El Mestizo had said, Camilo came out of the house. And headed toward the bus stop, just as he was supposed to.

Donzel stepped down from the bench and stretched his back, which had become a bit stiff from sitting hunched over for so long. Unrolled the gun from the cloth. Started to follow.

Soon. A real sicario.

PIET HOFFMANN SHOOK, inside. Not out of fear, not even from rage. He sank into the driver's seat, noted that the clock said 4:20, and tried to control the trembling that was unlike anything he'd ever experienced. It was as if everything had flowed together inside him and was now trying to squeeze its way out through his skin—three terrible years on the run, the threat of death ever-present, Zofia and Rasmus and Hugo, who he alternately exposed to risk and protected and had now left unattended in an apartment, and the child who had been sent to his house to take his life, and whose life he'd been so close to ending.

He should drive back. Now.

I don't like you leaving here. Not tonight, Piet. We have so little time left. To risk it . . .

He started the car, but the shaking was still there. Just like the cover of darkness. And he decided.

If he drove fast through the still sleeping city, if he avoided the brothel customers on their way in and out, it would only take him an extra fifteen, twenty minutes, tops.

He parked behind El Mestizo's black, square Mercedes G-Wagen, opened the trunk, and carefully shone his flashlight. He had everything he needed. Next to the no longer empty suitcase stood a bag with a remote control and four fastening magnets. And next to that—the bomb.

Cesar's work. Essentially, an ordinary car alarm. Now placed in a case with a black outer shell and a metal lid approximately the size of a box of chocolates, also containing one twelve-volt battery and a bunch of screw nuts and C-4 explosives.

Music from the brothel spilled out of a couple of open windows, he thought he could even hear the clink of glasses and bottles. A few customers, middle-aged men, were on their way out. After their lively discussion, they stepped into a waiting taxi and silence followed.

That was when he acted. A minute or so, total. He picked up the bomb, crept closer to the brothel owner's car, lay down on the asphalt, and turned the key on the bomb's cover, which switched on its battery. Then he crawled under the vehicle. The four magnets fastened it right where he wanted it—under the driver's seat. The last thoughts that passed through El Mestizo's brain would continue up through the car's roof.

Hoffmann crept out again, checked to make sure no one had noticed him, a couple of quick steps back to his own car. He rolled down the side window, aimed the remote at El Mestizo's car, and activated the alarm. That was why it was so important to keep the vibration sensor.

He would be far away when the time came a few hours from now, unable to take part—the sensor, however, would know when El Mestizo sat down in the seat and started the engine. And instead of sending the signal to the horn, the one that would normally set off the alarm, the signal would instead arrive in the cartridge and trigger the bomb.

AIRPORTS. HE HADN'T been in that many, hadn't been interested. Stockholm and the police station filled his days, evenings, nights. After two trips to and from Washington and now a sixth visit to El Dorado International in Bogotá, he was still convinced. Ewert Grens needed the world just as little as the world needed him.

Nevertheless. What he saw in front of him this morning was worth every moment of the trip, might even make him want to return to this South American country that he still didn't really understand.

A family. A father, a mother, a big brother, a little brother. And they were going home. And Grens would always know he'd helped to make it happen.

"Hello. My name is Ewert. Uncle Ewert." He crouched as best he could with his aching leg and held a big hand out to a small one. "And are you . . . Rasmus?"

"I'm Sebastian."

Grens winked, whispered. "I know your real name is Rasmus. A fine name. And after we've landed in Sweden, you'll be Rasmus again."

Rasmus glanced at his father, worried. Hoffmann nodded slightly, and also whispered.

"Uncle Ewert . . . he knows."

And the six-year-old face softened. "Rasmus. For real."

Grens nodded too—they had a secret together. And then he turned to the slightly taller boy.

"So that must mean your name is . . ."

"Hugo. I never liked William."

"And I've never . . ." Grens leaned in closer, whispering right into the boy's ear. ". . . liked Ewert. But your name is your name. And so it becomes you in the end."

They smiled at each other. They too had a secret.

"I'm Zofia. For real."

Zofia Hoffmann suddenly hugged him. He wasn't prepared, not used to that.

"Thank you, Superintendent. For everything."

So it wasn't much of a hug back.

"No problem. It was my attempt to make up for once trying to kill your husband."

Piet Hoffmann, however, neither greeted nor hugged him. They'd be spending time with each other after they landed at Arlanda. They could say good-bye then. Or whatever it was they needed to say.

The speakers crackled and announced something about a plane landing and another one that was getting ready to take off. Travelers wandered around, preparing for new meetings. And the small group of five Swedes headed toward the check-in lines. Each with their own suitcase. The woman behind the counter smiled at Grens's brown, patchy, outdated suitcase with its Eiffel Tower sticker in one corner. The two boys had considerably smaller and more colorful suitcases, red and yellow, and they made sure to carry them all the way to the scale on their own. Zofia's had a green ribbon tied onto one handle, he'd seen others use a similar trick because so many bags looked the same spinning around the baggage claim. Hoffmann's bag looked new, also big and brown like his own, but the leather was so shiny you could almost see yourself in it. The woman in an airline uniform weighed the bags and placed small stickers here and there, asked if they'd packed their luggage themselves, reminded them that bags should contain no explosives, and informed them their luggage would be inspected by detection dogs before passing through customs.

One hour to departure. Six hours to New York. Two-hour layover. And another eight hours to Stockholm.

Piet and Zofia Hoffmann were no longer carrying any suitcases; they held on tight to each other's hands and breathed as calmly as they could. It would be early morning when, after three long terrible years, they set foot on Swedish soil again.

PART FIVE

EWERT GRENS ALWAYS felt this fear just as they were landing. It seemed to confirm the insanity of it all. You were in the air. In a machine. With no control over your life or death. What if the man in the pilot's cabin—and it was a man, that much was clear from the announcements over the speaker—was having a bad day, or under the influence of something, or just inept? How could several hundred people who wore helmets when they rode their mopeds, used seat belts in their cars, who locked their front doors every time they left home, people who loved their own lives more than anything, put those lives into the hands of a person they'd never met, never had the chance to judge?

A quick glance behind him in the cabin. There they sat, the whole Hoffmann family—seats A, B, C, D, on both sides of the aisle. A little tired, a little happy, a little worried. He'd made sure to travel separately from them, with several rows of seats in between, so they wouldn't exit together, would arouse no suspicions, just in case the conversation Grens was about to have went to hell. Grens and Hoffmann had agreed to as much. If the short prison sentence the detective had promised was impossible to negotiate, then Peter Haraldsson would calmly say good-bye to his wife and two children, grab his shiny new suitcase, buy a ticket, and continue his journey elsewhere.

Grens closed his eyes as the wheels met the runway, clenched his hands as it bounced heavily, breathed slowly as the plane lurched from left to right. Only opened his eyes cautiously when they came to a complete stop. Never again. He always promised that to himself.

He stepped into the jetway that connected the airplane to the main terminal and nodded to all his fellow police officers and the customs officials lined up there. They had their detection dogs on a tight leash near the front, smelling each bag that passed by, and, after asking out of curiosity, he learned they often did that when a plane arrived bearing several passengers from Colombia. He continued on through the buzzing aisles of the international terminal, on to the hall with the spinning baggage claim, through passport control, and then on toward the tunnel that led to the parking garages and fresh air—Grens didn't stop until he entered a reserved room a bit to the right of the Arlanda airport police station. He wasn't worried about Hoffmann, who knew where to wait.

Chief Prosecutor Lars Ågestam was already sitting there. A handkerchief in hand, he coughed and blew his nose loudly. An empty teacup on the table, his blond bangs in unusual disorder, irritated eyes behind brown frames—he had arrived on time but the plane had been delayed forty-five minutes. Since their very first case together—a five-year-old murdered by a serial pedophile—the prosecutor had thought as little of Grens as Grens thought of the prosecutor, and at this point neither of them even tried to pretend otherwise. It had given the prosecutor great satisfaction to have the detective locked up in a wine-soaked suit. And now, an hour had been wasted as he slowly realized who he was waiting for. This hardly strengthened their relationship.

"Grens."

"That's right, yours truly. And you seem to have caught a cold, Ågestam. Heard you decided to go swimming with your clothes on."

"So it's for *your* sake I'm sitting here?"

Grens walked over to the simple—not quite clean—coffee maker, filled it with water and loaded it with Swedish coffee grounds. He'd started to get used to the richer varieties available in another part of the world. It was time to get back to what he could expect here, and this generic discount coffee served in a plastic cup was truly an excellent start.

"For my sake. For your sake. And for the sake of an old acquaintance. We have what the finance idiots would call a win-win-win situation on our hands."

"Grens, dammit! I was convinced to come here by Sven Sundkvist. Or rather lured! Because he told me I was going to meet the brains behind this week's record drug bust, which you missed while you were on . . . where exactly is it you've been . . . on vacation? You're looking a little sunburnt. Yes, the brains and maybe even get another tip. That's what he said. So now, Grens, I really don't understand."

"The brains? You flatter me. But you're not entirely wrong." The detective sat down in front of the much younger prosecutor, smacked his lips a bit as he filled the plastic cup to half.

"So here's how it is. There will be a new delivery in three days. I can give you the date, time, location. Not as big as the last one, but still enough kilos to qualify as one of the biggest Swedish cocaine busts ever. And it would be, if I were to choose to give it to you, Lars Ågestam's second huge bust in a very short period of time."

Ågestam ran his hands through his bangs as he always did when he was stressed, unusually disordered hair turning into chaos. "How do you know this?"

"Heavy reconnaissance. Unique reasoning. Razor-sharp analysis." Grens tried not to smile. He couldn't help it. He was enjoying himself too much. "Or, if I'm being honest, a tipster. The world's best tipster. He was the one who delivered that last bust to us. And he'll give us this one too if you cooperate. It's actually for his sake that I asked you to come here."

Lars Ågestam rarely looked this lost. Superior, irritable, overbearing, yes—all of which Ewert Grens had come to recognize and despise. But he'd never truly seen the prosecutor at a loss. Now he was.

"Please, Grens, I . . . what's this all about?"

"When a person takes a drug they become dependent on it. Want more."

"Dependent? More?"

"Like you. You want more. You know how this works. These big busts build careers. And this time, Ågestam, you won't even need to get wet."

Ågestam leaned back in his uncomfortable wooden chair to avoid Grens's smile. Sighed out loud. Stood up. Wandered around the table. Drank a glass of water. Stretched. Sighed again. And sat back down. "Okay, Grens. What do you want me to do?"

"You need to give me something in exchange."

"I'm listening."

"You have to use your—yes, I admit it, but will never confirm it outside this room—keen intellect. You need to find a rationale for why a murderer, who has been on the run from Swedish justice for several years, would end up serving a prison sentence of no more than a year."

ONE HOUR. THAT'S how long it took Lars Ågestam to understand, really understand, how a dead man had been resurrected in South America and had made his way to Stockholm. How he'd been marked for death again by another nation's highest leaders. How to avoid that fate he'd offered and then managed to rescue the world's most high-profile hostage. And that still he'd been ordered to die a second time, and so he'd done just that, died. And then to understand, truly understand, that that very man was now sitting somewhere in the airport with his family awaiting the outcome of this conversation.

"No, I have to follow the law."

"Another record-breaking bust, Ågestam. If you follow the law in such a way that the trial ends as we want it to."

"He took a life on Swedish soil. At least one person. Maybe two."

"He was employed by us, did so indirectly on our behalf. Just as he was employed by, and killed for, another authority in Colombia. And we've already put away the real bad guys—the minister of justice is at the Hinseberg Women's Penitentiary, a former national police commissioner and chief superintendent both in protective custody at Aspsås prison."

"He has to be punished."

"You know you want it, you know you want that tip. You'll never, ever get another chance at these kinds of quantities again. And you know it's possible, with effort, to find mitigating circumstances."

There stood a law book in an overlooked bookcase in the police station's break room. It was as if Ågestam had sniffed it out, almost gone straight for it when, mumbling to himself, he'd left the detective. He was carrying the thick book when he returned and sat down.

"I would probably . . . could . . . well, maybe . . . write that Hoffmann on x day in x month deprived so-and-so of life by shooting."

They both remembered. The world's smallest pistol smuggled in in pieces and reassembled in Hoffmann's prison cell. For use in case of an emergency, if he were to be discovered. If the Polish mafia he'd infiltrated behind those high walls were to realize he was actually working for the Swedish police. And then he was discovered. There was an emergency. And a shot through one eye was the surest point of entry for a weak weapon to trick the skull, the body's hardest bone, into allowing entry into the brain.

"And furthermore . . . strictly hypothetically, Grens . . . I could argue as the prosecutor—and get away with it—that according to mitigating circumstances this act should be considered manslaughter." Lars Ågestam flipped back and forth in the statute book, searching through its endless, onionskin pages. "I don't think you need to argue for the manslaughter itself—it's enough for the prosecutor to merely state that. Furthermore, I would explain to the court why I see it as manslaughter, probably during . . ." More onionskin pages. Those slim fingers burrowing through sections and paragraphs. ". . . the presentation of the case, and especially in my plea. Then I could—strictly hypothetically—explain that the situation was such that Hoffmann found himself in danger from a whole group, a lynch mob, and that there was no premeditation. That—and this sounds more like something from the defense, but sometimes a prosecutor defends as well—the weapon he used just happened to be there. And when he saw the mob—*mob* is a good term for a defense lawyer, but maybe not for a prosecutor, so I'd probably avoid that word after all—when he saw the crowd headed toward him, he had to make a choice between himself and them."

They'd sat like this once before. Cooperating. At home in Grens's kitchen, over a whiskey and with hundreds of wrongful convictions in front of them on the table, all of them the consequence of the illegal and therefore hidden work of Hoffmann and other criminal informants. It had felt good then, almost as if they could actually stand each other. It felt like that now as well.

"Therefore, Grens, he's ended up in a situation where I can neither prove nor disprove an act of self-defense—and it is the prosecutor who is *supposed* to disprove it. Thus, I would ask for a lower penalty. I'd explain that the situation was as I've described, and that it would have been close to impossible for him to alter his course, I therefore would ask for, say . . . three years. As the prosecutor. Then his defense lawyer would vividly describe the mob that came after the accused and how he was *lucky* enough to have a weapon on hand. Perhaps it wasn't the best choice to shoot to kill, but we're talking about manslaughter, his lawyer would say, even the prosecutor agrees. In addition, his lawyer would point out that Hoffmann voluntarily returned home and that should be reflected in the sentence—and then he or she would ask for six months."

Grens didn't hug Ågestam. But almost. "*Six* months, Ågestam?"

The prosecutor held up his hands as if to protect himself. He didn't want to get any closer than they were. "Yes. And then the court, with luck, would sentence him to a year."

"And he'd be released after maybe . . . eight months?"

"Yes."

Lars Ågestam had just lowered his hands. That was why he didn't have time to protect himself—again. As the burly detective threw himself across the table and hugged the prosecutor hard. Grens had moved so much faster than anyone would ever expect.

"You've earned your tip, Ågestam! I'll be damned if you didn't earn another hug as well!"

And so the slender prosecutor received a bear hug from thick arms that didn't let go until the cheeks of the man receiving the hug turned red from lack of oxygen.

The Hoffmann family sat in a corner at one of the small cafés that had sprouted up in the glassed-in hall between the international terminal and Terminal 4. Mineral water and some yellowish juice stood on the table in an irregular ring around crumbly, greasy, Swedish cinnamon buns. Grens didn't say a word as he approached—but Piet could see it on him anyway, they'd gotten what they were asking for. So four people held each other tight, while the detective went to a kiosk and took his time picking out newspapers. This was their moment, and it should last just as long as they wanted it to.

Hoffmann had been weeping when Grens returned—still standing there with his bag, looking as lonely and deserted and empty as he probably felt. They nodded to each other and headed to the small parking lot outside Sky City, temporary spots for a few vehicles, one of them held the police car Grens had requested for transport between Arlanda airport and the Aspsås high-security prison.

"Normally, Hoffmann, you'd have spent the night at the Kronoberg jail. But it was Aspsås you escaped from. And Oscarsson, the chief warden, had it pretty . . . well, tough after you left, since he was the one responsible for everything you managed to smuggle in and the subsequent explosions you arranged. He told me immediately that he had a place for you in the new protection department. Or maybe he created one. Either way, he wasn't difficult to persuade when I gave him the opportunity to lock you up—again."

A short trip, twenty or thirty kilometers, but enough time to talk about whatever needed to be talked about.

"And you understand this is where both the national police commissioner and Göransson are?"

"I understood that, Superintendent."

"It's important that you stay cool. Fighting back against the men who used me like an idiot, who manipulated me into taking a shot at your head, the men who exploited you, and made you dangerous, and then threw you away—revenge behind bars, now when they're the ones who can't escape, probably wouldn't be . . . so appropriate."

"The thought never crossed my mind."

"Good. Things like that are supposed to hurt terribly."

"And I'd just like to say that *now, unlike then, you know who I am.* If it were to happen. Which, of course, it won't."

"Of course."

Grens stood as close to the seven-meter-high wall as possible. Together they walked toward the prison gate, where a bell and a surveillance camera were waiting. This was where the prison guards would meet them and take over responsibility for a prisoner who'd once threatened their colleagues and killed and injured their prisoners, and who they now knew had been working undercover for the Swedish police. Grens extended his hand, Hoffmann his, they squeezed hard and then let go. The detective superintendent was about to leave when Hoffmann waved away the first prison guard, asking for a moment more.

"Just one more thing."

Grens smiled, not particularly surprised. There was always one more thing.

"Just this."

Hoffmann held out the brown, shiny suitcase.

"I should have sent it with Zofia. I won't need it in here. And locking it up in some dusty fucking storage space with a bunch of other prisoners' trash doesn't feel right. So I was wondering—can you take it? Put it in a corner in your office? Keep it for about eight months?"

THE NEXT DAY

THE NEXT DAYS

LATER THAN USUAL. But it felt the same somehow.

It wasn't often Ewert Grens was this calm, that terrible restlessness still plagued him, and despite his sixty-three years he'd still found no way to escape it. But on his way to her, to celebrate their day, his whole body had turned soft, warm, as if he'd never again have to face the fear or anger or loneliness.

He hadn't slept a wink. But with warmth and softness filling him up, he didn't need to. And even if he'd tried it wouldn't have worked, for other reasons—he hadn't yet figured out how to handle the time difference, he'd switched over to Colombian time just when it was time to switch back to Swedish time, and, apparently, it was too much of an adjustment for someone who was so stuck in their ways, holding tight to routine in order to avoid losing himself.

He'd left the wine auction with a plastic bag in his hand this morning and walked through Värta Port, which was as calm as him now, deserted, it was one of those days when people weren't headed anywhere. The cooler was already beside him in the passenger seat, and he made sure this time to put the bottles into it directly, tighten the seat belt around it, and fasten it tightly in case of any unexpected jolts.

And of course—a different route. Not through Östermalm or the city like a few weeks earlier, now he left the port area and drove through the new Northern Link tunnel, straight roads and far from where most taxis roamed.

This morning's obligatory conversation with a court-appointed alcohol and drug therapist—Grens had insisted it be completed before nine o'clock, he had more important things to do—had proven that

Detective Superintendent Ewert Grens certainly had many bad sides, but none of them were related to the consumption of alcohol. After just a few minutes of dialogue, the therapist stated that both the taxi drivers and the chief prosecutor lacked the expertise to evaluate him—that this was a man who rarely used alcohol, who was uninterested in intoxication, and that the two bottles of expensive wine that now sat in the seat next to him were about the extent of his drinking every year.

Magnificent ass.

Those were the words Grens had initially used to describe the chief prosecutor, and after an unusually short inquiry—two hours—he'd seen nothing to contradict the label. The preliminary investigation was closed quickly due to lack of evidence. Grens wasn't much for internal investigations, more asses would be called in to investigate, but he offered Ågestam—as thanks for yesterday's cooperation—the choice between that or a personal apology. The bastard had stood in Grens's office next to the worn corduroy sofa and the rickety coffee table, while Siw sang "Tunna Skivor," and stretched out a damp, limp hand.

Roslagstull became Norrtull became the E4 highway north. A cooler with two bottles of 1982 Moulin Touchais, which had been purchased even more expensively than ever before in a bidding war between three parties—the same suit as last time, and a lady in a wide-brimmed red hat. He checked the seat belt, pulled on it a few times to make sure, then nudged the bowl of two fresh, almost entirely golden peaches, which stood on the passenger-side floor.

Wine. And peaches. And the proud waitress at a guesthouse in the Loire Valley who served them on the very first day they'd shared a last name, who insisted on flambé peaches for dessert to draw out the flavor. She'd spoken at length about the wine and the vineyard, which had, since the early 1800s, placed a few cases in their cellars each year, and about how a century later they'd dug even more cellars so that they could set aside ten thousand bottles to mature. Until the Second World War. And the arches had been bricked up. And there they remained—complete, untouched vintages—and stayed put until the vaults were reopened in the '70s. Grens would probably be able to round them up two at a time and take them to her for the rest of his life.

Those first years they'd toasted with that particular wine, on that particular day, in a restaurant in Old Town or at home in their apartment on Svea Road. At the nursing home the glasses hadn't been quite as beautiful, just regular juice glasses, but the wine had tasted the same. In recent years, he'd made the trip to the North Cemetery, wandering among the stones toward a newer section with simple wooden crosses, block 19B, grave 603.

Anni Grens

That was all he'd had them engrave on that small metal plate. A row of heather and behind that a taller plant with pink clusters of flowers that could hardly be called beautiful, but he'd planted them because he liked the name—Love's Herb. He fetched a water jug that was hanging near a rake stand, filled it halfway, and started watering. Careful not to splash a drop on the rose bush that stood closest to the cross, the place that was the least shadowed by the surrounding trees. That flower was his alcohol clock. After filling two glasses, he first drank his own and then poured hers over the roses, making sure to wet some petals, which drooped immediately. It would take them two hours to stand up again. When they did, he knew his blood alcohol level was low enough to be able to drive again.

Grens walked over to a bench, which stood just off the asphalt path, dragged it over, and placed it on the grass in front of her cross. He sat down, and it sagged a little in the middle from his weight.

The stillness of a cemetery. He'd feared it for so long. But had learned to like it, depend on it. He opened the bottles, one each. He was celebrating late this year, but that would never happen again.

The first drops, and he remembered exactly how she looked when she drank this wine the first time, how she laughed, grabbed his arm, pulled him closer, kissed him, and whispered that they would never leave each other.

FOUR MONTHS LATER

HE COULDN'T UNDERSTAND why he'd chosen this path, walking down Pennsylvania Avenue block after block for more than an hour in black dress shoes and a warm suit, with nagging sore feet and hips that ached every time his heels hit the pavement. A new bodyguard walked a half step ahead of him. Another walked a half step behind. He didn't know their names, they were switched out regularly. If you got to know someone better, more deeply, then you become involved, had to go to their funeral, and he hadn't even visited Roberts's ceremonial grave—instead he'd seen him turned to ashes for real.

He was there. The fence. The gate. The lawn. The fountain. And the final arc-shaped piece of asphalt before the official entrance to the White House.

Morning spent at the NGA, then lunch at the House of Representatives, a normal day. Until now. He'd so far avoided coming here, to the meetings and briefings he was invited to once a week. He no longer wanted to know who was killed and how. Four months of freedom, that was why he was here—it was time.

He nodded and greeted the Secret Service guards who opened the White House door—no ID was asked for, no search conducted. As one of the country's most powerful politicians, he was used to being recognized by strangers—but since the kidnapping it had reached another level, Timothy D. Crouse was a bona fide celebrity now, and he could see this different level of recognition reflected in people's eyes.

"You stay here."

He lingered while his bodyguards—not quite convinced they were doing the right thing—left his side and sat down on simple chairs just inside the entrance. He then continued alone through corridor after corridor.

The day after his rescue and the press conference watched around the world, he'd been encouraged to meet with the House of Representatives team of trauma experts. But he'd declined, not willing to expose himself there, instead he sought private help—a therapist he met in connection with Liz's treatment, who helped both of her parents through their grief. Emotional memories. That was what they'd worked on, and it had been hell to call forth the feelings associated with seeing thirty-nine people die because of him. To relive being transported into the jungle on a truck bed, blindfolded, no idea where, why. A mock execution. Being locked up in a cage. Being tortured. Becoming an animal covered in mud and rags.

His therapist estimated he'd need at least one, maybe two years, to be able to handle emotions, thoughts, as he did before. But it hadn't turned out that way. What should have disturbed him after only four months no longer did. It didn't bother him in the same way anymore and he knew why—a man who had lost his only child had nothing left to lose. Those bastards thought they'd broken him, and might have before, but not now; they never got close to the fear that had already left him.

A closed door. He knocked, opened it, went in. It looked just as it did when he was here for a meeting the day before his Colombia trip. Sky-blue carpet, ocean-blue wallpaper. A mirror with a gold frame, a chandelier with candles that were never lit. Vice President Thompson behind her oak desk with her blonde hair put up and her red glasses on a cord around her neck. But the others hadn't been here last time. Chief of Staff Perry, CIA Director Marc Eve, and head of the FBI William Riley.

"Sit down."

The blue armchair, that was where he was supposed to sit. Near the fireplace, they thought maybe it would be warmer, safer for someone they assumed was fragile.

The Final War on Drugs. Kill lists. Colombia. It was not just meetings in here he'd opted out of, he'd consistently avoided any conversations with journalists, colleagues, or even his own siblings. Just like after Liz died. He didn't understand why then nor did he now. Maybe he just needed more time. Maybe he was the type who turned his emotions to thoughts, never allowing them to leave his brain for his chest. Or maybe this was just his way of surviving.

A large pile of documents lay on the antique table between them. On top of the stack—like the cover of a novel they'd soon read aloud to each other—lay an illustration of thirteen playing cards, on each of those cards stood one of thirteen portraits, and under that thirteen aliases.

Chief of Staff Perry leaned forward and pulled the pile closer, apparently it was his stack.

"The Ace of Hearts." Perry removed the book cover–like illustration and grabbed the next document. A black-and-white photograph. A dead man. Hanging in a noose. Crouse grabbed the back of the chair for support, no longer quite sure if he'd done right coming here.

"Ace of Hearts. Luis Alberto Torres, alias Jacob Mayo. Located in a port city called Buenaventura. And like the capture of Saddam Hussein, the Ace of Spades during Operation Iraqi Freedom, we gauged a trial and public hanging with an open flow of information would garner the most public support."

Crouse stared at the terrible picture, couldn't look away. From the black hood that looked so uncomfortable. And he wondered if the hood was for Torres's sake, or to protect those who were watching.

"Imprisoned at Camp Justice—which you, Tim, are quite familiar with—throughout the trial. The man we had stationed there, a Jonathan Woods from the embassy, described how, and I'm quoting now, *'the PRC commander in chief was led to the gallows, a trapdoor surrounded by red rails, while making small talk with his masked executioners.'* Furthermore, and I'm quoting again, *'a soft cloth was put around his neck before the noose was placed there and tightened, and the trapdoor was opened.'* Finally, Woods concludes his report *'the former commander fell to his death, and I heard his neck snap.'"*

Chief of Staff Daniel Perry kept a red marker in his right jacket pocket. Now he used it to cross out the picture of the Ace of Hearts, then sat the next document on the table. A new picture. A crumbling pile of black coal, the remains of a man in the sooty concrete foundation of a burned-out building.

"The King of Hearts. Juan Mauricio Ramos, alias El Médico. We used a drone. USS *Liberty*, firing from the Pacific, eight miles off the west coast of Colombia. The target—a building near Jamundí, south of Cali. Took out the whole family at the same time."

The red marker crossed out the King of Hearts's face. And a new picture. A large crater in the ground.

"Queen of Hearts. Catalina Herrador Sierra, alias Mona Lisa. Knocked out with a specially designed hybrid missile. USS *Dwight D. Eisenhower,* firing from the Caribbean Sea, twenty-two miles north of Colombia's coastline. The target—a property in La Cuchilla, west of Medellín. A two-pronged attack, which I'll return to."

The Queen of Hearts's face was stained red. And then—a new photograph. A burned-out car. Covered with black soot. At the edge of the photo, still in the driver's seat—the remains of a human being. And Crouse's gaze became stuck for a second time—on what he realized must be a head. So small. Like a newborn. Shrunken. He knew that heat was capable of that.

"Jack of Hearts. Johnny Sánchez, alias El Mestizo. A bomb. Which exploded one morning when he started his Mercedes G-Wagen in front of the brothel he owned. The technical analysis showed good craftsmanship—an ordinary car alarm supplemented with explosives, screws, and plastic explosives. We actually got the tip directly from former DEA Chief Sue Masterson, the last thing she did for us, gave us both the time and location, where and when we could find him. And best of all—we didn't even have to plant the explosives! According to Masterson it was an internal conflict, between two guerrillas."

The chief of staff buried him with two red strokes.

"A violent death for a violent man."

Crouse no longer held on to the chair for support. He was leaning forward, first toward the picture of a shrunken head, then toward whoever stood on the playing card. "Can I see that?"

Perry handed him the photograph of the burned-out car.

"Not that. What you crossed out."

He'd seen that face before. Via satellite when he'd executed and buried four soldiers. In person, when he stepped into a cage to carry out torture.

"El Mestizo. Isn't that what they called him?"

"Tim, what is it?"

Crouse, without realizing it, had stood up, and was equally unaware that he'd turned a flaming red from forehead to neck, and that he'd started to shake.

It was him. Who smiled as he destroyed me.

"Hey, Tim, are you okay?" The vice president grabbed his arm, held on to it.

But Crouse lifted her hand away, shaking off the unwanted physical contact. "Keep going. Now."

They'd all seen it. Crouse had gone elsewhere for a moment, beyond this, beyond communication. But none of them really knew or recognized where. So now they looked at one another, searching for answers they would never receive.

Crouse dried his neck and the top of his head with his white shirtsleeve, focusing his breath on his anxiety until he pulled the air all the way down to his stomach and forced it to remain there. Then he sat down again, and his trembling ceased, at least on the outside.

"Very well then, Tim. We'll move on."

Perry continued pulling paper out of his pile, plowing through document after document, now arranged in four piles on the antique coffee table.

"The remains of the Ten of Hearts—the other target in our two-pronged attack."

The first document—a picture of a crater. At least that's what it looked like. Like a black hole in the ground.

"Just like the Queen of Hearts, even though little remained, we're completely confident we got the right person, were able to extract some DNA—we found a femur, which is ideal, basically still intact. You can see one of them here."

The second document—Crouse knew what it was without having it explained to him—a bone crusher in a forensic laboratory at Langley. In the third document, part of the femur had been broken into pieces using a regular hammer, and in the fourth it had been placed in a rotary crusher filled with liquid nitrogen, twenty minutes of spinning and the leg had turned to powder, ready for DNA extraction.

"A red *X* over the Ten of Hearts—and there we have it: our royal flush." Perry smiled, gathered up the four images, making sure to put them in the right order. And then picked up the next two in the pile, before quickly putting them back again.

"Nine of Hearts. Eight of Hearts. Both our external and internal intelligence have yet to find them."

A new paper, a new image. And a quick glance at everyone.

"The Seven of Hearts."

A single document on the table. A naked body on an autopsy table. Lying on its back. Grayish skin with a wreath of bruises around his neck.

"This was left at the American Embassy in Bogotá. Lying in a trunk. Death by strangulation."

Marker and a red cross. The paper upside-down and the next document already in hand before Crouse interrupted.

"What did you say—in a trunk? Death by strangulation? Why did we strangle him and put him in a trunk?"

"Wasn't our work. He was dead on arrival."

Crouse stretched out an arm for the document. He grabbed it, examined the gray skin on a metal gurney for a long time.

"In that case, how do we know this is the right person?"

"He matched our description. Height, weight, body type, skeletal damage, distinguishing marks." Crouse should let go of the picture, let Perry continue his review of the kill list, so that everyone could make it to their next meeting on time. But the man lying there. Gray and stiff and lifeless. He wouldn't leave his hand.

"DNA?"

"No."

It felt as if they were trying to hurry this along.

"Fingerprints? Like the others?"

"Sorry."

Riley had been silent so far. Now he swept his arms wide as he spoke. "We simply don't have a match. Despite the largest DNA database in the world. Nine million profiles—but only suspects in criminal investigations. I've said it before, we should damn well get them all."

"The public isn't quite there yet. I think it's called integrity."

"Integrity, Perry? Why should criminals have privacy?"

The chief of staff didn't respond. It wasn't a question, despite how the FBI chief phrased it. He turned instead to Crouse and pointed to the man on the autopsy gurney.

"El Sueco. Alias based on origin, appearance, as is so often the case in Colombia. El Indio, El Mestizo, El Negro . . . ethnicity and race. We assumed El Sueco fit that pattern, so we sought out information from the police in northern Europe, Australia, New Zealand, Canada, South Africa, and probably somewhere else. No hits."

"Denmark. Now there's a damn good example, Perry. They save the blood of every newborn to test for diseases. And use it to compare suspects in criminal investigations. If they can—why can't we?"

It still wasn't a question. And the FBI director received no answer, while Perry indicated that it was Crouse he was speaking to.

"When it comes to the Seven of Hearts—we've made use of every tool available based on the information we had. The forensic experts and medical examiners believe there is sufficient circumstantial evidence to make a positive identification."

Like Riley, Marc Eve had been sitting in silence so far—watching, listening. Now he reached across the coffee table and gathered up the four images of the Seven of Hearts and put them in the pile of papers they'd already gone through.

"Now it's time to move on." He grabbed the red marker out of Perry's hand and crossed out the illustration of the Seven of Hearts for a second time, streaks turning into thicker streaks. "Perry?"

It was as if Perry was now changing his mind. The sudden hurry had made Crouse, the guest of honor, start to wonder. Perry met their eyes one at a time—Marc Eve, William Riley, the vice president. And picked up the documents the CIA director had so impatiently gathered, grabbed the red marker.

"We have to, for the sake of all parties involved, share this information."

"A dead criminal with no citizenship." The vice president did as the chief of staff had, made a point of meeting three other sets of eyes. "Isn't that enough, Daniel?"

"Surely we owe Tim the same background information that we have ourselves."

Crouse was no longer shaking. But he was still just as flushed. "What are you talking about? What are *all of you* talking about?"

Throughout the meeting a large black binder had stood on the floor next to Perry's left foot. Now he bent forward and picked it up, opened it, placed even more documents in front of him. Crouse, who was sitting across the table, tried to see, to read what stood there, but he was too far away, the font too small. The chief of staff lowered his voice, looked at him.

"Here, and exclusively in this room—we initially handled the Seven of Hearts a bit . . . incorrectly."

"Incorrectly?"

"The Seven of Hearts turned out to be an infiltrator and an informant."

"An infiltrator?"

"One of Sue Masterson's civilians with a criminal record. He was put onto the Most Wanted list based on false information in order to lend his undercover work credibility—enhance his status in the group he was infiltrating. A common strategy in these cases. But no one outside the DEA was informed! By the time we'd planned the Final War on Drugs in response to the attack, used the Most

Wanted list to build the kill list, and announced our plans to the whole damn world . . . well, it was too late to back out."

Speaker Timothy D. Crouse had stood up, still rattled, as again he could see a man stepping into his cage. Only a person who's been kept in a cage, forced to meet his torturers there, could understand how he felt right now. But at that point it had been all about him, his own damage. He still wasn't quite sure if he understood what Perry was talking about—but his body could feel it, this was about someone else who'd been injured, and someone whom he'd failed to protect, again.

"What group?"

"What?"

"What fucking group did he infiltrate!"

"The PRC."

"He infiltrated the PRC on our behalf?" He was no longer standing still. He walked around the ocean-blue room, a loop between the oak desk and fireplace, one lap, two laps. "So you're saying we killed one of our own?"

"We didn't kill him. We chose to keep him on the kill list."

"If I understand the images you just showed me, which I interpret as an autopsy, and what you're telling me now . . . He's dead?"

"He was on the kill list. That was all we accomplished."

Crouse didn't scream, nor did he whisper. He just stood there at the fireplace, next to the brass log-holder filled with birch, waiting. For something, he wasn't sure what.

"Tim—*t*hat's how it works! Those of us sitting here unanimously chose to sacrifice one life to save many, many more."

Whatever he was waiting for didn't arrive.

"Who was he?"

"We don't know. We know he wasn't American, had a criminal record, that he spent two and a half years infiltrating the PRC guerrillas and provided the DEA with a steady stream of information."

"Such as?"

Marc Eve was no longer just impatient, he was annoyed, bitter. "Let's move on."

"So really he worked for *me*? Died because of *me*? Listen, I was imprisoned like a fucking animal in the middle of the Colombian jungle. I have the right to know!"

Perry stood up. "Just wait. Both of you."

He left the room, but came back before the second hand of the golden clock on the wall, which was ticking so loudly, had time to make a full rotation.

"We got a summary from Masterson. She's the one who hired him."

A binder similar to the one that stood on the floor, maybe a little thinner. Perry flipped through it, handed it to Crouse. "There."

Crouse stood up as he read. Words became sentences and formed a picture of a person whose information allowed the US government to take credit for busting seven large cocaine kitchens.

"Damn."

And additional information that led to the seizure of fifteen huge shipments.

"Even Tumaco."

Not a month before the hostage abduction. One of the really big crackdowns.

"And we executed him?"

"Not us. Technically. But passed a death sentence, yes."

"Seven cocaine kitchens and fifteen deliveries of seven tons or more. I remember them all. This is exactly what the Crouse Model has been praised for! I even remember Masterson talking about this very informant."

The halls of the White House seemed to echo more than other hallways. It had always been like that, Crouse was sure of it, he thought about it every time he rushed through them. But he couldn't decide if the sound was actually louder, or if it was that particular power that was found only here that made them seem that way.

Listen, I was imprisoned like a fucking animal. Heels clacking hard against the stone floor. *So really he worked for me?* It wasn't anger, not irritation. *Died because of me?* It was the powerlessness of a man who was supposed to have just that, power. *I have the right to know!*

His two nameless bodyguards rose from their simple wooden chairs immediately as he approached the entrance. Half a step in front, half a step behind.

Then he stopped.

"I'm actually not finished here. A half-hour more. I'll be back."

He turned away from the door and headed back alone. But not to the right at the next corridor to the vice president's office, instead he continued on straight toward the stairs—he hadn't taken an elevator since he got home. One floor down, two floors, three floors. The basement and the archives. He said hello, identified himself, even though this guard also didn't ask for his ID or any other questions. And went in. To the smell of paper, folders, binders, dust, time.

He didn't make it far. It was the walls. They started to close in. Just like the roof, which started to press down. There was no room for him. He couldn't get out. The stench from the hole filled with a buzzing swarm of big, green flies, it fell over him, the powerful acid of red and black ants that sat in the banana trees and attacked by dropping their urine, which burned the skin until it was covered with blisters, even the cheese bread baked from yucca flour that lay in white bowls on the floor.

"Mr. Crouse? Is something wrong? Are you okay?"

A cage. And you need to get out of cages.

"Thanks. Everything's fine."

But he nodded toward the guard, continued farther in. He passed the section detailing the entire investigation into JFK's assassination, glanced at the slightly higher shelves labeled Vietnam and the slightly lower ones marked with white labels for Afghanistan, Israel, Iraq. Almost all the way in, under a makeshift sign, he found the FINAL WAR ON DRUGS. It was here he paused, lifted, moved, searched. And found a brown cardboard box—SEVEN OF HEARTS handwritten on one side.

He sat down at a small desk in the corner, opened the box. Blue folders from the DEA. Green folders from the FBI. Red folders from the CIA. All very thin. Then three DVDs, he coaxed them into the archive computer, which protested at first, but he pressed again.

A way of moving I recognize. Which I've seen before. That's how I met him the first time. From the perspective of a satellite in the offices at the NGA. On a chair next to an operator at the Colombia desk.

He kept searching. Loose plastic pockets, stapled documents, small and large photographs. He leafed through a report that compiled twenty-seven anonymous tips, which all placed the Seven of Hearts at specific locations—but for which the managing intelligence officer in every single case had judged as having a misleading purpose.

He leafed through a report on a Delta Force patrol that located the target at a brothel in Cali and prepared a crackdown—but it lacked any follow-up, just a supplementary document listing four names followed by the letters—MIA, missing in action.

He leafed through a report from the US Embassy in Bogotá, signed by Jonathan Woods, director of "The International Narcotics and Law Enforcement Affairs Section," which described in detail how a lifeless body, later identified as El Sueco/the Seven of Hearts, had been dropped off by a Swedish police officer on vacation in Colombia, delivered in the trunk of a rental car.

Finally, he flipped through the coroner's report. Which established that height, weight, and body type were all consistent with the estimates made on the basis of the visual material. Which described a tattoo matching—in appearance, size, location—the unique tattoo observed on the head of the Seven of Hearts. Which described cause of death—cardiac arrest due to asphyxiation. An interpretation based on a swollen and bluish face, an equally swollen tongue, multiple burst blood vessels in the eyes and mucosa, the stripe-shaped hemorrhages in the neck muscle and thyroid, the hyoid bone fracture. An overall picture that—according to the coroner—indicated strangulation with a neck snare.

And which, ultimately, described how the left index finger and the right middle finger were gone—the absence of the distal phalanges and middle phalanges.

Timothy D. Crouse had done it again. Without noticing. Stood up, flaming red from forehead to neck. And he shook. It was just like before. When he saw those moving images. *Something he recognized.*

He read that last part again. Left index finger, left middle finger, gone.

Which we didn't know. Which was lacking from our description of you, on the Most Wanted list.

But you let me know. Your greeting to me. Today.

"Excuse me—a glass of water, please."

The guard had been standing with his back to the speaker, at the end of the narrow passageway, just inside the archive's entrance. But it didn't take long, a glass pitcher, a large mug, which the guard filled, and Crouse wondered how he'd had time, and where he got it from.

Cold water down his throat, into his chest. The uniformed guard turned back around, disappeared, moved silently. While the speaker stood completely still.

You're safe now, Señor Crouse.

A way of moving I recognize.

We'll take you out of here, señor. Home to your countrymen.

An absence I recognized.

It was you.

A canteen with liquid on your hip. And two capsules of sedatives lying in your shattered hand.

It was you who saved me, gave me my life back.

That hand that was missing two fingers.

And we let you die.

ANOTHER FOUR MONTHS LATER

MORNING. HAZE. FAIRLY warm and humid. Piet Hoffmann took off the jacket he'd just put on, ran his hand through the hair he'd just combed. He was nervous. Time on the inside, in that other reality, does that to people.

It was fifteen, no more than twenty, meters between the central guard station and the giant prison gate. It could have been a thousand kilometers. Inside those walls, it was all about freezing time, forgetting time, out there, it was all about taking care of time, cherishing it. Inside you had to swallow your longing, keep completely still, out there everyone was on the move. He'd explained to Zofia that he didn't want her to meet him here with the boys, not once during his sentence and not today when he was released; he wanted to wait to hold them again, see them again, live with them again until they were all in their house in Enskede, their home. He needed to be alone for that hour or so—that journey between one reality and another, between being locked up and set free—to be without them in order to become one of them.

Seventeen meters. He counted the steps up to the gate. To Ewert Grens, who stood there waiting on the other side.

"Welcome back."

"Thanks."

"How've you been?"

"You don't really wanna know. What you *do* want to know, Grens, is that we've been having quite a nice time in our section, me and your former bosses. They were very surprised to see me still alive. We had many opportunities to socialize."

They walked side by side to Grens's service car, commandeered for the day, one of those black, discreet ones. This was no ordinary prisoner transport.

"Yes. *That* is what I wanted to know."

Hoffmann laid the plastic bag containing his few belongings on the back seat, and they rolled out of the prison parking lot toward the main road. Proud walls surrounded by a first layer of high barbed-wire fence, which in turn was surrounded by a second one—slowly disappeared in the rearview mirror, shrank to a past he was leaving behind. For good, this time. Never to be locked up again, never exploited, never caught between lies and even more lies. The trees they passed were real, as was the suburb, all those people in constant motion—the reality he was about to step into, live in.

They didn't say much. They had nothing in common, shared nothing that belonged to the future, had no intention of crossing paths. Just one last ride to the final destination of a three-year-long trip, and it was important to finish it together.

When they passed through Stockholm he felt a lightness in his stomach. All those times he'd pushed his thoughts in this direction in order to be able to stand it, finding reference points to his hometown in a jungle between hostages and cocaine kitchens, in markets among child sicarios, in morgues who sold places for unknown bodies to be cut apart piece by piece.

A little bit farther to the south—Slussen became Gullmarsplan became Nynäs Road. And Grens seemed to know where he was headed, veering off at a narrow street, passing by the flower shop, and on into a middle-class suburb filled with small houses. That was where the Hoffmann family had once lived. That was where they were living now.

He wept quietly when he glimpsed the roof, the garden, Rasmus and Hugo's bicycles and soccer goals, that small hole in the hedge still there, which they used to crawl through in order to save a few seconds on their way to the neighbors.

The detective stopped in front of a simple gate, standing ajar, as it was now, it was clear how much it had rusted over the last few years. Hoffmann climbed out, walked around the car, and stretched his hand through the window.

"Thank you. For everything."

"Take care of the people waiting for you in there. Do nothing from now on to expose them, or you, to danger. Every day, Hoffmann. Stay on the right side of the law. We'll never meet again. Right?"

The rough hand let go and pointed to the trunk.

"Your suitcase. It's in the back. It's been sitting in my office, between my corduroy couch and my uniform closet. And I haven't peeked inside once."

Ewert Grens exchanged a smile with Piet Hoffmann.

"That wouldn't have mattered, detective. The *contents* are of no value."

He stood at the rusty gate while the civil police vehicle disappeared, then searched through the windows, maybe caught a glimpse of someone in the kitchen. Or maybe it was just the shadow of the apple tree playing against the glass.

With suitcase in hand, he walked slowly toward the simple front door, which bore a plaque engraved on the day they moved in—HOFFMANN. He lifted his bag a few times up and down in the air, guessed it weighed no more than seven, maybe eight kilograms—knew that the far more valuable material that the bag itself was constructed from weighed exactly three kilos.

Their fresh start. In a couple days, after the kids headed to school with backpacks and expectant steps, after Zofia headed out to *her* school to work as a substitute Spanish teacher, he'd carry the empty bag down into the basement and work on that dreary, brown leather, which Carlos in Cali had made odorless. Using ether, permanganate, sulfuric acid, and a few other chemicals in plastic barrels, he'd bring the dead back to life, conjure a thick paste from leather and heat it to thirty-seven degrees, put it on a tray, let it dry.

The purest cocaine the world had ever seen. Three kilos would then be diluted to nine kilos—that was the quality of the powder he'd previously sold in Stockholm, and it had done very well. Nine kilos at seventy-five euros per gram. More than six million kronor.

Piet Hoffmann opened the front door, heard their voices.

He was home.

Heartfelt thanks from the authors

TO

S for letting us be part of your unique world for so long and with such trust—a reality few outsiders are allowed into.

AND TO

Lasse Zernell, editor-in-chief of *Allt om Vetenskap* (*Everything About Science*) magazine, for sharing his knowledge of satellites and other technologies that an infiltrator might need in a jungle. *Christer Lingström,* double Michelin-starred, for his guidance on wine vintages and peaches for the otherwise Spartan diet of a detective superintendent. *Anders* for his extreme expertise on submarines and aircraft carriers and how we might fool both. *Lasse Lagergren* for his knowledge on how to tattoo a corpse and other odd medical questions. And *Kerstin Skarp*, deputy attorney general, for her legal expertise regarding how a fictional murderer on the loose might end up with a short prison sentence.

About the Type

Typeset in Minion Pro Regular, 11.5/15 pt.

Minion Pro was designed for Adobe Systems by Robert Slimbach in 1990. Inspired by typefaces of the Renaissance, it is both easily readable and extremely functional without compromising its inherent beauty.

Typeset by Scribe Inc., Philadelphia, Pennsylvania.